FULL BLOODED

I was human again. I had no idea how that had happened, but I was relieved. I tried to move, but pain snapped me back to reality the instant my leg twitched.

With the pain came everything else.

The change, the escape, the poor farmer. I shuddered as the memories hit me like a flickering film reel, a snippet of my life one sordid frame at a time. I'd been there, I'd seen it, but I hadn't been in control for any of it—except at the very end. I hoped like hell the farmer was still alive. Saying *no* had taken so much effort, I couldn't remember anything at all after that. I had no idea where I was.

From everything I knew about wolves, not being in control was an extremely bad sign. If I couldn't subdue my wolf— couldn't master my Dominion over the new beast inside me—I wouldn't be allowed to live.

Holy shit, I'm a wolf.

By Amanda Carlson

Full Blooded

FULL BLOODED

Jessica McClain: Book One

AMANDA CARLSON

www.orbitbooks.net

ORBIT

First published in Great Britain in 2012 by Orbit

A CIP catalogue record for this book
is available from the British Library.

ISBN 978-0-356-50126-0

Printed and bound by CPI Group (UK) Ltd, Croydon CR0 4YY

Papers used by Orbit are from well-managed forests
and other responsible sources.

MIX
Paper from
responsible sources
FSC
www.fsc.org FSC® C104740

Orbit
An imprint of
Little, Brown Book Group
100 Victoria Embankment
London EC4Y 0DY

An Hachette UK Company
www.hachette.co.uk

www.orbitbooks.net

For Bill, Paige, Nat & Jane

1

I drew in a ragged breath and tried hard to surface from one hell of a nightmare. "*Jesus,*" I moaned. Sweat slid down my face. My head was fuzzy. Was I dreaming? If I was, this dream hurt like a bitch.

Wait, dreams aren't supposed to hurt.

Without warning my body seized again. Pain scorched through my veins like a bad sunburn, igniting every cell in its path. I clenched my teeth, trying hard to block the rush.

Then, as quickly as it struck, the pain disappeared.

The sudden loss of sensation jolted my brain awake and my eyes snapped open in the dark. This wasn't a damn dream. I took a quick internal inventory of all my body parts. Everything tingled, but thankfully my limbs could move freely again. The weak green halo of my digital clock read 2:07 a.m. I'd only been asleep for a few hours. I rolled onto my side and swiped my sticky hair off my face. When my fingers came in contact with my skin, I gasped and snapped them away like a child who'd just touched a hot stove.

Holy shit, I'm on fire.

That couldn't be right.

Don't panic, Jess. Think logically.

I pressed the back of my hand against my forehead to get a better read on how badly I was burning up. Hot coals would've felt cooler than my skin.

I must be really sick.

Sickness was a rare event in my life, but it did happen. I wasn't prone to illness, but I wasn't immune to it either. My twin brother never got sick, but if the virus was strong enough I was susceptible.

I sat up, allowing my mind to linger for a brief moment on a very different explanation of my symptoms. *That scenario would be impossible. Get a grip. You're a twenty-six-year-old female. It's never going to happen. It's probably just the flu. There's no need to—*

Without so much as a breath of warning, another spasm of pain hit clear and bright. My body jerked backward as the force of it plowed through me, sending my head slamming into the bedframe, snapping the wooden slats like matchsticks. My back bowed and my arms lashed out, knocking my bedside table and everything on it to the ground. The explosion of my lamp as it struck the floor was lost beneath my bona fide girl scream. "*Shiiiit!*"

Another tremor hit, erupting its vile ash into my psyche like a volcano. But this time instead of being lost in the pale haze of sleep, I was wide awake. I *had* to fight this.

I wasn't sick.

I was *changing*.

Jesus Christ! You've spent your whole life thinking about this very moment and you try to convince yourself you have the flu? What's the matter with you? If you want to live, you have to get to the dose before it's too late!

The pain buried me, my arms and legs locked beside me. I was unable to move as the continuous force of spasms hit me one after another. The memory of my father's voice rang clearly in my mind. I'd been foolish and too stubborn for my own good and now I was paying the price. *"Jessica, don't argue with me. This is a necessary precaution. You must keep this by you at all times."* The new leather case, containing a primed syringe of an exclusively engineered cocktail of drugs, would be entrusted to me for safekeeping. The contents of which were supposed to render me unconscious if need be. *"You may never need it, but as you well know, this is one of the stipulations of your living alone."*

I'm so sorry, Dad.

This wasn't supposed to happen. My genetic markers weren't coded for this. This was an impossibility. In a world of impossibilities.

I'd been so stupid.

My body continued to twist in on itself, my muscles moving and shifting in tandem. I was locked in a dance I had no chance of freeing myself from. The pain rushed up, finally reaching a crushing crescendo. As it hit its last note, my mind shattered apart under its impact.

Everything went blissfully black.

Too soon, pinpoints of light danced behind my eyelids. I eased them open. The pain was gone. Only a low throbbing current remained. It took me a moment to realize I was on all fours on the floor beside my bed, my knees and palms bloodied from the shards of my broken lamp. My small bedside table was scattered in pieces around me. It looked like a small hurricane had ripped apart my bedroom. I had no time to waste.

The dose is your only chance now. Go!

The bathroom door was five feet from me. I propelled myself forward, tugging myself on shaky arms, dragging my body behind me. *Come on, we can do this. It's right there.* I'd only made it a few thin paces when the pain struck again, hard and fast. I collapsed on my side, the muscles under my skin roiling in earnest. *Jesuschrist!* The pain was straight out of a fairy tale, wicked and unrelenting.

I moaned, convulsing as the agony washed over me, crying out in my head, searching for the only possible thing that could help me now. My brother was my only chance. *Tyler, it's happening! Ty, Ty…please! Tyler, can you hear me? Tyyy…*

Another cloud of darkness tugged at the edges of my consciousness and I welcomed it. Anything to make all this horror disappear. Right before it claimed me, at that thin line between real and unreal, something very faint brushed against my senses. A tingle of recognition prickled me. But that wasn't right. That wasn't my brother's voice.

Dad?

Nothing but empty air filled my mind. I chastised myself. *You're just hoping for a miracle now.* Females weren't meant to change. I'd heard that line my entire life. How could they change when they weren't supposed to *exist*? I was a mistake, I'd always been a mistake, and there was nothing my father could do to help me now.

Pain rushed up, exploding my mind. Its fury breaking me apart once again.

Jessica, Jessica, can you hear me? We're on our way. Stay with us. Just a few more minutes! Jessica…Hang in there, honey. Jess!

I can't, Dad. I just can't.

Blood.

Fear shot through me like a cold spear. I lifted my nose and scented the air. Coolness ran along my back, forcing my hair to rise, prickling my skin. I shivered. My labored breaths echoed too loudly in my sensitive ears. I peered into the darkness, inhaling deeply again.

Blood.

A rumble of sounds bubbled up from beneath me and I inched back into the corner and whined. The thrumming from my chest surrounded me, enveloping me in my own fear.

Out.

I leapt forward. My claws slid out in front of me, sending me tumbling as I scrabbled for purchase on the smooth surface. I picked myself up, plunging down a dark tunnel into a bigger space. All around me things shattered and exploded, scaring me. I vaulted onto something big, my claws slicing through it easily. I sailed off, landing inches from the sliver of light.

Out.

My ears pricked. I lowered my nose to the ground, inhaling as the sounds hit me. Images shifted in my brain. *Humans, fear, noise...harm.* A low mewing sound came from the back of my throat. A loud noise rattled above my head. I jumped back, swiveling away, searching.

Then I saw it.

Out.

I leapt toward the moonlight, striking the barrier hard. It gave way instantly, shattering. I extended myself, power coursed through my body. The ground rushed up quickly, my front paws crashing onto something solid, my jaws snapping together fiercely with the force of the impact. The thing beneath me collapsed with a loud, grating noise. Without hesitation I hit the ground.

Run.

I surged across hard surfaces, finding a narrow stretch of woods. I followed it until the few trees yielded to more land. I ran and ran. I ran until the smells no longer confused me, until the noises stopped their assault on my sensitive ears.

Hide.

I veered toward a deep thicket of trees. Once inside their safe enclave, I dove into the undergrowth. The scent pleased me as I wiggled beneath the low branches, concealing myself completely. Once I was settled, I stilled, perking my ears. I opened my mouth, drawing the damp air over my tongue, sampling it, my nostrils flared. The scents of the area came quickly, my brain categorizing them efficiently. The strong acidic stench of fresh leavings hung in the air.

Prey.

I cocked my head and listened. The faint sounds of rustling and grunting were almost undetectable. My ears twitched with interest. My stomach gave a long, low growl.

Eat.

I sampled the air again, testing it for the confusing smells, the smells I didn't like. I laid my head down and whimpered, the hunger gnawing at my insides, cramping me.

Eat, eat, eat.

I couldn't ignore it, the hunger consumed me, making me hurt. I crept slowly from my shelter beneath the trees to the clearing where the tall grass began. I lifted my head above the gently waving stalks and inhaled. They were near. I trotted through the darkness, soundless and strong. I slid into their enclosure, under the rough wooden obstacle with ease. I edged farther into the darkness of the big den, my paws brushing against the old, stale grass, disturbing nothing more.

Prey.

The wind shifted across my back. They scented me for the first time. Bleating their outrage, they stamped their hooves, angry at the intrusion. I slipped under another weak barrier, my body lithe and agile as I edged along the splintered wood. I spotted my prey.

Eat.

I lunged, my jaws shifting, my canines finding its neck, sinking in deeply. Sweet blood flowed into my mouth. My hunger blazed like an insatiable fire, and my eyes rolled back in my head in ecstasy. The animal tipped over, dying instantly as it landed in the dirty hay. I set upon it, tearing fiercely at its flesh, grabbing long hunks of meat and swallowing them whole.

"Goddamn wolves!"

My head jerked up at the noise, my eyes flickering with recognition.

Human.

"I'll teach you to come in here and mess around in my barn, you mangy piece of shit!"

Sound exploded and pain registered as I flew backward, crashing into the side of the enclosure. I tried to get up, but my claws slipped and skidded in the slippery mess. *Blood.* I readjusted, gaining traction, and launched myself in the air. The pungent smell of fear hit me, making my insides quiver with need.

Kill.

A deep growl erupted from inside my throat, my fangs lashing. My paws hit their target, bringing us both down with a crash.

Mine.

I tore into flesh, blood pooled on my tongue.

"Please...don't..."

No!

I stopped.

No!

I backed away.

"Bob, you all right out there?"

Danger.

Out.

I loped forward, limping along in the shadows. I spotted a small opening, jumped, and landed with a painful hiss. My back leg buckled beneath me, but I had to keep moving.

Run.

I ran, scooting under the barrier. A scream of alarm rent the air behind me. I ran and ran until I saw only darkness.

Rest.

I crawled beneath a thick canopy of leaves, my body curling in on itself. I licked my wound. There was too much damage. I closed my eyes. Instantly images flashed through my mind one by one.

Man, boy... woman.

I focused on her.

I *needed* her.

Jessica.

I called her back to me.

She came willingly.

Jessica! Jessica! Honey, can you hear me? Answer me!

　Jess, it's Ty. You have to listen to Dad and wake the hell *up!*

My brain felt foggy, like a thick layer of moss coated it from the inside.

Jessica, you answer me right now! Jessica. Jessica!

"Dad?"

I squinted into the sunlight filtering through a canopy of branches a few feet above my head. I was human again. I had no idea how that had happened, but I was relieved. I tried to move, but pain snapped me back to reality the instant my leg twitched.

With the pain came everything else.

The change, the escape, the poor farmer. I shuddered as the memories hit me like a flickering film reel, a snippet of my life one sordid frame at a time. I'd been there, I'd seen it, but I hadn't been in control for any of it—except at the very end. I hoped like hell the farmer was still alive. Saying *no* had taken so much effort, I couldn't remember anything at all after that. I had no idea where I was.

From everything I knew about wolves, not being in control was an extremely bad sign. If I couldn't subdue my wolf— couldn't master my Dominion over the new beast inside me—I wouldn't be allowed to live.

Holy shit, I'm a wolf.

I lifted my head and glanced down the length of my very exposed, very naked body. I focused on my injury and watched as my skin slowly knit back together. *Incredible.* I'd seen it happen before on others, but until now I'd never been in the super healing category myself. Young male wolves gained their abilities after their first shift. My body must still be adjusting, because my hip was still one big mash of ugly muscle. Dried blood stained my entire right side, and the heart of the gunshot wound resembled a plate of raw hamburger.

Thankfully there was no bone showing. If there'd been

bone, there would've been bile. Now that I was awake and moving, the pain had increased.

I closed my eyes and laid my head back on the ground. My encounter last night better not have been a normal night out for a new werewolf. If it was, I was so screwed.

Jessica!

My head shot up so fast it slammed into a pointy twig. *Ow.* "Dad?" So it hadn't been my imagination after all. I knew the Alpha could communicate with his wolves internally, but hearing his voice was new to me. I concentrated on listening. Nothing. I projected a tentative thought outward like I used to do with my brother.

Dad?

Oh my God, Jessica! Are you all right? Answer me!

Yes! I can hear you! I'm fine, er... at least I think I am. I'm in pain, and I can't really move very well, but I'm alive. My hip looks like it went through a meat grinder, but it's mending itself slowly.

Stay where you are. We'll be right there. I lost your scent for a time, but we're back on your trail now.

Okay. I'm under some thick brush, but I have no idea where. I can't get out because of my leg.

Snort. *You're not healed yet?*

Tyler?

Who else would it be?

Hearing my brother's voice in my head released a flood of emotion. I hadn't realized how much I'd missed it until right this second. *It's safe to say I wasn't expecting you back in my brain. We haven't been able to do this since we were kids, but it's good to hear you now.*

Tyler's thoughts shifted then, becoming heavier, like a low, thick whisper tugging along the folds of my mind. *Jess, I heard you calling me last night. You know, when it first happened. It sounded awful, like you were dying or something. I'm so sorry I didn't make it there in time. I tried. I was too late.*

It's okay, Tyler. We haven't been able to communicate like this in so long, I really wasn't expecting it to work. It was a last-ditch effort on my part to take my mind off the brutal, scary, painful transition process. Don't worry about it. There wasn't anything you could've done anyway. It happened mind-bogglingly fast. Almost too fast to process. My heart caught for a second remembering it.

I heard, or maybe felt, a stumble and a grunted oath. *You'll get used to it,* Tyler said. *The change gets easier after you do it a few more times. Hold on, I think we're almost to you. We lost your scent back at the barn. Jesus, you ripped that place apart. There was blood everywhere.*

An ugly replay started in my mind before I could shut it down. *I hope the farmer survived.* I shifted my body slightly and winced as a bolt of pain shot up my spine. My injuries would've killed a regular human. I was clearly going to survive, but it still hurt like hell.

My dad's anxiety settled in sharp tones in my mind. *We're close, Jessica. By the time we picked up your scent on the other side of the barn, we had to wait for the human police and ambulance to leave. It shouldn't be long now. Stay right where you are and don't move. Your scent grows stronger every moment.*

Yeah, you smell like a girl. It's weird.

Maybe that's because I am one. Or have you forgotten because you haven't seen me in so long?

Nope, I haven't forgotten, but you don't smell like a regular wolf, Tyler said. *Wolves smell, I don't know, kind of rustic and earthy. You smell too female, almost like perfume. It sort of makes me gag.* I could feel him give a small cough in the center of my mind, which was totally bizarre.

Then I should be easy for you to find.

Snort.

We'll be right there, my dad assured me. *Don't worry. We've got a car not too far from here waiting to take you back to the Compound.*

All this effort to communicate was taking its toll, and my head began to ache in earnest. The pain in my hip flared and a whooshing noise started in my ears. *I'm feeling a little woozy all of a sudden…*

Hang on—

2

I woke to white walls and the smell of disinfectant, latex, and coffee. The room resembled a typical hospital room, clean, bright, and sterile, except this one catered exclusively to were-wolves. It was underground because wolves weren't known for their calm cool natures, and dirt was damn hard to claw your way out of if you went crazy.

No one else shared the space with me, which made things easier. Newborn wolves meant chaos, and less chaos was prefer-able, since last night I'd managed to achieve the impossible. I'd become the only living female full-blooded wolf on the entire planet. My new identity was going to rock the supernatural sta-tus quo, and the sooner I could prepare for the fallout—which was inevitable—the better. Hauling my ass out of this hospital bed was a good place to start. "Hellooo," I called. "Is anybody there?"

While I waited for a response, I flexed my leg and tested for pain. A small twinge lingered high on my thigh, but otherwise it felt normal. I couldn't actually see the wound, since the top of my leg was wrapped with enough gauze to stuff a throw pillow. Recalling the mincemeat it'd been, I was more than happy to go without a visual. I had no idea if I would scar from the ordeal or not. I had a lot to learn about my new body.

A conversation started on the floor above me. My father's low baritone stood out. I cocked my head, half expecting to hear a bionic beep as I homed in on the conversation. It was amazing how clear it was, like they were in the same room with me. I tested my vision on a tiny container across the room. I could read the fine print on the label, no problem.

Footfalls hit the steps and my father, Callum McClain, the Pack Alpha of the U.S. Northern Territories, stepped into view. "Well, it's about damn time." I flashed him a big grin. It'd been a while since I'd seen him and I'd missed him. Since I'd left the Compound seven years ago, we'd only seen each other a handful of times. We'd been extremely cautious about our meetings, because being spotted together would've set off alarms in the supernatural community. Any gossip could have compromised my alias, abruptly ending the independent life I'd worked so hard to create for myself.

"Jessica, you scared the hell out of me." My father strode to my bedside. With a full head of dark hair and no wrinkles in sight, he didn't appear a day over thirty-five.

"I scared the hell out of myself." I chuckled. "Shifting into a wolf hadn't been on the evening's agenda. Plus I kind of thought I was dying, so that put a serious damper on the whole thing. My limbs felt like they were being sawed apart by a dull blade."

"The first time is always rough," my father said. "Especially if I'm not there to guide the transition. It's much better if you don't fight the process and stay calm. The tranq would've eliminated the pain. Why didn't you use it?" My father slid a chair over and pulled it next to the bed and sat. "That was our agreed-upon failsafe if you ever started to shift. You were to inject yourself, knock yourself out, and we would find you. No damage to you in the process. You could've died jumping out of your apartment and it's lucky the gunshot didn't sever your spinal cord. I put my trust into you, into our agreement. I expected you to follow it to the letter."

"I'm sorry." I plucked at the bedsheets like an errant child. "I tried to reach the dose, but I didn't make it. I have no one to blame but myself. I transferred the case from my bedside stand to the bathroom cabinet a few years ago. I thought it was close enough, but honestly, I never thought I'd need it. It's been over ten years since I hit puberty and we'd always been told I wasn't genetically coded to shift." I paused for a second. "I'm sorry. I thought you were being overprotective as usual."

"Dear Jessica!" Dr. Jace entered the room, his familiar white hair fanning around his face like a fragile halo, his expression full of open amusement and wonder. "You gave us quite a fright! You're a miracle, young lady, truly a miracle." He shuffled to my bedside, grabbed on to my hand, and patted it affectionately. "Who would've thought it possible? A true female among us. Amazing! Truly amazing!"

"Doc Jace." I tilted my cheek toward him so he could give it a quick peck. "It's great to see you again. It's been too long. You're looking well." This man was the closest thing to a grandfather I'd ever known. He was an Essential human in our Pack, like his father and grandfather before him—meaning he knew our secrets, worked for us, but was not supernatural himself. Essentials were a necessity in every supernatural Sect, since the human race had no idea we existed. They were doctors, teachers, lawyers; individuals recruited to play a special role within the Sect. Doc Jace was a brilliant doctor, an extreme asset to our Pack. "I'm so glad you're here"—I flashed him a grin—"because you're just the man to answer a burning question."

"Of course," he said. "I will always do my best to answer your questions, Jessica."

"How did I survive? I thought I wasn't coded for wolf, that it would be impossible for me to make a full transition, and if my body chemistry did change late after puberty I'd likely die from the ordeal. But I'm alive."

Doc absently stroked his short beard. "Males carry their wolf markers on their second Y chromosome, very uncommon indeed, but they are there, coded very clearly. You have never had any such indicators and no second chromosome. My best guess is your body must carry the gene, the one that marks you as a wolf, elsewhere, perhaps in a noncoded region. But as you can guess, I will be doing exhaustive research on that very topic." He patted my hand. "Exciting work it is." Puzzling over our genes was his life's work. "Having you make a successful transformation as a female is revolutionary. We are blazing a new trail with this research. It will be marvelous indeed."

I already knew it was revolutionary, because females didn't exist in our race. My birth had sparked a frenzy of discontent, which was enhanced to a breaking point by a certain unsubstantiated but extremely well-circulated myth proclaiming I was pure evil, a menace placed on earth for the sole purpose of bringing down the race of wolves. Once the Pack found out about my new status as a full-blooded wolf, there was going to be a huge uproar, and everything I'd built for myself would slide straight down the drain. Without going into all that with the Doctor, I asked instead, "What time is it? How long have I been out?"

"It's seven o'clock in the morning," Doc answered. "You've been asleep for nearly eighteen hours, which is not uncommon for a wolf recuperating from a traumatic injury. I'm guessing you're ready for some coffee and some breakfast? You must be famished. Shifting utilizes an incredible amount of energy, and newborn wolves are more hungry by nature."

"Yes, coffee and food sound heavenly." My stomach growled on cue. "I'm actually starving." Dr. Jace left and I turned back to my father. "I've been asleep for eighteen hours? Are you telling me it's Monday morning already?"

"Yes, it's Monday." My father leaned forward in his chair. "But don't worry about missing work. I've already been in contact with Nicolas. He's already on his way. You've actually been asleep with a little extra help from the Doc. He wanted to be perfectly sure you would heal completely with no complications, and I wholeheartedly agreed with him. Injuries like yours take time to mend, especially for a newborn. I'm just thankful you came back to us in one piece. That was a hell of a ride you took us on."

I was relieved to hear my business partner and best friend, Nick Michaels, was on his way. It would be good to have another ally here, since I had no idea how this was going to play out. "The whole transition was insane, but I don't really remember how it went down." I corrected myself. "No, that's not exactly what I mean. I do have a clear memory of the pain, but for some reason I can't remember the actual turning very well."

My father sat back. "It's not uncommon to disengage with your wolf during your first turning. Your change was an unexpected, traumatic event. As we discussed, fighting the process can make it excruciating. Your wolf likely took over while your human side remained in a shocklike state. It happens. It's not ideal, but it happens."

I was mildly surprised by his reaction, but ultimately happy he wasn't going to hatch an immediate plan to chain me to a bed until I could master more control. "It didn't feel like I was in shock, but I guess I could've been. In the end she toggled something between us and handed me control again. I'd been a passenger up until that point, but when I finally slid into the driver's seat, I took one sniff of my injuries and passed out." My first tough werewolf moment and I'd passed out like a champ.

My father regarded me quietly for a moment. He ran a single hand through his thick dark hair. It was a gesture of stress, and he didn't do it often. "Well." He cleared his throat. "I'm not sure what happened there, but it can take a wolf many years to master Dominion over their wolf. If your wolf willingly handed control back to you, it seems you're not going to have a problem with mastery." He leaned in closer, his eyes alert. "It's a sign your human side is strong, and that's a damn good thing."

A wolf was required to prove Dominion over his inner wolf before being allowed to reenter human society. By instinct your wolf wanted complete control—demanded it. The human side had to be powerful enough to override the wolf's urges at all times. No exceptions.

I bit my bottom lip.

That wasn't exactly how it'd happened. I knew I'd stopped her from killing the farmer, but I had no idea how to do it again if I had to. But I was content to drop it for now, and asked instead, "How did you know I changed? How did you find me?" I grew up on the Compound, so naturally I knew a lot about wolves, but I'd been kept in the dark about a lot of things too.

Before my father could answer, my brother bounded into the room. He'd grown even taller since I'd seen him last. "We found you because you stink, and stink is easy to track." He dropped himself onto my bed, edging me over without a thought.

"Be careful, you big ox. I'm recovering from a serious injury here." I chuckled as I shuffled my barely hurt leg out of his way to make room for him, but it still wasn't enough because he was massive and the bed was tiny.

"Then you must not be that strong, wimpy girl, because if that was my leg it would be as good as new already." He grinned, flashing teeth and dimples. My ever competitor.

"That's easy for you to say," I said. "You didn't just get your leg almost blown off in a gunfight with an angry farmer." I leaned over and gave him a playful shove. He didn't budge an inch. At six foot five, he was built like he was trying out for a spot on the WWE circuit. Tyler resembled our father, we both did, except Tyler had blond hair instead of our shared darker shade. He'd also inherited a pair of shameful dimples, also courtesy of our late mother. But the one feature marking us so clearly as siblings was our matching sky blue eyes.

"Face it, Jess. I've gotten into a hell of a lot more scrapes than you have, and the next day I'm always fine," Tyler said. "You're just wimpier because you're a girl."

"Yeah, right. Remember that time with Danny in the mountains? You had to be carried out on a stretcher. And if I remember correctly, you were out cold for three days straight."

"My skull was split open and my brains were leaking out. That hardly constitutes a *minor* injury."

"The last time I checked, getting a leg blown off is not exactly *minor* either."

"Oh, please. That"—he pointed to my hip—"it's nothing more than a flesh wound."

Flesh wound my ass, little brother.

Comprehension lit his face. Our shared mental capacity as children had always been tenuous at best, blinking on and off like a loose wire. Most of the time it had run unfairly one way—from Tyler to me—and when Tyler had changed at puberty the connection stopped for good.

Now it was back.

Time for a little payback, huh, brother?

"Okay, that's enough," my father ordered. "Tyler, I need you to behave. Your sister's going to need our help; what's happened here is unprecedented. We've managed to dance around the seriousness thus far, but now we need to determine the right course to follow to minimize the fallout. The wolves are restless and we must tread carefully."

My brother sobered instantly. He took Pack business seriously, he always had. At twenty-six, he held an unusually high Pack status; the only other wolf with more status was my father's second-in-command, James Graham, who'd been by my father's side for more than a century. Tyler had fought a lot of bloody battles to move up so rapidly in the Pack ranks. He was a strong wolf and I hoped it ran in the family.

My father stood and paced to the end of the bed. "The wolves know something, but there's still a good chance they don't know you've turned. Most are unsure of what they heard last night, because I snapped the line quickly. We're going to use that to our advantage and try to hold off sharing the news of your shift as long as we can—possibly indefinitely if we're lucky."

"What do you mean, 'what they heard'?" I asked. That didn't sound good.

"A new wolf signals his first shift to the Pack. It's a built-in safety precaution and your wolf sent out that very same alert." My father turned to face me. "At first change, your body triggers a beacon, and hundreds of years ago we found wolves all over Scotland and Wales exactly like that—wolves who didn't know what they were prior to their first shift."

"The whole *Pack* heard my shift?" The thought of having a pack of werewolves inside my brain sent a rush of panic racing through me. "Can they hear me right now?" I tried to contain the waver in my voice, but it shot around the edges anyway.

"No, they can't hear you now," my father assured me. "The Pack connection is always established by me first, and by me alone. Wolves cannot talk internally on their own. You and Tyler are a rare exception, which is undoubtedly because of your close blood-bond, and not because of Pack. I am the conduit of communication only because I'm Alpha. The alert you sounded was only heard by the Pack for a few brief moments. Once I realized it was you, I shut it down completely. As of right now, they aren't positive it was you and that runs in our favor." He ran his hand through his hair again. "I can reasonably deny my knowledge of your change without triggering an untruth, because I never saw you. Nobody actually saw you in your wolf form, therefore no one knows for sure if you've changed. If we're lucky, they'll think it was a beacon coming from a new wolf in the Southern Territories, which is a possibility. We've heard one once before. The distance is a factor, but because it's happened we can use it." The U.S. Southern Territories controlled everything south of the Mason-Dixon Line down into Mexico, my father, everything north into Canada.

My brother nodded in agreement.

Making sure my father didn't have to lie to his Pack was important. Wolves could sense a lie, because the body betrayed itself every time. The heart raced, pupils dilated, and you perspired. My father, being a strong Alpha, could mask a lie, but if his wolves questioned him too deeply, his emotions could betray him.

"It's a relief they can't hear me, but they have to be curious why I'm home in the first place? I'm assuming they know I'm here." Keeping me a secret on the Compound would be too hard. I wasn't supposed to be here, I was supposed to be in Europe. When I'd finally departed for good several years ago, I'd started a new life under the alias Molly Hannon. The Pack was informed Jessica McClain had headed to Europe for good. I'd actually spent a short time overseas recuperating from injuries I'd sustained fighting just before I'd left the Compound, so it wasn't untrue, and it'd worked like a charm. I'd come back stateside as Molly, and my new life was two hours south of here, in the Twin Cities, and it had been blissfully uneventful. Nobody knew who I was, and I desperately wanted to keep it that way.

"I told them you were in town for a few nights for a rare visit with your brother, and you'd been staying down in the cities with Danny. You arrived on Compound late last night, which was purely a coincidence." Danny Walker, my brother's best friend and another of my few allies. He worked policing the cities' boundaries for errant wolves, and he was damn good at it.

"And they bought it?"

"You haven't been back in seven years. It was time."

"When, and if, the news of my shift gets out, it's going to be hard to convince them I'm not their enemy after all the years of the Cain Myth infecting their minds. They're finally going to have the hard evidence they've been waiting for to accuse me of bringing down the Pack."

"Your presence here right after the beacon went out is not ideal." My father walked across the room. "Any extra time we obtain will allow me to ready the Pack to better handle the news. Some of the wolves have cooled their position on you over the last few years, but finding out your new status as a full-blooded wolf is going to shake their beliefs once again." He turned at the stairway. "I'm heading back out to talk to them now. After your breakfast, and Doc has finished his testing, we meet in the main lodge to discuss the next step."

Tyler patted his hand on my knee as he stood. "Don't worry, Jess. We'll figure this out. And for the record, I don't think you're a freak at all."

Um, thanks?

3

After scarfing down the most food I'd ever eaten in one sitting, I went through a battery of tests involving every spare tissue sample I could part with. "I told you, I'm fine. I don't need these." I was perched on the edge of the bed, wiggling a needless pair of crutches in my hands. "My leg feels great."

Dr. Jace stood next to me, scrutinizing my every move.

"Watch." I bent my leg and extended it. "See, it works just fine. No pain." I'd changed into an old pair of pajama pants and an ancient Radiohead T-shirt of mine someone had scrounged from my old bedroom at the main lodge. As my pajama leg eased up, I caught a glimpse of the thick dark hair coating my once cleanly shaven leg and stifled a gag. "And, um, other than all this gross hair, I'm totally good." No amount of money could make me look under my arms. My eyes had remained firmly closed. Apparently after a full change, your hair came back. *All* of it.

"You will use these for now." Doc nodded toward the

crutches. "If you prove to be better later, well then, we will reevaluate at that time."

A head of lettuce would've been easier to convince, so I took the damn things and stuffed them under my arms as I stood.

The walk from the infirmary to the house I'd grown up in was a short distance across a nicely manicured lawn. No one else was out, likely on my father's orders. This spring had been unusually rainy and the grass was a bright, startling green.

The Lodge, as it was affectionately known, had been built in the late '30s and had served as the Northern Territories home base ever since. The worn red cedar plank floors were a welcome sight as I entered. Doc stepped in ahead of me. "Jessica, would you care for another cup of coffee or perhaps some tea?"

"Coffee would be great. Thank you." He veered toward the kitchen and I continued into the enormous two-story living area. The fireplace, set with stones quarried directly from the lake, covered the entire eastern wall.

It was beautiful, but it wasn't as good as what was awaiting me.

"Nick!" I dropped the crutches without a thought and jumped immediately into his arms. "I'm so glad you're here."

"Easy there, Jess." Nick enveloped me in a big hug, and then stepped back to give me a careful perusal. "*Hmm*, you do look pretty good. No lingering fur or fluffy ears to speak of, but how's the leg?"

"All healed." To prove my point, I slid down the side of my pajama waistband to reveal the top of my hip. The only thing still visible was a slight red discoloration. "See? Pretty cool, huh?"

"That *is* impressive."

I pulled him down on the couch beside me. Along with being my best friend, Nick was a werefox, not a wolf. In the world of shifters, your strength and size matched your animal, so he wasn't a huge guy, topping out at around six feet. His father had been First Nation Canadian, his mother white. He had light copper skin and shaggy dark hair. He was a welcome sight after all the craziness.

"I'm really glad to see you," I told him. Nick calmed me in a way no one else could, and he had since we were children. "This whole thing has been slightly insane. I'm having trouble believing it actually happened."

"Well, I'm just happy you made it through the transition in one piece." Nick's eyes were an amazing dark golden color naturally and they lit for a moment with a hint of emotion, making them appear even more brilliant. "You could've been killed."

Before I could respond, my father and James Graham, his second-in-command, strode in. James wore his standard-issue black T-shirt and camouflage cargos, the same uniform I'd seen him in my entire life. The ensemble matched his short dark hair and olive skin perfectly, adding a unified blend of menace and strength to his tall frame. James was an impressively large wolf, with a pair of huge shoulders, and would've stood out in any outfit, but I was glad to see he hadn't changed at all.

My father acknowledged Nick with a quick nod. "Nicolas."

"Hello, sir," Nick answered, scrambling to stand.

"How's your leg, Jessica?" my father asked as I rose.

"All healed."

He looked me over for a few seconds, then gave me a quick nod.

James approached me. "It's good to see you, Jessica," he said as he encircled my waist in a warm embrace. His rough Irish brogue was still infectious after all this time. "Glad to see you are well."

I gave him a hug. "It's been too long, James." I smiled as I stepped back. "Far too long." He'd been instrumental in my final departure from the Compound seven years ago and I was happy to see him. Without his support I might never have left, and it had cemented a bond of friendship between us that hadn't existed before.

"Let's head into my office." My father strode into an adjacent opening off the living room and disappeared inside.

The rest of us followed. As we came in, my father set two chairs in a semicircle in front of the leather couch facing the windows. His office had originally been the old library, and rows of beautifully crafted bookshelves lined the walls. It also had a superb, unobstructed view of the lake.

"Jessica, please take a seat on the couch. Nicolas, you sit beside her."

We sat immediately.

Without needing to be asked, James took the chair next to my father, leaning over and bracing his forearms on his thighs, ready to start the discussion.

My father sat straight and imposing. Physically he was a few inches shorter than James, but his body held more mass. His strong arms spilled out of his rolled-up dress shirt. My father was always dressed for the occasion. I'd never seen him run a serious meeting in a T-shirt and jeans. My father was a leader. There was no mistaking it.

"Nicolas," he began. "After this briefing I want you to find out everything you can about the rumors circulating in the supernatural community concerning Jessica or a recent shift. See if any news has spread outside of this Compound. If you find anything out of the ordinary I want to hear about it immediately." My father continued, "That will be your top priority. But for now, let's start with a replay of what happened early

Saturday morning when you first arrived at Jessica's apartment. I know you've already relayed it to me, but I want to hear it again from start to finish." He nodded my way. "And I'm sure Jessica would like to hear what's happened in her absence."

"Yes, sir." Nick turned toward me.

"This should be interesting," I joked, hoping to ease some of Nick's tension, which smelled like burned toast to my new nose.

"Tyler called me around two-thirty a.m. the night you shifted," Nick said. "He was worried and thought you were in trouble. I jumped into my car and immediately called Marcy, and told her to meet me there. I knew if there'd been some kind of a disturbance at your place there was a strong chance your neighbors had already called the police. Having her there would make things easier."

"Good thinking, ace," I said. That was the best news I'd heard since I jumped off my three-story balcony. Marcy Talbot, the secretary at our firm, was a very talented witch, even though she refused to give herself any credit. Marcy hated working under pressure, and had the misfortune of constantly misfiring her spells in stressful situations, which kept any coven from accepting her. But when she did perform, it was completely mind-blowing.

"Marcy and I arrived at your complex at about the same time," Nick continued. "It was a total miracle we made it there before the police. It was a mess and people were milling around all over your hallway. Marcy conjured a spell on the spot, something that made everyone think they were needed elsewhere. Once they cleared out, we slipped into your place unseen."

"Go, Marcy," I said. "How did the apartment look? My wolf busted up a lot of stuff trying to get the hell out."

" 'Busted up' is on the tame side." Nick flashed me a cynical grin. "It looked more like you laid a bunch of C-4 around the place and blew it up. There were piles of demolished furniture everywhere and the floor was trashed with huge gouges. Your bedroom was the worst. But we didn't have time to clean it all, because the police sirens were getting close. Marcy had a brainstorm to make it look like something busted *into* the apartment, instead of you jumping *out*. So she made your sliding glass door look like it had been punched from the outside in."

I nodded along. "Brilliant."

"After that she was almost drained." Witches needed to refuel when they conjured consecutive spells. "So we ran back to your bedroom, because we knew it had to be clean or it would've launched a huge investigation. That much unexplained blood would have to be accounted for."

"Did you make it?"

Nick nodded. "Yes. She had enough power left to make it look like you hadn't been home at all, bed made, everything tidy."

I murmured, "Perfect."

"We barely made it out before the police arrived, but we couldn't leave the building without them spotting us, so we ducked into Mr. Stubbard's apartment next door." Nick glanced at my father. "Jess's neighbor directly to the east. Then it was my turn to do a little bespelling of my own. I convinced Mr. Stubbard to go back to sleep after he let us in. Marcy and I stuck around and watched bad TV until the police took off, and that's it in a nutshell."

Nick possessed the extremely useful gift of mind persuasion. Lots of supes had special abilities to go along with their true natures. A power like persuasion usually only worked on weak-minded humans, but was handy to have nonetheless. As far as extra abilities went, my brother was able to run twice as fast as any other wolf, and James could heal in half the time it took anyone else, which was amazing to watch. There were no guarantees you'd inherit a special gift. It was all a matter of what was already coded in your genes. I was hoping like hell I'd get one, but I had no idea how long it took for them to surface.

"Marcy's going to need a raise. Witches don't work for free," I told Nick. "Without her I'd be completely screwed. It's going to be hard enough to come up with a statement to give to the police, but this will help immensely. A break-in is much easier to explain than a break*out*."

"Oh, and here's your phone." Nick pulled it from his jacket pocket and handed it to me. "I found it on top of a pile of debris. I just happened to see it on the way out. Nobody leaves town without their phone these days."

"Thanks." I took it and tucked it into the waistband of my pajama pants. "Did you happen to see my purse too?"

Nick looked stricken for a moment. "No, I—"

"Don't worry," I interrupted quickly. "Nick, honestly, you did a perfect job of covering my ass, as usual. Guys never have purses on their radar." Marcy would've grabbed it if she'd seen it, I was sure, but it was probably buried underneath a pile of rubble. I glanced to my father. "Do we still have a stockpile of backcountry camping passes? I'll use a last-minute overnight camping excursion as my excuse for not being home." We were surrounded by deep woods and national forests up here.

"That shouldn't be a problem," my father said. He turned to Nick. "You did an excellent job, Nicolas. You've proven yourself time and time again as an asset to this Pack."

Nick bowed his head at the compliment. My father didn't mete them out often.

"The break-in will allow us to take care of the first step with the human police," my father said. "Now comes the hard part, and James and I have already discussed some of the possible scenarios." He turned toward James. "There are dangers attached to keeping you here and allowing you to go home. Each option gives me pause."

James picked up the thread, his Irish lilt giving it a rough, pleasant texture. "If you stay here, Jessica, I feel it will announce to the Pack, in no uncertain terms, that you've already become a full-blooded wolf. I think it's an unnecessary risk to take. The wolves here are agitated already. They know they heard something last night. They're just unsure what it was. If we can possibly keep your shift a secret, and give you a shot of going back to a normal life, we should do that."

"There's one more thing in favor of you heading back home," my father added. "Anyone in the supernatural community who had an idle suspicion that Jessica McClain was really Molly Hannon will be on high alert. They will be looking for you to be missing. If Molly disappears, right as rumors of Jessica McClain turning into a wolf surface, you might never be able to go back to that life, and preserving your alias is a high priority. It would be extremely hard to give you another identity at this point. Supes are tricky, and many are familiar with you from your chosen line of work." He held his tongue, but I knew what he wanted to say—that I'd been reckless and made poor choices regarding my career path, and as it sat right now he'd be right. It'd been a tough battle to convince him to let me involve myself in the supe community in the first place, but after I ended my short stint as a police officer, I had only a few options left open that made any sense. In the end, and likely against his good judgment, he'd allowed Nick and me to open Hannon & Michaels Investigations, with the understanding that I would act solely as Nick's Essential, his human companion, and we would take only low-risk cases. It'd worked, and now I was on the brink of losing my hard-fought-for life. It scared me. "Letting you go back to your life until we see how this unfolds may be the safest place for you. But I don't like it," he growled. "Keeping you here under lock and key is what my gut is telling me to do."

"If news of my shift leaked today, how many wolves do you think would actually be a serious threat to me right out of the gates?" I asked.

My father studied me closely. "Out of the hundred and fifty-nine wolves under my immediate directive, not including out-lying Canadian or Alaskan wolves, I believe there are only a few—ten to twelve at most—who still hold tightly to the belief that you will bring about the ruination of the Pack if you become full blooded. The majority are undecided, but could be swayed quickly if the loudest of the opposition gained momentum before we were able to shut it down. I don't want to worry you any more than necessary, but this morning the Cain Myth resurfaced on several U.S. Pack sites. It could be a coincidence, it does come up once in a while, but it's likely tied to the unease. We haven't figured out where it was generated from this time, but we're working on it."

"Already?" I exhaled the breath I'd been holding. "That can't be good."

"In this instant age of technology," my father shook his head, "I have no way to stop it. It infuriates the hell out of me, but it proves beyond a doubt there's already speculation and unrest within our own ranks, and getting you back to your old life and out of danger is an absolute priority. If we can stop the momentum and keep your shift under wraps, we have a chance to calm the uprising; if not, we may possibly have a civil war on our hands. It's my job as Pack leader to keep that from happening at all costs."

The goddamn Cain Myth.

A few nonsensical verses typed on a plain sheet of paper had shaped my entire existence. The Myth had been mailed to the Compound with no postmark exactly one month after my birth. Whether it carried an ounce of truth had never mattered. It had achieved its goal from the start—to seed unrest inside the Pack, while ruining my life in the process. I knew the lines by heart. They were etched in my mind permanently, like a bad stain:

As a Female in Wolf Skin rises, the unborn Daughter of Cain is born;
In her the beast shall lie, well hidden in True Form;
And from this day forth, the Wolves of the Night shall pay;
Blood and flesh of their bones, her mighty hand shall slay;
The end of the race will be close at hand;
When the Daughter of Evil rules the land.

Did I believe I was the daughter of Cain? Of course not. But fear was a powerful motivator, especially for the extremely superstitious wolves. When the Cain Myth arrived, I'd been told it sent the wolves into a frenzy, many calling for my father to end my life. It'd taken a few years to quell that unrest, but the Myth had lingered, rearing its ugly head throughout my childhood, causing never-ending trouble for me. Things had finally leveled off, but only because I hadn't shifted into a wolf at puberty, and ultimately I'd fought my way off the Compound. Out of sight, out of mind.

Now I was back.

"It can't be a coincidence," I muttered. If our entire history wasn't structured around myths and legends, and wolves weren't the most superstitious beings on the planet, my life would've been a hell of a lot easier.

My father cleared his throat. "The wolves can speculate all they want, but until they have absolute verification—which can only come from *me*—they will continue to be unsure, which is why I'm leaning toward sending you back. But honestly, Jessica, not having you near me, not being able to protect you myself, goes against every fiber of my being."

I scooted to the edge of the couch. "Dad, listen." I touched his leg. The contact felt good. "This is the right thing to do. I know it's going to be a rough road, and things are uncertain, but I have to at least try to salvage my life. If I stay here, there's still no guarantee of my safety. You can't hold my hand or lock me in my room forever, and with the wolves on edge it's better for me to leave now. We have to give it a chance."

My father stared at me for a long time. Then he turned to James, and without words they made a silent agreement. "Okay, we'll give it a chance." His words held a solemn note. "But I'm not sending you back without adequate protection."

I nodded, accepting his decision. Having bodyguards would likely be my new norm from now on. I could live with that.

He straightened in his seat. Now that we had a plan, it was time to delegate. "Nicolas will take you home immediately," he said. "Tyler and James will follow you down shortly. Danny is already there, and I'll put him and his team on high alert within the city limits. It's my feeling we will know within a few days what the fallout will look like. I will be in contact with you daily."

I took a breath. "I completely understand the need for backup, especially now," I said carefully. "But like you said, if anyone suspects Molly Hannon is Jessica McClain, now would be the perfect time to snoop around in my life. If they spot wolves near my building, we can bank on trouble sooner rather than later. Molly Hannon isn't known to entertain wolves." In fact, nobody entertained werewolves. They were an elusive bunch, with a hefty dose of superiority. They didn't mix well with others.

My father gave me a hard look and answered me briskly. "James will stay at the Safe House. If you are in danger, he can be there in less than two minutes. If you're on an assignment, I expect you to let James or your brother know. If you're not with Nicolas, you will take one of them with you. No exceptions. Tyler will be in charge of all security operations and will be your link back to us. You will keep in contact with him throughout your day. This is the only option, so I'd suggest you take it."

I took it.

4

Tyler was in the kitchen. A stack of sandwiches waited neatly on the counter, along with some coffee to go. I'd never gotten my cup from the good Doctor before the meeting had started. Nick and I picked up the drinks and snatched a few sandwiches and followed Tyler out the door. My father and James had already gone to deal with the other wolves, and our plan was to get out of here as quickly as possible.

I licked my lips. "I'm hungry every five seconds, is this normal?" I took a huge bite. *Jesus.* Ham and cheese had never tasted this good. It was like it was laced with some kind of supernatural MSG.

"Get used to having an appetite." Tyler chuckled. "Wolves eat a lot."

"I can get down with eating a lot," I mumbled around a full mouth. "But it's not that—it's like superfood. It tastes so much *better.* The cheese is actually . . . *cheesier.*"

Nick laughed, but it sounded more like a snort. "Those are

your new and improved taste buds in action. Not only do they work better, but now you have more of them. But be careful, because when you bite into something nasty, it's like licking the bottom of a garbage pail."

We headed toward the main driveway. I had nothing to pack, since my departure had been a tad unplanned. We rounded the final curve in the lawn, and to my surprise a couple of wolves, in human form, were waiting for us at the edge of the lawn, where the parking lot started.

Tyler's voice rang in my brain. *Hold tight. That's Hank and Stuart.* He slowed his pace, and Nick and I followed his lead. *What the hell are they doing out here? They're supposed to stay in the commons until after you leave. Those two have been the most suspicious since everyone learned you were back.*

That's hardly a shocker, I replied. *My main enemies-at-camp are suspicious? I wonder why?* Hank Lauder and his son Stuart had been against me since day one. Hank was nearly as old as my father, but he'd only been a member of this Pack for the last twenty years. Before that he'd been a Pack wolf in the Southern Territories, but had been expelled for some reason unknown to me. Hank was strong and loud, and had led the biggest initiative against me when I'd lived on Compound, riling up the younger wolves and maneuvering them in line to do his dirty work, which ranged from foul taunts to fist throwing. If anyone would be pointing the finger, it would naturally be Hank.

My brother's voice filtered into my mind again. *None of the wolves are sure what's going on, including these two, but they aren't as stupid as they look.*

There's no one on earth I despise more than Hank Lauder. He made my life a living hell while I was here. As we closed the gap, I could tell by their dour faces they weren't going to buy any of our excuses. *We're going to have to be careful not to give anything away.*

Hank's nostrils flared as we came to a stop. "You smell different," he accused, not wasting any time. The charming southern drawl should've sounded like a good ol' boy full of apple pie, but instead it was like a pie full of buzzing wasps. "Kinda like a werewolf, but somehow off"—he inhaled again, tasting— "more like a mongrel bitch in heat."

Well, that was a pretty picture.

Without my consent, my fight-or-flight response flew to the surface as adrenaline rushed through me, spurred on by the strong scent of Hank's aggression. My muscles began to twitch inside the tight wrapper of my skin and my nerve impulses sparked like a million tiny fireworks. *Shit.* I had no idea if I'd be able to stay in control or if my wolf would fight me for it. I couldn't handle a battle for Dominion right now, not to mention I wasn't supposed to give myself away to these two losers.

I forced myself to take a step backward.

Fight. My wolf flexed in my mind, pushing for control.

I curled my fingers into fists, crushing the empty foam coffee cup into tiny bits. With effort I steeled away the urge to hand Hank his ass on a platter. My nails dug into my palms. It was all I could do to keep myself under control. *Down, girl*, I hissed. *This isn't the time or the place. If we fight Hank, we lose everything.* I stood my ground, but the power was dizzying. She pushed back with the force of a tornado.

Hank's eyes widened with a hint of surprise, but he recovered quickly. "Yep, just like a dog in heat." He forced a chuckle through his clenched teeth. "But not a true werewolf, because no self-respecting wolf would stink like that."

He was playing me for dominance.

It was his wolf's natural instinct. I knew it. He knew it. We all knew it. Whether or not he thought I was a wolf at this point didn't matter. This was a stressful situation, and a wolf like Hank emitted dominance constantly, always fearful of losing his place in the pecking order. Unlike James and Tyler, who had solidified their dominance by sheer force, earning respect and ensuring other wolves were wary of a fight they weren't likely to win. A wolf could sense power, and the rites of passage in this race were fierce. Fighting for status happened on a regular basis. Pack dynamics were fluid and only one constant remained: the weak fell below and the strong rose above.

I exhaled on a shallow breath and clarity struck like an arrow. If Hank and I fought right now, I would win. No contest. It didn't matter if Hank was older and stronger. It didn't matter if his status was rightfully above mine.

I *knew*.

The rush of the knowledge tipped the emotional scales to my wolf and a slow smile crept over my face before I could stop it. Without being totally aware of what I was doing, I brought my head up, my eyes at half-mast as I let the ecstasy of my new wolf wash over me.

The power was a drug. And I liked it.

My eyes pinned Hank's shit-eating grin with a glare, and as the smirk fell from his face it sent a new jolt of adrenaline racing though my veins, the impact hitting me so hard my fingers exploded in sensation, my nails expanding to sharp points in the time it took to take a breath. For a wolf, holding eye contact was the ultimate challenge.

My gaze didn't falter.

Something brushed against my brain and my brother's voice held mild panic. *Hey, eeeasy there, Bonnie. No need to start slinging your guns just yet. You need to back the* fuck *down right now. Do you hear what I'm telling you? This has already gone way too far. You're not even supposed to be a* full-blooded wolf, *remember? You need to back off!*

Says who? I half slurred.

Hank held my stare with defiance, his eyes flashing amber. Half a beat later they blazed full yellow.

My brother stepped into my shoulder, jostling me. *Snap out of it! Drop your stare. Let him be. You're* not *supposed to be a wolf! This is typical status behavior, and if Hank pulls you in, you can kiss your freedom goodbye. Lower your goddamn gaze! Act like it's a mistake and you have no idea what you're doing.*

I tore my eyes from Hank.

My wolf howled inside my mind and I quaked with the need to finish the fight, but there was no other choice, it had to end. Tyler was right, fighting now would be like showing my royal flush before everyone had a chance to place their bets.

I took another step backward, trying hard to fasten a chastened look on my face. I kept my eyes averted, skittering over Hank's smug smile and over to Stuart, Hank's only son, looking positively gleeful at my sudden withdrawal. Breaking eye contact first suggested a weakness that went against every grain in my new body.

My wolf snarled in my mind.

Not here, I scolded. *We can't fight.* It was totally crazy, but I could hear her in my mind clearly, separate from me, yet the same.

Out of the corner of my eye, Hank crossed his arms, menace emanating off him in noxious waves.

Now what? I asked my brother. My fingers twitched as the smell of a challenge hung in the air. It had a sharp tang to it, like something bitter mixed with smoke. My nails slid back to normal. My wolf was holding back, but just by a hair. She was taut, ready to pounce, still itching for a fight.

"See you later, bitch," Hank said, turning abruptly on his heel and starting up the hill, Stuart following behind like a puppy.

Way to go, Jess. Tyler sighed once they were gone. *You did a superb job of riling up the natives, just like we said we weren't going to do. God only knows what they're going to think. There's no way Hank doesn't suspect you're a wolf now. But at least he thinks you're weak.*

I expelled a long frustrated breath, still trying to calm my wolf. *I know. I totally blew it.* Damn it. *I just couldn't get a hold of it. This crazy emotion shot up out of nowhere. Then there were all these smells and it was confusing. I wanted to fight. It took everything I had to rein her in. Next time I'm not even sure I'll be able to.* It made me nervous to think of having something inside me I couldn't control, some sort of loose cannon that could go off at any moment. I hoped my father wasn't making a mistake not chaining me to the bed.

Well, if it makes you feel any better, it took me a hell of a lot longer to control my own wolf. It was a bastard of a fight and still can be. Given the circumstances, I guess I can say you did a better job than I would've in your position. Hell, I wanted to rip Hank's head off.

I chuckled, feeling slightly relieved. *Thanks, little brother.*

Harrumph.

It was more than time to get the hell out of here.

"Man, Jess," Nick said as we took off in his Honda. "The smell coming off of you back there was toxic. It was like pure adrenaline mixed with rage. I've never smelled anything so strange in my life." He shook his head and glanced at me from behind the wheel. "I honestly didn't think we were going to make it out of there in one piece. Did you see the look on Hank's face?"

"I know." I laid my head back against the headrest and shut

my eyes. "Honestly, if it'd come to blows, Hank would've torn my head off and asked questions later. I have no idea what I was thinking. For a moment there my wolf thought she'd win, but he's hundreds of years my senior. I didn't have a chance of winning, even though my wolf was absolutely positive we would." I rubbed my hands over my face. "Ugh, how is he not going to think I'm a wolf now? Apparently I stink like one—or at least stink like something awful—and we both know no human can rile up a wolf like that on their own. I'm so screwed."

"It's true, you smell, but you don't exactly smell like a wolf. That works in your favor. Hank won't know for sure based on smell alone. And, on a positive note, at least you're not going to be some loser werewolf," Nick mused. "Going head-to-head with Hank Lauder takes some serious gonads. If he faced me like that, I'd likely just piss myself and run away."

"We can pick you up some Depends on the way home." I chuckled, turning to check the backseat. Someone had placed a small tent, a sleeping bag, and a backpack, along with a back-country pass, on the seat. I turned to Nick. "Do you think whoever's in charge of my apartment investigation will buy the whole last-minute camping story?"

"It depends on who's assigned to the case."

I was not a fan favorite on the police force by any means. "God, I hope it's not Ray." I ran my hands down my legs. I was fidgeting with a nervous energy, coming down from my adrenaline high. The twitchiness was bugging me, but I couldn't help it. "That would be the single worst thing that could happen. We don't need to pile any more stress on top of this already stressful situation." I was starved again and felt like I could sleep for a week. My stomach let out an embarrassing howl.

Time to focus on something else.

I fished my phone out of my pajama waistband, where I'd stashed it back at the meeting. Then I stopped, glancing down at my lap, phone in hand.

And I started to laugh.

Before this very second I hadn't realized I'd just had a show-down with an extremely dominant wolf in faded pink plaid pajama pants. "*Aarrrgghh*," I sputtered between breaths, my laughs sounding like manic hiccups. I clutched my stomach, bending forward. I'd just gone up against a powerful werewolf in grungy pajama pants and an old ripped T-shirt. "Oh...my gods...oh...my..." I hacked between gasps.

"You going to let me in on the joke?" Nick glanced at me from the driver's seat. "It looks awfully funny."

"There's...no...*joke*," I managed. "I promise. The insanity of the whole situation finally...just got to me." I laughed again. "*Whew*, I feel better now. I had to release it somehow, or it was going to eat me alive." I wheezed. "And speaking of eating, can we please pull over and grab some takeout? I'm freaking *starving*." More giggles.

"Anything you need, Jess." Nick grinned. "Wouldn't want you to crack too soon, because whether you like it or not, this is just the beginning."

That was comforting.

It took me well over an hour and several Big Macs to fully calm myself. I'd dug a pair of jean shorts out of the backpack and managed to squeeze myself into them in the bathroom. It was a damn good thing Daisy Dukes were back in. The shorts were old and tight, but at least they weren't plaid. I'd happily dumped my pajamas in the garbage can on the way out and prayed my hairy legs weren't going to overly offend anyone's delicate sensibilities in the restaurant. The crowd inside hadn't appeared to be overly grossed out and I'd made double sure I didn't stick out by ordering my food in an affected European accent. My talents were vast, and Europeans loved their hair.

Nick eyed my legs as I climbed back into the car, his one eyebrow arching perfectly above a dark golden eye. "Forgot to pack your razor?"

"Shut it." I plucked my phone from the center console where I'd left it. "Hey, do you have a phone charger in here? This thing is dead."

Nick pointed to the glove box and I fished out a charger. We always bought the cheapest phones at Hannon & Michaels, since we tended to break them on a monthly basis. The bad guys never cared if your pockets were full when they trounced you.

I plugged my phone in, gave it a quick moment to gather some charge, and powered it on.

"Are you going to call the PD now?" Nick asked as he nosed us back onto the highway. "Or wait until you see the damage for yourself first?"

"I'm actually hoping there's a call from Pete on here. I'm sure word spread through the precinct once my address came through, and Pete should've noticed fairly quickly. I definitely want a heads-up to who's in charge of the case before we get back, and I'm still crossing my fingers like crazy it isn't Ray Hart."

Pete Spencer was the only supe I knew of on the human police force. Or at least the only one I'd ever detected. I'd never been very good at picking out other supernaturals when I hadn't been one; they were good at blending in. Pete was an avian shifter and a damn good beat cop. He knew me as Molly Hannon, a human Essential who used to be a cop who now worked for a supe. He'd kept his distance from me on the force, but once Nick and I had started our P.I. firm, we'd set up an information swap to benefit both of us. I'd just helped him on a case, providing him with information on a group of pain-in-the-ass juvenile sorcerers who'd been causing trouble around town. He owed me, and if he had information, I knew it would already be on my phone.

Once I got a signal, I keyed in voicemail and punched in my codes. I had seven new messages. The first one was from my building super, Jeff Arnold, a low-budget guy who got by without doing much of anything. "Um, hi, Molly, this is Jeff. Just wanted to tell you your apartment is kind of trashed. There was some kind of break-in. So call me if you need anything…" *Click.*

The next message was from Nick, who did a great job sounding alarmed and worried. I glanced at him with the phone pressed to my ear and gave him the thumbs-up, knowing he could hear every word.

"I know I'm the bomb." Nick grinned. "How many times can I save your ass? Lemme count the ways. One…"

I rolled my eyes.

The next call came from my landlord, Nathan Dunn, which surprised me. I'd only met him once about a year after I'd moved in. I guess if your apartment gets ransacked, you have a vested interest, but I was still surprised by a personal call. "Hello, Ms. Hannon, this is Nathan Dunn, the owner of your building. I'm calling regarding your break-in last night, and am hoping this message finds you in good health. The police have informed me that you were out of your apartment at the time of the burglary." They were calling it a burglary. My first piece of good news. "That was very fortunate. The damage seems to be…in the extreme. Please let me know when the apartment will be available for cleanup. I'll send my carpenters over at your first convenience. I am anxious to get this fixed, as I'm sure you are as well."

I raised my brows. Nick shrugged.

The next call was from Marcy. She sounded panicked, which was likely genuine. Marcy Talbot loved her routine more than the Queen loved her tea, and even the smallest upset put a serious wrinkle in her demeanor. She was the only gal pal I'd ever had—or even toyed with having. We didn't do sleepovers or get pedicures, but there was a connection there. She ended her call with, "...and if you ever scare me like that again, I'll make your life a living hell. You can count on it, princess." *Click.*

The next call was from my neighbor Juanita Perez, a fifty-something Latina divorcée who'd never quite gotten the hint, like everyone else in my apartment building, that I despised small talk. Instead, she behaved quite the opposite. "Hola, Chica," her heavily accented Spanish stretched across the phone line, then dropped to a rough whisper. "Dees is Juanita Perez, jour neighbor here. *Somteen baaad* has happened. The police, they tell me you are not at home when the crashing and the banging start, but I know you are still in there. I hear you come home in the night, but I weel not tell. I weel keep it quiet from them. Since they did not find you in there, I theenk you must get away anyway. I keep jour secret, but oh, Chica, the damage, it es sooo much. I weel pray for you." *Click.*

I pressed lucky number seven to erase her message from my phone forever. Then made a mental note to thank her by buying some of that Patrón tequila she always talked about. Maybe then she'd forget she ever made this call. Though having a neighbor who would gladly lie to the police for me, without my asking, was definitely a huge bonus. Juanita could be a thorn in my conversational side, but now I knew for sure she had my back. If anything, this phone call should teach me to be a better neighbor. It paid off.

The next call was the one I'd been hoping for, and Pete's

voice came on the line calm and precise as usual. "Molly, it's Pete. Looks like there was some trouble at your place over the weekend." I could hear him in the background shuffling papers. "It says here you weren't at home during the time of the...assault." He read off the page, "Bed was made, no sign of struggle, blood in your living room, rope fragments on the balcony. Lots of speculation here. Looks like the place was roughed up quite a bit, possibly by someone's...*pet*?" I could hear the surprise in his voice.

The police wouldn't have a good way to explain the massive amounts of fur or the gouged claw marks all over my floors. Bringing your pet to a crime scene was highly unusual. Anyone with a brain would know that the fur samples taken from my apartment could be matched to their pet exactly, making them guilty.

Pete continued in his monotone. "Your purse was found at the scene, but you were MIA. Looks here like a call to your office found you were...camping?" The inflection in his voice showed this piece of information was still under speculation by all. "Ray's got your case. Call me." *Click.*

"Oh, for fucksake!" I yelled, throwing the phone onto the dashboard in disgust. "Just drive straight to jail and drop me off. If Ray's on the case it's not going to be a fair investigation anyway, so we may as well save the taxpayers some money." Anyone but Raymond Hart and I'd have a shot of talking my way out of this mess. I glanced at Nick and he shook his head in sympathy. "Is it too much to ask to get someone who doesn't have a wicked vendetta against me to take the case?"

"Apparently it is," Nick answered. "Do you really think he'd pass up the opportunity to nail you to the wall? He probably had to trade all his good cases in order to get your crappy one."

I sighed. "I don't know why I was dumb enough to think he

wouldn't do exactly that. Of course he'd want this case. He can use it as his final grandstand against me."

Ray Hart hated me. If he could finally prove I was the dope freak he thought I was, or at the very least engaged in something highly illegal, it would make his whole existence. I'd unwittingly become his number one focus during my short eighteen months on the police force. In hindsight, joining the PD had been the most foolish vocation I could've ever chosen. But I'd been young and eager to show the world what I had to offer, and unfortunately, even though I hadn't been full blooded, I'd still been a female born to an enhanced gene pool, which meant I could run faster than any of my human male counterparts, jump higher, lift more than I should be able to, and to top it off, I had better instincts.

According to Raymond Hart, the only rational explanation for "stunts like that" was my being a total crackhead or speed junkie. I must've been doped up on some kind of a superdrug to perform feats like that, and even though I'd willingly subjected myself to multiple drug tests, and worked actively on my defense—in the end, the only option left for me was to quit.

But it'd been too late to shake Ray.

After I'd departed from the police force, along with Nick, who had joined with me, Ray had kept me in his sights. For reasons unbeknownst to me, he wasn't willing to let it go. There were rumors he still took home police footage of me in unexplainable situations, either clearing a six-foot fence with relative ease, or of me explaining how I tracked a perp to an undisclosed location with nothing but my eyes and ears to guide me.

The man was irrationally obsessed, which was a dangerous thing for him to be, especially in light of my recent lifestyle changes.

I glanced at my phone on the dashboard, laying where I'd

tossed it. "There's one more message on my phone," I said. "It said I had seven, but I only listened to six." I knew without having to check it was Ray. I glanced over at the driver's seat. "I'm going to have to listen to it, aren't I?"

"If you want a decent heads-up, you do. If not, feel free to let it go."

I reluctantly plucked my phone off the dashboard. "I need some alcohol for this."

Nick laughed. "Sorry, but all the Jack is at home."

Ray's tenor spread like oil into my eardrum. "Hannon, it's Hart. By now you should know your apartment has been trashed by someone and their goddamn pet. You appear to be *camping*." He let that one sit for a second, his glee prickling me through the phone. "When you get your ass out from wherever you are, call me. I need a formal statement. No more fucking around." *Click.*

That was it.

A good cop knew a crime like this one was personal, and unfortunately Ray was a good cop. Nobody trashed your furniture and personal possessions except a scorned lover, a drug dealer you owed serious money to, or a sick bastard with a vendetta—and they'd brought their *pet*, no less. Who brings their animal to a premeditated crime? The only thing running in my favor, the one thing casting a shadow of doubt on the investigation and my possible connection to it, was thanks to the talented Marcy. My most personal space, my bedroom, had been left intact. The place you lay your head is the first place someone goes for revenge.

Damn, I was really going to have to pay her more.

"Ray's never going to buy that a stranger did that to your place," Nick said.

"I know." I ran my hands through my hair. "The only solution is to continue with the personal angle. We'll have to dig up a former pissed-off target who had motive to break into my house—which shouldn't be too hard. There wasn't an actual burglary, so there'll be no need to press formal charges."

"And will this mystery person we dig up happen to have a pet whose fur matches the samples taken from your apartment exactly?" Nick chuckled. "Ray's not going to back off that easily. I'm sure he'll be lurking in your hallway for the next year until this is solved to his liking. He's a bloodhound. You haven't given him a whiff of anything in five solid years, and now you just dumped the best load of crap *ever* into his lap."

"Ugh, I know." I gave Nick a sideways smirk. "But if he doesn't back down eventually, I can just beat him up with my new guns." I brought my arms up and flexed my biceps. They didn't seem any firmer than usual, but I knew they'd inflict a hell of a lot more damage now if applied correctly—and I planned on applying them very correctly. "Or I could grow some fur, or take a swipe at him with my new, handy-dandy claws." I wiggled my fingertips. The claws weren't out, but it was cool to know they were there somewhere.

"Those would be…effective tactics." Nick chortled. "If you were insane. And I'm sure there wouldn't be *any* consequences if you chose to go that route."

I sighed. Of course there'd be plenty of repercussions, but the real problem was none of them would really affect me in the long run. Now that I was Pack, I had a secret to guard and Pack would enforce it without thought. If Ray kept digging his nose where it didn't belong, the Pack would have no problem taking care of him—permanently.

I hated the guy, but I wasn't ready to sign his death warrant.

"I'll just have to soldier on without my new muscles," I said, reconciling myself to my boring fate. "I've got the camping bags and the passes. It's weak, but it should hold and cast enough doubt into my involvement, which is all I'll need in the end. I'll just have to find a scorned lover who has a penchant for big dogs."

Nick smiled wryly at me. "I'm sure that won't be a problem, Jess. It just so happens we have a lot of big dogs to choose from."

Now it was my turn to snort. "We can't frame a werewolf, and none of them would cooperate on their own anyway. They'd just as soon have me thrown behind bars so they didn't have to deal with me. Not that a jail cell could hold me anymore." I grinned. That was pretty sweet.

I picked up my phone and dialed Ray. It was better not to put off the inevitable. It went to voicemail, which was a small victory. "Ray, I'm on my way back into town. Should be hitting the city in two hours," I said. "See you then."

I had no doubt he would be waiting in my hallway in one and a half.

5

Ray Hart had one shoulder braced against the wall, both his arms loosely folded in front of him like he didn't give a shit how long he had to wait. To a passerby out on the street, he would've appeared to be waiting patiently for his wife to finish up her shopping so they could catch a movie.

Except, of course, he wasn't married and probably hadn't seen a movie since *Rambo* hit the big screen.

I wasn't fooled.

Ray was just under six feet tall with a full head of steel-colored hair. It was cut close to the scalp in a style that would've been military if he'd ever joined up. He had mean muscle, the kind that looked beefy and aggressive. His square jaw matched his thick eyebrows perfectly. He wore plain clothes, a pair of dark khaki pants, and a blue dress shirt, and his hazel eyes bored directly into mine as I walked down the hallway.

I had to hide my grin, since Ray's easy stance was in direct contrast to the foul odor he was emitting. If the strong scent of leftover curry, the garbage that needed immediate emptying, or the stale smell of uncirculated air wasn't enough—the smell of Ray could've knocked me over on its own.

He reeked like a potent mix of satisfaction laced with heavy aggression, and it blew into my nose like a leaf blower aimed straight at my face. This man was not going to accept any of the bullshit I'd planned to dish out. I had to come up with plan B.

Ray exaggerated a look past me, bending his head forward, like he'd expected me to arrive with someone else. When he saw no one behind me he feigned surprise.

But I was alone on purpose.

Both Nick and I agreed it would be better if he stayed out of this for now. Ray knew Nick and I were partners. He knew where to find him.

I plastered on my best smile and sauntered up to him without dropping my eyes. With the sarcasm he'd be expecting, I dripped, "Hello, Ray." I adjusted my hold on the backpack and shifted the sleeping bag I carried in my arms. I'd rubbed dirt on my clothes at the last pit stop, to add to the authenticity, but the hair on my legs and the pungent sweat was completely mine alone. No need to up that ante. "It's so nice to see you again. It's been a little too long in between stalkings. I've missed our happy fun time."

"Cut the crap, Hannon," he said. "Looks like you got yourself into some serious trouble this time. Care to explain?" He levered himself away from the wall in one clean movement, his eyes flickering over my ensemble with little interest.

"Ray, you know perfectly well I can't explain something I haven't seen yet. I just arrived back in town from the wilderness five seconds ago. From what I've *heard*, someone took advantage of my absence and trashed my apartment."

Ray crossed his arms. "That's a convenient way to look at it."

"Gimme a break, Ray." I dropped my bags by the door and gave him my best pissy look. "You know damn well in my line of work I make enemies all the time." I turned toward my door. "Something like this is not *exactly* out of the ordinary, but I shouldn't have to explain that to you. You're the detective."

Ray grunted his response and shifted his body so he stood directly behind me as I reached for my doorknob.

I paused mid-grab.

Holy crap. I didn't have a key. I'd totally forgotten about a key.

Oh, for *shitssake*.

Instead of reaching into my shorts, where I knew I wouldn't find one, I continued reaching for the knob, praying the door would miraculously be unlocked.

I casually turned the knob.

Nothing.

The knob had in fact turned, but the deadbolt above it was engaged, so it didn't give an inch. Jeff the super had a set of keys and must have buttoned it up after the cops left. Inside the door, my lock was sticking its thick metal tongue out at me and laughing. I couldn't shoulder it either. The bolt was top of the line, courtesy of a certain Alpha father, and fashioned from some sort of unbreakable titanium. I could probably rip the door off the hinges without much effort, but that would be a tad too suspicious in front of a detective when I was gunning for complete innocence of any wrongdoing.

I hesitated for a moment, trying to muster a reasonable way out of this.

"Looking for these?" A ring of keys bounced in front of my face like a cat toy.

I glanced back at Ray. His face was inscrutable, but his eyes were focused on me like two beady lasers. Hoping, I'm sure, to note some kind of major reaction on my part. And to add insult to injury, the smell wafting off him now was pure, unmitigated delight.

I was getting good at this sniffing game, the rat bastard.

When I didn't answer, he said, "These were found in your purse—along with all the other goodies you'd think someone would need on vacation. Like your wallet and your sunglasses." The cynicism dripped heavily. "Not many women I know who'd leave town without their purse tucked under their arm."

I turned to face him, leaning back against my door. Then I crossed my arms in front of me, because I was already tired of this game and we were just getting started. "Listen, Ray. I realize you think I had something to do with this whole mess." I jabbed my elbow into the door, indicating the mess in my apartment. "And you think I'm hiding a big, juicy secret from the world. Possibly hidden somewhere behind that door. In fact, you've been dogging me for a very long time trying to find out exactly what it is, making my life hard and increasingly more miserable along the way, but here's the truth—are you ready? I'm *not* hiding anything." Well, other than the fact that I'd just turned into a scary werewolf. "I'm not on drugs and I don't deal them. I don't have ties to the Colombians, and more importantly, I haven't broken *any* laws. The truth is, my boyfriend and I decided to go camping at the last minute simply because the weather was beautiful." Thank goodness it wasn't tornado season. "It was just one of those happy, carefree decisions people make. He took care of bringing the keys, and I forgot to get them back. And while we were gone, someone trashed my place. That's the end of the incredibly juicy story." I reached up and snatched the dangling keys from his grasp and turned to unlock my damn door.

Ray's voice hummed with contempt. "Really, Hannon? And

where in the hell is he right now? Shouldn't he be here with you, so he can unlock your door with his *key*? And help you see about all your troubles?"

"Nope," I said as the deadbolt snapped open. "The last time I checked, I was a big girl who could handle her own problems."

He wasn't buying any of it, but I didn't have much choice. Telling the truth was not an option and I had no other alibi at this point. Ray didn't have any legal right to harass me in my hallway anyway, and as a former cop I knew my rights—but if I tossed him out I might as well just buy my own orange jumpsuit. I could call a lawyer, but lawyering up was just short of admitting you did it. I was hoping my apartment would be a big enough distraction, so we could focus on a new topic, like how I had nothing to do with any of it.

The door swung open.

My apartment was more than a helpful distraction.

It was a fucking showstopper.

My breath hitched in my throat. The devastation was complete. The apartment looked exactly how I'd imagine a frat house would appear after a night of disruptive partying by an army of hooligans bent on total destruction. There wasn't a scrap of furniture in my living room left standing. The only nice thing I owned, an antique sidebar, which used to run along my living room wall, was now lying in a heap of broken wooden chunks.

I must've barreled into it from the side. A few times. Now it resembled a collapsed cardboard box, all the broken bits lying haphazardly at odd angles.

The rest of my furniture was scattered around the apartment. Literally. It was like a grenade had exploded my life into complete chaos. My gaze landed on my shredded couch. Stuffing erupted from the cushions like fluffy intestines, and both armrests were completely mangled. I must have pushed off hard, because the couch was clear across the room.

Damn, I liked that couch.

"I've never seen a place trashed this badly in my entire career," Ray said smugly. He stood just behind me once again, peering over my shoulder at the wreckage.

I ignored him and scooted my bags inside the door with my foot, displacing debris as I went. Then I started to pick my way around the room. The police had dusted for prints and there was residue everywhere. Unfortunately for them, they weren't going to find any suspicious fingerprints. I rarely entertained.

I headed straight across the room to the sliding glass doors that led out to my tiny balcony. Sheets of plywood stood in place of the glass. Huge shards of broken glass scattered the floor *inside*, right by the opening. Yeah, Marcy.

I unlatched the doorframe and slid it open. It still worked, which was surprising. I must have hit it cleanly, since only the glass had shattered. The frame was intact.

I stepped onto my small balcony.

I'd chosen to come out here first for two reasons. One, because that's what Ray would expect me to do. A good cop investigates the entry point of the crime scene first, and even though Ray was not buying my camping story, I still believed he thought this was a true break-in. A break-in I had something to do with, but still a break-in. I also believed Ray thought I'd been home when the attackers came, and had subsequently fled, thereby leaving behind my much-needed keys and purse.

The second reason? I wanted to see if any incriminating evidence lingered so I could try and get rid of it quickly.

Ray stepped onto the balcony with me, crowding us both.

"Hannon," he said. "There was a car in the parking lot with significant damage to the roof. It was all scratched up with what appeared to be…claw marks. The diameter and size matched the gouges all over your floor exactly. It's like they threw their fucking dog off the balcony when they were done. Except there was no blood. We should've been scraping a dead carcass off that roof." He managed to sound accusing, like I'd been there to witness the dog-throwing. "But the techies told me a regular canine wouldn't be heavy enough to inflict that kind of damage. The mutt would've had to be attached to a boulder to crush it that far in. The steel frame warped."

"Hmm. I didn't hear about a car being wrecked," I said in a distracted tone. I was casually examining the top of my railing for gouges. There should be some there, which would give some legitimacy to an animal launching itself off of here, but there were none. Marcy had swept the entire balcony.

"We also found evidence of grappling-hook marks and some rope, but not a single person in the whole building saw anyone shimmying up or down three stories. Pretty strange, don't you think?"

"Yep. Strange." I turned and headed back into my apartment, sidestepping a large pile of broken things on the way in. "It's a mystery. You'd think at least one person would've spotted a body climbing up or down three stories."

"That begs the question: how in the hell did they get their pet in here if they climbed a fucking rope? Now that would be a great circus act if you ask me."

"Maybe there were two people. One who shimmied up and unlocked the door for the waiting dog owner," I suggested winningly. I might as well go along with the probable scenario like a good P.I., since there was no arguing that an animal had been in my apartment. I had no idea what the fur samples would come back as, but I was hoping for "undetermined species." Having it come back as wolf would be a pain in the ass, and would raise more questions than it answered. The human police would never in a million years think "werewolf," but it was best not to raise any complicated questions.

"Crash like that"—Ray indicated back to my shattered sliding glass door—"is bound to bring your neighbors over in a hurry. Not much chance to open the door for an accomplice, and then still have time to trash it all up like this."

Without answering, I headed toward my bedroom. I passed my galley kitchen on the left, the only place my wolf hadn't entered. The small space had been spared because my wolf had ignored it in favor of getting out of the apartment. I loved my tiny kitchen. It was clean and white, with black granite countertops and small stainless steel appliances. It had a large breakfast nook cut into my living room, set with a countertop, which gave the space a larger feel.

I stepped over what was left of a table in the hallway, all the knickknacks that used to sit on it destroyed. I maneuvered around some of the bigger pieces as I edged closer to my bedroom door, which was shut.

I held my breath and turned the knob.

Ray lurked behind me, taking every opportunity to size up my reactions.

The police had spent time in here. Fingerprint residue skimmed the top of my dresser and dotted all the drawer knobs. The police were gathering evidence to prove an intimate crime had been committed. Otherwise my bedroom looked unmolested.

I approached my dresser and pulled a drawer open, knowing Ray was still scrutinizing my choices. I scanned the contents, reaching in and lifting the clothing to do a thorough check. I closed the drawer and pulled open my meager jewelry box, which sat on top of my dresser. It contained only a few pieces of cheap costume jewelry. I was not a bling girl. I glanced in for a cursory check. Ray would expect it.

"We couldn't find anything disturbed in here. It seems to be clean." Ray peered over my shoulder as I closed the box. "You missing any jewelry?"

"No."

"What we can't figure is, why didn't they come back here first? Crimes like this, personal space gets hit first. Kind of like slapping someone in the face. If they wanted to hit you hard, they come here. Cut up the sheets, stab the mattress, shred your underwear. But it's all clear."

I walked toward my bed. "I have no idea, Ray. With a loud crash like you said, they only had limited time to do any significant damage. Guess they just couldn't get back here in time." I slid open the tiny drawer on my completely fixed bedside stand. It was only big enough to hold one small paperback book, or a leather case full of a useful syringe. A stupid mistake I was paying for in spades. I closed it and I ran my hand over my pristine covers. Marcy's work was flawless.

Ray crossed his arms and grunted. The scene didn't match the typical scenario for a crime like this, and it pissed him the hell off. He also understood I was seeing it for the first time, which I was.

Perfect.

I was famished again, my stomach already knotting in on itself. I was also exhausted in the extreme. I was done with Ray and the dance for the day. I strode purposefully back to the living room with him predictably traipsing after me. I spun around in the middle of the chaos, all business. "Okay, Ray. Do you have any leads? Anything concrete you'd care to share with me? If not, I'll get you my statement tomorrow. I'm calling it a day. I've got to clean up this mess and I'm tired and hungry. You're not going to want to be here in another five minutes, because my cooperation time with the police is officially over."

"We're working a couple angles," he hedged. "I'm going to need a full disclosure of all your contacts, specifically anyone you'd suspect capable of doing damage like this. Then I'll need the name of that mysterious boyfriend of yours. I'd like to ask him a few questions." Ray shot me a smirk. "When and if he shows up, of course."

"That's fine, Ray. I'll fax mine over tomorrow and talk to James. I'm sure he won't have a problem chatting with you. Is that it?" *James?* Well, I guess I couldn't exactly date my brother. Men were minimal in my life and the thought of James and Ray having a real face-to-face made me smile. James it was.

Ray headed toward my door on his own, but I wasn't at all surprised when he turned back around with another smug grin on his face. "Oh, and the horse tranq full of shit we found in your bathroom cupboard? We'll need your full explanation on that. *In writing.* It's still at the lab, but once it comes back and we tag it, your ass is mine, Hannon." He left without looking back.

Of course they would find the syringe! That was Ray's big coup de grâce. Why he'd gone a little easier on me once we'd gotten inside. He thought his dramatic exit would bring down the house, that the crippling news of them finding suspicious drugs would leave me quaking. And I had to hand it to him, horse tranq wasn't actually too far from the truth. Dr. Jace had spent a good chunk of his career perfecting a sedative strong enough to prove effective on werewolves. The lab reports would likely contain a laundry list of ingredients, all with doses high enough to effectively knock out not just one horse—but a dozen.

I'd put a call in to my father. Dr. Jace would need to invent a medical necessity for my having it, some rare disease requiring heavy sedatives, and fax the info down to the precinct. That sounded feasible. The needle had never been used, which would be easy enough for the lab to see, and even if they suspected it was illegal, it wasn't like I shot up every night, since there was just the one dose. But Ray was still going to make a big deal about it. Like a thorn stuck in my ass. I sighed and turned, considering my living room and the mess surrounding me. "Okay, now what?" I said out loud to a roomful of my broken possessions. Sadly, nothing responded.

I spent the rest of the afternoon cleaning and stacking as much as I could into various piles. My walls were going to need some major repairs. Big chunks were missing where things had smashed into them. I couldn't even think about the floors without weeping. The gorgeous hardwood was so deeply scarred it would be a miracle if it ever looked the same.

When I finished, I made a couple of phone calls, then devoured every scrap of food in my kitchen, which amounted to an assortment of cheese, crackers, pickles, and microwavable entrees—before falling into bed. Everything else would have to wait until tomorrow.

I slept like a newborn.

When I opened my eyes it was noon the next day.

Fuck.

6

I hustled out of bed and showered quickly. While still slightly damp, I yanked on a pair of jeans and a black cotton top. I tugged my long black hair back into its customary ponytail and slipped into a pair of soft leather flats. I always went to work casual when I wasn't meeting with clients.

Marcy had briefed me yesterday in a short phone conversation about the schedule for the rest of the week. I had several cases requiring my attention today. It seemed the office had received an interesting call from a prospective client yesterday morning, and a response on my part was necessary as soon as possible. It felt like I'd been gone for weeks, not days. Sleeping in had not been on the itinerary.

I'd also chatted briefly with my father before bed. He informed me that he'd positioned several trusted wolves around my neighborhood, several blocks away. The plan today was business as usual. Molly Hannon had to convincingly pick up where she'd left off on Friday if we had any chance of keeping a lid on my shift.

I was glad for the distraction of work, because lingering on my change would drive me batty if I was left to my own devices. My wolf had been quiet in my mind since returning home, but the plain fact that I'd become a full-blooded werewolf was going to alter my life completely—my current reality would eventually become unrecognizable. I wasn't ready. Truth be told, I was ill prepared for any of it. I'd lived as a human for the past twenty-six years. I had no idea what it meant to be supernatural. But since I'd left the Compound seven years ago, I'd taken each day as it came and today I was going to do just that. So help me.

I grabbed my errant purse, the one I had to scrub down last night so it was usable, and slung it over my shoulder. I wove my way through the path I'd cleared to my front door. Once I got outside, I made a cursory glance around the lot. There was no evidence of the car I'd crushed. There weren't even any bits of glass or stray pieces of chrome lying around. That was a little disappointing. It would've been interesting to see the damage. Crashing out of a three-story balcony was impressive by anyone's standard.

I walked toward my black Nissan and pressed the unlock button. The car gave a gratuitous beep. I pulled the door open, but before I could slide in I heard a noise. Footsteps sounded on the asphalt behind me. I inhaled, but strangely I couldn't scent anything. The air carried no smells. I tossed my purse in the front seat and spun around, ready to fight.

"No need to be worried then." A heavily accented English voice hit my ears a heartbeat before I spotted him. "It's just me. I'm checking to make sure all is well with you this fine bright afternoon, and you're still all in one piece." Danny Walker, my brother's best friend, and one of my father's most trusted, sauntered up to me smiling. His brown hair fully covered one eye, which he remedied with a flick of his head. He was a lanky wolf, thin but powerful.

"Danny," I said. "You snuck up on me. I'm going to have to get better at detecting, but it's great to see you." Even though Danny was a friend and ally, and one of the few who knew my secret, our paths never crossed in the city. It had always been too risky. Even now it was risky. "Why can't I smell you?"

"I rang up that witch of yours last night when I received my orders from your father. I asked her for a favor and she willingly obliged. Positioning wolves around the perimeter of your place was bound to raise suspicion to anyone who happened by with a keen nose, even if they were a few blocks away. She fixed us up quite nicely. Seems to have done the trick."

"Great plan." I inhaled again. All clear. Marcy must've conjured some kind of stripping spell, making it impossible to detect any smells within its boundaries. I couldn't even smell the grass. It was likely the quickest and easiest way to spell such a vast area.

"It only lasts a day or two at most, so we'll have to have her come round again." Danny grinned. "You're looking very well, by the way. I have no idea why there's a big uproar about your safety, since no one's bloody told me anything, but don't worry your little head about security. Tyler arrived in the wee hours of this morning and we're all on top of it. Nothing but the very best protection for you. We will make sure you stay safe from whatever it is that's plaguing you." If Danny hadn't figured it out from the beacon, maybe there was hope it had gone unnoticed after all. He knew me and my voice.

"Thanks, Danny. I appreciate that. I hope the whole thing will be short-lived and we can go back to normal as soon as possible."

"Ah, but then I won't get any more chances to see your gorgeous face. Best for us to keep vigilant so we have ample opportunity to keep our clandestine parking lot visits ongoing. This will likely be the highlight of my very long, very boring day."

I chuckled. "How is it possible you never change, Danny Walker? At least you didn't comment about my ass this time."

"What's wrong with your bum, then? Eating too many biscuits?"

"No." I laughed. "I haven't been eating biscuits, but that does sound damn good. And my ass is just fine." I grabbed on to my door handle. "I hate to break up our reunion, but we should end this illicit meeting before it gets noticed. It was good to see you, Danny. I mean that. Thanks for the backup. I appreciate it."

"It's my pleasure." He gave me a mock three-finger salute. "Hope our paths cross again soon." He turned and left like the professional he was. But not before he snuck a glance over his shoulder to check out my ass.

I got into my car, smiling as I slammed the door. Once I was on the road my stomach gave a deep, disgruntled grumble. I'd eaten myself out of food last night and I needed coffee, but it would have to wait. I was already late. My small, nondescript office building wasn't far from my apartment, by design, and I made it in under five minutes.

I pulled into the side lot, closest to the door. The low concrete complex hosted a variety of other businesses—dental, insurance, and chiropractic. Very unnoticeable. Our offices were on the main floor.

I swung open the opaque glass door, marked with the white stenciled lettering "Hannon & Michaels Investigations," and walked in.

Marcy pushed back her chair and stood. "Well, well, well,

look who the cat finally dragged in." She mocked checking the big clock on the wall.

"I know, I'm late," I said. "My cell phone died sometime during the night. I need a new charger; my old one is one of the many casualties of my ransacked apartment. No alarm. But I bet you knew that already. How many times did you try to call?"

"Contrary to what you think, O blessed taskmaster, I thought it best to let you sleep. I'm only your keeper part of the time. My other starring roles include—but are not limited to—the fun-loving gal pal, the beautiful chirpy sidekick, and your brilliant bookie. And I can be all those things because I'm so unbelievably gifted." Marcy walked around to the front of her desk.

"I haven't gambled a day in my life." I chuckled. "And to think, all this time I thought you were all work and no play."

"Nope, that, my friend, would make me a very dull girl." She wrapped her arms around me for a brief second, and then held me out at arm's length, her bony fingertips digging into my shoulders. "And if you ever scare me half to death like that again I will quit this job. I swear. Forever." She shook me. "As in never coming back. Got it?" Then she dropped her grasp and headed back around her desk.

"Marcy," I chided. "Your deep concern about my safety and well-being makes me all tingly inside."

"I don't care. It just seems like I do. But scaring people isn't funny. I almost had a heart attack. You're putting my health at risk if you do something like that again." She sat down and pulled her chic glasses out of her rich red curls—hair I could only dream about—and drew a sheet of paper off the stack in front of her, back to the day's agenda. "You have some calls to make about the Craig case. The one you finished last week. The warlock wants some sort of compensation for his broken nose." She ran through the details. "Oh, yes, and the new potential client, the one I talked to you about yesterday, his name is Colin Rourke. Sounds like a solid case, plus he sounded totally cute." She shuffled through a stack of notes marked "Molly." "And tonight you and Nick are slated for another Drake surveillance run. While you were gone, Nick hired Gary to watch him. The report is waiting on your desk. Oh, and Nick wanted me to tell you, and I quote, 'when she gets her ass out of bed tell her I will be out of the office all day trying to figure out that mess with the paint store owner and the graffiti,' end quote." She handed me the stack. "That about covers it."

"You're a goddess like no other." I grabbed the notes and quickly flipped though them. "This looks like it will keep me in my office all day, which is a good thing, because I'm supposed to lay low."

"Yes indeed. No going outside for you."

I started for my office. "Oh, and by the way." I turned. "I need an enormous amount of food delivered here as soon as possible—and I mean anything and everything you can get your hands on: burgers, fries, shakes, Chinese, whatever. And while you're at it, let's relocate the coffeepot closer to my desk. Like on top of it."

Marcy didn't even blink. "Got it."

"Oh, and Marcy?" She snapped her head up from the pile of food menus she'd already plucked from her filing drawer. "I'm upping your pay by thirty percent, effective last Friday. I wouldn't want to lose the best-kept secret in town because I'm too cheap to notice the value of your extensive talents. And that includes the favor you did for us last night. Good technique with the smell thing, by the way. It totally worked." Witches charged exorbitantly for their crafting services. There were no freebies. And we both knew it. "You can file it under 'saving the boss's ass' or 'awesome spell casting under extreme pressure,' whichever works best for you." I chuckled as I walked down the hallway.

"Just doing my job," she muttered after me.

"I can hear you."

"Stupid werewolf hearing."

I was still smiling when I entered my office. Marcy would take my secret to the grave, and after what she did for me and my apartment, there was no sense trying to pretend it didn't happen. I felt a small pang, because by knowing my new secret she was involved in this whether she wanted to be or not. But knowing her, she wouldn't have wanted it any other way. In fact, she'd probably choke the life out of me if she found out I'd been keeping such a thing from her. We didn't have to have a conversation about it; she was smart and knew the stakes.

My office was small and decorated with standard-issue furniture from the previous tenants. There was a conference room down the hall with a bigger table to accommodate larger groups, but on the whole, we usually met with our clients in a convenient spot of their choosing. The biggest selling point of this particular space, other than its nondescript nature, had been the big windows.

I plucked a thick folder off my desk as I sat down. I shoved my purse by my feet and set Marcy's notes to the side to go over later. Getting back to work was a godsend. Making sure my mind stayed off everything was the key to keeping myself sane.

I opened the case file. The imp we'd been tracking the night of my change, Drake Jensen, was a forty-seven-year-old lowlife slimeball, and it looked like he'd been busy these last few nights.

I scanned Drake's background in the file. It was the first time I'd seen any of this, because he was a new target and the report had taken time to generate. An imp was the lowest demon on the totem pole, which meant he was stronger than a human, but not impossible to catch. By nature, an imp was half demon, half human, his demon side usually inherited from his father. Male demons were known to have the occasional fling with a human counterpart. Female demons were rare and reclusive.

Drake, it seemed, got his rocks off on sex and fear, which was not unusual for certain kinds of imps of the sex demon variety. It fed them the way food feeds the rest of us. But instead of consenting adults, his chosen targets had been young innocents, which made him worse than slime.

He'd recently been released from a human jail for soliciting underage sex and he was already back to his old filthy habits.

We actually had quite a few files on imps because they typically caused the most trouble. They were one of the few supernatural Sects who didn't care if they got caught. An imp usually had a specialized skill, depending on its parent demonic origin. But they all typically had weak magic, because demon magic was born of the blood, and human blood was extremely diluted. Like pouring a shot of vodka in a gallon of water. Hard to get yourself drunk.

Drake's abilities were still unknown. It was a shame birth certificates weren't more helpful, indicating things like "great-grandfather was a fire demon" or "child may have lingering perverse sexual tendencies, from twice-removed sex demon uncle." Because of the sex fixation, we were fairly sure he'd come from an incubus, which meant he most likely possessed the power of sexual persuasion, a dangerous skill to have.

I glanced through the last pages. Drake was on the move. He'd gone to the same movie theater parking lot the past three nights in a row and had been agitated last night in particular. He'd actually left his car, but hadn't physically approached anyone.

I set the folder down on my desk.

If Drake had left his vehicle, his sexual need was coming to a head. Literally. Most incubi had to have sex once every few weeks to fuel their life force. If Drake was still targeting innocents, I was looking forward to catching him and making him pay for his crimes.

Almost immediately a clear image of me pummeling Drake jumped into my head and a sudden jolt of satisfaction surged through me. I grabbed on to the edge of my desk to steady myself, leaving little half-moon nailprints in the cheap laminant wood. I had him by the neck. He was struggling, but it was no contest. A tide of endorphins rode through my bloodstream, dizzying me.

My wolf growled happily inside my head, snapping her muzzle in agreement.

Hold on there, sister. One step at a time.

I needed food.

I spent the remainder of the day making calls and eating. I shoveled in as much food as Marcy could lay in front of me. My hunger was insatiable.

It was sad, really, because at this rate I'd have to eat in private from now on. There was no way I could go into a restaurant and order three cheeseburgers at a time and then gobble them down in front of anyone with any sense. And there wasn't enough time to go to three different restaurants for a normal-sized meal every time I was hungry. It kind of sucked, because I hated cooking, but I was going to have to learn in a hurry; either that or be resigned to the bleak fate of eating prepackaged food or takeout for the rest of eternity.

Marcy was positively gleeful as she dropped another greasy takeout bag on my desk.

I ripped into it without hesitation.

"Good Lord, woman," Marcy said. "At this rate you're going to be twice your size by the end of the week."

"Be quiet or I'll make you eat with me," I managed between bites. "Not all of us were lucky enough to be born with the body of a supermodel." Marcy was tall, svelte, and had incredible curves, which is exactly why normal women referred to women like her as "bitches." It was completely unfair. She could ingest anything she wanted and still look phenomenal. I was hoping my newer, faster metabolism would shape me into a Marcy over time. Doubtful, but I could hope.

She took one look at my face and made a hasty retreat, but not before throwing over her shoulder, "If I ate like that, my stomach would explode. Then you'd be sorry."

"Quiet, hot stuff," I said, my mouth already around another burger.

After my third dip into food, I finally had time to call Nathan Dunn, my landlord, back. It was a quick conversation, and I heartily accepted his offer to help clean up the mess in my apartment. I briefly explained about the piles of furniture and he assured me he would have a team out there shortly to take care of it.

I was mildly surprised I hadn't "heard" from Tyler yet. Communicating telepathically was handy. I gave a small tweak outward in my mind.

Tyler, are you there?

Nothing.

I wondered if there was a distance range. Weird.

Next I wrote my statement for the police and faxed it over to the station. I hadn't had a chance to talk to James in person, but my dad was going to fill him in. Ray hadn't shown up today waving an arrest warrant, so that meant the tranq findings hadn't come back yet. Or they'd been inconclusive. Even better.

The last thing on my agenda was to retry my potential new client. I'd tried calling him earlier in the day, but hadn't gotten through and there'd been no voicemail option, which was a little strange. Everybody had voicemail. I picked up Marcy's note, which had his name highlighted as "the cute-voiced Colin Rourke" and a phone number.

"We'll just see about that," I mumbled as I dialed.

"Hello, this is Rourke," a very strong male voice answered on the first ring.

I had to admit, it held a very nice bravado. There was also an intriguing trace accent I couldn't readily place. "Hello, Mr. Rourke. This is Molly Hannon, of Hannon & Michaels. You contacted us yesterday about a possible problem? What can I do for you?"

"Ah, Ms. Hannon." I could detect a hint of a smile behind those words. "Thanks for getting back to me. It seems I'm having some issues with my business partner, and I'd like to retain your services."

"What kind of problems specifically?" I asked. We took most cases, but sometimes things weren't nearly as dire as people originally thought.

"I believe he's embezzling money from our company."

Well, that sounded dire enough. "Okay, we'd be happy to help. Let's see what we can do."

"Ms. Hannon," he said. "I want to make this extremely clear from the get-go. I'm retaining *your* services, and your services alone. This is a highly sensitive matter and I'm not interested in making it a three-ring circus. Privacy is of the utmost importance."

I cleared my throat, immediately tamping down my annoyance. "I assure you, Mr. Rourke, Hannon & Michaels is a very professional firm. We treat everything we do with *extreme* privacy. Performing circus acts won't be anywhere in your contract, not even in the fine print."

Rich laughter echoed over the line. "I sincerely hope not." Then his voice dipped, taking on a low, gravelly tone. "I'm looking forward to meeting you, Ms. Hannon. You come *highly* recommended for this line of work."

"Thank you." I think. "I look forward to meeting you too, Mr. Rourke. We can set a time to further discuss your situation right now, if it's convenient. When are you available next?"

"It's Rourke, no need for the 'Mr.'"

"Excuse me?"

"My name. It's just Rourke."

"Um...okay, Rourke. When would be a good time to meet?"

"I'm heading out of town on business for the rest of the month Thursday morning, so the only possible time I can meet is tomorrow night."

"That should work." We arranged to meet over drinks the next night in a nearby bar.

"Looking forward to it," he said.

If I was being honest with myself, I'd have to say I was intrigued. My wolf had taken notice too, surprising since she'd been relatively quiet since we'd come to work. However, the moment Rourke had come on the line, she'd begun to prowl. Having her in my head was beyond strange. It was like two separate parts of myself were alive and could operate independently. It was going to take some getting used to. But I pushed it out of my mind for now. I couldn't afford to dwell on it, since my top priority was still business as usual. Once things settled back to normal, like I was madly hoping they would, I was going to allow myself to take as much time as I needed to figure everything out.

I stood and stretched. It was after five and I needed to run a few errands before Nick and I met with the lovable Drake Jensen. I was eager for him to make his move tonight, so we could be done with it.

"Have you talked to Dreamsicle yet?" Marcy asked pointedly as I passed her desk on my way out.

"I have. And he did sound pretty darn dreamy. I'm meeting with him tomorrow evening at eight o'clock to discuss the case."

"Okay, I'll jot it down." I watched her simply mark tomorrow night's calendar date with a big heart. Smartass. "And just so you know, I have a good feeling about this one," she said with a saucy wink.

"You say that about everyone." I rolled my eyes. "You're starting to lose credibility. Plus, you know I never date clients. It goes against my high ethical standards."

"When you're done with the job, he won't be your client anymore. Voilà," she said. "And I'm bound to be right one of these times. I have witchy instincts, you know."

I chuckled. "If Nick calls, tell him I'll pick him up at six-thirty." He'd been gone all day, which wasn't unusual. We were both out of the office a lot. His current case was trying to track down a mystery graffiti artist whose art enthralled those who came too close. It was a tough one.

"I'll be sure to do that," Marcy said.

I walked to the door.

"And, Jess?"

"Yep?" I turned.

"I'm really glad you're back."

"I'm really glad to be back." I smiled.

"No need to get a big head about it."

7

I shut my car door and a soft ping floated through my head, followed by my brother's voice. *Heading home already?*

Yep, but I'm leaving on another assignment in a couple of hours with Nick. It should be no big deal, just a stakeout. Are you nearby?

I'm a couple blocks away. I can see your car from where I'm standing. Everything's been quiet on all fronts.

That's a relief. I glanced out my window and down the street. I couldn't see Tyler or his completely unsubtle shiny red Mustang anywhere, but that didn't mean he couldn't see me. *I wasn't sure what to expect, but nothing sounds perfectly great to me.*

Nick is in charge of covering you tonight, so if you two decide to split up you have to give me a call.

Okay. Have you heard anything new from up north? I was hoping the wolves on the Compound had calmed down overnight.

I haven't heard anything specifically. Dad still has everybody on lockdown now. They were going to have several meetings about it today. I don't think they're buying you haven't changed, and Hank has been on a rampage, shouting garbage about you as usual.

Shit. That's not good. Well, to top off that crappy news, Ray Hart is the detective on my case.

The asshole who gave you trouble on the force?

The very same. He also found my tranq. They have it at the lab as we speak. He thinks it's highly illegal and is hoping to pin it on me.

We should've taken care of him years ago.

Killing people is not always the perfect solution to everything. Dad didn't think it was a problem and has Doc on it already. They'll come up with something plausible. I also told Ray I wasn't home because I was camping with my new boyfriend, James.

He half snorted half coughed.

Yes, and to top it off, we were so madly in love he made me forget my purse and all the necessities a normal person needs on vacation.

Tyler laughed. *That's a good one. I'm sure James will play along; he's a good guy, even though that's the funniest thing I've heard in a long time. And don't worry about trouble cropping up, one of us will be close by from now on, including Danny. I'll get you a Pack cell phone shortly. You can use that to get a hold of the rest of us.* The Pack changed their cells more often than an infant soiled their diaper. I'd never bothered with one. Honestly, if I'd had a problem big enough to bother Pack with prior to this—I might as well have just used my own damn phone.

I know, I saw Danny today. It was nice to see a friendly face, especially if a storm of discontent is on its way. He was exactly the same. Nothing ever changes with him.

Danny is loyal to Pack. You can trust him with your life.

I was curious about our brain connection. When we were kids, we were never farther than a few miles away from each other. *How far away do you think we can do this mind thing from? Do you think there are stipulations? Like mind-wave distance boundaries or something?*

Pretty far, I'd assume. I was outside the city limits all day, just got back. I wanted to touch base before you went home, so this was the easiest way.

It was my turn to snort. *You mean you were ordered by Dad to check up on me to see if I was still breathing once you got back into town? To make sure no rogue wolves or trusted Pack mates have torn me to pieces yet?*

That too. He chuckled.

I sobered. *Tyler.* I paused. *How long do you think we really have until my shift to full blooded blows up in our faces? Before there's no turning back? I desperately want my life to go back to normal, but it doesn't seem remotely possible. I want you to tell me the truth. The honest-to-goodness, in-my-face truth.*

Honestly? He sighed. *I don't have a clue. If we can quiet the Pack, we gain time. If not… I don't know. What happened to you is completely unprecedented. None of us have any idea what we're dealing with yet. We have no way to know how the community will react to the news. The wolves have always feared the Cain Myth, but other supes might have that information too. I have no idea what they'll choose to do with it, if anything.*

I'm fooling myself, aren't I? Thinking I can just go back to my normal life like nothing's happened—like I'm not a freak of nature. Like there's not going to be an army rising up against me at the first opportunity.

No. I don't think you're fooling yourself. You're not the type. He paused for a moment. *I think we're doing the right thing here. If we have any chance of keeping the biggest secret in supernatural history under wraps—and us werewolves are known for our secrecy, make no mistake about it—then you need to be right where you are now, pretending nothing has happened. If it does happen to get out, it happened to Jessica McClain, who is currently in parts unknown, not to Molly Hannon, who's been minding her business while this story unfolds.* He cleared his throat, which sounded odd. *I think if we keep your alias intact, we have a shot. I really do.*

A shot. That's not saying a whole hell of a lot.

Well, it's more than saying we're fucked right out of the gates.

I laughed. *That's very true.*

And, Jess? Now that you're a wolf, you know you're going to have to make a full change soon, right? A new wolf feels the pull often. Your body will ache to run. We usually head down by the river after midnight. Next week at the very latest.

I shivered remembering my change. Not in my top ten fun moments. *Got it. Other than hunger, I'm not feeling much of anything.*

It'll come.

I'll take your word for it.

If you need me, you know where to find me.

I opened my apartment door and found a surprise. All of my broken furniture, which basically meant everything I owned, had been cleared out. Including the shredded couch. The floor also appeared to have been swept and mopped, and other than the deep, angry gouge marks and a few ragged dents in the wall, it looked like a new apartment.

Dunn had been good to his word.

I lugged two bags of groceries I'd just purchased into my kitchen. I quickly put everything away, and then made myself two pounds of spaghetti and stuck a whole loaf of garlic bread in the oven. Thank goodness for take n' bakes.

It took me under ten minutes to eat the entire meal, and five to clean it up.

I headed into my bedroom. Time to get ready for the Drake run. I opened my closet doors and gave a happy sigh. Finally the fun part of my day. Anticipation rippled across my spine and soft tingles raced down to my fingertips. I reached in and selected a few hangers, smiling like a fiend.

Time for a little kickass.

There were a lot of things in my closet I was fond of, but my stakeout clothes were by far my favorite. I'd learned the hard way, being unfettered and fluid was a necessary part of my job.

And it was a purely fortunate accident that my ass looked fantastic in spandex.

I dropped my jeans and slid on a pair of silky black leggings. They fit like a second skin and were supposed to be tear-resistant, water-resistant, and somewhat flame-resistant—if someone threw a lit match at me, not if I were to become engulfed in flames. They were satiny and insanely comfortable. A small pocket was sewn into the waistband just big enough to hold my ID, which was handy since regular pockets don't work well on skintight.

I matched them with a long-sleeved spandex top of the same material. It had tightly woven mesh under the arms, to make it breathable, and extra padding running halfway down the sleeves. There were also two loops sewn onto each arm, right below my shoulders, to hold weapons of my choosing.

I wasn't carrying any throwing weapons tonight, however.

Incubi weren't known for their fighting skills. I wasn't going to need much more than my fists, especially since they were packing extra heat these days.

I finished the ensemble by pulling on a tight black knit cap and I knotted my hair at the base of my neck. My hair was a problem, and by all rights I should've chopped it off a long time ago. It had gotten me into trouble in the past, and being incapacitated by hair-pulling could prove a fatal mistake. But vanity was a bitch and I liked my hair long.

I laced up a pair of custom-made black cross-trainers, which boasted extremely thick treads and a line of thinly molded steel running protectively around the toes. They also sported tiny Velcro pouches sewn discreetly on the sides. Very handy for sneaking in a wire undetected.

You could custom order just about anything if you had the money. An extra thousand and I could've had my outfit spelled. Though, depending on who you were up against, the spelling didn't come with a guarantee. A higher demon or sorcerer could smash right through most things if they had enough strength. Plus, the last time I had a thousand dollars to spare was, um, never. My dad had offered to supplement me on many occasions over the years, but I'd never accepted. It'd taken a lot for me to finally earn my independence off Compound, and I took it very seriously.

I hadn't heard any different from Nick, so I assumed we were on schedule. I grabbed my cell phone, pushed my ID into the front of my pants, and headed out.

In the lot, I opened my car door and slid inside. I leaned over and pulled open the glove box first to check my handgun. My licensed-to-carry, palm-sized 9mm Glock 26 looked brand-new. I'd hardly ever needed it. I did a cursory check of the sight line and the magazine. It shot jacketed silver hollow-point bullets, with added silver shavings at the tip. The bullet was meant to explode on impact and send silver streaming into the blood of whoever was pissing me off at that very moment. It was deadly, because silver worked on most supernaturals. Not all myths were true—which I knew firsthand—but silver was spot-on. Silver, in its purest form, had the highest electrical and thermal conductivity of any metal and reacted like fire to whatever magic fueled the blood of a supernatural. Only the oldest vampires and shifters could fully recover from silver poisoning without massive intervention.

I could hit a running target dead-on, but a gun would never be my weapon of choice. It was too clumsy. But it was nice to know I had a little something-something in reserve when the going got tough. I put it back, closed it up and headed out.

Nick lived only a few minutes from me. He was waiting at the curb. His outfit was black, but was lacking in the shine department. His loss. He opened the passenger door and climbed in. "Feel good to be back?" he asked. "Or do you wish you'd kept right on running Saturday morning?" He held a bag of goodies that smelled suspiciously like the pecan cinnamon rolls from my favorite bakery around the corner from his place.

"What, and leave all this behind?" I spread my arms over the wheel in mock exaggeration, then I nodded toward the bag. "Is that what I think it is?"

"Yep. I figured if yesterday's forty pit stops were any indication, you'd be hungry within the first ten minutes. When I went through my transition, if I went without food for more than an hour I was in danger of gnawing on my own leg. Plus, I knew if I fed you these sticky, sweet things at regular intervals, I could keep you relatively happy and focused on the task."

"Good thinking, ace," I said. "Now open that bag and toss me one."

The movie theater Drake had chosen to haunt was located just outside the city limits. It was one of those mega–theater complexes, situated at the edge of a long flowing suburb that used to be nothing but farmland. It boasted eighteen screens and three full snack bars.

We pulled into the main parking lot and drove to the overflow lot, located a hefty distance from the main entrance.

I swung the car into the farthest space available, right next to a grassy knoll. Over the top of the small hill more undeveloped land stretched across the landscape—most likely awaiting a future Home Depot or Wal-Mart. There were a few young trees and bushes dotting the boundary, but otherwise it was pretty bare. It was the perfect location for someone like Drake to take someone unaware. Which was exactly why we were here.

"How do you want to run this?" I asked, turning to Nick, before snagging another sweet, delicious roll. I licked the sticky caramel from my fingers. He was the levelheaded-planner type and I was the take-action-and-ask-questions-later type, so Nick usually ran the points.

"When it gets dark, one of us stays," Nick said. "And one of us heads back into the trees until he shows. If he's agitated, he won't be able to hold out long. Once he finds a suitable target, he'll move."

"Okay, I'll take the trees. I'm too pumped to sit still anyway." More cars pulled into the lot. "I hate when we have to deal with the lowlifes. It's always so depressing."

"I know, but a world without Drake on the streets is a better world. If he does decide to make a grab and tries to take her back to his car, I'll be the diversion. I'll maneuver him back to the trees instead. He'll have no choice but to head there if I'm too close. We take him once he's over the hill."

We both knew Drake would not surrender. In a case like this, it was within our rights to use a "reasonable amount of force" to bring him down, which is how it was worded in the description of a citizen's arrest. I loved the ambiguity, since "reasonable" for an imp meant a considerable amount.

"Here." Nick held out a small black device. It was thin and about the size of a pack of gum. It worked like a vibrating pager between the two of us. If I depressed my button, the one Nick carried would go off. Small, easy, and effective. "One buzz for visual contact, two for a change of plans, continuous for backup. We rendezvous at the southeast corner of the building if anything goes wrong."

"Got it." I took it from him and swapped out my ID, which I stuck in the glove box next to my Glock. I maneuvered it into my pocket, positioning the device facing out, so I could activate it through my spandex.

Slipping from the car, I disappeared over the knoll.

I picked a place with the best vantage point. There was still time before the last of the daylight vanished. Drake wouldn't come until full dark. I inhaled, curious to see what I could identify with my new nose. I immediately caught stale popcorn, a mixture of greasy fast food, and more than a hint of human urine. Gross. It wasn't a surprise with everyone slurping a super-sized soda. I just didn't need to know about it. I picked up a family of rabbits nearby. I was surprised to find I liked the smell. It was a sweet musk and it made me hungry—hungrier than I already was, which wasn't saying much.

For the next hour and a half, cars entered the lot but few left. Around nine, the main area stayed full. It was late summer. At nine-fifteen the streetlights blinked on, triggered by the fading light, spreading dull pools of light over the asphalt. Ten minutes later, when the sky settled into darkness, our man Drake pulled into the lot.

I knew it was him by the make and model of his car. The

battered Lincoln Continental floated up the lanes, right into the overflow area. My hip buzzed a second later, Nick alerting me to his arrival. Drake swung his boat into a spot not ten feet from where I crouched.

His features through the car window were sharp and hawkish. Once he turned off his engine, his fingers immediately started drumming the steering wheel. He glanced over his shoulder every two seconds to survey the lot.

You're not getting any tonight, boyo.

He'd make his move tonight. There was little doubt.

The thought of permanently wiping that smirk off his face sent a sweet rush of adrenaline racing through my veins, much stronger than it had been earlier today.

Prey.

The word flashed through my mind like a rocket and suddenly my wolf stood at attention, front and center in my mind. She wanted a fight. *Uh-oh.* I couldn't fight a Dominion battle now, all hell would break loose if I lost.

She growled. It was a low menacing sound.

Shit.

Drake chose that moment to ease himself from the car. He half slouched, half crept his way through the parked cars. I had no choice but to follow, but I tried to reason with my wolf as I went. *You have to let me have this one.* I edged along the tree line, staying low, keeping him in my sights. *I can't let you have control again. We already did that, and I'm not looking for a repeat of the farmer fiasco. This is too important, you have to let me lead.*

The wind shifted and I caught a whiff of something faintly sulfuric. A beat later an overwhelming sense of Otherness hit me, climbing along my skin like a warning. The hair on my arms rose to attention and my body gave an involuntary shudder. My sensing had kicked in and I'd picked up Drake's magic, clearly marking him as a supe. That was handy. My wolf sat up straighter, scenting real danger for the first time. *Crap.*

I knew the moment Drake picked his target, because the scent of his lust wafted over me. His pheromones were repellent, like stale moldy bread. I wrinkled my nose and tried to breathe through my mouth as I crept closer. His lust scent, mixed with the rotten egg smell—the demonic part of his Otherness—was now officially burned into my memory banks like a bad acid trip. My brain efficiently categorizing it away for later. Wolves could recognize scents, even years later. Not exactly a smell I wanted in my arsenal, but it was good to know that if he got away, I could track him down.

Drake's victim, or victims in this case, were two girls of no more than fifteen or sixteen. The girls giggled as they walked, totally consumed by their discussion of the boys they planned to meet inside. They were perfect targets. Too totally preoccupied with their upcoming adventure to notice the odd man lurking a few car lengths away from them.

I slid in closer, shielding myself behind the last tree at the edge of the lot. It wasn't much of a cover, but Drake was fully absorbed. The noxious amount of lust he was emitting told me he was using all of his primary brainpower on seizing his victims instead of keeping alert for possible danger—which made him a dumbshit, as well as a pedophile. I was only four car lengths away from the group now.

Drake eased forward, and I dropped to the ground. The girls were chatting more animatedly as they approached a large gap separating this lot from the main parking area. Drake would lose them if they cleared the last row of parked cars.

"Can you believe how Danielle acted last night? She just threw herself at him. I was so embarrassed for her."

"I know, it was ridiculous. As if he would..." The skinny blonde in the light blue sundress stopped talking in midsentence. She faltered for a moment, shaking her head. "Becky, I...I think I left something in the car. I...I need to go back." Her voice was stressed.

"What do you mean? What'd you leave?" Becky was a foot taller, with long brown curls.

"I dunno...but I have to get it. I'll be really quick...I promise."

So our friend Drake did have persuasion skills. I hoped like hell that was all he had.

"We're already late, Jen," Becky said impatiently. "Just forget it. Honestly, it can't be that important if you can't even remember what it is."

"Um." Jen struggled. She was hearing one thing from her pal, and another in her head. "No...you go on ahead...I'll catch up. I'll be really quick. I promise. I just have to get...this thing."

Becky clearly wasn't willing to leave her friend alone. *Go, Becky.* She started trailing after the now departing Jen. "I don't know why you're doing this. We're already late." Two paces in Becky stopped abruptly. She shook her head. After a short pause, she mumbled, "Um, okay, Jen. You go get it and...I'll wait for you...in the theater." Even though Becky was clearly getting a missive from Drake to leave, it took her more than a few seconds to actually tear herself away and head in the opposite direction. She was warring with herself. People with strong will were always harder to persuade than those without.

Controlling two individuals was going to be a double struggle for Drake. It sapped a lot of energy to do a dual persuasion, as Nick could attest to, and I hoped he was motherfucking tired.

Becky trotted off toward the movie theater, while Jen wandered back toward her vehicle. Drake followed behind her like a shadow, keeping a single car in between them as he went. Another shot of sweat-laced, moldy pheromones wafted up my nose. He was getting more and more aroused. It made me want to tear his arms from his body.

I was still on the grass, waiting for an opportunity, when my wolf lunged to the surface with no warning whatsoever. She barreled into my psyche like a hammer exploding down on a nail, demanding control in a rush of power. My arms shot forward and I sprang onto the balls of my feet.

She wasn't going to take no for an answer this time.

With gigantic effort, I forced myself to my knees in the grass. I was furious. *Goddamn it, I'm not going to lose control again! Do you hear me? This is my body and we do what I say when I say it!* I plunged my hands into the earth hard enough to break all my nails to the quick. I clutched at the dirt like a lifeline, trying to ground myself in my *humanness*. As she fought for control I closed my eyes and pushed back as hard as I could. I couldn't let my wolf take control, it wasn't an option. If she ruled me, I could kiss my life goodbye.

My arms trembled with the need to change, my muscles shifting under my skin. I clenched my teeth. I couldn't believe I'd been stupid enough to think I could come here tonight. I was a newborn. A ticking time bomb. I had no control. What was I doing here?

I opened my eyes and glanced frantically around me. I had to get out of here. Right now. Nick could handle Drake by himself. I wrenched a hand out of the earth and was about to push the vibrate button twice, when Jen's childish sound of alarm rent the air.

Drake had made his move.

I spotted them quickly. He had her around the waist. Jen was struggling, fighting for her life. In his anxiousness, he must have dropped his persuasion over her. Either that or he just wasn't strong enough to manage both girls at the same time after all.

There was no way I was letting sweet, blue-sundressed Jen become Drake's latest victim.

No more time to think; I had to act. I closed my eyes once again, and with all the power I could gather I grabbed my human side and shoved it into the forefront of my mind in one massive mental heave. My wolf rose against the tide, snapping and growling, doing her best to block my human instincts as she fought for her own. She wanted to win.

But I wanted it more.

Beads of sweat broke out along my skin, prickling my forehead. I continued forcing the pressure forward, making it count, not relenting. It was like pushing against a giant rubber band, I had no idea if I was gaining ground. It bowed one way, and then back the other, as we both fought hard for command. I threw one more shock of energy into it and a loud tearing sound reverberated along my senses, like a massive sheet of paper being ripped in half. My mind pulled apart like a photo negative, one side gray, the other side black. Both still the same image, but now fully separate.

No time to worry about it.

I was in control and that was all that mattered.

I jumped up and started moving. *I'm in the driver's seat now, got it?* She was still in my mind, but now she sat just behind an opaque film that hadn't been there a moment ago. *Fighting humans and imps is mine*, I told her as I slid between the parked cars. *You can have the nasty werewolves.*

She let out a howl of frustration.

We're searching for harmony here, so feel free to help a girl out. I stopped and crouched lower. I was one car length from Drake and Jen. He had a grimy hand covering her mouth and one solidly around her middle. He was fully occupied.

I shimmied to the edge of the fender. As much as I was aching to jump in right away, I had to be patient. We had to pin Drake with everything we could. If I jumped too early, especially since he had the gift of persuasion, he could easily convince Jen that nothing had happened and get away scot-free. I couldn't risk that.

Jen bravely kicked and slammed her head into his shoulder over and over. She was fighting a good fight. It was all I could do not to attack then and there. Drake was obviously struggling to keep his hold. He finally grabbed her face and hissed something in her ear. She stopped moving instantly.

He hurried her back toward his car.

I followed closely, keeping myself low and out of sight. I spotted Nick across the road. He was right on time, whistling something under his breath, making a good show of a man heading back to his car from a night at the movies. Drake saw him immediately and arched himself around, Jen still in his arms, changing his plans instantly. He started toward the knoll to get out of sight, just like we'd thought.

Drake, although not full on brains, would've had a loose plan in place. If he failed to get his victim to his car in time, the hill would provide a cover from any human interference. That's why he'd picked this particular theater complex.

Only he had no idea that the only female werewolf on the fucking planet was coming after him.

The moment he disappeared from sight I took off. There was a small cry followed by the sound of a body hitting the ground. I jumped the curb, leaping into the air, clearing the knoll in one jump. Drake was already on top of her. From my angle, it wasn't clear if he was trying to keep her quiet or if he was going to satiate himself right then and there.

It didn't matter, because I was on him one beat later.

I hit him hard, smashing into him from the side, and we both went flying. "Take that, asshole," I growled. I rolled once and was back on my feet. Drake readied himself just as quickly, snarling at me, flashing a set of stained, yellowed teeth that looked remarkably sharp.

Hmm, maybe he had a bit more imp in him than we'd previously considered.

He let out an enraged yowl and came at me with impressive speed, but he wasn't nearly as fast as I was. When he was within an arm's length of me, I swung my right leg around and connected with his ribs. They popped with a satisfying crack and he flew backward ten feet in the air.

My wolf gave a delighted yip. *See, I'm not a pansy. You're going to have to start trusting me.*

Despite his injury, Drake was up and on me again. "You little bitch," he hissed. "I'm going to make you hurt for that."

He seemed to have increased strength, as well as persuasion. I was now a hundred percent certain Drake Jensen was genetically more imp than human. If I hadn't just become a full-blooded wolf, I was pretty sure he would have the upper hand and my ass would've been in serious trouble.

I needed more strength.

I made a split-second decision and opened myself a little to my wolf. I cracked the opaque barrier a tiny bit and she gleefully burned through me, pumping me with more strength, giving me a satisfied growl in return.

Drake came at us again, and I dodged him easily. He wheeled around, changing his direction quickly. I braced myself for the impact and we both exploded to the ground. He landed on top, grinning down at me, mistakenly thinking he'd caught a lucky break. He threw a punch, connecting hard with my left shoulder. It rocked me into the dirt, but as he recoiled to throw another punch, putting space between us, I shimmied my knees up under him and rolled back on my hips. I threw him off in a rush, crossing my fingers that he would hit something hard. I jumped to my feet.

My shoulder hitched for a second, healing from the blow. Another shot of adrenaline raced through me, courtesy of my wolf. The surge of new power was more than the small opening I'd just made could sustain for any length of time. The little crack was on track to become a gaping fissure. With my new infusion of strength, I felt fire kindle in my irises. I was certain they were blazing full yellow.

Drake lunged at me again, feral madness in his own eyes. I spun quickly, pivoting back around, bringing my arm up. Using the power in my upper body as a fulcrum, I smashed my fist into his face as we collided.

Drake's face imploded in on itself as he flew backward, crashing directly into the small tree behind him, shaking it to its roots. He slid down the base, collapsing into a scumbag heap on the ground.

I stood staring, my mouth open, eyes wide for several beats. The thrill of the fight wound tightly inside me like a loaded spring ready to explode. I felt no pain, only pure elation. I forced myself to bend over, bracing my palms on my thighs, taking in several quick breaths. I had to calm down, shut myself off from the adrenaline. But my wolf wanted more, rubbing against my mind like an itch I couldn't scratch. She demanded we finish what we'd started here.

I had to settle her. *We did it, the bad guy is down. Now we have to get ourselves under control, because it's going be crazy around here any minute. People will be crawling all over. Honestly, I couldn't have done that without you, but I need to be fully in charge now, and I can't do it if you fight me. It's too damn hard to concentrate when my brain is divided. Do you understand?*

She gave a frustrated bark, but eased back down.

Someone was calling my name. "Jess! Jess, are you okay?" Nick jogged in my direction. "Jesus Christ, Jess! That was completely insane. I've never seen anyone fight like that. I couldn't even track you, you were moving so fast. I think you might have killed him." He looked from me to the listless pile of Drake.

I met his eyes and he gasped.

"My God," he breathed. "Look at your eyes. They're fully changed. How in the hell are you doing that?"

"They're still lit?" I gasped between breaths. "I've got to calm myself down. When the crowd comes I can't have glowing yellow eyes. That would be a teensy bit suspicious."

"Um, Jess?"

"Huh?"

"They're not…exactly yellow," Nick said quietly. "They're actually kind of…purple…"

I rose to a standing position so quickly I almost tossed myself ass backward. I stumbled to get my footing and opened my mouth to tell Nick he had to be out of his frigging mind, but a voice inside my head interrupted me before I could get the words out. *Jessica! Jessica, what's going on! Jessica, are you okay? Goddammit! Answer me this instant!*

It's okay, Dad! I'm here. I put a finger up to Nick and turned and walked a few paces away. *I'm fine. There was just…I had a little trouble at work. Are we on an open line here?*

No, of course not. Your wolf called to mine and I answered, like

I've always done when one of mine is in need. Then for some reason... I couldn't connect with you. I could feel his confusion. *I've been trying my damnedest to reach out to you ever since. What in the hell is going on down there?*

Well. I surveyed the scene in front of me. Jen was quietly weeping and Drake was still unmoving against the tree. *It seems I just won a fight against an angry imp who was gunning to kill me. At least I think he was an imp. He was actually stronger than we'd originally anticipated.* I wasn't sure what to say about the next part. *And because I underestimated him, I sort of needed... well, I guess you could say I brought my wolf to the forefront to help me get rid of him, but I didn't shift. If I hadn't used her, I'm not sure I would've won.* I glanced over at the pile of Drake bleeding profusely from his face. *I think I may have killed him by accident.*

There was dead silence in my mind.

Dad? Listen, I'm so sorry! I didn't mean to do anything wrong. I honestly don't know what happened, it all went so fast. A fight like that should've taken an hour, but it seemed to happen at warp speed. There was no time to slam on the brakes. I just reacted as best I could. I never should have come out tonight on this run, but I thought I could handle it.

After a long pause, my father said, *Jessica, we'll discuss this later. We have strict Pack rules and guidelines that must be followed. No exceptions. You don't know our ways yet, so I am going to give you some leeway. Using your wolf is acceptable, but shifting is not. But I'm more concerned about your safety right now. It's my top priority. Do you need a cleanup crew? I can have James and Danny there in five minutes.* All supernaturals had a strict "cleanup" protocol. If we called in the human authorities every time a fight happened between us, our secret would be out with the first dead cadaver. When something with fangs, no working organs, yellow eyes, or pointy ears showed up in the morgue it tended to get noticed. There were breaches, but for the most part every Sect followed the rules.

I considered taking my father up on it. I'd never used a cleanup crew before, and it would be so much easier to have Drake disappear. *No, this one will have to be aboveboard. We have a teenage civilian.* Something streaked by my peripheral vision. It was Becky. She took one look at Jen, who was lying where Drake had left her, and dropped to her knees, wrapping her arms around her pal crying. *Make that two civilians. There's going to be a huge scene in about ten minutes. Police, ambulances, concerned parents, the whole nine yards.*

What can I do?

There's nothing you can do here. Are you at the Compound?

Yes, I'm here. The wolves are still… in some unrest. I am occupied for the moment.

What about the tranq? I knew Ray would be breathing down my neck as soon as my involvement with Drake came over the wire.

Jace is putting together medical papers for you and he'll fax them down tomorrow. He's confident the lab won't be able to identify the serum. He's going to label you as having some kind of a seizure disorder.

Got it. Becky was beginning to get hysterical. *I have to run.*

Jessica? There's one more thing. I heard—or rather felt—tension in his voice.

Yes?

What I say to you now has to be kept between us at all costs. I can't stress this enough. Do you understand? Anxiety thrummed through the connection.

Yes, of course I understand. I won't repeat it.

Tonight? What you did? Blocking me like that? He took a

breath. *It's never been done before. There has never been a wolf strong enough to block me the way you just did. I'm fairly certain that's what you were doing—whether you intended to or not. No matter how much power I pushed toward you, and even though your wolf had called to mine, I couldn't break through. I felt his fear then. Jessica, I felt all your emotions…and I couldn't do a damn thing to control them.*

Well, fuck.

8

As predicted, the scene was chaos in under ten minutes. Huge spotlights drenched every inch of our little pocket of grass. It was lit up like a stadium during the Super Bowl. The place was crawling with reporters, cops, firefighters, curious moviegoers, theater staff, and a double set of furious parents.

Nick and I sat half perched out of a squad car, giving our statements to the attending officers. Thankfully, Ray hadn't shown up yet, but there was little doubt he would materialize soon enough.

I hoped I'd be excused before then, but it seemed doubtful.

"Okay, Ms. Hannon. We have what we need for now. Someone will be in contact with you soon. Mr. Jensen's final condition"—the female cop nodded toward the ambulance—"will affect this process, as you know." She meant, if Drake managed to survive, I would be expected to testify in court, and if he died, well, there would most likely be a detailed investigation into his death. I wasn't looking forward to either scenario.

Before we put a call in to 911, Nick had persuaded both girls, changing the story of what had really happened to something easier to swallow. Poor Jen would retain most of her "before" part clearly—but watching me almost kill her attacker bare-handed with stupefying speed had been tweaked as necessary. In the spirit of things, Nick had even coaxed her out of severe shock before the paramedics arrived, which had been a big task because he'd also had the wailing Becky to contend with.

My right hand, where it'd connected with Drake's jaw, had completely healed in a matter of minutes, so blaming hand-to-hand combat on what had happened to Drake's face was completely implausible.

While Nick was busy tending the girls, I'd devised a quick solution with an appropriately sized rock. I pressed it into the contours of Drake's face, smearing the surface of the stone with an adequate amount of blood and tissue. Thankfully Drake hadn't stirred during the process—and to my relief, he hadn't been quite dead either. Supernaturals, on the whole, were tough to kill. But that didn't mean he'd be waking up anytime soon. His injuries were severe—even for a supe.

The story I told the police was that I'd snuck up on him with the trusty rock, interrupting his attack, and hit him with more force than I'd intended. The story hadn't accounted for any of the other injuries to his body, but there was a chance Drake would heal some of his own wounds by the time he arrived at the hospital. That would certainly help.

I glanced over the officer's shoulder as they loaded Drake into the back of the ambulance. He'd already been in a human jail, but I had no idea if he'd ever been in a hospital. An imp's blood wasn't exactly a red flag. Most of the time their blood was classified as hemophilic.

The officer handed back my ID. "I understand the process," I said. "Is there anything else?"

"Will we be able to contact you at this number tomorrow?" She read back my cell phone number.

"Yes."

"Then you're free to go."

Nick was still giving his statement, so I stood outside the car and waited. Our story should hold as long as the persuasion held and Jen didn't decide to change her side of the story to, "The girl with the glowing violet eyes beat him to death with her fists."

Unfortunately, blue-sundressed Jen would likely have dreams containing pieces of the true events her entire life. The subconscious was a powerful thing, and this had been an extremely traumatic event for her. Lucky for us, and her, Nick was one of the strongest wielders of the gift. There were only a few humans who hadn't succumbed to his efforts, and the guy heading straight toward me was one of them.

Cripes.

No matter how many times Nick had tried, Raymond Hart's mind had never taken to persuasion. The alterations in his line of thinking never stuck for more than an hour at most. And Ray always acted crazy for the next few days. He had no idea what had happened to him, just that something had, and he always blamed me, his anger becoming more intense every time we tried. It was a lost cause, so we'd stopped trying.

"Ray, it's such a nice surprise to see you here," I said. "I'm assuming you rushed all the way over here, nowhere near your jurisdiction, to make sure I was safe after my awful run-in with a pedophile. Thanks for caring so much, big guy." I mocked punching his arm

"Cut the shit, Hannon. This has your name written all over it," he said.

"Well, yes it does, doesn't it?" I smiled. "I guess it makes sense my name would be attached to it, since I'm the one who took the creep down a few minutes ago. If it had someone else's name attached, we'd be in a quandary."

"You don't fool me for one minute. Destruction follows you like metal to a magnet. I don't care if you have some lousy, half-concocted story about why you happened to be here tonight. Or why you knew exactly when an attempted teenage rape was going to take place. Or why there's a man over there with half his face caved in." Ray took a step forward, getting into my personal space. He was actually pretty good at intimidation for a non-wolf. I wasn't shaking in my boots, but he'd made me think twice. My wolf wasn't the least interested, which was nice. I didn't need that complication right now. But if Ray continued to push, there was no doubt she'd want in on the action at some point. "I know," he continued in a harsh whisper. "I *know* you have something more to do with this than you're letting on. I can *feel* it in my bones. And when I find out what it is, I'm going to throw your ass in jail, make no mistake about it. And when I do, I'm gonna sing to the high heavens. You're going down, Hannon. And there's not a damn thing you can do to stop it."

He turned on his heel and stalked away, his swagger assuring me he meant every last word. I knew he was going to stick his nose into the Drake investigation, and I also had a sinking feeling if he made a lot of noise our thin story wouldn't hold up. A coroner would know better, if he or she was forced to make a serious assessment about a possible murder weapon. It most likely would not come back in my favor.

If Drake lived, my life would be much easier.

I yawned. I needed some sleep. "Let's get out of here. I'm

beat," I said to Nick, who'd just finished up and was walking around the car.

"Beat doesn't cover it. What a crazy-ass night," Nick said. It was only ten-thirty, but it felt like three a.m.

We walked across the parking lot and I poured myself into the passenger side. Nick slipped behind the wheel. I mindlessly grabbed the bag of pastries and fished the last one out and took a bite as Nick drove away.

Nick was quiet for a while before he finally turned to me. "Jess, now that you're a full-blooded werewolf everything is going to be different. You get that, right? Especially with a serious threat like Ray Hart. Before, he was a mild inconvenience in your life, but now he'll be viewed by Pack as a direct threat. You'll be protected at all costs whether you like it or not." Nick kept his eyes on the road. "That's Pack Law to the letter. We all follow it. If there's even a slight chance Ray might find out what you are, or if he comes too close, or threatens you physically..."

"You mean, I'll be protected by *some* at all costs," I answered with a snip. "I have a distinct feeling Pack Law won't fully apply to me. There's no precedent for a female in Pack, and the wolves are in an uproar already and they only *suspect* I've changed. I can name quite a few wolves who'd be elated to let Ray do their job for them. It would be much less dirty that way."

Nick gave a faint *psst* sound. "Please. Do you think your father is going to let Ray Hart—or anyone else for that matter—threaten you outright? You're his daughter, for chrissake. Anyone dumb enough to lash out at you will be paying a huge price—like with their life. Wolves won't take that risk easily no matter how much they grumble. Waging war against Pack is no small thing. Some wolves may be pissed now, but when it comes time to choose, they won't leave Callum McClain. Your dad is the strongest Alpha on the planet. They're going to come around and accept you...eventually. They have to. Ray doesn't stand a chance if he doesn't back down."

Nick was right. Ray had catapulted himself into a game he couldn't possibly win. Even though I disliked him for a thousand reasons, I didn't want to be the impetus of his death. I'd joined the police force all those years ago not only because I was good at it, but because I actually *believed* in the notion of justice. The right to live and be free. Without those two things, I wouldn't be alive right now.

Unfortunately, that viewpoint wasn't embraced among wolves. In fact, it didn't even exist for them. They had no philosophical debate going on in their minds about humans; it'd always been cut-and-dry. Humans were necessary, but not equal. End of story.

I'd lived up to this point as a human, and killing one for no other reason than to keep his silence wasn't going to happen if I had anything to say about it. When the time came, and if it was up to me, I'd find another way. There had to be another way.

"Well," I said. "We'll just have to make damn sure Raymond Hart doesn't step in any deeper, then. We're going to have to make sure he follows up other leads. The ones we plant." I closed my eyes both physically and figuratively on the topic. My eyes burned and I needed sleep. It was safe to say I could add exhaustion to my list of newborn traits. My body was still adjusting to the changes. It was going to take time, and I planned to use that time curled up in bed.

The ride home took fifteen minutes and I dozed off completely. Nick pulled into my parking lot and turned off the car.

I opened my eyes and yawned. "Thanks for the ride. But now you have to walk—" Screaming ripped through my consciousness. I lunged forward, grabbing on to the dashboard. My fingers punched right though the plastic. *Shit*. This night was just getting better and better.

WHERE THE HELL ARE YOU? Jessica! Jessica! Can you hear me? Jessica…

Tyler, I'm here! You can stop yelling now. I yanked my fingers out of the dashboard one at a time. Molded plastic didn't puncture uniformly, it cracked. *What is it? What's wrong?*

Nick glanced over at me, one eyebrow slightly raised. I lifted my freed index finger and placed it on my forehead.

He gave me a sympathetic smile.

What's wrong? Tyler grumbled. *What's wrong is I've been trying to get into your head for the last fucking hour. You start calling some guy an asshole and then I feel this wicked pulsating anger thing, and then nothing. Completely blank. You blocked me. How in the hell did you cut me off?*

My dad's words rang as a warning in my head. I trusted Tyler with my life, he was my brother, but the last thing I was going to do was place him in jeopardy. Caution was my new best friend. The less any wolf knew at this point, the better, and that included Tyler. I selected my words carefully, knowing he'd be able to sense a lie if I didn't believe what I was saying to be true. *I have no idea, Ty. Blocking you wasn't a conscious thing on my part. I can assure you that much. I must have cut you off accidentally when the fight started.*

What goddamn fight? His impatience was loud and clear.

I fought the imp we were tailing tonight when he grabbed a teen. He turned out to be more than I bargained for, but I won.

How in the hell can I possibly protect you if I can't even find you? Tyler shouted. I put a finger up to my temple and pressed. Being yelled at inside my head was making my head ache. *Nick was supposed to be with you tonight! Where the hell was Nick?*

He was with me. It was my choice to go after the imp. Nick had nothing to do with it.

My brother's emotions simmered as images of my death

floated through his subconscious. It startled the hell out of me. *Quit doing that! I can see what you're thinking!*

Jess, I thought you died tonight. His voice wasn't above a whisper. *Again.*

My heart jumped. *Tyler, honestly, I'm so sorry. I didn't mean to scare you. It wasn't anything I did on purpose, I swear. If I would have heard you, I would've answered. I promise. Even if it was only to tell you to get the hell out of my head so I could concentrate on the fight.* I formed the next thoughts carefully. *I think it's safe to say a female werewolf is a complete unknown, just like we talked about today. My mind may not work the same as yours. I have no idea what's happening to me. Or what will happen in the future. None of us do.* I took a deep breath. *I have a feeling this is going to be one giant clusterfuck, just like everyone has always predicted, and I'm recommending we wake ourselves up. It's time to face facts.*

Well, shit. The old Tyler was back.

My sentiments exactly. But right now, instead of trying to fix everything and figure it all out, I'm going to sleep on it. And while I'm at it, I can hopefully scrub the bloody pictures of my grisly death courtesy of your brain out of mind. I yawned.

James and Danny are still trying to track you down. I'll give them a call and tell them you're safe.

Thanks, I appreciate it. I know you haven't had to watch my back since I left the Compound, but it feels good having you there again.

It's what I'm here for, sis. Just do me a favor and don't get yourself into any more trouble tonight.

It's not on the agenda, trust me. I can promise you that much. I'm going inside and getting some much-needed sleep.

There was a brush against my senses and he was gone.

I laid my head back on the headrest and turned to Nick, who had patiently waited for me to finish my conversation. He frowned with concern, and his eyes held a questioning look that hadn't been there a few moments ago. "Oh no," I said. "You can't start in on me tonight. Please don't say anything. I don't want to hear it." I swiveled my head toward the ceiling and closed my eyes. "Please, Nick. I don't think I can take any more tonight."

"Um..." he started. "It's just..."

I waved off his sentence with my hand. "I mean it, Nick." My eyes were still closed. "In all honesty, this whole wolf thing is completely freaking me out. I've kept a lid on it all day so I could stay focused on pretending to be normal. I don't need you to freak out along with me. You're my rock. You're my best friend. I need that right now. I don't need an interrogator. I have no idea what's going on, and I don't have any answers for you anyway. So let's curtail this question-and-answer thing until I know more."

Nick reached over and grabbed on to my hand. For the first time, I realized I'd been smelling Nick's scent clearly for a while now. He smelled like a mixture of cedar and fresh rain. It fit him perfectly. And, as an added bonus, it calmed me and made me feel happy. I guess it always had, and I just never knew it.

"Jess, I'll always be here for you. No matter what," he said. "I pledged my life to you, and to this Pack, a long time ago—but even more than that, I love you. You're my sister and my best friend. I'd gladly fight anyone to the death if they ever threatened you. Well, except for Drake, who you got to handle on your own. But, honestly, there is nothing I wouldn't do for you."

"I know, Nick. I love you too." I smiled at him. "I promise, we can talk soon, but I'm going to need time to process everything. It's been so much at once and such a major change in my life. I just need to figure it out before I'm ready to dissect it and put it all on the table. That's all I'm asking."

"I hear you." He released my hand. "But, honestly, can we just talk about the eyes for a minute?"

I laughed. There was nothing about Nick I didn't love. "Nope." I stretched my arms out in front of my body, trying to rouse myself. "No eyes, no strength, no weird anger smell, no nothing. It's all off the docket for now."

Nick eyed me. I could feel him evaluating my mood, wondering if he could push the issue a teensy bit more. Instead, he shifted in his seat, leaning over and placing a small kiss on the top of my head. "Do you want me to walk you in?"

"Nope. I saw Danny today and they have it covered. Go home. I'll see you tomorrow."

"Gotcha. I think I'll go for a run." Nick slid out of the car. "I could use a good run right about now, let the stress out. Try to make it in before noon tomorrow, okay?"

I laughed. "The alarm will be on."

He shut the door and I watched him take off through the parking lot, his graceful body moving fluidly like the shifter he was.

I slumped back in my seat, thinking about everything that had happened tonight. My brain still whirled and I wanted to put everything to rest. Blocking your Alpha was impossible. It was clear evidence that something was wrong—I was officially a problem my father couldn't control. If that information got out, the Pack would *never* accept me. The Alpha was in place for a reason; he was at the top to control all others. If I didn't fit into the hierarchy, they would take me down. Wolves needed structure and hated change. They feared the unknown and hated anything they couldn't explain.

I was the epitome of those things wrapped into one.

I was so screwed.

9

I was almost to my apartment door when a rich, unfamiliar voice reverberated along the folds in my mind. I stopped in my tracks and glanced around.

Nobody else was in the hallway.

The voice brushed along my brain again like a soft, steamy caress. It was less concrete—more like it was being manifested from *inside* my brain, rather than outside. It didn't sound like my brother or my father's voice at all. Thank goodness, because what it had just said to me was filthy as hell.

It came again, whispering along my senses, and I finally recognized the timbre. The voice in my head was Colin Rourke, my potential new client. I listened for a moment and then blushed like a madwoman.

What's going on? This has to be a trick.

Rourke's throaty voice washed over me again and tingles erupted on the pads of my fingers all the way to my toes, hitting all the important parts along the way. I couldn't help shivering.

Um... chocolate syrup goes where?

Sex *and* food. It was too much. I shook my head, trying to knock it out of my brain. Marcy had to be playing a joke on me, getting me back for making her worry. It was the only real explanation. What else could it be? What a minx. I glanced down the hallway again just to make sure she wasn't giggling behind someone's door.

The voice continued without pause. Graphically.

No, no, caramel can't go there. It's too sticky for that.

Before I could do anything to stop myself, my nipples budded to hard peaks under my shirt. I was totally and completely turned on. *Damn you traitorous body parts.* No guy's voice should be in my brain without my permission, but it didn't stop me from imagining what he smelled like. Rich pine boughs or salty ocean was my best guess, possibly with a hint of fresh rain. *Yum.*

A rush of wetness hit my panties.

Jesus Christ!

This was too much. The joke had gone too far. *Marcy, if you're in my head, get the hell out! It's not funny. I'm going to practical joke you to death. Do you hear me? To death!*

I had to be temporarily out of my mind to get that turned on by an imaginary voice. I straightened and walked briskly to my door, keys out at the ready. I didn't even know what the guy looked like, hot voice or not; this was not an appropriate reaction. It was wrong on so many levels. Marcy's scrawny ass was mine.

I stopped in front of my door and a low growl escaped my diaphragm with no provoking on my part.

Did I just growl?

I growled again.

Suddenly it all made sense.

Marcy hadn't been messing with me.

Why would you possibly *do something like that?* I asked my wolf, even though I already knew the answer. This was payback for winning my Dominion.

She snapped her teeth at me.

If you start playing games with me, how in the hell am I supposed to trust you? Last time I checked, we were in this together. We share the same mind and body, for better or worse. If I'm horny and unsatisfied—you're horny and unsatisfied. Got it? I grumbled. *We have to get this we're-playing-on-the-same-team thing figured out. If not, it's going to tear us apart. And guess what? I'm holding you completely responsible if we can't. Hear that? Your. Fault.*

She huffed at me like I was an idiot. Then fed me an image of her lying on her back wiggling around like she was trying to scratch an itch. She got up, paced a few times in a circle before lying down with her head on her paws.

Then she closed her eyes and shut me out.

Just like that.

Very mature, I told her.

No response.

I shook my head and unlocked my apartment door. I pushed it open and inhaled an unfamiliar scent.

Werewolf.

Then he was on me.

He lunged at me from my left side, where he'd been hidden by the shadow of the door, plowing into me with the force of a battering ram, slamming my door shut in the process. My upper body jerked backward and we both crashed to the floor. We skidded, me on the bottom with a two-hundred-pound werewolf anchored to my chest.

Unimpeded by a single lick of furniture, we crashed into the opposite wall, blowing out the bottom Sheetrock. I was pinned.

He was in his full animal form, and it was all I could do to keep his snapping jaws from my face. My hands clung to the fur around his neck and I held on for dear life as we rolled back and forth across the floor.

"Get *off* me," I gasped as we took another turn. My wolf's ears were pinned back, a fierce snarl reverberating through my psyche, adrenaline and strength pounding through me. The same psyche she'd just been messing with a few seconds ago.

The werewolf's foul, mangy breath wafted over me, his eyes radiating a fierce, pulsating yellow.

I absorbed everything she sent me as quickly as I could. Without it, I'd already be dead. The constant infusion of power gave me a small edge. My arms hardened, growing stronger by the second. I managed to wrench my attacker's jaws backward a few precious inches, twisting my fists farther into his fur, like I was wrapping my hands up in a dish towel. When my hands were strung into his fur as far as they could go, I gave a little.

Just enough.

He came down hard, viciously snapping at my face, his jaws within a hairsbreadth of tearing my skin. Then I extended my arms forward, snapping my elbow in a quick motion, at the same time twisting his head to the side. There was a small but satisfying crack. One angry yowl and he went still, the weight of his head falling heavily into my arms.

"That's what you get for messing with me," I panted, my hands still firmly planted in his fur. Adrenaline pumped through me at a steady pace. It was delicious. The strength dizzying.

One twitch, and the wolf's head shot up off my chest. *Shit*. This one must heal faster than normal. I hadn't really thought I'd killed him—that would've been too easy—but a girl could dream. My arms were still firmly entwined in his fur, so I kept him back as his teeth gnashed inches from my face. He unleashed a low, nasty growl as his jowls dripped thick saliva on my chest.

Well, hell. Fear pierced me deep in the chest for the first time. I might lose. This wolf was too strong for me. As quickly as the thought entered my mind, a massive tide of power surged up inside, pushing against me so fiercely I almost let go.

In an instant, my fingers pulsed, my nails morphing to sharp points. My canines followed, lengthening to deadly spears in my mouth. My muscles danced under my skin, pulling and shifting. Fur sprung heavily along my forearms.

No pain this time. Instead it was exhilarating.

My attacker lifted his nose and scented the air, growling as he registered the power shift. His eyes blazed with a cold fury.

My wolf was not going to be denied a fight this time. She slammed against the barrier that still held, even though it was cracked, whining and barking. *Be my guest. I don't think I'm going to win this without you anyway.* I focused hard to drop the wall between us. It didn't fall easily, but the small fissure that I'd made before finally ruptured under the force and our minds snapped together like a slingshot as we merged.

Then all hell broke loose.

I reared up and sank my new fangs into the side of his neck and ripped happily. He let out a strangled howl and tried to scramble backward. I'd missed his jugular by an inch. My new claws were now fully embedded into his neck and blood flowed in rivers down my arms, coating us both.

He howled again, trying to shake himself free.

In one powerful heave, I flung him away and sprang to my feet, power rushing through me in a sweet continuous current, hitting every single nerve ending. My wolf was in control of the fight, she was leading, but I was there. It was different than before. We were united this time, but she had the wheel.

My attacker paced back and forth in front of me. Blood coursed down the wound in his neck, dripping onto my recently mopped floor in thick dark streams.

He leapt without warning.

I was ready.

My body launched itself into the air and we clashed in the middle. The only way to kill a wolf was to sever the vertebrae completely. No more impulses from the brain and you were done. I'd only cracked his neck before. Anything other than killing him at this point was not an option. If he gained the upper hand for even a moment, I was dead.

We rolled again, my arms coming around his body tightly. As we fought, my body continued to change and morph. We rolled twice before smashing against the plywood inside my sliding glass door. It wavered for a moment before it crashed down on top of us, startling my attacker.

It was the edge I needed. As the werewolf lifted his head and shoulders up to dislodge the wood, I slid my feet into his soft underbelly. Then I punched my legs forward, tossing him, and the board, off me in one powerful thrust.

Blood ran down my legs. As I brought my legs back, I saw that my claws had ripped through my running shoes, tearing into his belly, eviscerating him.

Foot claws were definitely a dandy new feature.

The plywood crashed into my breakfast bar a split second before my attacker hit it, snapping the board in half with a decisive clap.

He was up in the next moment, and so was I.

His dirty yellow eyes narrowed on me and he shook his head. The toss and the stomach wound weren't going to stop him, but he was more leery of me now.

"Not what you were expecting, huh? You filthy piece of

crap." My voice came out low and gravelly, surprising me. It sounded nothing like my normal tone. My eyebrows shot up and I glanced down the length of my body.

I was partially changed.

It hadn't occurred to me, but if I had to stop now to finish the shift, I'd be dead before I woke up and old yellow eyes over there would chuckle as he let himself out my front door.

I extended both my arms in front of me. The werewolf growled, but stayed put.

My claws were fully formed, sharp and nasty-looking. The backs of my hands, all the way up my arms, were covered in a smoky gray fur. Muscles bulged where I had no idea muscles should be. I brought a finger up to my jaw, patting it carefully against my nose. My snout had extended, giving room to my new massive canines, but it wasn't a full muzzle. My hair was down, flowing all over the place. It had burst from its keepings at some point and was irritatingly long. I was thankful my attacker didn't have hands.

I lifted a leg. Thick muscle stretched my shiny spandex to its absolute limit. Holes dotted the seams where the fabric had started to give way, and gray fur shot through in patches.

Even though I was busy taking inventory, my wolf was deathly focused on our intruder. The werewolf circled us slowly, sniffing the air and growling fiercely. He was healing at an alarming rate. He was massively injured, and my self-examination was aiding his recovery time. I couldn't risk a drop and change now, and I had no idea if my body would force a shift on me, but I had no choice but to continue fighting and hope I could beat him before he killed me.

"Didn't think I could kick your ass, did you?" I growled. "You should've thought of that the first time. Now it's time to come and get it." I didn't wait for him to respond. I lunged at him quick as lightning, my arms locking around his neck before he could register his surprise. I went for the kill. He struggled hard as I yanked him up, my elbow cocked under his muzzle, his bulky head forced back against my shoulder with no wiggle room.

I wrenched back, dragging him with me as I pivoted on the floor, my new claws digging into the floorboards to stabilize me. I spun hard, gaining momentum. My strength amazed me. There was no way I should be this strong. Manhandling the weight of this werewolf didn't even register.

In one clean motion, I twisted his neck and flung him straight at the brick wall my apartment shared with the outside. He crashed into it like a wrecking ball. The bricks held as several pops rang out and he fell to the floor.

"Good riddance," I snarled. More like gurgled. My hand went to my neck, still surprised by how I sounded.

My head turned toward the noise a second before my door exploded inward.

James, my father's second, barreled into my apartment, his eyes glowing amber. "What in the bloody hell's going on?" His accent was thick, and it echoed off my walls like a shot, making me quiver. He was a very strong wolf, even in human form.

I stared stupidly at him.

Then I turned and pointed a clawed finger at the mass still lying inert on the floor.

James reached the fallen wolf in three steps, putting a hand into his fur, searching for life. "Neck's broken. No pulse."

I spun around to face the door as my brother shot into the room, followed closely by Nick and Danny.

Tyler came to a screeching halt in front of me, his eyebrows at his hairline, his mouth open. "*What the—*"

Nick pulled up just short of plowing right into him, but steadied himself quickly. He locked eyes on me.

Danny stopped beside Tyler's left shoulder, covering his mouth in a gesture he usually used when he was trying hard to stop himself from uttering something completely vulgar.

Everyone was motionless for a few seconds.

Then Danny dropped his hand and uttered one single word in a thunderstruck whisper. "*Lycan.*"

I had no idea what was happening. The adrenaline still pumped through my veins like a raging river, but very slowly my body eased itself back to normal. My teeth and nails receded and my muscles softened. When I found my voice, it sounded normal again. "What's the matter with you guys?" I asked. "Shut the damn door before my whole floor knows what's going on! We need to clean this up. Yes, I didn't finish my shift, so the hell what? You can stare at me all you want later! Let's get moving before the cops arrive."

Nobody moved.

I stared at Nick, who still looked confused. "Get out to the hallway! There was enough screaming and banging in here to raise the goddamn dead. You're going to have to use your gift quickly before there's a herd of people clamoring on my doorstep."

He continued to stare at me with a dumb look on his face.

"Now, Nick!" I yelled. "Go!"

He shook himself and turned on his heel, darting back into the hallway. Voices were already gathering. Maybe they weren't sure which apartment it was coming from. That would be a miracle.

It felt like the fight had gone on for hours, but in actuality it had only been about five minutes at the most. If the police weren't here in the next five, it really would be a miracle.

I turned to Danny. "Danny, if you haven't already guessed, there's a breach in your security. No way this guy should've gotten through, unless he was somehow spelled. Now get the hell out there and help Nick while we cover our tracks. If the cops show, we're screwed. We're going to need time to get him"— I pointed to the dead wolf—"out of here as soon as possible."

Danny's face broke into a wide grin. "Will do. I'll get to the bottom of it, and whoever's responsible for letting him in will pay in full, I assure you." He ducked into the hallway.

James still crouched next to the dead wolf, who was now in the process of changing back into his human form. When wolves died, they reverted back to their humanness. It was an adaptation insurance policy.

Tyler was the only other person left in the room.

He stared at me. "Cut it out," I accused. "You're freaking me out."

He took a step toward me. "It can't be." His voice tinged with fear. "Jess, this just can't be possible."

"Tyler." *You're pissing me off,* I said inside his head. Out loud I continued, "I honestly have no idea what you're talking about. But if you haven't noticed, we're kind of in the middle of a crisis here." I gestured angrily toward the dead body, and then to the hallway. There were twice as many voices out there as before.

He still didn't move.

"Okay, fine," I said, crossing my arms across my chest. Thank goodness my shirt was still in one piece, even though it had ripped in a few places. "You want to label me a freak because I didn't finish my shift? Fine, I'm a freak. But, honestly, it's a damn good thing I didn't have to drop to change, or I'd likely be dead right now. Then all your gruesome death visions of me would've been accurate, and my bloody, broken body would've haunted your dreams forever. Do you really think Furry Joe over there would've waited patiently for me to finish my shift? There was no time!"

"Jess, that's not—"

"Tyler!" I yelled. I was finished with this conversation. "We can talk about this later. If we don't get this body out of here before Ray arrives, he will bring the *entire* police force down on our heads. If he finds a dead man in my apartment—I go to jail. *Period.* We cannot kill the entire police force!"

Tyler physically shook himself and walked over to the body. He crouched beside James and asked, "Do you recognize him?"

"No." James took in a deep breath, mouth open, nostrils flared. "His scent doesn't register at all, so I know I've never met him face-to-face either."

My cell phone rang.

It was on the floor in the corner, where my purse had been flung when I'd been attacked. I was surprised it was still intact. I walked over and punched the talk button without looking at the number.

I knew exactly who it was.

"*Jessica!*" my father roared into the phone. I pulled it several feet away from my eardrum. "What in the *hell* is *going on*? Your wolf called to mine for a second time tonight, and you cut me off *again*! *Goddammit!* I can't help you if you keep doing that!" His anger was palpable. It sent a searing, physical wave into the room and attacked my emotions on so many levels.

James's face was inscrutable. Tyler looked away. They both went back to figuring out how to get the mystery man off the floor, ignoring my conversation completely.

I paced away, back into my bedroom. "I'm sorry, Dad. Honestly, I have no idea what's going on. I didn't mean to block you again. It's nothing I'm doing on purpose. I don't feel a trigger from you or anything. If I did, I would've answered right away."

"Jessica, just tell me what's going on down there," he said, forcibly trying to calm himself. "I'm trying to keep you safe, and it seems I've missed the godforsaken mark entirely. This can't keep happening. I feel you, I know something's wrong, and I can't figure out what's going on. It's maddening."

"Dad, my secret is out. There's no slipping under the radar anymore. Someone knows. There was a rogue waiting for me when I got home. I was careless, thinking about other... things"—there was no way I was going into that—"and I wasn't paying attention. I have no idea how he got in. It must've been the balcony, because I didn't smell him in the hall. It was a mistake thinking I could fly undetected for even one day." I sat down on my bed, feeling defeated.

"We made a grave mistake," my father said. "*I* made a mistake when I sent you home. I should've listened to my gut. I knew it was going to be risky no matter what we did, but I should've kept you here, where I could've protected you myself. I was dreaming, hoping the wolves would stay calm. It was a mistake."

"There was no way you could've known for sure," I said. "None of us knew. We had to try. I don't regret trying. I liked my life. I'm sorry to see it go."

After a beat of silence. "Tell me what happened," he said. "All of it."

I gave him a complete replay of the entire evening. I started with the imp and ended with walking into my apartment, minus the sexcapade.

When I got to the part about changing only partially into my wolf form, I faltered. "Then I gave physical control over to my wolf... and I started to change... *but*... I sort of stopped midway through... Um, I'm actually not quite sure what happened..."

His silence was so deep it scared me.

I waited a few beats. "Dad?"

"Did you hold this form for long? Were you able to fight in it?"

"Yes."

"I'll be down there first thing in the morning. I'm calling a Pack Council meeting tonight. The entire Council should be able to make it into the city by eight a.m. if they leave now. If your secret is officially out, we will address it then to the whole Pack. This thing will be out and we will deal with it accordingly."

"Dad!" I shouted. "You can't leave it like that. What's going on? You have to tell me what's going on. Danny said a word... he said 'Lycan' to me. What did he mean? I know what a Lycan is, but why did he call *me* that?"

Lycans were our ancestors, the original werewolves. We evolved from them thousands of years ago. We were different from them now, but I didn't know exactly how or why.

"Jessica, we will talk about this tomorrow," he said firmly.

"I want to talk about it now."

After years of dealing with each other, we'd both learned some very valuable lessons. If my father had no intention of telling me over the phone, he would hang up and that would be that. I would either accept his decision or hold it against him later, making his life harder than it needed to be.

I waited.

He sighed. "Jessica, I don't know anything for sure, because I haven't seen it myself, but I think it means you are able to do something no other werewolf has been able to do for thousands of years. There have only been myths and legends floating around about what our ancestors were truly capable of doing."

"What do you mean?"

He sighed. "A True Lycan has not been witnessed in my lifetime. The term 'Lycan' specifically means you are able to maintain a perfect suspended form between beast and human. You are able to shift at will, while maintaining your human form. No other wolf can do such a thing." He paused. "Including myself."

Holy crap.

"It's the ultimate fighting weapon, and it is revered in our legends as unparalleled. In the days of old, Lycans ruled the supernaturals. There were none stronger. We've evolved over the centuries to accommodate man, and have lost some of those great abilities." My dad sounded tired as he added, "There is an old proverb among us that states, '*He who holds the power of Lycan will be lord over all.*'"

I was stunned into complete silence.

"I will be there in the morning. I will stop at the Safe House for an update from Tyler first. You are to stay in your apartment and you are not to leave. Do you understand me?"

"Yes."

"Jessica, that is a direct order."

"I understand."

"Hand the phone to James."

I did.

10

I ran a wet washcloth over my face and rinsed the last of the smeared blood down the drain. I'd been avoiding the mirror. Trying to imagine what I looked like as a half wolf, half human didn't come easily to me.

I squared my shoulders over the sink. It was now or never. The mess in my living room wasn't going to wait indefinitely.

Lifting my head, I gazed into my reflection.

I looked like my normal self, only more worn out.

My hair was messy, falling everywhere, but it was back to my regular length. I had contusions all over, but they were healing fast. I leaned in closer and saw a violet fleck flash like a banked ember in the farthest reaches of my irises. Calling them yellow now would be silly. There was nothing yellow about them.

I had violet eyes.

Just like my father.

I hadn't remembered to tell my father that bit of news, but

my eye color was the last thing I'd been thinking about. I grimaced in the mirror. Lycan must've been a horrid sight. A wolf in its full animal form was the most unbelievably beautiful creature in the world. But half a wolf?

Likely the worst.

The most captivating wolf in the world was my father. The image of him in his true form had been as much a part of me as anything I could remember as a little girl. He was glorious—his fur dark as coal, towering above all others, strong and dangerous, but breathtakingly beautiful at the same time. Truly magnificent.

I stepped away from the mirror, tossing my shredded running shoes into the plastic bag I'd grabbed from under the kitchen sink. My clothes would soon follow.

I tied up the contents and opened the bathroom door and headed out into the new chaos.

"The coast is officially clear," Nick declared, turning to prop my broken door in the jamb behind him as he and Danny came back in. The door had been unlocked, but knowing I was in danger, James hadn't waited to see, he'd simply come through it. "We corralled your neighbors and ushered them back inside their apartments quickly."

James and Tyler had rolled the dead body into one of my spare sheets, and were in the process of discussing the best way to remove it from my apartment.

Danny chuckled. "Yes, we told the lot of them out there in the hallway that we were having a *huge* party and it had gotten a little out of sorts. And they bought it hook, line, and sinker."

Nick snorted. "They bought it after I told them to buy it."

"The only other issue was the police outside, but Nicky here took care of that as well." Danny slapped Nick on the back. "Mighty fine gift, persuasion is."

"The police were here?" I asked in alarm.

"Relax, Jess." Nick came over and put his hands on my shoulders. "It wasn't Ray, and they were just here to investigate a 'noise' disturbance—not a gruesome werewolf killing. I convinced them they were at the wrong building. Everything's fine now."

"Thanks." My wolf paced inside my mind. She and I were both still agitated. "We have to get him out of here quickly." I glanced at the rolled-up corpse. "And then we have to figure out what the hell is going on—why he was even here in the first place. I've only been a werewolf for a day. It seems too quick to have someone after me already, almost like this guy had been sitting by the phone."

"We need to bring him back to the Safe House so we can look into his identity and figure out what's going on," James said.

"Agreed," Tyler said. "We'll take him off the balcony. Danny and I'll go down in front and you can drop him out to us."

I raised an eyebrow and interjected, "Um, that seems a little on the unsubtle side, don't you think? Tossing a body-shaped object off my balcony is bound to be noticed by someone."

They stared at me blankly.

Reasoning with wolves was going to require patience, but right now I had none. "Well, how about this, then," I said. "If it *does* get noticed—and subsequently reported—I can't afford any more scrutiny on me right now. In case you've all been living with your heads up your asses the last few days"—my voice rose several decibels as I spread my fingers apart and started emphatically ticking off—"I just finished killing a werewolf we know nothing about. I will likely have to testify in court about killing a pedophile imp. My apartment has already been the scene of a vicious, unexplainable break-in, which happened…oh, that's right…four *fucking* days ago. An identified drug that could knock out a stable of animals was taken from my home"—my voice peaked as I slammed my pinky finger—"and I just made some freaky, impossible transformation into a beast, bound to have every superstitious werewolf in the entire goddamn universe gunning to end my life. So I refuse, *refuse* to add tossing a human body wrapped in my own *bedding* from my balcony to that damn list! Are we clear?" Tension radiated off me like a furnace. It swirled around the room, hot and palpable.

Three pairs of wolf eyes locked on me, each of them sparking with more than a hint of amber. Only one pair of calm golden ones in the mix.

Wolves did not function well in heightened emotional situations. It certainly didn't help when my muscles started to vibrate and soft fur began to sprout along the backs of my hands once again.

My wolf stood in a protective stance, legs apart, muzzle up in my mind.

Danny broke the tension and strode forward. He walked to me in a surrender pose, shoulders hunched, eyes carefully downcast. "Easy there, Jess," he murmured as he knelt down in front of me. "I promise you the lot of us here aren't going to do anything to bring you any harm. In fact, it's quite the opposite, really. Wolves can be really bloody stupid, it's true. We're stubborn and aggressive, and we never take kindly to change. But I promise, you're safe with us." He placed one of his hands over his heart. "I swear to it on my own life."

I stood very still. I didn't trust myself to respond. My wolf watched Danny carefully. The lines between her and me were still blurred from our encounter with the rogue. I'm not sure what had happened during the fight, but for now she was on this side. There were no dominance issues between us at the moment, only an equal unity to keep us both safe.

Danny's eyes met mine for a moment and skittered away. He glanced quickly over his shoulder at James, Tyler, and Nick, who stood slightly behind him. "I think I can speak for everyone in this room, the very ones who watched over you as you grew up"—his face changed to a devilish grin—"and may I interject here to say you grew into quite a ravishing beauty." He winked. "All of us plan to stand by you and we are fully prepared to lay down our lives to protect you, Jessica McClain. We always have been." Leave it to Danny to defuse an awful situation with a pseudo pickup line and end with a heartfelt statement.

I smiled warily. My wolf relaxed a tad at his words and fur stopped sprouting along my arms.

"We have always known," he continued, "that having a female among us would be risky. I knew it when I joined this Pack, and we all chose to stick it out despite the myths and rumors. Any one of us could've left anytime we wanted to, but we didn't. We chose to stand by you and your father. Callum McClain is a great leader who deserves our respect, just as you do." Danny bowed his head. "I gave my vow of fealty freely to my Alpha. I swore to follow this Pack to my death. Now I give it to you. I intend to hold up my end of the bargain and to protect you at all costs. I promise, you have nothing to fear from me, Jessica McClain."

Shockingly, he dropped his head back and exposed his neck to me.

My wolf responded immediately with a rough bark. She accepted his posturing like it was her right, and growled with pleasure, nudging me to accept what he was giving us.

I blinked. My human side was wildly uncomfortable.

I trembled where I stood. I didn't understand any of this.

This was all wrong. It had to be. Instead of moving forward,

I took a small step backward. My wolf responded with a sharp, angry yip.

My eyes darted to my brother. He met my stare for a second before his voice sounded in my mind. *It's okay, Jess.* Tyler was quiet. *This is normal. Danny's wolf has recognized your dominance over him, so he's acting as he should. He can either choose to fight you for status or he can yield to you. He's choosing not to fight you, which is extremely smart of him, since I would rip his goddamn throat out if he tried.*

Tyler, my voice vibrated with emotion, *I don't understand what's happening to me. This can't be true. None of the myths and rumors were supposed to be real. I'm not supposed to be strong. I'm a female, which means weak in our world. I've always been less. A wolf like Danny should not be submitting to me. It has to be a mistake.*

Jess, it's going to be okay. When Dad gets here, we can sort it out. I have no idea what's going on either. It's going to take us some time to figure it all out. When you changed, your wolf was fully realized. It came the way it was meant to be. Your job is to shape and control it the best you can. We were both alpha-born. It's not something you learn. You just need time, and I promise everything will fall into place.

I'm not sure I have that kind of time. I glanced at the dead body rolled up like a mummy in my lavender sheets. Then to Danny, who was still on the floor in front of me, neck back, waiting patiently for me to do something. *What am I supposed to do now?*

Flash him your teeth, meet his eyes for the count of five, and then walk away like you don't give a damn.

That's it?

Tyler snorted. *That's it, sis. Then we try to get back to fucking normal as fast as we possibly can.*

I did what he told me to do. I flashed my teeth, growled, courtesy of my wolf, and turned my back and walked away. I headed purposefully into my kitchen. What I needed was a bottle of whiskey, but I settled for a glass of water instead.

My brother headed back to my bedroom. I heard him open my closet doors, and he came back to the living room a minute later carrying a big navy blue canvas duffel I used for carting my dirty laundry. I followed him into the living room.

"We can cram him in here," he told James. "Then we toss it off the balcony. It isn't body-shaped, and if anybody asks, we're headed to the Laundromat."

Everyone was moving around like normal. I pointed to the body. "He's not going to fit in there. He's twice as long as that." I ran my eyes over the shrouded shape on the floor to make sure I hadn't missed anything.

"Not for long." Tyler grinned.

Right. I excused myself and went back to my bedroom to change out of my dirty, bloodstained clothes. Hacking up bodies and tossing them off balconies was hardcore. Life as a wolf was going to take some getting used to.

After I changed, I headed back to the living room slightly more refreshed, just as James and Nick stepped in from the balcony empty-handed. The deed was done.

Time to clean up. That was something I could do.

I grabbed a mop and bucket from my kitchen closet and went to work. Even though I was still trying to calm myself down, my limbs hummed with adrenaline, which made me jittery. The endorphins in my system nipped at my nerve endings in quick, staccato beats. There was nothing I could do about it. I had too much buildup between my fight with Drake and the rogue. I was hopped up with no place to go.

Half an hour later, with more muscle than necessary, the room appeared spotless to the naked eye. The smell of blood and werewolves still permeated the air, but to a human the scene would look and smell normal.

Tyler had already left with the body. Danny had gone to tighten security around my building. Nick had left, taking my bloodied bag of clothes and shoes with him, presumably to burn. He'd also bolted my front door back into place with a toolkit I kept for emergencies. The door wasn't going to keep anything of substance out, but I had a big wolf with me for the night to help me maintain order.

My father had ordered James to stay with me, which was fine by me. If anything else happened tonight, I wasn't sure I could physically handle it, and having company was nice.

"Here, let me get that," James said as he plucked the bucket, along with the rags I'd been using, and walked them out onto the balcony.

I rested my back against the brick wall and ran my hands through my hair. It'd been a long night. One of the longest of my life.

James stepped back into my apartment empty-handed. He was wearing almost the same thing I'd seen him in yesterday, a black T-shirt and a pair of faded green cargo pants. I'd never really seen him in anything else. Both pieces of clothing were stretched tightly across his body, producing the maximum effect of powerful man. He had no clue how good he looked.

My wolf's ears perked and I shifted slightly.

James stopped midstride, his gaze snapping to mine.

My breath hitched without my permission. I stared back. There, just below the surface, a hint of yellow danced across his irises.

Hmm.

When wolves fought, adrenaline raged through their veins, as it did through mine now. With the excess buildup from all the stress and excitement, they often ran for hours to get their systems back to normal.

Or sometimes they just had sex.

I dropped my eyes and fiddled with the hem of the tank top I'd changed into. "So, here we are," I said quietly.

He growled in response.

My skin pricked and lust shot to the surface, hot and fierce. My wolf let out a long agonized howl, ending in a series of short, frantic barks as a dam inside me ruptured. Everything ached at once. My fingertips gripped the wall tightly so I didn't fall down as the lust wrapped around me, tugging at my body, pouring through me with its urgent craving.

James stayed where he was. Waiting.

I didn't dare look at him again. I knew his eyes would be blazing.

My wolf whined. She wanted this. There was no question.

But did I?

I knew feeling lusty was part of the newborn deal; add in all the chaos of the night and nobody had to spell it out to me. I needed a release. I also knew wolves had sex a lot. They didn't view it as humans did. It was something to be fulfilled. A base urge. No emotional ties needed.

But I hadn't grown up a wolf, I'd grown up human.

Hold on, Jezebel, I told my wolf. *I'm not sure if I can do this—* check that—*if we can do this. I'm not interested in becoming a slutty werewolf, no matter how good it sounds right now. Being the only female wolf around, we're going to have to watch it. And James is not our mate.*

Don't ask me how I knew that fact, because the man could fit the bill, there was no question about it, but James was not ours. I'd always heard finding your true mate was a gift, something rare. It didn't mean James and I couldn't sleep together, it just meant there was a slim to none chance we would ever pair up permanently.

My wolf gave a frustrated huff and threw a picture in my mind of an Alpha wolf taking his pick of females.

We are not the Alpha!

Huff.

Another flash of an Alpha wolf choosing a female, and—*Helllooo, that's enough of that! I get it. You want him.*

A fierce growl.

It was a little too late to argue with her. The scent we were leaking into the air was pure, unadulterated sex, fueled for the most part by my horny wolf. It was so thick, I could almost see it. *Geez, can you tone it down a few notches?*

I inhaled and caught a new smell.

A wild, earthy scent flooded my senses like a sweet, inviting offer. All the cells in my body simultaneously popped and everything that was already aching started pulsing with a new, delicious heartbeat. My skin erupted in a million inviting tingles. I tightened my hands into fists, my regular nails pricking my palms.

I was losing myself to the overwhelming sensations.

And I liked it.

James moved, taking a single step closer. I lifted my head slowly and pinned him with a heated gaze. He was a warrior, his irises locking on mine, blazing full gold. A new tide of desire ran through me, his eyes triggering something deep inside me. His hands were fisted, his body tight with strain, his wolf at the very forefront. I'd never in my life noticed him like this before, but no one could deny he was a beautiful man. His olive skin shone, his dark hair just long enough to be deliciously tousled, his jawline strong and masculine. He looked thirty at the most, all of us destined to stay young forever.

I opened my mouth and a growl-laced purr came out.

My consent.

One step and he had me pressed up hard against the bricks. He snarled, his lips taking my neck, his tongue ran along my shoulder blade, his wolf seeking my taste. I groaned at his rich scent, pressing my nose and lips into him as far as they would go, inhaling deeply. His wolf sang directly to mine.

He pulled away and I mewed at the loss of contact. He brought his hands down and with one fierce tug my shirt was off. He stripped his away in the next motion, and my hands immediately found his chest, my fingers stroking the defined grooves, caressing the soft skin. I licked my lips in anticipation. My wolf yipped. James growled and put his head down in front of me, snapping my bra with his teeth. I dropped my arms and it fell to the floor.

His head was still bent, and I writhed on him like a drunken siren, dragging my hands through his hair, grabbing fistfuls, pulling him closer. My wolf howled in ecstasy.

His lips sought my nipples. He took one into his mouth with a fierceness that made me shudder. My head rolled back and I moaned. He lapped and pulled on the sensitive peak, making the sensations inside me strum and heighten at an exhilarating rate. I'd never experienced anything like this before. Everything as a wolf was more amplified, each touch a greater flood of sensation than the next.

He broke the seal on my breast and slid his lips slowly up my body, his mouth and lips running over my neck, growling in my ear, "This is it, Jessica. I won't be able to stop myself if we go forward. So say your piece now."

I couldn't answer. Instead, my nails raked up his back and into his thick hair then traced back down to his backside, urging him closer.

He took his delightful lips off my skin and cupped his hand around my neck, tilting my face up to meet his, his thumb languidly caressing my jaw.

It took me a second to focus on him.

"Jessica...my wolf is too far gone." His voice gruff with need. "You must tell me right now if you want this. I won't be able to stop otherwise. If you don't want this, all you have to do is tell me and I will leave your apartment and return in an hour."

The adrenaline pounded in my veins, demanding a release. It was either this or change and run for hours with him.

"I want this," I said simply.

He bent his head, his mouth finding mine. I opened myself to him, tasting, pulling, sucking. His lips were hot, firm, and lusciously soft, but there would be no sweetness between us, no wooing. This was going to be exactly what it needed to be.

I rubbed against him, lost to the delicious lust. He nipped my lips, my neck, and my breasts over and over. His body was so hard, so full of strong angles. The only thing keeping him out of me was the fact that we were both still wearing our pants.

I reached down between us and yanked blindly at his buttons. I buried my tongue in his warm mouth again, lapping at him while I eased the soft cotton down around his hips.

He gave me a throaty growl as I freed him. My hand ran

along the smoothness, and he moaned into my lips. I rubbed my fist along the length as his hands slid around to my back, his thumbs dipping into my waistband. He flexed once and the flimsy yoga pants I'd chosen ripped apart at their seams, dropping around me in a pool of material.

He guided my hips forward, my shoulders tilted back against the wall, and entered me in one smooth motion.

I arched to meet him, taking his fullness deeply. I was more than ready and the pressure of him was delicious and intense. He stroked in and out, his hands pressed tightly into my hips, gripping me, guiding us together faster with each meeting.

I laid my forehead against his chest and cried out. My hands clutching the back of his arms, his muscles flexing in my palms. My nails dug in, following his movements, urging him. I whispered, "More...Please, *more*."

He broke his hold on my waist and ran his hands down to my wrists. He grabbed hold and stretched them above my head, pinning me fully to the wall, pounding into me fiercely with his hips. The strength and power radiating between us made me dizzy. Each thrust sent shock waves though my body, amplifying everything until I screamed with pleasure.

"Jesus bloody Christ," James ground out, releasing my arms and encircling my waist. "I'm not going to be able to keep up this pace for much longer. It feels too damn good."

My hands found his firm ass and I grabbed his finer, tighter curves, pulling him closer to me. "James," I breathed. "I want it harder...please." I guided him faster, my nails urging him on. I met him thrust for thrust. We were both coated in a slick sweat.

He threw his head back and roared, the intensity between us reaching its peak. "Jessica, please...you need to come now...I can't..."

Two more and I was finished. I cried out, pressing my face against his chest as I came. The orgasm hit so powerfully I clung to him as frantic spasms rocked every cell in my body.

His response was immediate.

He let out a savage howl, crushing me back against the bricks as he pumped his furious release into me. My body exploded again as I came for a second time, delicious currents raging though me, my nerve endings pulsing with heat. With the last thrust we collapsed against each other, panting heavily.

My body rang with pleasure.

We were both satiated, exhausted of all remaining usable energy.

So we did what wolves do.

We made our way back to my bedroom and crawled into bed together naked and satisfied, curling around each other for warmth and comfort.

Neither of us moved a muscle until the next morning.

When we were rudely awakened by incessant pounding on my still very broken door.

11

Someone was jackhammering their fist against the wood. I was amazed the door still held. If they were trying to wake the dead, they were succeeding. I jumped out of bed and threw on the first robe I could find. It was a smooth black silky number with large pale flowers and a decidedly geisha feel. I didn't have time to be picky, since the pounding reverberated around my empty apartment like an echo with a vendetta.

James rolled off the bed behind me, running an absent hand through his hair. He looked completely unfazed by the early morning wake-up call, which was good news. It meant our visitor wasn't a serious threat. I was happy to know I wouldn't have to start the day off with my fists.

"Morning, Jessica," James murmured as he strode toward the bathroom. "Call me if you have any trouble." He shut the door behind him.

The pounding intensified as I belted my robe. I hurried out of my bedroom wondering who the mad knocker was. It could be my father, but I hadn't sensed him. That didn't mean much, since I hadn't sensed last night's attacker either. I sampled the air, but there were still too many other lingering scents in my living room from last night. A residual blast of pheromones gave me a little jump. *Yikes.*

I stopped in front of my nailed-together, barely still upright door and paused. It was probably an angry neighbor coming to give me grief about all the racket I caused last night. But there was no way I was making the same mistake twice.

I pressed my face up against the door right by the defunct deadbolt and inhaled deeply through the tiny opening.

I barely needed a full breath to figure out who was on the other side.

Crapola.

I wondered for a second if I could get away with not answering. This so wasn't how I wanted to start my day. It was six-thirty in the damn morning.

Another stream of fist-pounding, followed by a muttered curse. "I know you're in there, Hannon. I can wait out here all day if I have to. There's nothing on my agenda today more important than nailing your ass to the goddamn wall. Now open up!"

Dammit all to hell. How was I going to get the door open without causing a scene? "Hold your horses, Ray," I grumbled. "I'm here, but at this ungodly hour I was asleep like most of the other normal people on the planet. Gimme a minute."

Most likely, when he arrived at work this morning he discovered that a police car had been dispatched to this address last night, so he hightailed it over without thinking it through. Now I had to deal with him.

"I'm going to wait for exactly five more seconds, Hannon. Then I'm going to kick it in."

"Ray, are you holding a warrant for that?" I called. "If you have one, you've been a very busy boy this morning. If you don't, kicking my door in would mean lots of nasty paperwork for you—not to mention some serious legal hassles. I'm not sure I'd rush into that direction if I were you, but honestly, be my guest..."

He grunted his response, adding a few choice words.

Cripes, this man pissed me off. I should let him break down the door. He would get reprimanded and if nothing else, maybe someone without an evil grudge against me would be assigned to my case. But deep down I knew there was really no way to get rid of him; like a homing pigeon, he would always come back.

So I did the only thing left I could do. I braced my silky geisha-clad shoulder against the door, grabbed on to the knob with both hands, and gave it one swift, hard yank.

The door popped instantly free of the opening. I stumbled back a few steps ungracefully as it wobbled against me. I'd used too much strength, but I recovered nicely, and calmly placed it a few feet to the right of the opening.

I turned back to Ray with a sunny smile on my face, like nothing out of the ordinary had just happened. "Hi, Ray. So glad you could drop by."

Ray was momentarily stunned. He tried to recover himself, but it took a second. "What in God's name is going on here now?"

"You know, Ray, people keep asking me that and I don't really have a good answer. But I promise when I have one you'll be the first to know." I turned and headed to my kitchen to make a pot of coffee. Ray chased after me, lecturing my retreating back.

"Did you happen to know a police car was dispatched to this

location last night at approximately eleven-fifteen p.m.?" he barked. "And they left without even coming in. The officers who responded actually said they 'forgot' to file a report. Doesn't that seem a little strange to you, Hannon? A little too out of the ordinary for this quiet building to get hit again so soon?"

"Ray, right now nothing seems strange to me." I dumped some fragrant Colombian coffee into the filter and poured enough water to fill the pot. Ray situated himself outside my breakfast nook to better harass me.

"By the looks of your mangled door," he went on, "it seems you're the source of the complaint. I can find out who called it in with a quick search of your neighbors' phone records. You can't cover all your tracks, Hannon. No matter how hard you try. Or have you forgotten what you learned when you were still on the straight and narrow?"

I braced my hands on the kitchen counter to give me strength, and then turned my tired eyes on Ray, giving him a full dose of my stare. He wiggled immediately and dropped his eyes. It was damn satisfying. "I never left the straight and narrow, Ray. You only choose to believe I did to pacify your own overactive imagination. I left the force because it wasn't the right fit for me, and because I didn't like dealing with overzealous cops who thought they knew everything. Cops who dogged me, made my life hell with their craziness, cops who can't seem to leave well enough alone. I'm not the bad guy here, Ray. You're the one with the vendetta. I'd say it's more than time for you to drop this whole damn thing so we can both get on with our lives."

"*My* imagination?" he barked. "You're the one who's living in la-la land, Hannon. For one, your apartment's been royally trashed by someone who hates you—hates you enough to bring in their fucking *pet*. Your door's been blown off its hinges since the last time I was here. You had enough horse tranq in your possession to put out an army of Clydesdales, and your made-up camping buddy has yet to show his face." He must've called in several favors to get the lab results that quickly, if he wasn't just guessing. "Then there was that guy you beat up at the movie theater—a mere nine hours ago—who was DOA." *Dammit*, Drake's death would definitely complicate things. "And you're worried that *I'm* the one with the overactive imagination? Now that's hilarious, Hannon."

A throat cleared behind me. "I'm sorry, but were you just referring to me?" James asked, his voice gravelly and rough with sleep and menace. "You know that part about the 'made-up camping buddy'? I assume you meant me."

I turned to see James framed perfectly in my kitchen doorway like a page out of one of those hard-bodies calendars.

He was naked from the waist up.

Droplets of water from his shower still lingered on his chest. His hair had been slicked back with his fingers, because, I guess, brushes were for sissies. He'd managed to find his pants, which was probably a good thing. I didn't really feel like explaining Ray's heart attack to any of the attending officers when they came to remove him from my apartment.

James leaned his half-naked, wet body against the doorjamb and casually crossed his arms, making his biceps jump. He had a small smile on his lips. He was enjoying this.

But I wasn't fooled for a second.

Tiny hairs on the back of my neck and arms stood at attention when our eyes met. He was every inch a lethal predator, and in about half a second Ray would know it too. James wasn't going to mess around. This was all business.

Ray had inadvertently stepped backward into my living

room when he had seen James. I bet he hadn't even realized it yet. It was a common reaction. Humans instinctively wanted to get away. Ray's mouth opened a few times, but nothing came out.

"I can assure you I'm not make-believe." James continued the conversation as if nothing were amiss. "You know how it is, when you just want to escape with your lover for a few nights. All your careful planning goes straight out the window. Wouldn't you agree, darling?" He gave me a wicked grin.

"That's right … honey. See, Ray, we just got caught up in the moment."

James's gaze locked on mine as I spoke and a line of goose bumps erupted along my arms. James growled, "And it was quite a moment, wasn't it?"

Ray physically shook himself. His hands shot toward his chest, I'm sure itching for the gun I knew was tucked inside the ill-fitting sport coat he had on today. I caught a whiff of surprise emanating from him, as well as a heavy dose of frustration.

James didn't wait for Ray to respond; instead he paced slowly into my kitchen, stopping immediately behind me. He reached above my body, his arms brushing my shoulders. He pulled down a coffee mug and placed a kiss on the top of my head before turning around and busying himself pouring a cup of coffee.

When he finished, he settled his hips against the counter and took a lazy sip. He wasn't playing fair. "I apologize we haven't had a chance to chat sooner, Detective. It is Detective, isn't it? We've been a bit busy trying to clean up after the nasty break-in." He took a long swallow. "By the way, do you have any leads? Anything you care to share with us? It would give Molly some much-needed peace of mind to hear how the case is shaping up."

Ray fought for control, but I could see he wasn't going to give up easily. He squared his shoulders and took half a step forward. I had to give him props for trying. He cleared his throat. "Well, maybe you do exist. So what? That doesn't mean anything. The last time I checked it doesn't explain away everything else that's happened around here." He nodded toward my bare living room, littered with gouges and trashed walls. Point taken.

"No, it doesn't," James agreed. "But if I'm not mistaken, isn't that your job, Detective? To find out exactly what *has* happened here and why? Correct me if I'm on the wrong track, but as I understand it, the victim is usually not the one harassed by the investigating officer. It's your job to track down the perpetrators and find the clues. Do you honestly think Molly would trash her own apartment like this?" James's tone became steely. "I also don't believe there've been any formal charges filed, and from my understanding there has been no theft here, no serious crime, only some unfortunate vandalism."

A trickle of sweat made its way down the side of Ray's face, right next to his hairline. Receiving the full attention of a dominant werewolf was taking its toll. "It doesn't matter if she files," Ray managed to spit out of very clenched teeth. "This is my case until it's closed. And you still haven't adequately explained the illegal concoction we found in your bathroom either. It's highly suspicious to have a breaking and entering, and the victim just *happens* to have a stash of drugs in her bathroom cabinet."

James took a hold of my hand, pulling me against his side. His Irish brogue purred just above my ears as he leaned in. "Now why haven't you told Detective Hart about your condition, dove?" He nuzzled my neck. "Seizure disorders affect a huge percentage of the population, just like the doctor told us.

It's nothing to be ashamed of." Then he turned to Ray. "Has the lab actually confirmed your ridiculous claim of 'horse tranquilizer'? Or are you going to keep hounding us with that in favor of trying to solve the *actual* crime committed here?"

Ray had the good decency to look slightly abashed. "Um... no, they haven't confirmed it exactly. But they couldn't rule it out either. It seems that the makeup of the liquid was... well, let's just say it was highly *unusual*." He sneered. "And that only adds to the strangeness of this case, and to Hanno—*Molly* herself. The truth will come out soon enough." He staggered a bit, this little speech taking every ounce of gusto he had. Then he turned and lurched abruptly toward the door.

He'd lasted longer than most men I'd seen in his position. I could file a harassment suit against him for this visit and we both knew it. He had nothing solid on me, and James had just reinforced that.

When Ray reached the doorway, he pointed an accusing finger at me. "If she has this so-called mystery seizure disorder, which I'm sure no one on earth has ever heard of before, then why isn't it on file with the state? Huh? She was a cop. All her physicals are on record. Her records are clean. They state she's in perfect health."

"Ray," I said, walking out into my living room. "If you bothered to check, the paperwork for my very real seizure disorder should've already been faxed to the precinct by my physician. It's an affliction I've acquired in the last year. I guess I was a late bloomer." I crossed my arms in front of my chest, keeping my robe closed. I didn't want to flash Ray for the finale. "Have we given you enough to get you off our backs this morning, Ray? 'Cause if we have, I'd just as soon jump in the shower and start my day."

James came up behind me, a cup of coffee in his hands.

Ray was within an inch of disappearing out the door. "The two of you don't scare me. You don't intimidate me, and you don't make me sweat." *Oh, on the contrary, Ray.* "I know what I feel and I've been spot-on my entire career for eighteen solid years. There's something more than meets the eye with you, Hannon. Ever since you tagged Milo Curtis, I've known something was off. When you're around, strange things happen. You do things normal people can't—*and shouldn't*—be able to do. You're like some kind of doped-up circus freak. You can't hide forever. At some point you'll fuck up in a big way, and I'll be waiting." He turned and stumbled out of the apartment.

James handed me his cup so he could right the door.

"That's it!" I cried as James effortlessly propped the door back in place. "After all these years, I get it. I've been so stupid."

"Get what?" James took his cup back and headed toward the kitchen.

I followed. "Ever since Ray Hart zeroed in on me like a bloodhound, I've been trying to puzzle out the real catalyst. One day I was living my life, and the next he was dogging my every move. He just inadvertently revealed what set him off. It was Milo Curtis. I don't know why I never put that together before now." I stopped at the kitchen doorway. James had his hand on the fridge door, the muscles in his back flexing. I was momentarily lost.

"And who is this Milo Curtis bloke?" James set food on the counter.

"Um." I cleared my throat. "Milo Curtis was Ray's first big case, that's who." I walked over and started helping James with breakfast. "Milo was a big-time cat burglar doing all these huge heists around town. He stole millions. All these rich people with lots of power were getting hit, and subsequently putting pressure on the mayor and police department to find him. Everyone in the precinct was on edge. Evidentially, and unbeknownst to me at the time, he must've been Ray's ticket to the top."

James grabbed a pan off my hanging rack. "And let me guess, you got this Milo Curtis fellow your first time out, and in the process made the good detective look like a wanker who couldn't find his own arse with both hands."

"That about covers it." I chuckled. "I found out later Milo was a shifter of some kind. He disappeared soon after his arraignment, which is why I thought Ray never cared too much about the case, because it remained unsolved with the suspect on the loose. But the robberies stopped altogether, and it turned out that was all that had mattered to the chief. They didn't care about an arrest, they just wanted the hits to stop. And they did."

"Ray Hart is a bloody idiot." James started to whip the pancake batter. "He could stand to learn a lesson or two."

I needed a shower. Watching James make pancakes with no shirt on was going to ensure it was a cold one. I headed for the bathroom, calling over my shoulder, "Yes, but now that same idiot wants payback, and by the looks of it, preferably in the form of my personal demise. He's going to do everything in his power to get me."

I heard an egg crack against the pan. "Let him try."

12

The phone rang while I was in the shower. We were set to meet my father, brother, and the other wolves who'd made it into town in my office conference room in an hour.

Not using my place of business as the meeting location had apparently been discussed briefly, because a truckload of wolves descending on the premises would be a screaming beacon announcing to the world I'd changed. But if a werewolf had already found me in two days, my secret was already out. There was no stopping the train now, even though I would've loved to derail it completely.

We stood in the kitchen eating breakfast, because there was no furniture for sitting. I watched James eat, his powerful body up against the counter. A small pang surfaced in my chest about what we did last night. I didn't feel in any way attached to him, even though he was an unbelievable specimen, but it was kind of weird to be slutty and okay with it.

Do you feel any flutters? I asked my wolf.

She yawned at me and closed her eyes.

I didn't want it to be strange between James and I, so I tried to clear the air. "Um, James, about last night…I hope that was…you know…okay with you…"

James let out a throaty laugh. "No need to worry yourself. My wolf couldn't have denied your wolf anything in the world last night. I don't regret our little tryst one bit."

"I don't either," I admitted truthfully. "It was a nice way to end an extremely stressful evening. I felt better immediately." I had to ask one more thing. "James, do I…I smell different to you? Not just because I'm a wolf now, but I mean, different than other human females?" I shifted uneasily. It was totally embarrassing having this conversation in my kitchen. "I'm asking because it sort of seemed like…I don't know, I was giving off some weird hormonal thing last night I had no control over."

"Jessica, last night you smelled like nothing I'd ever come across before. It set me right off the moment I entered your apartment. It sent my wolf into a bloody frenzy. It was actually hard for me to get you out of my mind so I could sort out the rogue. My wolf paced with a constant need to satisfy you, to comfort you, to enjoy you thoroughly. It was all I could do to keep a rein on things. By the time we had the place to ourselves, your scent intensified by three hundredfold. There was no stopping it."

I smiled sheepishly. What had happened in the hallway moments prior to entering my apartment must've made me smell like a harlot on steroids, but I wasn't going to go into that here. "I don't smell like that now, do I?" I asked, a little panicked.

James took a gratuitous sniff even though we both knew he could smell me just fine. "You do smell different than a regular wolf—not bad, mind you, just a bit different. Definitely sweeter.

But, no, you don't smell anything like you did last night. Last night was…" His face hardened. "…Let's say it was intense. When you give off a smell like that, male wolves will come running. There's no doubt about it."

"Danny, Tyler, and Nick didn't seem to have a similar reaction to me," I said, feeling a bit stricken that I might be a dinner bell for salivating horny wolves without knowing it. "Maybe you're just more sensitive to it."

James laughed. It was a great sound. "Well, I should hope Tyler wouldn't be feeling very amorous of you. You two are bonded as kin. I'm betting your smell was quite sour to him. I can't speak for Nick, because he's not a wolf, but I would actually think you would smell like danger to him in that state. As for Danny, well, your wolf is very dominant, and while he might have liked to act on your scent very much, his wolf wouldn't have been so bold as to come on to yours directly. He would need permission from you first—some kind of a signal it was okay to make an advance." There was a slight growl in his voice. "I believe in the future you will only have issues with the most dominant of us." James regarded me for a moment over his plate of eggs. "The rest will likely be a bit worried."

As I ate my breakfast, I reflected on how much I *didn't* know about wolves. I was a newborn in every sense. "James, can I ask you something else?"

"Of course."

"How do you mate with human women? Well, I know *how* you mate, of course, but what about babies? I know it's hard for humans to carry them to term." That's how I lost my own mother. Carrying one wolf was hard, two was impossible. She died shortly after our births, and it was a miracle she'd held on for that long. "That's why there are so few new wolves around. But if a human woman actually does get pregnant, how does it all work? Especially if you're not mated. What do you tell them?"

"In the beginning, there's no need to tell them anything," he said. "We go on a few dates, woo them if we're so inclined, go through the process, and then see if we're lucky enough to procreate when it's all said and done."

"That sounds...*um*...promising."

James chuckled. "Actually, we have a bit in our saliva that helps keep a woman in the dark if we're not interested in a long-term commitment. Over time, if we choose to stay with them, or they are carrying our child, their bodies make up antibodies and they become immune to it."

I choked. "What do you mean by 'a bit in our saliva'?"

"Our saliva contains a drug to keep them a bit hazy about the whole thing, so they're not exactly sure if they've been with us or not the next morning. It's necessary, since with emotion our eyes tend to light up; it makes coupling a little tricky."

"What in the *hell*"—I coughed, swallowing my eggs wrong—"are you talking about? It sounds like you just said we have roofies built into our saliva."

"Think about it, Jessica. There are only a few women in the entire world who are compatible with us genetically—who can even be impregnated to begin with. And there are even fewer who are capable of carrying our baby to full term, and even less who can survive the actual birthing. So in order for us to find a woman who meets all those criteria, we have to..." He cleared his throat "...Well, let's just say it takes a lot of trying on our part."

I thought about it for a moment. It made sense when he put it like that, but still. "I take it you've had a lot of *tries* over the last few centuries."

"Yes."

"What about finding your mate? Wouldn't that be easier than sleeping with hundreds of women hopped up on roofie-saliva? Aren't true mates supposed to be able to bear your children with no problems?" I moved over to the sink to rinse my plate.

"That's what it states in our lore, though I've witnessed very few couplings through the centuries." He sounded suddenly weary. "If each of us waited for our one true mate, we would cease to exist as a race—and we don't exactly have that luxury. Without offspring, our species will become extinct."

"A fair enough point."

"You don't need a true mate to have tikes," James said. "You just need a gal who has something lingering in her gene pool from long ago, when villages used to be situated close to Pack boundaries. There were plenty of women back then who could birth strong pups. The lads even stayed with their mums until their adolescence. Then, over time, the lines became diluted as the gene pools spread out. We've lost our ability to reproduce easily." James was deep in thought for a moment. "True mates weren't as important to us back then. Once a woman had your child, she was considered your mate and you protected her and your son as such."

Was there a touch of sadness lingering behind that last part? To my knowledge James had never fathered a child, but I wasn't sure. I'd only been alive for twenty-six years, not the last few hundred. "A true mate is supposed to provide you with more than just a child, though, right? Supposedly compatible to your wolf in all ways. She is able to give you children, but she can also calm a part of your wolf like no other, and from what I understand, she alone can keep you from making a change."

"Aye. And your wolf, in its true form, is supposed to be able to spot her from a great distance. Your blood sings for her."

James walked to the sink and started to fill the basin. "'Tis the rarest gift to receive."

"My mother wasn't my father's true mate, was she?" I'd always wondered but never had the nerve to ask my father. Since I'd never known her, she was only a figment attached to a few photographs. I'd grown up in such a male-dominated world, I'd never had a chance to dwell on it too much. If she had been there, I'd be a much different person than I was today. Maybe I'd be softer. Who knew?

"That wasn't entirely clear to outsiders, even in the end." James dipped his hands into the sudsy water he'd drawn and grabbed a dish off the counter. "Callum was crazy for your mum. Followed after her like a lovesick puppy. Though when Annie died in childbirth, he didn't go through the deep, dark depression they say happens to a wolf when he's deprived of his mate. He also didn't end his own life, which is commonly spoken of in the lore. He was already Alpha then, though, and had a pair of twins to look after. Your father has always done things his own way." That sounded about right. "He's a man worthy of following. The strongest I've ever known."

James washed the dishes and handed them to me to dry. He'd always been fiercely loyal to my father. He would make a wonderful mate to a female, strong and valiant. I found myself hoping he would find her someday, aching for him to find his happiness.

He caught me staring. "What is it?"

"Nothing." I glanced at the clock. "We should get going. We don't want to leave my father waiting."

"No, Jessica, that wouldn't be a good idea."

13

James and I headed out of my apartment together. James discreetly forced my door back into its rightful opening, while I knocked on Juanita's door. I hadn't seen her since before my apartment had been trashed, and I was hoping she'd be home. She usually left early for work, so she was probably up.

The door whipped open before I had a chance to knock.

Juanita pulled me into a fierce hug. "Ooooh, Chica! I have been so worried! It es *soooo* good to see you here in the live." She pushed me in front of her and then grabbed me back into another bear hug. For a tiny person of roughly five feet two inches—in heels—she was a lot stronger than she looked. I also noted, when she finally let me go for the last time, that her ensemble today consisted of a bright pink sleeveless blouse accentuating her ample breasts, coupled with an orange miniskirt. Her hair and makeup were flawless. Her scent, I quickly found after I separated out the myriad other smells, was equal parts eucalyptus and lime. She smelled tough, and I liked it.

"It's good to see you too, Juanita," I told her, stepping out of reach of any more hugs.

She pushed up on tiptoes and glanced over my shoulder. James was still wrestling with the door. "*Oooooh*, Chica! *Muy bien!*" She gave me a saucy wink. "I was beginning to worry, you know, when I don't hear from you." She bobbed her head toward James and then leaned toward me for a conspiratorial whisper. I obligingly met her halfway. "Es that who you were fighting weeth last night? I hear some noises again coming from jour place." She laughed and elbowed me in the stomach.

"Um, yes, he's the one." What else was I going to say? *Nope, it was a scary rogue werewolf trying to kill me*?

"I keep jour secret, Chica. You know me, I weel always have jour back. We"—she motioned between the two of us with her cherry red nails—"we have to stay together when the tough get going."

"That's great, Juanita. Thanks." I felt like a chump asking her for a favor when I had so obviously shunned this nice woman's attempts at friendship over the last few years. "Um, I have a favor to ask you, Juanita, if you don't mind."

"No problem." She smiled at me with no misgivings. "I do it for you, whatever it es."

"As you can see, I had a little problem with my door last night." James grunted under his breath at my choice of the word 'little.' "I'm going to call the super, but I was hoping you could maybe keep an ear out if anyone who happens to come by when you're around?"

"*Sí*, thees es my day off, so I weel keep up guard for you no problems!"

I eyed her outfit again, wondering what motivation got you

out of bed and into full dress and makeup on your day off. But who was I to judge? This woman was turning out to be a great ally, and I was kind of running short on those at the moment.

"Listen, Juanita." I leaned in closer and she immediately followed, her forehead almost touching mine. "It's very important you don't open your door if you hear anyone out here, no matter who it is." As I said it, I looked straight into her eyes, trying to force some Vulcan mind-meld mojo at her—a gift that I might or might not have, but it was worth a try. I was interested in Juanita's help, but I had no intention of forfeiting her life for it. Whoever hired rogues meant business. They would not hesitate to take her out. "I mean it, Juanita. No door opening under any circumstances. Use your peephole and call me if anything seems…um, I guess…strange." *Well, stranger than what you heard last night.* "Or *overly* unusual."

"Okay, Chica. I weel not open the door to no one, even if they say to me es okay, *sí*?" She was obviously completely unpersuaded by my nonexistent mind-meld skills. A pang of disappointment ran through me. Not having an arsenal of super new gifts was going to make it hard to navigate in the supernatural world, where power was a must. I was really hoping for persuasion; it would've been a great asset.

James had finished propping the door into the opening and it looked fairly good at first glance, however, one push of a fingertip would likely topple it back into my apartment, but it would do for now. I'd put a call into Jeff, the super, as soon as I could. I had nothing to steal, as my apartment was bare, but allowing access to anyone who stopped by was tricky. If Juanita alerted me to anything suspicious, I might have an advantage.

We were late.

I quickly jotted my number on the piece of paper I'd brought out and handed it to her. "Remember, Juanita. It's extremely important that you do not open your door for any reason. Are we clear?"

"I weel no open, Chica. I weel keep watch with all my strength for you." She leaned in to me one last time with a sly look. "But for my repayment, you weel need to come to my house to have a drink, *sí*? Juanita weel keep jour secrets for you, but in return you have to tell Juanita what es happening here in thees crazy place." She shook her head at me. "Es too much. I worry for you."

Juanita was sharp as a tack and I admired her spunk. "Okay, Juanita, you have a deal."

I pulled into my office parking lot a few car lengths ahead of James. There were a ton of cars already in the lot. No one was waiting to jump me outside, so I figured my father had them under control. I parked and headed into my building. There was no need to wait for James with plenty of able-bodied wolves inside. A supe bent on attack, even if it was another rogue, would be foolish to come here. The smell outside was a swirling tide of male aggression.

I pushed the doors to Hannon & Michaels open and Marcy strode toward me anxiously. "You're late." Her eyes gleamed with the sparkle of adventure, not a typical sight. Her signature scent of fresh lavender wafted up my nose, making me smile in spite of the situation.

I glanced at the clock behind her desk. "You can barely call this late. I'm a little tardy."

Marcy raised her eyebrows in a manner indicating she pitied me immensely. "Everyone's in the conference room, but there's hardly any room left." She took my arm, guiding me down the hallway at a brisk pace. "And in case you were wondering, I've already cast a spell around the perimeter of the building. It's set to go off if any other supernaturals feel like crashing the party. Oh, and I also took it upon myself to jump-start the rumor mill. My aunt Tally, that crotchety old bitty, now thinks Callum McClain is hiring Hannon & Michaels to look into a *murder investigation*," she whispered excitedly, despite the fact she just told me the whole supernatural community was already in on it.

"You've had a busy morning." I chuckled. "Good thinking on all counts." We stopped in front of the conference room. "And, Marcy, if I didn't know any better, I'd say you were enjoying yourself." I leaned over and whispered, "And, honestly, it's a good thing at least one of us is having fun. This may be the end of my life as we both know it. The chances of me coming out of this room alive are slim to none."

"Oh, please." She swiped her arm in a dismissive gesture. "You'll be fine, and for your information I haven't enjoyed myself in years. Now get in there before the Alpha of the U.S. Northern Territories starts gouging holes in the furniture because his ungrateful daughter made him wait too long."

"I'll admit to 'overly harried' or 'exceptionally talented,' but never 'ungrateful.'" I gave her a wry smile.

I opened the conference room door.

A cloud of hostile testosterone engulfed me completely. The shroud of stale air saturated the room. How could they stand it? I'd taken one step inside but was forced to stop in my tracks in the middle of the open doorway. I had to mentally snatch my hands back before I placed them on the jambs to steady myself. I couldn't afford to look weak. Instead, I dug my nails into my palms. Pain over asphyxiation. Nails in the palms were becoming my norm. The pain centered me, and lucky for me the room was crowded, so not all eyes found me immediately, mostly because they couldn't see over the six-foot-plus wolves standing in my way.

Marcy was still behind me. "Are you okay?" she whispered. When I didn't respond she murmured, "Hold tight, I'll be right back with some water." She took off down the hallway.

With as much composure as I could gather, I closed the door with a snap behind me. Keeping Marcy out of the volatile conference room was now a top priority. The water would have to wait. Agitated werewolves in a small space were not good for anyone's health, least of all my skinny, breakable friend. If the smells swirling around were any indication, we were just short of an all-out riot.

As I stepped forward, the wolves in front of me parted slightly. I stopped a few paces in, meeting my father's gaze across the conference table. He was seated at the head of the table, looking regal and completely in charge. My brother was on one side, Danny and Nick on the other. Since this meeting was specifically about me, and involved Hannon & Michaels, it looked like Nick would be included on the events. I was relieved.

I ran a quick glance around the room, careful not to meet any direct gazes. The room contained every wolf I'd ever known, and many more I'd never met. They were keeping themselves in check for the time being. My father had called the cavalry in to settle important business. I wasn't surprised he'd done it, since it was protocol when the Pack was in danger, but it was still shocking to see so many wolves gathered in one place.

Our conference room at Hannon & Michaels was a fairly large space, but now it resembled a crowded subway car.

Marcy had brought in extra chairs, but there weren't enough. The wolves who ranked highest in status sat around the table. The rest lined the walls.

My gaze settled back on my father. Wading through a sea of agitated werewolves didn't seem like a very smart idea at the moment. They were bound by their Alpha's orders right now, but I didn't want to stir up a frenzy, so I gave my father a small nod to let him know I was good to go where I was, and he took the cue and slowly stood.

His movements controlled the room. All eyes focused on him as he leaned forward, bracing his knuckles on the tabletop in front of him. He swept the room with a severe gaze, meeting each and every eye individually. It took a while, but the effect was clear. "This is my daughter, Jessica McClain." My father's voice rang out, calm and authoritative. "She has gone under the alias Molly Hannon and has been living in this city for the last seven years." There was some murmuring. Many in the trusted inner circle had known, but for security reasons it hadn't been common knowledge, so most of the wolves in the room had no idea. "A little over three days ago my daughter became a full-blooded werewolf."

Well, that was one way to sort it out.

The murmurs turned to commotion as my father continued, "If anyone here objects to her directly you must make your presence known to me immediately."

Many of the wolves darted looks my way and a few, Hank included, looked very put out, but no one uttered a word. The wolves nearest me jockeyed for position, some of them peering at me curiously.

James strode into the room behind me.

He came up close, stopping only inches from my back. He radiated some much-needed strength in my direction and it calmed me by a few degrees. I ventured a quick peek over my shoulder. His nostrils flared, a growl reverberating deep in his chest. His face was as steely as I'd ever seen it. He knew what it was going to take to convince this Pack I was not their enemy, and his face told every wolf in the room where his loyalty stood.

A new smell permeated the air.

It was strong and acidic, the scent of anger mixed with aggression—*almost* a challenge. The hairs along my arms bristled and my wolf began to pace agitatedly in my mind. She growled a low threatening sound. *Easy*, I warned, *we won't win this one. It's not the time to wolf out, believe me*. She quieted, but ignored my words completely as she kept watch.

James's body stiffened behind mine as the smell grew more dense. I darted a glance at my father, who continued to quietly scan the room with a watchful eye. He was allowing his wolves the opportunity to take in the new information, and while they processed it, he gauged their reactions.

My brother, seated next to him, had assumed a similar vigil, most likely waiting to see which wolf's neck he'd have to snap first. I couldn't tell which wolf had issued the challenge, because my senses were stuck on werewolf testosterone overload. Likely it was more than one. And because there were so many wolves in here, I was almost certain no one could pin an accurate read on the aggressor.

James stepped forward, coming shoulder to shoulder with me.

His voice was strong and clear. "Jessica is not weak. I've seen the results of her fight firsthand. Those of you who perceive her to be an easy target will be sadly mistaken. From this day forth, she will be protected by the Rights of Laws of this Pack—*to the death*." His eyes targeted certain wolves, and they dropped their gazes one after the other. "I vow it in my name." He clapped a fist to his chest above his heart.

There was an immediate stirring.

The Rights of Laws was our bible. It contained all of our lore, passed down through generations. It was a physical text outlining the ways of the wolf, dating back several thousand years. When my father had become Alpha it had been entrusted to him, though to my knowledge it had been damaged in a fire more than three hundred years before he'd inherited it. I'd never seen the book, but it was said chunks of text were missing and some pages had been burned and charred beyond recognition.

A Primary Law stated that no werewolf, with the exception of the Alpha, or at the Alpha's directive, could attack another werewolf without just cause, outside of a challenge to Pack status. Pack challenges were their own event, and treated with great ceremony. The penalty for attacking without provocation was death. No in-betweens, just plain death. If a wolf broke this law, his punishment would be meted out by the Alpha, or a wolf designated by the Alpha.

James had just in effect told a roomful of wolves—his Pack mates—that he would kill any wolf who chose to lash out at me without just cause. It was a heavy threat since James was the second most powerful wolf in the Pack. His strength and killing prowess were legendary.

My father gave a curt nod of approval to James, before he added, "There will be no Pack challenges issued against my daughter until the matter of the dead rogue is addressed. There will be no exceptions. A direct threat against my daughter, by this rogue, will be treated as it should—as a threat against *Pack*."

The buzzing in the room reached a feverish peak. Wolves hated change and their body language clearly showed it. Many tensed, growling under their breath, shuffling their feet. They weren't going to be won over easily, if at all.

There was a wisp against my consciousness. *Don't worry, Jess,* Tyler said softly. *Even if it doesn't look that way, the majority of us are behind you and will protect you no matter the cost.*

Won't the cost be too much, Tyler? I couldn't bear to think of something happening to my brother or father, to any of them, because of me.

That's what Pack Law dictates, Jess. And that's what we'll do.

I think someone forgot to tell the wolf who attacked me last night that he was bound by Pack Law.

He wasn't one of ours. We don't know who he is yet, but Devon's working on it. He was definitely a rogue, but there's a good chance he was hired by someone outside of any Pack.

That was news. For the first time I noticed Devon with his laptop in the corner of the table. Devon Lee was the resident computer wiz and one of my father's top advisors. He wasn't a wolf, he was an Essential. I had no doubt that given enough time he'd come up with the rogue's missing identity. He had a brilliant mind for solving issues.

Rogue wolves were extremely dangerous. They were wolves who'd been thrown out of a previous Pack because they couldn't play well with others, or had broken some law—which really meant they couldn't play well with others. Some rogues, like Hank, moved to another Pack immediately, which was allowed if the new Alpha deemed them worthy. If they were accepted, they were given another chance to play by the rules.

The Rights of Laws mandated that rogue wolves be given a one-year respite from harm so they could rehabilitate into a more suitable Pack. Most rogues chose a new Pack, because if they didn't, within a year to the day, they had a standing kill order on their heads. I didn't know the exact number of rogues now on the run, but I assumed, at the very least, it was in the double digits. In the old days, assimilation into a new Pack worked, these days it wasn't a sure thing. A rogue who chose to stay a rogue on purpose had few redeeming qualities.

And anyone who would hire a rogue to do their dirty work

was also no friend of Pack. It was a severe crime in our world, and would be enough of a catalyst to start a war with the Sect responsible.

My father commanded the room again, effectively cutting off any rebuttals, as well as my internal conversation with my brother. "This *Pack* has been attacked by an outsider—a rogue wolf. A wolf who chose not to live by our rules. Our laws state this is a direct threat to all of us, and it will predispose any other action until it is resolved. There will be no further discussions about it."

There were some surprising murmurs of agreement, and some nodding. I hadn't thought any wolf would agree. A little relief ran through me until I heard a chair scrape back.

Hank stood with a snarl and pointed an angry finger at me. "How do we know this rogue wasn't just one of her jilted lovers gone bad? Huh? Someone she got tired of and decided to kill? There's been no proof she was attacked in the first place, and there's been no proof that the wolf in question was even a rogue."

Leave it to Hank to start us off with a bang. He had some gargantuan balls—he and Ray should have a tea party sometime. They'd bond over their shared hatred.

Another wolf piped in on Hank's heels, a voice I recognized as Rich Garley. Hank had officially opened the floodgates. Rich was one of the older wolves seated at the conference table. He'd spent time at the Compound during my early years, but now ran a small successful equipment business in South Dakota, where he spent nearly a hundred percent of his time. He wisely stayed in his seat. "Callum, I respect what you're saying here. But do we *really* know for sure what happened last night? From what I understand, the presumed rogue wolf in question has not been identified. I will stand by you, but I am unwilling to wage a war without some physical proof or complete certainty that this was a direct attack on Pack."

A younger wolf with shaggy brown hair and a decidedly aggressive edge boldly stepped forward. "How do we even know for sure if a female can *be* Pack? Why would we stick our necks out for her without proof she's Pack?"

My father snarled. The insolent wolf's eyes widened and dropped, all aggression in his features died in an instant, his surliness replaced by a pandering look. In his wolf form, he would've nipped my father's mouth with his tail between his legs. His indiscretion would not be forgotten.

Served the bastard right.

My father snapped his teeth fiercely. "Malcolm, because you are a relatively young wolf, and aren't familiar with our laws due to your residence off Compound"—a low noise issued from the back of his throat, alerting the young Malcolm to what he should've known anyway—"I will forgive your indiscretion. *This time.*"

Malcolm squeaked a response.

"A child born directly to the Alpha is Pack by bloodline." My father turned to the room, his voice echoing with power, making every syllable jump. "It has been so since the beginning of our existence. My children need not prove alliance, it is given freely. They need not swear to the Pack. It matters naught if Jessica is female. My blood flows through her veins. She is my kin. She is *Pack.*"

Hank still stood, a blatant disrespect to his Alpha. James growled and took a mock step toward him.

Hank sat down with a thump.

"Jessica," James declared, looking fierce as yellow light shot across his irises, "was attacked last night without provocation by a rogue wolf. I saw him myself. She was injured, but had already killed the wolf on her own." He dared anyone to challenge him. "The rogue was in full wolf form during the attack. He sprang without warning the moment she entered her apartment. Jessica should be dead by all accounts. It was a cowardly show of aggression, beneath us as a race, but she bested the wolf on her own and won"—he gave a big pause—"in human form."

Glances whipped toward me immediately, appraising. Most were skeptical. James hadn't mentioned the word "Lycan" and I had no idea if any of them were thinking it. I was a girl. How could I beat a werewolf as a human? Lycan was likely far from their thoughts, but they were thinking of something, there was no doubt.

The door cracked open behind me. Marcy delivering the water.

Before I could shoo her away, James spun on his heel too fast to track. He scooped Marcy around the middle and pounded out of the room, slamming the door firmly behind him.

All I'd heard from Marcy's retreating body was a diminutive "Ooof."

My father ignored the brief interruption, and instead motioned me over to him with a quick nod of his head.

Okay, then.

Danny quickly vacated his seat as I made my way around the table. Wolves parted aggressively, but kept themselves under control. My wolf was issuing a low-level continuous growl as we moved through the room. She was on the defense, ready to protect us. I calmly took the chair on my father's left, Tyler on his right.

Our seating arrangement presented a fierce showing of where we stood in Pack.

The faces around the table, to my surprise, displayed both

acceptance and rejection. Once again, I hadn't been expecting anything positive.

My gaze followed James as he strode back into the room and without a sound paced around the table and stood behind my chair, legs splayed wide, his wrists clasped in front of him. His fighting stance.

Having the support of many significant wolves would help eliminate some of the dissension, but any wolf who felt my position would affect their place in the pecking order would choose to fight me eventually no matter who supported me, or why. And when the official status challenges came, it would be me fighting alone. Not even my dad could circumvent those laws.

I couldn't worry about future challenges. I hadn't made it out of this room yet. I had to focus on what was going on here, and eliminate the white noise.

"The next step is to formulate a plan," my father said. He didn't touch on what James had just said about me besting the rogue in human form. I was relieved. "The Circle will stay to discuss the main options, and the other wolves will be brought up to speed once a decision is made on how the entire Pack will proceed. You are excused until further notice." He nodded to the wolves lining the walls.

I watched as the wolves filed out of the room.

I caught a brief glimpse of Marcy as the door opened, her eyes wide. Then without missing a beat she said, "Right this way, fellas." I didn't have enough money in my coffers to pay her enough.

Behind me, there was a barely audible growl. It was coming from James. I turned to him, but his gaze was pinned on the last wolf leaving the conference room. As the door closed, I wondered if I should be worried. The wolves should behave themselves out there. Marcy shouldn't be in any real trouble. I was the problem, not her. The smell of aggression diminished considerably as the wolves left the room, but before I could ask James what he thought, my father's voice filled the space.

"We will start this meeting with Jessica. She will brief you on the details of her first change, up until she arrived here this morning. After we've heard from her, we will hear from both Tyler and James. Then the Circle will decide what action is to be taken."

The Circle was the formal name for the werewolf Council, made up of roughly thirteen wolves including my father, one for every cycle of the moon in our original calendar. My father had supreme ruling over all decisions, which went without saying, but throughout the past few centuries wolves in every Pack had employed an advisory council of some kind. The Circle was short for "Circle of the Moon." The full moon has always been our most sacred symbol.

When it began, the Circle originally consisted of the Alpha and the twelve oldest werewolves in attendance at that given time. Nowadays, with technology and modern human development, my father had assigned specific wolves to the Council, to go along with the oldest.

There were nine wolves left sitting, not including Nick, me, and Devon, who was part of the Circle but not a wolf. Besides my father, my brother, and James, in attendance were Grady Carson; Rich Garley; my new super supporter, Hank, who I wished to hell wasn't here, but because he was one of the eldest he ranked a seat whether I liked it or not; Danny, who had a spot due to his status as the enforcer of the city boundaries; and two other older wolves, Cliff Delano and Elliot Murphy. Three wolves were missing, all of whom resided in Canada.

I had no idea how any of the Council members felt about me, besides Hank and Grady, but we were going to find out in about five minutes. Normally the Council meetings were held on the Compound, but because of the rogue attack, and everything that had gone wrong, my father had come here.

My father turned to me with his eyebrows raised expectantly.

I told my side of the story. I recounted to the Circle everything that had happened to me over the past few days, up until James busted through my door last night. James picked up the thread after that, and then my brother followed.

Nothing was mentioned about our brief interlude. Neither James nor I would be expected to share our coupling. Some things were private, even for werewolves.

My being a possible Lycan was also not specifically mentioned by name either, but it was implied. James told the room I had begun to change, but never finished. When Tyler finished describing the scene there was a long silence.

"What do you mean she *started* to change?" Hank, not surprisingly, asked first. "Did she finish, or did she get locked?" He looked at me hopefully. Getting locked or stalling partway through the change was typical with newborns, and extremely painful. Or so I'd heard.

I deferred to my father with a glance. I didn't feel it was my information to share; I barely understood what was going on my own self, much less trying to explain it to a group of wolves.

Callum McClain peered seriously around the table at his inner Circle. The anxiety in the room had amped up a few degrees. I suddenly felt light-headed. I had no idea what everyone was going to do when they found out. It couldn't possibly be good.

"What I am about to tell you will stay in this room until I deem it Pack business. Vow it."

Around the table a chorus of voices chimed, "I vow it."

14

A pulse of power flowed through the room as my father accepted an oath from each wolf. If they broke their vow he'd know it. Vows were binding in our world. The link from an Alpha to his wolf was a physical one, and when it came to a vow, it manifested between them in a tangible way.

"I have not seen this for myself, but it has been witnessed by my son and my second." He met the curious stares of his Council straight on. "It seems Jessica was able to change partway and hold that form for a considerable amount of time. She fought the rogue that way...and won." He lifted his eyebrow slightly, challenging his wolves to say otherwise. "She did not get locked. She did not stall. She was able to function with complete control."

There was dead silence.

Some of the wolves darted looks at each other. I wiggled in my seat, uncomfortable now that my secret was out. Receiving the news I was a Lycan had to be the equivalent of proving the

Cain Myth true for these wolves. I knew my father had to address it, there was no other way around it, but I just wished I'd had a few more days to digest everything first before it all came crashing down around me.

The soft clacks of the computer keys came to a halt. "*Lycan*," Devon breathed. "You're talking about a Lycan, right? I didn't think that was even possible. I mean, there's plenty of legend surrounding it, but no one in the last thousand years has ever witnessed one."

Everyone held perfectly still.

Emotions passed over each wolf's face as they grappled with the news.

A hesitant cough came from across the table. "But, Callum, if you didn't personally see it, they may have been mistaken," Rich said calmly. "No one has ever seen a true Lycan. How could it be accurately judged so quickly? It's possible that a female werewolf can't even change fully to begin with. Changing partway may be the only thing she can manage."

He had a point. If I hadn't made a full change my first night I would be questioning it as well.

"I would agree with you, Rich. Caution would be the right way to tread with this," my father said. "This is not information I share lightly with all of you. Jace did a full blood workup on Jessica when she came back, and her chemistry has completely changed. I received the results before I left the Compound. He is still working on isolating the gene, but according to her blood, at this time, she is full wolf and that's confirmation enough." He let his voice trail off as he gazed around the room. It was still absolutely quiet. He continued, "There have also been a few other indicators pointing to Lycan, which have made me solidify my judgment."

Cliff Delano, a steady wolf with chocolate skin and serious

eyes, stared at me in open wonder. "What other indicators?" he asked my father in a sedate tone, which underscored the fear quietly emanating from him.

In fact, the stink of fear began to fill the air from several directions. That wasn't good.

"Jessica, it seems," my father told his Circle, "is able to block me from her thoughts unconsciously. I am unable to reach her. I cannot break through her barrier, though I have tried to do repeatedly."

There was an audible gasp and a few open growls.

I felt like a fish in an aquarium, right before the cat dips his paw in and gobbles her up. I burned under the weight of their gazes. *What do you think about that, boys? Huh? I'm an unknown risk and the most powerful Alpha in the world can't control me. I'm your worst nightmare come to life. How do you like me now?*

I closed my eyes. My internal senses shifted as Tyler spoke in my head. *Jess, it's gonna be okay. We will figure this out. If they retaliate, we will quell it and move on.*

That's easy for you to say. Quelling a few wolves is one thing, but once this gets out, my life will be up for grabs. You can't stop all of them at the same time. The wolves who fear what a Lycan will mean in Pack, having never seen one before, will hate me for no other reason than that, and those who deny I'm a Lycan will fight me for status.

My brother's emotions swirled near the surface. In my mind, it appeared like an ethereal arc of colors. I had no idea the thought process could work like that. Fiercely loyal green, purple for his fears, and the scarlet of his heart. He had no words for me, but that was enough.

I glanced up from the table. My gaze landed solidly on Hank. Naturally. His facial features went from shock to revulsion in one second flat.

He shot up from his seat before he could contain himself, so fast he stumbled back a few steps, his chair clattering. "I will not take orders from that," he said as he pointed at me. "I will *not* be ruled by a *female*." He was so angry, spittle gathered at the sides of his mouth.

My father stood from his chair slowly, taking his time to rest his hands on the table and lean forward. "No one is asking you to take orders from Jessica, Hank Lauder. I'm the Alpha of this Pack. I will remain the Alpha. There's been no shift in power, nor do I expect there to be. There is much for us to learn about what a Lycan means, but I assure you Jessica will not be seeking to challenge me. Not now, not ever."

You've got that right, Dad. I had a very clear sense my wolf wasn't the Pack Alpha type. Yes, we were alpha, strong and bullheaded, but running Pack was for Alphas. There were very few true Alphas born. It took the strongest alpha-born personality, coupled with cunning, power, and the ability to run a Pack to make a true Alpha. Just because you were alpha-born didn't mean you were strong enough to control a bunch of unruly wolves. Don't ask how, but I was certain it was not our role to take over Pack leadership. My wolf snapped her jaws at the thought, dismissing it. I was definitely missing something here. *I don't get it. I know we're alpha-born, but not Alpha. None of it makes any sense.*

Elliot Murphy spoke for the first time, interrupting my inner thoughts. His red hair and freckled face looked friendly enough but I wasn't sure if he was on my side yet. "Let us hear from Jessica, then. She can tell us for herself she will not seek to rule us as Alpha of this Pack."

My father looked to me and I stood up. He was still standing, since he wasn't going to sit until Hank did. "I can assure everyone here I do not wish to be Alpha." My tone was clear and even. "Being a werewolf is very, very new to me, but my wolf clearly holds my father as Alpha of this Pack. I have absolutely no intention of fighting my father for his place. Ever."

"Then prove it to us," James's voice intoned from behind me, mingled with a little regret. "Swear to us right here, right now. Swear to it on a Blood Oath."

I turned to him, my mouth gaping slightly. His face remained still, no emotion showing, but from my proximity, only a foot away, I could see a pinprick of amber flicker in his eyes.

I knew exactly why he'd made the request, but it still made my heart skip a beat.

If I didn't swear to these wolves, right this minute, the panic and unrest would seep into the Pack at a rate that would ensure my elimination by challenge or other means by night's end, starting a civil war within our Pack. Maybe if the news had only been full blooded, I might have scraped by, but Lycan? No. This news was too much, and I could not let the Cain Myth come true. I'd be damned if I was going to be the catalyst that broke this Pack apart.

No fucking way.

If I swore a Blood Oath never to challenge my father for Alpha status, I could lessen some of the insanity right now. I had no other choice. "Of my own free will," I stated, "and before you all, I will swear a Blood Oath to never challenge my father for Alpha status of this Pack."

A vow resonated with power, making it binding. If a wolf broke their vow, the Alpha would mete out punishment as he saw fit. A Blood Oath was deathly.

Nothing in Pack was more powerful than the Alpha. The Alpha's blood was the key to that power. When a wolf's blood mingled with his Alpha's, and an oath was spoken, it sealed an unbreakable deal. If I were to try to go against my word, to fight my father, my death would be instantaneous. My father's blood would stop my heart, or clot my brain, or something akin to that. Who knew exactly how it all worked? I just knew it did. And so did everyone else in the room.

Few wolves ever swore Blood Oaths, because they forfeited their lives if they ever changed their minds. I wasn't going to change my mind. For the sake of my family, I couldn't and wouldn't.

My father turned to me, his eyes steady. I could see regret in them, but also acceptance. He knew as well as I did that we had no other choice but to move forward like this.

There was a sharp intake of breath from across the table before the caustic words hit the air. "If she's able to block your power in her mind already, do we know if the Blood Oath will even work?" Hank sneered. "She could fake it."

My father looked directly at Hank, rolling his shoulders forward. Hank had exhausted his get-out-of-jail-free cards. I'd never understood why my father put up with Hank's antics—he was a constant pain in the ass—but he must've had a good reason. Or Hank would already be dead.

My father growled, and Hank dropped his eyes and sat. "Blood works differently. Both Jessica and I will feel the oath as it binds and accepts us. I will know." His voice was a command. No one else spoke.

James stepped from behind my chair and handed my father a hunting knife from its resting place on his belt. My father handed me the blade after making a quick incision in his palm. His blood ran thick and dark, but would be open on his hand only a few moments before it healed over.

I took the blade, staring straight at my father, and said what I hoped would be enough. "I, Jessica Ann McClain, will never challenge Callum Sèitheach McClain for his rightful place as

Pack Alpha of the U.S. Northern Territories for as long as I live and breathe. I swear it on this Blood Oath, with this Pack as witness. If I so do, may I die."

I sliced my palm open. Bright red blood flowed like a river. I grasped my father's outstretched hand. He closed his eyes and arched his head backward. Power radiated between us in a pulsating mass of energy. I was sure the other wolves could feel it as well. His blood rocketed through my system like a meteor, hot and dangerous.

My body shuddered with the impact. My wolf howled. Every single molecule of my being stung like it'd been seared. His blood was unbelievably strong. My body raced to process the influx of his power as it mingled with mine. My wolf barked and scratched her claws along the floor of my mind, shaking her head like a bee had flown in her ear.

We stayed like that for another few seconds.

"It is done." My father unclasped his hand, breaking the connection.

His wound was completely healed. Mine continued to bleed. Nick handed me a set of napkins from the coffee cart.

My father sat down without looking at me.

I resumed my seat and blotted the napkins into my still healing skin.

Rich Garley snorted. "Well, if she can't heal a flesh wound like that"—he pointed at my still dripping hand—"she can't be that much of a threat. I, for one, am satisfied." He looked around the room to other nods of approval.

Danny and Devon nodded their heads up and down in unison. My gaze landed on Grady, who hadn't uttered a word since I'd walked into the room. He appraised me carefully with open speculation. His wise eyes lingered on my hand, his face drawn in an inscrutable line. I hoped like hell he hadn't already discovered what my father and I were trying so well to hide during our little demonstration.

If he knew already, the others wouldn't be fooled so easily.

Power had swirled as our blood merged. That part had not been a lie. But I knew in my soul, just as my father knew.

The Blood Oath did not claim me.

15

"Devon"—my father was back to business in the span of a heartbeat—"give us an update on what you've found about the rogue who attacked Jessica last night."

My father was clearly not going to risk taking any questions about what had just gone on between us. We both knew he should have shared it with the Circle, but he'd chosen in an instant to protect me against all other rational thought.

He was my father and I love him for it, even though it put us in a dangerous position. The Pack could wage war on him for the betrayal, if they ever found out.

On my life, I would just make sure they never did.

"The photo"—Devon tapped his computer screen—"I just uncovered seems to match the wolf we're looking for. According to this, his name is Robert Lincoln. He was booted from the Southern Territories about ten years ago, and not a lot is known about him. The last entry speculates he spent time in

Russia." Devon paused to let the weight of that sink in. "And the last physical sighting of him was in Spain two years ago."

Devon, and a few other computer-gifted wolves across Pack lines, had spent some time compiling a database of sorts. It let the six World Packs share information with each other for these very reasons. If a wolf went rogue, or chose a life as a lone wolf, his picture and profile were automatically entered into the database. Lone wolves were wolves, usually extremely old, who chose to live out the rest of their lives in wolf form, instead of in their human form. There were very few of them, all of them low-threat betas, and there were strict rules, but they did exist.

The database was the only "cooperative endeavor" the major World Packs did together.

There wasn't a lot of trust across Pack lines, but it was meant to ensure everyone's safety, both werewolf and human. The World Packs consisted of the two U.S. Territories, both Northern and Southern, which included Canada to the north and Mexico to the south, South America, Europe, Asia, and Russia.

Russia was the most wild and notoriously unpredictable territory. The wolves there were born mean and were known for their unscrupulous behavior. It was said they valued human life very little, if at all. A rogue come and gone from Russia solidified himself as a threat, it being one of the few remaining places for a rogue to run wild and, with enough bribery and viciousness, survive for any length of time.

There were many small factions of wolves scattered around the world, but they were not considered fully operating Packs. They were usually tied to an Alpha on one of the main continents. My father controlled a small contingency in the Aleutian Islands. Their leader was required to check in once a year, and they were not bound to our Pack like the other wolves. Meaning they were not required to wage war for us. They also ran their clans differently, more loose and organic, like the old ways. But unlike the rogues, they were beholden to rules and they still answered to their Alpha.

"Go on," my father said.

"There has been a kill order on him for the last nine years," Devon continued. "And it looks like several wolves in Europe have gotten close. A bounty has never been issued." If you killed a rogue, the Pack that rogue last came from paid a hefty reward. It was money well spent to keep rogues from running wild, and for other wolves to get the idea if they went rogue, everyone was going to be clamoring to kill them. "There has been no recorded kill. Well, until today, that is." He tapped the keys to fill in the appropriate data, I assumed.

It looked as though Robert Lincoln had stayed alive longer than most. This wasn't good news for our Pack. Someone obviously had hired him. And they'd hired him quick, since I'd only "technically" come out as a werewolf today.

The rogue had also known where my apartment was located, which was leased under the name Molly Hannon with no records leading to Jessica McClain or Pack whatsoever. It pointed to a rather large breach in our Pack ranks, which didn't bode well for any of us.

My father took the news seriously and was quiet for a long moment. "If this rogue came from Russia or Europe, our Pack faces a major threat," he said. "I will contact Julian to see if he has any additional news about this particular wolf. From now on our Pack will be on high alert until we discover who and where this threat is coming from and why." He rubbed his chin absentmindedly. Julian de Rossi was the Pack Alpha of the European Territories. His wolves had been involved in a civil war on and off for years. It was just a matter of time before they split into two. Too many wolves in one Pack bred all kinds of trouble. "My gut feeling is someone has been waiting for Jessica to turn, with plans in place all along. All they needed to do was enact these plans once receiving confirmation of her transition. Any other scenario would've taken too long. I've been extremely foolish and lax in my assumption she would go undetected for so many years. I blame myself for this and no other."

"You can't possibly take all the blame," I said, not knowing if I should jump in, but doing so anyway. "I don't accept that. I insisted on a life outside the Compound. I fought for my life for it. Literally. And I'd do it again if given the chance, whatever the cost."

"That's where we differ, Jessica." My father turned toward me. "If I'd known the cost we're facing now, I would've restrained you and kept you under my watchful eye all this time. There is nothing on this earth worth the possible risks we face now." There was a softness in his eyes that I hadn't seen since I was young. "Jessica, you are the only female werewolf in existence. We have no known record of such a thing ever happening before. You are priceless among us, and something we cannot even begin to understand. I've been remiss in how I've dealt with you, and I will compensate by making a vow on my life that you will survive at all costs."

Tyler added, "Jess, we're going to find these assholes and eliminate them quickly and efficiently. Even if the threat is coming from overseas. We have enough power in our Pack to crush the opposition."

The U.S. Northern Territories were known around the world as the powerhouse Pack not to mess with. Unlike Russia with its brutal wolves, our Pack took cunning and paired it with strength to become an undefeatable force for the past three hundred years.

Grady's voice came slow and steady from across the table. "It is my belief we must first determine if there is a traitor among our own Pack." Unease fluttered around the table, each wolf looking warily at the other. "My humble suggestion is we keep every detail of this Council meeting private until that point has been determined. Letting this information out may risk the only edge we may have."

"Agreed," my father said. His tone brooked no further discussion on the matter.

"Agreed," a chorus of voices chimed in around the table. No one was going to risk being the one to disagree now.

I rested my arms on the table, the wound on my palm finally sealed. "If I understand all this correctly, my mind was wide open during my change for a few moments. Correct? If that's the case, any wolf in this Pack could've figured out what was happening last Saturday morning. That leaves hundreds of possibilities."

"The message I received from your wolf came in the wee hours of the night," Danny said, speaking for the first time, "and it was very short and muddled. I was unsure it was really you—and I know you." He continued, "The wolf who decided to take that very scant knowledge acted quickly on an unfounded assumption that you'd made a full change. There was no physical proof you'd actually become a wolf." He leaned forward, his accent deepening. "Until today, none of us knew you were the real deal. Whoever sold you out is no friend of ours. We must act immediately, and strike high on the vertebrae—Pack brother or not."

Danny was proving to me why he'd been entrusted to run the protection of this city. He carried no fear and was boldly sure of himself.

Keeping the news of a possible traitor to ourselves would enable us to sniff them out. Literally. If the wolves in this room played their cards right, the traitor in question would grow nervous.

I thought about it for a moment. "If we keep this private for now, it may be the best way for us to find him. If we act like nothing's happened, like the rogue was an isolated incident, we may be able to sniff him out sooner. If we put pressure on the Pack right away, he may run and we'll lose our chance to nab him and find out what's going on. If I leave here and go back to my life as usual—with bodyguards," I added before anyone could object—"we can downplay this meeting as my official 'coming out' party and pretend it's business as usual. He may not be able to resist his good luck and keep gunning for me."

"That has possibilities," James murmured in agreement.

Nick cleared his throat and spoke for the first time. "None of the Pack has any knowledge of how we conduct business here. Things run differently here. If we tread carefully, we may be able to monitor Jessica's movements without detection. We focus our assumption that the Russian-based rogue was an outside interference, not an internal search. Jessica goes back to her life, and we tail her quietly to find him. He won't be able to sit still. If the traitor wants her gone badly enough to hire a rogue, he will strike again. Likely sooner than later."

"I don't like it," my father grumbled. "We should be able to find him without a bunch of charades. If I have a traitor in my Pack, he will *not* be able to hide from me for long. If I apply pressure, it will only be a matter of days before he is forced to betray himself. The only uncertainty is whether he has already aligned himself with another Sect altogether. That unknown makes it risky. I feel strongly that until we have more information, Jessica should go underground, kept safe where we can watch over her."

"I understand your caution," I said, addressing my father directly. "But if I go underground we are essentially telling Pack, and whoever's on my tail, that we know something is wrong and we're investigating. It may force an ugly situation before we're ready. Or the traitor will run, taking away our only chance to find out any information about a possible connection to another Sect—one that may or may not be after me. If I spend a few more days acting like nothing's happened, we may be able to gain a jump on who's after me quickly, and without risk."

My father wasn't nearly convinced.

"Just give me two days, Dad. That's all I ask. Nick will be with me during the days, Tyler, Danny, or James during the nights. There's enough power in this room to do backup surveillance on all our movements. I have no doubt whoever sent that rogue will continue to come after me. If we're inconspicuous enough, we can turn the tables on him and come away with information we need in less time than it will take you to pressure him out. He has my scent and he isn't going to stop now."

I looked at Nick for help. "What do the next two days look like for you, Jessica?" he asked me, and I loved him for it. "I'm fairly free and can manage all your details with you."

"Actually, I have a meeting tonight with a potential new client," I said. "Drinks at a public place to discuss a future case." I looked to my father, who still wore a grim expression. "It would be a perfect location for someone to follow me in unseen."

"Which case?" Nick asked. "I haven't heard of any new client."

"His name is Colin Rourke. I spoke with him yesterday for the first time."

The uproar was instantaneous.

Everyone in the room began talking at once, a few of the wolves jumped from the table and started pacing, including my brother. Devon let out a small gasp as his hands furiously clacked away on the computer keys.

"What? What did I say?" I shouted over the din, startled by what had just happened. I raised my voice a few notches. "What's going on? He told me he ran an accounting firm. He suspects his partner of embezzlement, or something equally uneventful. What's the big deal?" I ended lamely with nobody paying any attention to me.

"This really is bad," Devon said, more to his computer screen than anyone else. He shook his head slowly. "If Rourke knows, then Jessica's already on the open market. We have more to worry about than just one traitor in the Pack."

James loomed behind me, his knuckles stark as he gripped the back of my chair. The wood bowed and cracked beneath his fingers, and he was muttering a colorful string of nasty words under his breath—words I hadn't heard him utter since I lit my father's toolshed on fire by accident when I was thirteen. I turned from him to my brother.

"How in the hell did he get here so fast?" Tyler shouted. "And he told Jessica his real name! He knew she would find out who he was, and he still gave it to her. What's his fucking angle?"

"Who *is* this guy?" I yelled, making sure I was heard this time. "Why are you all freaking out? Somebody better fill me in before I lose it." Then I immediately felt foolish for not researching my own client myself. At the very least, I'd been off my game yesterday, but if I let the truth be known, I hadn't really planned on researching his legitimacy until *after* I'd accepted the job. *Dammit.*

These rookie mistakes were going to cost me. There was no way my father was going to have any faith in me now, and by the looks of it, he was gearing up to tell me just that. I'd just showed myself as an incompetent and foolish private investigator. I was the only female werewolf on the goddamn planet, and I hadn't thought for two seconds about changing the way I did my business moving forward. I should've been on high alert, not dillydallying around eating cheeseburgers.

This guy must be incredibly talented if he could cause a roomful of lethal werewolves to go crazy.

Well, *shit*.

Nothing about this looked good.

My father answered me first, scowling. "Colin Rourke is the most notorious supernatural mercenary in the entire country, possibly even on the planet. He only gets hired when people want the job done, meaning they want it finished, tied up tight with no loose ends. The fact that he's already here escalates this issue to a new level. Your secret, it seems, has not been much of a secret at all. Other Sects, not just wolves, must have been waiting on your change, with plans put in place. It's the only possible way he could be in my territory so quickly."

"What is he?" I asked. "If we're this up in arms, he has to be something big, right?"

"He's a werecat of some kind," my father said. "But his exact species is unknown. No one has seen him in his true form and ever lived to talk about it. It's speculated he's the last of his kind, which is why we're unfamiliar with his scent. The cat population has decreased to the point of extinction over the last few hundred years, and he is much, much older than that. He's ruthless and extremely dangerous. His common aliases are David West, Dean Raith, and Connor Dade. And those are only a few." My father eyed me. "He rarely uses his given name, and most don't even know it."

"How do you know it, then?" I asked.

My father looked past me. "I hired him to fight with us a long time ago."

"He came to battle with you?"

"He did. He killed everything in his path without shifting.

He fulfilled his duty to me. I paid him. He left. We forged no further bond."

I mulled this over in my brain. He must've been skilled with a sword or some weapon to go to war and not shift. James and my father were that strong, depending on who they were up against, but not relying on your true form to aid you in battle was almost unheard of these days.

My father added, "And you won't be going anywhere near him this evening. Or any other evening after for that matter."

Well . . . *hell.*

I'd heard of Connor Dade. In my profession, you came across notable stories about bounty hunters and mercs all the time. Connor Dade's reputation was well known. The last thing you always heard after a recounting of one of his exploits was "*Whatever you do, don't fuck with Connor Dade.*"

I was less familiar with his other aliases, but the one I knew was more than enough. "Let's look at this logically for a moment, shall we?" I said, fighting to be heard. "If Colin Rourke used his real name, and he knows who I really am already, he'd most likely count on me finding out who he was." If I was a smarter person to begin with. "He can't be out to kill me if he told me his real name. Right? He dealt us a hand, and now he wants to play." Sneaky sucker.

The noise level quieted as the wolves chewed on that.

"Listen, he deliberately told me who he was," I pointed out again, not wanting to lose my audience. "He could've used any name on the planet, especially if he was trying to lure me away. Screw that, he could've jumped me himself instead of the rogue. And if what you're telling me is true, he would've been successful, and all this would be a moot point right now because I'd be dead."

My father grumbled but stayed silent. Tyler stopped pacing.

"This is reading like a go-to, not a jump," I insisted. "Maybe he has something to share, or knows who's after me. Who knows? But telling me who he was when he's had known contact with my father doesn't make any sense. And how did he know I wouldn't recognize his name from the start? That you hadn't shared it with me a long time ago?" I looked over at my father and raised an eyebrow. "Which may have been a good idea in retrospect, with me being a P.I. and all."

Tyler reluctantly said, "Jessica has a point. There has to be some kind of angle here. Someone like Rourke doesn't just pop in and announce himself to the world like that. He's a threat to our Pack, and just being in our territory without permission is enough for us to go after him."

Sly bastard. He knew I'd meet with him, even when I found out who he was. He was banking on it.

"He's not stupid," Elliot Murphy added. "He'd know without a doubt the Pack would recognize his name." His pale, freckled skin now seemed a few shades lighter. "It also seems he knows who Jessica is already. It's a ballsy move. I have to agree, he must have something to share, because calling to announce he's here is not his standard M.O. He's a brutal bastard. If he was hired for a kill, he would not give fair warning." He finished with a little lingering awe in his tone.

"He honored our contract during the war," James stated. "He showed up and fought hard for our side. He did not strike me as a man who would kill a female without provocation and I don't have that impression now. He doesn't take jobs because he has to; he takes them because he wants them. Killing Jessica doesn't feel like something he would sign up for."

"How do you know that?" Cliff Delano asked.

James shrugged. "Because that's not what I would do."

"The bloke doesn't have to kill her," Danny interjected. "He could be hired to kidnap her. That's what I'd do if I wanted her. Pardon me, Jessica, but who better for a heist than a psycho killer with a penchant for playing mind games?"

"Yes, that's exactly why he called her and announced to the world he was here," Tyler scoffed. "If he was going to grab her, he wouldn't go through the trouble of setting up a meet first. Hell, he most certainly wouldn't have given her his real name. My bet is he's hired to do a job, but doesn't want to stir up trouble in Pack. He's playing both sides. Smart bastard. If he arranges a meet, he can cover his ass if we catch on, claiming he was just here to chat. If we don't catch on, he's scot-free, back out of town before we even knew he was here."

Most of the wolves agreed. Grady appeared deep in thought again, his brows drawn in a frown, eyes aimed at nothing in particular. Hank, of all people, stared blankly into his coffee cup. I couldn't decide if he looked guilty or just defeated, but I was happy he kept his mouth shut.

My father listened to the back-and-forth, a vein throbbing in his temple. When he spoke again, the room quieted. "If Colin Rourke has legitimate business with my daughter, the protocol would've been to call me first. This is my territory and he knows that. He's playing with us. If he had important news to share, aboveboard, he would've shared it with me first."

"But maybe coming to you would've shown his hand," I argued. "Maybe he had to contact me first because others are watching?" That made sense to me. If Rourke was playing both sides, contacting the Alpha when you're hired to kidnap his daughter would be the wrong move.

The protocol for entry into this city was not dialing up the Alpha of the U.S. Northern Territories on your cell phone to chitty-chat, the protocol was to take your ass up the Compound and beg for permission to be seen and subsequently allowed to stay.

My father growled. "I still don't like it."

"I know it doesn't make much sense," Nick said, coming to my defense once again. "But I think I have to agree with Jessica. If Rourke is as lethal as you say, then calling Jessica and announcing his presence would negate a serious threat. At least right now. I think we should go ahead with the meeting as planned. It sounds like there's too much at stake to pass it up."

Tyler added, "We could put every available wolf on the outside once Jessica was on the inside. He won't kill her in a public place. Not his style. If he tried to grab her, we'd be waiting."

"Tracking me won't be a problem," I said, solidifying my part. "Not that I think he's going to snatch me." I glanced at my father to see if he was warming to the idea. His stony expression said otherwise. "Nick and I use small button vibrators to communicate when we work together." The vibrators were actually called "panic buttons," but who could take you seriously when you called it that? "If I sense any trouble, I'll push it to ring the alarm. If we head in prepared, there's very little chance he can follow through with an evil plot to snatch me." I sighed. How many more targets were going to be on my back? Too fucking many.

My father's features didn't flicker with any emotion. He remained stony and unmoving in his seat.

I knew if I didn't win this, I was on my way back to the Compound to be kept underground until the traitor was found and this mess with Rourke was resolved. Meeting with Colin Rourke and keeping our suspicions about a traitor quiet was the best chance I had to solve this quickly, without being kept under lock and key. No one was really speaking, so I continued,

"Listen, we don't really have much of a choice here. If Rourke is as good as you all say, he's going to hunt me down eventually. Even if you try your best to squirrel me away. I don't think Compound boundaries are going to keep him out. Going into this meet with him, and being as prepared as we can be, is our best shot at trying to gain the upper hand in this situation—and while we're at it, figuring out why in the hell he's here and who in the *hell* sent him. It can't be a coincidence that he wants to meet with Molly Hannon to discuss a real case so soon after my change. He knows, and whoever hired him knows too. I don't know about the rest of you, but I want to know who that is."

"Sir, I think your daughter's correct on this one. This is too dangerous to ignore," Devon added meekly. "If what's listed on file is the truth, ignoring Colin Rourke's request for a face-to-face meeting could be very bad indeed. It seems this might be his way of waving a flag of truce for the time being. It's in her best interest to go and meet with him—with protection, of course. Otherwise he comes to us."

I held my breath.

My father looked around the room at his wolves. "Then we go."

16

Rourke and I had arranged to meet for drinks at a trendy local bar. After the Council meeting finally adjourned, I, Tyler, Danny, and Nick went over plans for the meet. Tyler was in charge of corralling the wolf backup around the bar. He'd picked a handful of wolves he trusted and left to figure out the logistics. Danny was assigned to be my personal bodyguard for the rest of the day, Nick had left to scout the inside of the bar, and my father and James had left for the Safe House to deal with the rogue and any leftover fallout from my coming-out announcement today. The wolves were not happy, but so far they were cooperating.

My father wasn't taking any chances of a budding unrest due to the news, so he dispatched all out-of-town wolves back home. The wolves outside the Council had no idea I was a Lycan yet, but everyone now knew I was a full-blooded were-wolf. That was enough until we dealt with the traitor and Colin Rourke.

The final agreed upon course was to keep a steady "business as usual" attitude and hope the traitor didn't run. It was five o'clock now. Danny and I headed to my apartment so I could change and get ready.

When we arrived, I was surprised to see I had a new, fully operating front door. "That's strange," I said, checking my cell phone. There were no missed calls.

"What's strange?" Danny asked, coming up behind me.

"My door was completely broken this morning, from when James ripped it off its hinges last night, but I forgot to let anyone know." I'd totally spaced on calling Jeff Arnold, the building super. My brain had been a little preoccupied. It was hard to believe Jeff had come to investigate on his own. It just didn't seem likely with his slack personality, but maybe Juanita had called him after all. She might have been tired of watching my place for me.

"That's part of living in a building, right? They come and fix things for you."

"I guess." I walked over and knocked on Juanita's door to see if she'd seen anything or talked to Jeff. I rapped on it, but there was no answer. I put my ear to the door just to be sure. I shrugged, turning to Danny. "Well, she didn't have to stick around all day to keep watch over nothing if the door got fixed. She must have been the one to call Jeff."

"Who?" Danny asked.

"Nothing." I was actually relieved she wasn't here. I'd felt bad all day thinking she might get into trouble at my request.

"Look here," Danny said as he bent down and grabbed on to the edge of an envelope lying halfway under my door.

He handed it to me and I ripped it open. It was a new set of house keys.

By the time I'd showered, changed, and eaten, it was only six. The meeting wasn't until eight. I walked into the living room, where Danny sat propped against the wall reading a newspaper he'd brought with him.

He whistled a catcall as he stood, folding the paper neatly under his arm. "Hold on a minute. We're only trying to dismay this sot so he gives us information, not render him useless with desire." Danny grinned.

"Give me a break." I laughed. "I'm not trying to render anyone useless. If he's as tough as everyone says, I hardly think he'll be swayed to the point of silly by a black pantsuit."

I'd actually chosen my outfit with care, knowing I'd be able to hide the weapons I might need with relative ease. The pantsuit was a tailored number. The bodice was tight across the middle, but cut loose enough in the sleeves to hide the two Bo-Kri throwing knives I had strapped to each arm.

The accompanying pants were snug at the waistline, but the flared legs concealed a small holster for my Glock, and a particularly evil-looking dirk. This time I was arming myself with as much as I could. I wasn't going up against a known killer without adequate protection. I pinned my hair up in a chignon instead of a ponytail, the outfit carried an air of don't-mess-with-me professionalism.

"Then you don't know men," Danny answered. "If you wore that pantsuit any better, I'd have to have you bloody arrested myself." He came closer, leaning his head toward me. "Is that a wee bit of white lace I see peeking out of your very ample cleavage?"

"It's called a camisole." I snorted. "And for your information, it's completely *necessary* with this outfit."

"I'm certain it is, luv." Danny chuckled. "Pairing that suit with anything less would be a complete travesty."

"It only has a dusting of lace," I said as I walked over to my purse. "Now get your pretty mind out of the gutter, Danny Walker, and let's get out of here. I want to do some reconnaissance at the bar to get a better feel for the area before the meet."

"Whatever you say. I'd follow that outfit anywhere."

The bar was a relatively new hot spot, fairly close to my apartment building. Every Tuesday night, it seemed, they hosted an extended happy hour, so it was already hopping by the time we arrived. Minnesotans were notoriously after-work-happy-hour kind of people. For the most part, we liked to be home and tucked in by ten, and there was nothing like cheap drinks to lure out the masses.

Tyler met us across the street, handing me a button vibrator immediately. "We have every entry point covered within a two-block radius, and Nick is parked behind the bar. He's got the other piece." He nodded at the button. "But remember, now we have this"—he tapped his temple—"so you can let me know what's happening immediately. I'll be in close range, so it shouldn't be a problem. Whatever you do, Jess, don't leave the bar with him. Understand? He's dangerous as hell, and completely unpredictable."

"Got it." I slid the panic button into my suit jacket pocket. "I'm not interested in finding any more trouble, Tyler. No need to worry about me, I'm all over the plan. Have you decided to stake the inside?" It'd been discussed but not determined.

"Nope, I decided it was too risky. If Rourke gets one whiff of wolf on the inside he may decide to cut and run," Tyler said. "The plan is to track him when he leaves. But he's a quick bastard, so I'm only giving us one-in-three odds of keeping a tail on him at all. You have to pump as much information as you can while you're with him."

I nodded. "My sole purpose is to gain information. I want to know where this threat is coming from. I'm not expecting him to divulge much, but anything we can get will be more than we have right now."

"It's not his style to snatch you here anyway, but keep your head up. You have to stay alert at all times." Tyler ran a hand along the back of his neck. He was agitated. "Man, I don't like it. I want to know what this guy is up to."

"I don't like it either." Danny frowned. "This man is a known killer."

"I know we can handle it," I said. "And remember, if I don't meet him, he comes to me. I don't want a highly trained killer sneaking through my broken sliding glass door. My quota this month for nasty break-ins is passed its full mark."

"I still don't like it," Tyler grumbled. "Something feels off."

"Have either of you ever seen Rourke in person?" I asked curiously.

"Nope, he was around before my time," Tyler said.

"No," Danny added. "But I've heard my fill about the wanker."

"Do you actually believe all the rumors?" I asked. "Some of the stories about Connor Dade are so outlandish. Tying people up by their entrails? Severed body parts spelling out words? Some of that has to be fiction. It's just too creepy to be true." It was common for mercs to inflate their profiles—plant stories to make them seem worse than they were. Fear went a long way in keeping yourself on top, and it sounded like Rourke had plenty of years behind him to do just that. If nobody ever saw him, it would be easy to fabricate stories of grandeur.

Tyler grunted. "I don't need to believe any of the stories. I've seen pictures."

"What pictures?" I asked.

"Of some of his kills."

"Where did you get a hold of pictures?" I made a face. "How do you know they were his?"

"Doesn't matter. The man's a brutal-ass bastard." Tyler folded his arms.

"Hmm," I said. "Sounds a little unsubstantiated to me. I could hand you any photo I wanted and give you a good story. Doesn't mean it's true."

"I've seen glimpses of the pictures too," Danny said, ignoring me. "In one, the dead bloke was missing all his fingers. Every one of them had been cut down to the nubbin, each to a different knuckle. And on the middle stump he left a finger puppet behind."

"What kind of finger puppet?" I asked out of grotesque curiosity.

"The bloke's own nose with a smiley face drawn on it."

Jesus.

The restaurant was covered in sleek, hard lines, and the walls were coated with dark paint. The lighting was minimal, giving it a calming ambiance, and it was packed to the brim.

I pushed my way through people waiting for tables and veered left toward the bar. We hadn't specified dining options, but I figured the bar would be the best place to check first.

Is he there? Tyler asked in my mind. He was on edge. None

of the wolves had scented a fresh supe trail anywhere around the building. If he was here, the cat had snuck in without the wolves knowing. And no one was happy about it.

Gimme a minute. I just got in here. My wolf was on high alert. As I worked my way through the crowd, I scanned the room for possibilities.

Then I spotted a lone shape at the end of the bar. He was huge, so it was a likely pick. He was clad in a black leather jacket, his forearms splayed casually on the bar, a tall draft beer sitting between them. The well-worn leather he wore was in stark contrast to the yuppie dress clothes around us.

I wove my way toward him slowly. *I think I have him.*

Be careful. If it's him, ask him how the fuck he got there without us knowing, Tyler griped.

First things first, little brother.

His guy's head was angled down, but as I eased closer, it swiveled without hesitation in my direction.

His eyes lit on me.

Then he smiled.

My stride hitched momentarily. *Holy Christ. That can't be Rourke.* I recovered myself by the next step, thankfully.

What? What do you mean? Tyler asked.

Um. *Nothing, it's just...he's not what I was expecting a killer to look like.* This man oozed power, it was true, but he was beautiful. Honey-colored hair brushed his collar in the back, and he had a set of the clearest eyes I'd ever seen. Even from a distance, I could see they were ringed in a sliver of deep green. They were completely breathtaking, and most definitely not on any normal color chart.

Snort. *Who cares if he doesn't look like a killer, just be sure—*

Tyler, I have to go. I'll get back to you. I cut him off with a single thought.

Rourke's gaze intensified as I came closer. I blinked a few times, but refused to look away. I slid onto the empty barstool next to him and sat down without being asked.

He appraised me with open curiosity. More than a hint of humor flashed behind those ridiculously gorgeous eyes. Up close his skin was flawless, tanned deeply from the sun. He had a short blanket of blond stubble running over a defined chin.

So *not* what I was expecting.

His power vibrated around me, sending little pinpricks of energy into my skin. It came from somewhere deep inside him, I could sense that much. He was old, there was no question. Power like that took a long time to accumulate.

"Hello, Rourke," I said, taking in my first full breath of him. I almost choked as my nails shot into the underside of the bar to steady myself. *Hooooooly shit.* My wolf started barking incessantly. *Quiet, I can't think. Be quiet!*

He smelled like the woods, like I'd originally guessed, but there was no fresh-cut grass about him. What emanated from him was thick, dark, and rich, like some kind of molasses mixed with cloves. Its deliciousness made it hard for me to concentrate. My wolf was still yipping excitedly. *You have to calm down. We look completely unprofessional and he's not going to take me seriously if we keep this up. Get a grip.* She quieted begrudgingly so I could get down to business.

Rourke shifted in his seat slightly, turning his body to face mine. He gave me an unabashed once-over without uttering a word. By the amused expression on his face—a lazy grin highlighting two faint dimples—he recognized my distress, indicating that this kind of reaction to him was par for the course.

"Pompous ass" came to mind.

He caught me off guard by extending his hand. "It's a pleasure to finally meet you, Ms. Hannon. Your reputation for

being the *best* in the business precedes you." His voice held the
same deep bravado I remembered and a tingle wound its way
up my spine. The accent was more discernible in person, but I
still couldn't place it. Possibly South African?

I contemplated shaking his outstretched hand. Or not shaking it. I'd already lost valuable street cred by acting like a bab-
bling teenager, so I grabbed on to his hand and was rewarded
with a jolt of power up my arm. *Dammit.* I clenched my teeth
and tried to ignore it. I couldn't risk any more foolishness. "If
my reputation precedes me, then let's cut the shit, Rourke.
There's no need to keep the act going. I know you know who I
am." I was going with bad cop. It usually worked in my favor.
Nick was good cop. "I'm just not exactly sure why you're here
and what you're looking for, which is why I decided to keep our
meeting tonight." I lowered my voice. "Why exactly are you
here, Rourke?"

Mild surprise shot through his expression. "No beating
around the bush for you, huh, sweetheart?" He took a swig of
his drink and placed it in front of him. Then he settled his full,
clear gaze on me again.

Holy balls.

He had to quit doing that. All the hairs on my arms rose to
attention and my wolf had taken to constant whining. Before
he looked away, I saw an almost imperceptible tiny green spark
in the depth of one of his irises. *Interesting.* I cleared my throat.
"Why would I want to beat around the bush? It's a waste of
time. And you haven't answered my question yet, so I'll ask it
again. Why are you here?"

"You already know why I'm here."

"Do you honestly think I'd be sitting here if I knew?" I
cocked my head, making my own show of giving him a once-
over. "I'm assuming you're not going to break my neck in front

of the after-work crowd at dinnertime, but other than that, your sudden appearance in this city is unclear. No more circles, Rourke. I want to know *exactly* why you're here." I tapped my index finger on top of the bar to emphasize my point. "Right here, right now. With me."

He waited before answering. Then he leaned forward, his huge leather-clad arms brushing my fingertips. "I'm here, beautiful, because I was hired by an extremely interested party to retrieve all the information possible, and by whatever means necessary"—his voice lowered to a soft, gravelly purr—"about the *only* female werewolf in town."

I sucked in a breath.

Motherfucker. "Are you implying *I'm* a werewolf?" I gave a caustic laugh. "I have no idea what you're talking about. You may have me a bit confused with being the *daughter* of a werewolf, which I am, as you well know." I wasn't worried about being overheard. The noise level in the bar was enough to cover the conversation. The fact that Rourke knew I was a wolf was more than a bit staggering. "Your employer must have their facts wrong."

He threw his head back and laughed.

I folded my arms across my chest and slapped on a pissy expression.

When he was done with his fit of mirth, he motioned for the bartender. "Bring us a round." He held up two fingers. He turned back to me, his eyes still crinkled at the corners. "Listen, even if I hadn't heard it with my own two ears, on good authority, I'd still have known you were a wolf from the moment you walked through those doors. Your power climbed up my skin like a bad rash, and your scent is so powerful, I'm surprised these humans around us"—he jerked his thumb absentmindedly—"aren't coming up to congratulate you on your recent change."

Harrumph. "Very funny." I narrowed my eyes. "Now you get to tell me how you got your hands on this very secret and *extremely* unsubstantiated information in such a short amount of time."

"A pro never divulges his sources." He winked. "But you already knew that, didn't you?"

I leaned forward in my seat. "You're kidding me, right? Then why meet me here at all? Why tell me your real name? If you're so notorious, why didn't you just take what you wanted by force? Isn't that your usual mode of operation: snatch and grab and ask questions later? Instead, we're sitting here—at your request—so we can…*what?* Chat about the fucking score of a ball game? You came to me, remember?"

I might have glimpsed some grudging respect, but it could've just as easily been annoyance. A low growl issued from his chest as his features dropped their playfulness. The predator was lurking just below the surface. I would do well to remember it. "I knew your father long ago."

I waited for more, but nothing came.

"So I heard. So what? You're supposed to be a ruthless badass, why would you respect an ancient connection to my father now?"

"Because your father is deserving of great respect."

"Respect enough to kidnap his daughter?"

"My job is not to kidnap you."

"Then why the *hell*—"

Two things happened very quickly.

One, Rourke pushed back his barstool and jumped to his feet. Two, Tyler came screaming into my brain. *Jess, you have to get out!* Now! *This is a setup of some kind. Goddamn*—he was breaking up—*Southern... all fighting... get the* fuck... *out...*

Tyler! What's going on? I don't understand? Answer me! I sprang from my seat, but I had no room to move. I was stuck in the small space between my stool and Rourke, who was now emitting a very lethal snarl over the top of my head.

No answer from Tyler. *Goddammit, answer me!*

I twisted by body around to see what Rourke focused on.

Five werewolves I'd never seen before were weaving menacingly through the crowded bar. Their combined scent of aggression hit me as my wolf howled in rage. Adrenaline shot through me lickety-split. I knew what was coming next. *Wait, wait!* I told her. *We can't change in here, and we can't take all those wolves alone!* I had no time to reason with her. My fingertips pulsed close to the tip, my muscles starting their telltale dance under my skin. *Just wait a min—*

Something grabbed me from behind and I landed hard.

I glanced up and found Rourke glaring down at me, his features twisted furiously, his hands gripping my wrists like steel cuffs. His eyes shone like two diamonds, veins of green blazing across his irises like an electric storm. "I gave you that one"— he jerked his head behind him, snarling savagely—"but trying to get a jump on me was the wrong choice, sweetheart. It seems you haven't done your homework on me after all. I *don't* play nice. Now you're going to have to say goodbye to all your buddies."

"What are you talking about? What *one*?" I stood on my tiptoes and peered around his massive shoulder to see what he was talking about, and surprisingly saw James closing the gap behind us quickly. I hadn't even known he was here. "Rourke, we're *not* jumping you. I've—"

Rourke's hot breath cut me off as it landed firmly in my ear.

It wasn't above a whisper, but I could hear it perfectly. "This deal is changing. I tried to play fair with you, but now your options are officially up. I don't give out second chances."

My anger, fueled by a hardy dose of my wolf, surged inside me. "Get your hands *off* me," I spat. "Deal with this, *asshole*. I have *no* idea who those wolves are coming at us. And if you knew *anything* about my father and the way he operates, then you already know putting a jump on you isn't his style. Now, if you're interested in continuing our little chat where we left off, as *planned*, then stop this posturing bullshit and help me take out this threat." Before he could respond, I finished bitterly, "And if that's not enough of an incentive"—I pressed my finger-nail into his chest—"I'm certain your employer would like it if I remained *alive* so you can continue to extract your much-needed information."

Rourke's eyes widened. Not from my harsh words but most likely from my eyes, which I could feel were sparking violet. It didn't matter. Aligning myself so quickly with Rourke might be a mistake, but my gut, which was almost entirely made up of a grouchy she-wolf, was telling me the greater threat to us was the wolves who were almost on us.

I'd made my choice, now I had to live with it.

Instead of responding, Rourke whipped his torso around and took James by the throat in the time it took me to blink. "What the hell is going on, Irish?" Rourke growled. "Trying to take me here was the wrong choice, and you know it. I let you in here out of respect for Callum, but it ends right here, right now."

James knocked Rourke's fist away from his neck like it was nothing more than a mild irritant. "Wrong answer, cat," James snarled. "There's no jump. Jessica's in danger, but you bloody well knew that already, didn't you? Coming here and announc-ing yourself was well noted, but now we'll see if you can be as trusted as you once were all those years ago. I have no other choice left." His face held a hint of a grimace. "I need you to get her the hell out of here," he said, his amber eyes blazing, "and I'll take care of this lot." He gestured at the approaching five wolves. "As of four minutes ago our Pack went to war. We need every wolf to fight, there are none left to protect Jessica. Whoever sent you here used you to get to us, and they used you well. They knew right where to find us. Now get her out of here, and if you harm her in any way I swear I will kill you myself. Slowly."

James didn't wait for an answer. He shot around us, lunging into the five, scattering them like bowling pins. At that, the bar erupted into chaos. The humans hadn't noticed the threat before, but they did now. They would all assume it was a bar fight, not a supernatural showdown.

I turned and took a step after James, eager to join the battle. I didn't care what he'd just said, there was no way I was leaving with Rourke. This was my fight and I was staying. Before I could go more than a foot, my wrist snapped backward and once again I was pressed against Rourke's jacket. The leather was tinged with the scent of oil, along with sweat and delicious cloves. And it pissed me *off*.

I jerked my hands up, breaking his hold on me. With everything I had, I shoved him back. He moved less than two inches, but it was enough. "I'm not going anywhere with you. This is my fight, dammit! I caused this, and I will not abandon my Pack to wage a war without me. Got it? So don't even think about getting in my way."

I dismissed him completely, wrenching myself from his grasp entirely, turning back to the fight.

He let me go.

As I spun around, I met a powerful, piercingly blue stare.

It stopped me in my tracks.

The gaze held me across the sea of pandemonium. My father strode through the bar like he was strolling through the woods, like nothing was amiss and a war hadn't broken out all around him, humans shrieking and things breaking.

His eyes held one word.

Go.

Rourke stilled behind me, reading the message clearly too.

I opened my mouth to protest, but nothing came out. This order wasn't from my Alpha. It was from my *father*.

Go.

His command swirled through me, pushing me, urging me. I realized with a start that sharing my father's blood during the oath had somehow connected us, bonded us in a new way. His emotions raced through me, and I felt compelled to follow his directives. My wolf cried in my mind. She felt it too. I tried to resist, but I was frozen in place.

Go.

"Sorry, sweetheart, what you want doesn't look like it's in the cards tonight," Rourke muttered from behind me.

I took a step forward, trying my hardest to break the command, pushing as much power into it as I could. I didn't want to leave, *dammit*, I wanted to fight.

Before I could get away, Rourke lunged, bending and twisting, snatching me up by my waist and tossing me effortlessly over his shoulder. His arm clamped around my middle like a vise.

Then he turned, ignoring my howls of rage, and raced out of the bar.

17

In the back alley behind the bar, Rourke set me down roughly but kept a tight grip on my forearm. Then he started ushering us forward at a quick clip, his nose scenting the air as we moved, his posture guarded.

"You've got to be kidding me!" I tried to wrench my arm from his grasp, with no luck. His hands were like stone. "You can't just pick me up like a fucking caveman and make my choices for me. How dare you!"

Rourke stopped, spinning around. "Keep your voice down," he snarled, "and listen up." His irises blazed an ethereal green. "In case you haven't noticed, none of this was my idea. But here are the facts. You're a one-of-a-kind werewolf. The *only* one of its kind. That means you're now in a position of extreme interest to all parties involved. And I mean *all* parties. There's not one Sect on this planet who won't be interested in getting a piece of you now. Do you hear me? All of them—wolves, shifters, vamps, witches, everyone. If you die now, whatever you are dies with you. Understood?" He shook me a little to emphasize his point. "Now stop whining like a pansy-assed little girl, because we need to get clear of this area right now."

My anger bubbled over and I had to tamp the rage back in order to speak. I had no intention of backing down. My Pack was fighting. I wasn't going to leave them behind just because this guy told me to. "What do you mean, *what* I am? Just because I have breasts doesn't mean that's not my Pack in there. Those wolves happen to be in the middle of fighting a war because of me. Now let go of me! I'm going back to join them." My words sunk in. I was the catalyst for this war.

"Wrong answer." Rourke started down the alley, yanking me behind him.

It was full dark. I tried to anchor my feet into the ground as he toted me down the alleyway like a three-year-old. I couldn't get away unless I shifted, and even a partial shift now would be extremely risky out in the open. Not to mention I had no real idea how I'd done it before. *I could use a little outrage here*, I told my wolf. Rourke continued to haul us along, and I could feel her on the edge of anger, but not nearly as pissed off as I was. *I thought we weren't supposed to leave the bar with the scary predator. He's a no-no. And he's tugging us along like a petulant toddler. He's kidnapping us! Get mad.* Her ears perked and my muscles tensed for a quick second. I got excited.

But she wasn't focused on me at all, her eyes were directed ahead of us, scanning for the next threat.

Some help you are.

As Rourke continued to drag me farther down the alley, I tried to reason with him. "Let's start this again, Rourke. I think we've made a mistake here. I need to get back to my Pack—"

He turned on me in a flash, snarling, his face inches from mine. I flinched, my back pressed against the brick wall of a building. "I already told you I'm not playing around here. If your Pack is at war, who do you think they're fighting against right now?"

I hadn't been expecting a question.

"Um... I'm not exactly sure, but most likely the Southern Territories..." I finished lamely.

"Right on the nose, sweetheart. So at this very moment your city is flooded with more werewolves than you can fight on your own, and more than I can fight while I babysit you. So our only real option is to get the hell out of here, and we're wasting precious time *talking* about it." His breath was laced with cinnamon.

I bristled. "*Babysitting* me was your choice, not mine, and it's not a *mandatory* position, by any means. You can let me go anytime you'd like. Then you'd be free to go back to whatever place it is you came from and we can forget this whole thing ever happened."

His eyes glittered with emotion. "No."

"Rourke," I breathed. "Just let me go."

He studied me for a long moment, his face so close to mine I started to squirm. He opened his mouth to say something, and then, just like that, we were back down the alley again, him pulling me along like a child.

He led us across a few streets, ducking and dodging through parked cars as we went, finally slipping between another pair of buildings. There were no streetlights here. It appeared to be a delivery space with a narrow path leading out to the other side. There wasn't more than a sidewalk space between the two structures. Rourke was too big for us to walk side by side, but he had no problem tugging me behind him.

"Rourke, where are we going?" I whispered.

"To my bike."

I knew he wasn't talking about his bicycle.

He meticulously scanned every building around us as we went, scenting the air continually. I was scenting too. Every once in a while I caught a whiff of werewolf in the air, but it was never too close. They should be swarming us. "Rourke, why aren't they out here?" I asked. "We should be covered in angry Southern wolves. They should've been all over the building when we came out."

Rourke glanced over his shoulder at me, his eyes completely green. They glowed like two emerald pools in the dark. "Either your wolves were keeping them occupied, or something else is going on here." He sniffed the air and his brows creased. "I don't like it either. It's too easy. Something is off. It doesn't feel like a full war, they're looking for something."

I tested his grip on my arm again, and earned a low growl in response. "Keep it up and I'll put you back over my shoulder."

We emerged from between the last two buildings onto a frontage road and slid quietly along the deserted storefronts, making our way down the street. This place was familiar. It was the last block before the neighborhood dead-ended into the train tracks across the street, which were down in the culvert, and it was exactly how you'd expect it to look. A long line of old, run-down buildings, most of them vacant, and had been for years. On the other side of the tracks the highway overpasses looped off into the distance. No more neighborhood.

Down the street in front of us, I spotted a lone motorcycle parked on the sidewalk pushed tightly into an alcove against a shuttered storefront.

"How'd you get from here to the bar without being seen tonight?" I asked curiously.

"I've been here since yesterday. Slept on the roof of the bar and came down through the fire escape."

"That's one way to do it." Tricky cat.

He shrugged. "It wasn't hard. Once I gave you my name, I knew your Pack would stake out all the strategic locations, but this isn't one of them." He pointed. "Up ahead is a dead end, nowhere to go but back the way we came."

"If we're trapped, how are we getting out?"

He nodded toward the giant culvert. A rusty chain-link fence separated the tracks from the neighborhood, not doing much to keep people out. Grass and dirt ran until about halfway down and then the ground changed to old, broken concrete.

"The old tracks? And how exactly are we getting down there?" There weren't any real crossing points for about a mile and a half in either direction.

"We drive, sweetheart."

"Huh?"

Shouts broke out behind us. Rourke tightened his grip on my arm and started jogging us forward faster. We were almost to a vintage Harley-Davidson when I wrenched my head behind me right as a runner flew around the corner, shouting a curse over his shoulder.

Ohmygod. "*Tyler!*" I screamed.

He slid to a stop, his eyes blazing full gold. His shirt was ripped and stained dark.

"Is that blood all over you? Are you hurt?" I yelled, struggling to get loose, but Rourke held me fast. "Tyler, answer me!" Then I turned back. "Rourke, let me go!"

Tyler started racing toward us. "Let her the fuck go, cat!"

Rourke tensed for a fight, his muscles tightening under his jacket, but he didn't yield his grip on me.

Before Tyler could get to us, a U-Haul truck swerved around the corner behind him. His attackers, it seemed, had hitched a ride. The truck slammed on its brakes with a tire-squealing screech, sliding the whole van sideways, cutting off the road completely.

Dead end in front of us, U-Haul full of Southern wolves in back.

"It's a goddamn trap!" Rourke roared. "Get on the back of the bike." He yanked me against my will the last few paces to his bike and tossed me at it while he jumped on from the other side, flipping the kickstand up and starting it with a roar. "Get on the bike. *Now!*" he yelled over the noise of the engine.

I didn't move and Tyler closed the gap between us in two strides, grabbing on to my arms. "What the hell's going on? Why did you leave with him?" I could see him processing what Rourke had just said.

"James decided to trust him," I told him quickly. "And Dad backed him up. Rourke took me out of the bar fight and brought me here." I left out *against my will*, because Tyler could see the scenario as it stood. My father was likely still occupied with his own battle or the wolves would be updated on my whereabouts, or at least who I was with, by now.

"Jess, you have to get out of here," Tyler pleaded. "We're in the middle of a war—and you're their prize. You have to go right now, even if your only option is to go with the...goddamn cat." His face held revulsion, but I knew if his Alpha had already sanctioned it, he would go along with the program.

Dammit. "Tyler, I don't want to go, I want to stay and fight. My place is here fighting alongside my Pack, not being protected like some breakable object."

The U-Haul doors sprang open and a half dozen unfamiliar wolves in human form touched the ground running. No time to think about formulating a plan, they would be on us in two seconds.

Tyler whipped me behind him, pushing me inadvertently

toward Rourke as he went, yelling, "Go! Just get out of here while you still can."

"No, I want to fight. Let me help you," I cried. "I can fight!"

"No!" *No.* He flipped to my mind. *Jessica, please, you can't do this. I can't protect you and fight at the same time. You're not trained for combat yet. You're putting us both in danger by staying here.*

"I can't leave you. I'm not going to leave you here alone." *I'm not going to fucking leave, do you hear me?*

Tyler ignored me as his gaze shot to Rourke. "Get her out of here, cat. There's no one left but you. But if you lay one hand on her, I swear I will rip you apart with my bare hands. Do you hear me? I vow it on my life." Tyler looked back at me. "That's an order, Jess. Now go!"

The motorcycle revved in response, tires screeching behind me. But before Rourke could make a move, I tore out of Tyler's grasp, pulling both throwing knives from my sleeves at the same moment.

My body bent forward, and without any hesitation I launched them straight into the two wolves in the lead barreling down on us. One landed with a *thunk* in the fleshy part of the trachea, hitting home, and the wolf went down with satisfaction. The other missed its mark entirely, embedding itself without harm in his shoulder. It didn't do anything close to dropping him; it only pissed him off more. He stopped and yanked it out, snarling at me as he did it.

It's on now. My wolf howled.

Tyler sprang forward with no other choice to tackle the next two. I crouched in a fighting stance, muscles rippling under my skin—*finally*—pulling, shifting, readying me for the fight. The angry wolf I'd hit in the shoulder was almost to me, and when his filthy hands reached for my throat, he was going down. My eyes were trained on him like lasers. He thought I was weak.

He thought wrong.

But before he could reach me my body flew backward.

My attacker bellowed his rage.

What the hell? The road was moving beneath me, Rourke's arm locked firmly around my middle, my ass barely on the edge of the seat.

"Get on the goddamn bike!" Rourke yelled.

I didn't have time to protest. In the next moment we hit the curb, the bike flying upward toward the sky. On the way down, I shot my leg over the seat and grabbed on to Rourke's jacket with everything I had. We cleared the embankment at the top, crashing through the rusty fence like it wasn't even there. The bike plunged nose first down the grassy slope leading to the tracks at top speed, each bump on the ground like a giant mountain crashing up to greet us.

Rourke maneuvered the bike from side to side like a slalom course, pulling us parallel at the last minute before we hit the concrete at the bottom. Coming onto the ground at the right angle lessened the blow, but it left us reeling nonetheless. The shocks groaned and crunched, but they held, keeping us upright for the most part.

As we bounded onto the concrete of the culvert floor, I pried my eyes open and screamed, "*Sonofabitch*, Rourke. If I wanted to die, I could've just stayed and fought!"

He wrenched the bike hard to the right, all his muscles contracting at once underneath his jacket. Power emanated from him as his boot came off the pedal, stabilizing us, sending sparks up from his skid pads. When we were finally fully upright he called over his shoulder, "We're not dead yet, sweetheart."

"Smartass," I yelled back. Over my shoulder, two wolves, still in human form, were scrambling onto the tracks. A third made his way down the embankment behind them. Relief flooded through me, because if they were after me, that meant they'd abandoned Tyler. "Rourke, they're coming after us. I hope you have a plan."

I reached out to my brother. *Ty, are you okay? Can you hear me?*

There was a familiar brush. *Jess…fighting…can't hear you. Be safe…* The connection died.

We must not be able to hold a conversation and fight at the same time. It made sense, because fighting used a lot of brainpower. My father hadn't reached out to me either, which meant he must be equally engaged. Maybe that was the reason I'd been able to cut them off when I was fighting. I couldn't manage both at the same time.

The wolves behind us dropped to the ground to shift. Once they were finished they'd be crazy fast. And they'd have our fresh scent.

"They're changing on the tracks," I yelled to Rourke. "This place is going to be full of wolves in about three minutes."

"Then it's a good thing we're getting off here," Rourke shouted back as he turned the handlebars hard, tearing up a small grassy hill. The sides of the culvert had tapered off along the way, making it possible to escape. The bike bounded over the top, crashing through another fence, and then we were back on the road, the tires squealing as Rourke twisted us in front of a highway underpass. One more quick turn and we were wheeling up a ramp.

Three wolves in their true form, two in the front and one trailing, ran behind us full tilt, but they'd have to abandon the chase at the highway. Wolves on the road wouldn't work. But it didn't matter. They had our scents. Their buddies in the U-Haul would pick them up in a few minutes.

Unless Rourke had an unbelievable plan, we would be running from them indefinitely. A weirdly pungent female and a one-of-a-kind cat on the back of an open motorcycle meant we were going to be easy to track.

I relaxed my death grip on Rourke as we flattened out on the freeway. I likely wouldn't die if I was tossed from the bike. I was used to being human and it was going to take me some time to stop reacting like one.

Rourke had no such issues, clearly.

My hand dipped into my suit jacket pocket as Rourke weaved expertly in and out of traffic. The smooth panic button brushed against my fingertips. I rubbed it a few times for luck. Then I depressed it. It wasn't going to help me now, but it felt good to hold it in my hand. "Nick, I'm going to need a pickup soon," I said into the open air as it blasted by my helmetless face.

"What?" Rourke called over his shoulder.

"Nothing," I muttered. "Just praying you have a decent plan."

18

"This is your brilliant plan?" I stood knee-high in the middle of a swift current, my lovely pantsuit swirling around my legs. "You know, man-eating werewolves aren't afraid to go swimming. If our trail leads to a river, they won't hesitate to get in."

"Don't worry, they aren't following where we're going," Rourke said from behind me. "At least for right now."

"How can you be so sure?" I glanced over my shoulder in time to see him step into the stream. I forgot my question for a second because he was bare-chested, his shirt and boots wrapped in his leather jacket, which was tucked safely under his bulging and ridiculously muscular arm. He had to be bigger than any wolf by a few good inches and a lot of mass. The man was a beast.

All my things were wrapped in my blazer jacket too, only I wasn't naked from the waist up.

Thank the good heavens above I'd worn the damn camisole. The fact that it was white hadn't escaped me, and if Danny could see me now he'd be laughing his ass off. I'd drawn the line at dropping my pants, and Rourke had kept his on without question. It would've been a lie to say I hadn't been a tiny bit interested in seeing what he had underneath his jeans—or more accurately, my wolf had been *extremely* interested in what was there, but I was ignoring her.

We had far more important things to worry about.

Somewhere along the line, after trying to fight it repeatedly, I'd realized my father's command for me to *Go* had been a strong one—*too strong*. I wasn't going to shed it easily. It wrapped around me even now, compelling me to stay with protection and not turn back. The blood I'd taken from him during the oath had bonded us in a strange way. I had no idea if it had done the same for him—if he could feel my emotions or not. I couldn't read all the notes and emotions clearly just yet, but I knew without a doubt that if he had died, the new things I felt inside me would stop. I prayed everyone was okay and safe. I hated not being there.

My wolf gave me an irritated snap, directing me back to her thoughts.

I'm sorry, but you're not getting your way. We're not lifting tail for every good-looking guy we come across. Plus, this one happens to be a highly trained mercenary. Remember? We are here against our will. Don't forget it.

It was safe to say my wolf and I were still coming down from a major adrenaline rush, and knowing how the last one had ended, I was being extremely careful to keep my lusty thoughts in check.

Instead I'd plied myself with a bucket of beef jerky I'd bought at our last stop. Too bad I didn't have any left. It wasn't a comparable substitute for sex, but I'd had to work with what was available.

I watched the water tease the legs of Rourke's well-worn jeans as he waded deeper into the stream. I tore my gaze from his completely defined stomach as he hoisted his clothes higher in the air. As his arms went above his head, I noticed two tattoos flowing along the inside of each forearm. They were geometric, and beautifully drawn in a deep black ink. My wolf licked her lips. I did love tattoos. *Damn*.

He stalked, he didn't walk. And honestly, if I hadn't been raised around supernaturals, and hadn't just become one myself, his presence would've been almost too intense.

"Up ahead about ten miles"—Rourke gestured—"is a sulfur stream, and about a mile beyond is a small cabin. The only way to get there is to climb straight up. It'll take the wolves some time to pick up our scent again after the stream, but by the time they arrive, we'll be long gone."

We were currently somewhere in the foothills of the Ozarks, according to Rourke. Nothing looked familiar. Day had broken around us and the morning light seeped between the trees. My guess was it was around seven-thirty or eight in the morning. Rourke had taken a series of back roads, trying to throw any pursuers off our scent, but we both knew it was only a matter of time before the big bad wolves caught up to us.

"Did you just say ten *actual* miles?"

Rourke chuckled. "Yes, and the last one is straight uphill." He sloshed over to me. "Here, hand me your jacket."

I unrolled my shoes, gun, and dirk, and handed the jacket to him without question. He took it and passed me, continuing up the bank on the other side. "And don't worry, I have a feeling you can handle the climb just fine. I'll be right back. I'm going to lay a scent trail on the other side to buy us more time."

I watched his powerful body run up the short grassy hill, my jacket dangling from his right hand as he disappeared into the dense forest along the edge of the embankment.

The cold water lapped at my ruined clothing as I stood in the stream for another few minutes waiting for him to return. At this point, what else was I going to do? His bike was stashed a few miles behind us in a shallow cave, and for the last half hour we'd trudged through thick forest to this riverbank. There was no going back now.

It was way too late for that.

I shifted in the water, wading a little closer to the shoreline. I glanced up and down the river. There was dense tree growth running along both sides as far as I could see. Some large rocks dotted the creek bed, but otherwise the river looked fairly tranquil, running no more than a few feet deep.

"Miss me?" Rourke rejoined me by leaping from the embankment to the edge of the stream. He strode forward, splashing though the water with little care, extending my jacket out to me. I took it from him and rewrapped my things.

"In your dreams," I said. "Where to now?"

"We head upstream until we hit sulfur, and then take a hard right straight up into those mountains." He pointed over the tops of some of the trees. The peaks were barely visible.

He dropped his arm and took off.

I sloshed after him. "You couldn't have picked an easier hidey-hole to get to?"

"Easier means company."

"The wolves will catch up to us eventually," I grumbled right as I slipped on a medium-sized rock, catching myself before I tumbled all the way in. My reflexes were much better now as a wolf. Thank goodness, or my ass would've been soaked. "Wolves are tenacious, you know."

"By the time they find us, we'll have come and gone."

"Rourke," I called to his quickly retreating back. "You know I'm not staying with you for more than a day, right? Once I get confirmation from my Pack, I'm heading back the way I came. I'm not jumping from hidey-hole to hidey-hole with you."

He grunted a response.

After long miles with not a lot of rest, we came to a natural pool framed by a number of large boulders, a strong eddy swirling at its center. It was fed by a steady trickle of extremely stinky water erupting out of a crack in a giant rock. The smell of rotten eggs permeated the air. I took another whiff. "Wow, that's awful," I said. "Does it smell this bad to humans?"

Rourke climbed onto one of the rocks bordering the pool. A lock of his sand-colored hair fell over his forehead as the sun reflected on his still bare chest, illuminating the tiny droplets of water stuck to him from walking in the stream.

That man should be arrested, I grumbled at my wolf. It was a grumble kind of day.

My wolf let off a low growl, her eyes tracking Rourke's every move, but they were sounding less like growls and more like purrs. The hair on my arms began to stand on end without my permission. I hugged my jacket-wrapped weapons tighter to my chest. I hoped like hell he didn't notice the effect he was having on me. It was embarrassing.

When he didn't answer my question about the sulfur, I asked, "What?" a little defensively. "It's a legitimate question. It's getting harder for me to remember how I smelled things before as a human. Things are muddled."

His eyes danced for a moment and I caught a quick flash of green, like a lighter sparking right before it jumps to full flame. "It smells more mild to humans, not like it does to us. Sulfur is a powerful natural element. It does a good job of masking our scent naturally. When the wolves arrive here, they'll have a hard time picking up our trail with a nose full of sulfur." He grinned mischievously. "Now I'm going to need you to submerse yourself in the pool." He gestured out to the middle. "Completely."

"Is that really necessary?" I eyed the pool. "Can't we just splash ourselves with that?" I pointed to the stream trickling out of the rocks. "It smells much worse."

"We will need to do both." He set his jacket and boots down on an exposed rock. "The water in the pool will strip us of our sweat, the sulfur stream will mask us on the way out."

He didn't wait for a reply, instead he dove straight into the deepest part of the pool, surfacing a good distance away. It appeared to be quite deep. The sunlight glinted off his wet hair, making him look like some kind of water deity when he surfaced.

It so figured.

"I thought cats hated to get wet."

He gave me a cagey grin. "There's nothing I like better than being wet." He dove under, his broad, powerful back skimming just under the surface.

"Fine," I muttered, resigning myself to my fate. "Whatever you say." I set down my jacket wrapped with goodies and picked my way to the edge of the pool.

My white camisole had stayed dry for the most part, but my black pants were completely soaked from splashing my way through the river. I bit my lip. On second thought, I went back and plucked up my jacket, untangling it from the pile, leaving my weapons and shoes sitting exposed on the rock.

I picked my way over to another area, the one closest to the sulfur stream, and hung it carefully on a dead tree branch jutting over the pool so I could grab it when I emerged soaking wet.

I turned back to the pool. Rourke was grinning at me again. "No need to be smug about it, cat," I growled. "I'm getting in the damn water."

Rourke's laughter bounced off the boulders and echoed back into my ears. "Nothing smug about me, sweetheart." He turned onto his back to float. "Just taking some time out of my busy day to enjoy the beauty around me."

"You're lucky I grew up around a bunch of wolves. I learned early on to check my modesty at the door." Well, mostly anyway. I glanced at my dangling jacket.

It was nice to have a backup plan.

I turned back to the pool, contemplated my fate for a second, and dove off the rocks.

Right into a pool with a predator who looked like he wanted to eat me for breakfast.

19

"Rourke?" I asked as we swam. "With what you know about the supernatural world, do you think my Pack is winning this battle? I absolutely hate that I'm not there. I know very little about the Southern wolves, but from what I do know, it seems surprising that they're this efficiently organized. Redman Martin is an arrogant asshole from the stories I've heard over the years, so it's understandable, but it seems strange that he would wage a war so soon, after what happened with the division of Pack lines all those years ago." Red Martin was the Alpha of the U.S. Southern Territories and he and my father were enemies. It was because of Redman that there were two U.S. Packs instead of one.

"I have a hard time believing any other wolves can best your father and his Pack," he answered. "He's a powerful leader and his wolves are fierce fighters. I don't think you have anything to worry about. I've only ever had a few run-ins with Red, but as much as he is arrogant, he's equal parts lazy. He likely wants to ransom you to the highest bidder or has some other slimy, easy-to-profit-from plan in place. It may even be as simple as he wants to pay back your father for any perceived wrongdoings. My guess is the fighting won't last long once they find out you're gone. You're their prize. No prize, no fight. He knows he won't win a combat battle, which is why no wolves were fighting on the streets. They were looking for you. You did your Pack a favor by leaving."

I hoped what he said was true. We didn't swim for very long, time being of the essence. Rourke emerged first, and I watched him from my spot on the other side of the pool. He picked his way over the rocks with ease, his jeans conveniently sticking to all the important parts. Water sluiced off his shoulders, running down his back in cascading rivers. His hair looked much darker wet than it had dry.

He tilted his head at me, like he was enjoying the weight of my stare. Cocky bastard. At that precise moment, the sun glinted perfectly on his irises and they flashed the palest green, almost white.

"Rourke, your eyes are completely insane." I swam over to the edge closest to where he was standing and stared, shielding my eyes to the sun as I glanced up. "Humans must comment on them all the time. How do you explain them away?"

He shrugged like having diamonds for eyes was a normal everyday occurrence. "If I think they deserve an answer, I usually tell them I have my mother's eyes," he said. "And if I don't, I tell them it's none of their goddamn business."

"And they actually believe you?"

"Humans already know they're going to have to accept whatever excuse I give them, before they even ask. Thinking I'm 'Other' is not an option. So they ask with the idea that they'll get a logical explanation, and once I give them one, they usually take it without question." He gave me a lopsided grin, which made him seem more human. "But sometimes it takes a little more finesse on my part to win them over."

"Are they really your mother's eyes?" I asked, choosing pointedly to ignore my wolf, who bristled at the "finesse" part. *He's not ours*, I scolded. *He can finesse anyone he wants.* She bit the air.

"I guess you could say that," he said. "My shifter genes came from my father, like everyone's do, but my mother had very unusual eyes to begin with, or so I'd been told. I don't remember her much. It was a very long time ago." He grabbed his clothes and started around the pool toward the sulfur trickle coming out of the large boulder.

I swam over to where my jacket was hanging and hoisted myself up. I turned away demurely and was about to put it back on to cover myself when Rourke cleared his voice right behind me. "Um, sorry, sweetheart, but I'm going to need that jacket now."

"Huh?" I asked, dripping wet, arms crossed over my chest.

"Scent trail. Our scent stops at this pool."

I took my jacket off the branch with my index finger and reluctantly swung it out to him. He took it and walked to the edge of the pool, grabbed a large piece of floating wood and draped my jacket over, and sent it off. I watched with a heavy heart as my coverage floated down the stream. "Wait, you just sent my jacket downstream where we just came from. How is that going to help?"

"It will eventually float to shore. Hopefully that's where they'll think we got out. Having a buildup of your scent downstream can only help us." He headed to the sulfur without looking back, and started cupping the smelly water and splashing it all over his body.

I made my way over to him. "You just sent my modesty downstream for a two-minute diversion?"

"Hey, I'll take any advantage I can get."

"That wasn't an advantage, that was sneaky." I walked up next to him and started pouring water over my head, cupping my hands tightly to catch it. It smelled awful this close, like rancid eggs right in my nostrils. Rourke stayed focused on his task. At least he wasn't trying to ogle my breasts. Though it would've been easier to dislike him if he had. Instead I was feeling quite the opposite. He was just so...normal. Not at all what I'd been expecting. It was throwing me off. *We have to remember he's dangerous, right?* My wolf huffed at me, and instead of agreeing, she flashed me a picture of him getting out of the pool without his jeans. *Stop it! You're not helping! He could snap at any moment and try to kill us.* She turned her back on me. *Plus, he doesn't seem to be that into us anyway.* Other than a few lighthearted comments, and some dazzling smiles, he hadn't sent us any real signals.

I cleared my voice and hoped I sounded normal. "Rourke, what kind of werecat are you?"

He seemed genuinely surprised by the question. Then he narrowed his eyes, flashing me a toothy grin. "I never kiss and tell on the first date."

He turned back to the putrid water and splashed more of it on his chest.

My wolf licked her lips and let out a mew. *We don't mew.*

She snuffed at me.

"Come on, you can tell me." I moved in beside him, cupping more water between my palms. "I won't spill your secret. I've got enough to worry about, why would I have any reason to tell?"

We stood close and heat from him radiated into my body, along with his strong power current. It prickled my skin again like a million tiny pressure points tapping at the same time. Standing this close to him was an at-my-own-risk kind of deal, but I was doing it anyway. Rourke turned, tendrils of water snaking their way down his body, disappearing under the lip of his denim. A spark ignited somewhere deep in his eyes, and chills ran down my spine. That had been a little on the "real" side.

He said, "I haven't told a single person in over five hundred years what I am, and I'm not planning on breaking my streak now."

"Why the big cloak-and-dagger?" I asked. "It can't matter that much if people know what you are." I poured a palmful of the stink over my head. I tried to face away from him, toward the rock, so my see-through camisole was aimed at something innocuous.

"If they know what I am, they can better anticipate how I may react in a certain situation. Secrecy may aid me only a little in that respect, but the unknown tends to be more frightening than reality anyway." He grinned. "As a rule."

He literally towered over me, but the weird thing was, I didn't feel threatened by him at all. It bugged me, because he was a predator, most likely a natural enemy of mine. I should feel threatened nonstop. My hackles should be raised and I should be baring my teeth. Shifters rarely got along with other shifters. We were animals. Animals fought. They didn't hang out in a creek together splashing around. My wolf should want to rip her canines into him and sever his jugular, not mew at him like a lovestruck teenager.

Instead of ripping his heart out, her tongue lolled out while she enjoyed the view. *Put your tongue back in your mouth. You're embarrassing me.*

I stopped dumping water over my head to take in what he'd just said. "So, let me get this straight. If people think you may be…let's say, a saber-toothed tiger, they'll be more afraid of you than say…if they found out you were a common house cat? Is that the real reasoning behind all your mysterious mystique?"

Rourke chuckled. "Jessica, you're no shrinking violet, that's for damn sure." He shook his head back and forth, water spraying us both. "My 'mysterious mystique,' as you so nicely put it, has gone a long way in facilitating my reputation as a resident badass. If you build up the rumors and the fear, it makes your job a hell of a lot easier. I like easy." He pinned me with his eyes. "And I can promise you I am most certainly *not* a house cat." He chuckled again.

I stopped moving.

When he'd used my name in the familiar, blood had thundered around in my brain. My wolf and I had both snapped to immediate attention, the effect of his words had been physical. My blood pumped wildly and little tremors broke out all over my body, making me twitch. *I don't even know this guy. He shouldn't have any effect on us. What just happened? Why is our body doing that?* My wolf was too busy running in circles excitedly yipping to answer me. Plus I was having trouble focusing on what I'd just been saying as Rourke raised his arms over his head again. Water coated his face and ran freely down his body. A low sound emerged in the back of my throat. I brought a hand to my neck. *Jesus, you have to stop doing that. Calm yourself down!* I seriously hoped that sound had not been uttered out loud. *Listen, you have to get a hold of this. We're not sleeping with every single person we meet.* My wolf was just short of jumping up and down. *You can't be into this guy like that. He's a mercenary who was hired to stalk us, possibly even kidnap us. We are not going there. Do you hear me?* She wasn't listening because she was lost to her own personal frenzy.

I left her there.

We climbed straight up. Our wet clothes and shoes dried fairly quickly in the heat—thank goodness. Rourke had taken the lead and so far hadn't glanced back. I had no idea if he was being chivalrous or if he was just anxious to reach a safer location. After a couple hours, I picked up my pace and lessened the gap between us.

The sulfur had definitely helped mask us for a while, but as it dissipated I clearly smelled the deep clove musk emanating from every pore on Rourke's body.

There was no way to get rid of it. Our scent was intrinsic to us; you couldn't turn it off.

The wolves had it in their memory banks and could absolutely track it, it was just a matter of time. We had a day at most.

Rourke paused beneath a tall tree. I trailed behind him, coming to a halt right as my stomach grumbled like rocks were being ground up in my intestines. Rourke arched an eyebrow.

I shrugged. "What? I'm hungry." Another rumble. "Actually, scratch that, I could eat an entire restaurant full of food."

"We're almost there, and there's food at the cabin." He started walking again. "When I made my first change, I was insatiable for a solid year." His voice held a soft purr. "In more ways than one."

I caught my footing in time and managed not to nosedive into the ground as I followed after him. "So I have this to look forward to for a full year?"

"Pretty much."

I complained after him. "You know . . . It's not like a normal hunger. It's more like I'm trying to feed something else— something craving so much more than I can give it. Food doesn't fill it. It's like a gigantic void and nothing I seem to do can satiate it."

"You're craving fresh blood."

I stopped in my tracks. "What do you mean, 'fresh blood'? I'm not killing someone just to calm my irritable stomach. That's not happening, like ever."

"No, I mean you need to hunt." He slowed, turning around. "You know, rabbits and squirrels? The hunt is what your body is craving, and a fresh kill staves off true hunger. Your body craves the blood." He squinted back at me, bringing his hand up. When I didn't respond, he said, "You don't know what I'm talking about, do you?"

I shook my head. "No. I've only made one change…and let's just say it didn't go exceedingly well. I'm not actually sure I can make a successful change again…*um*…without help. I haven't had any Werewolf 101 tutorials yet. If people stop trying to kill me long enough, I may be able to squeeze some in, but so far, other than what I've witnessed as an outsider all my life, I don't know much of anything."

He turned and continued picking his way up the rocky slope. I followed. "Maybe you can make a change when we get to the cabin," he said. "I'm certainly not a wolf, but I've been a shifter for a lot of years, too many to count. I might be able to help."

"Maybe." Making a successful shift could be the ticket back to my Pack. As a wolf, it would be easy for me to find another way out of the mountains quickly. "But, just so you know, there's a strong possibility I would eat you instead of the rabbit if I change. I don't have the greatest control and I can't promise things won't get out of hand."

"I'm counting on it."

He laughed all the way to the next clearing.

The cabin was simple. And beautiful. The aged logs on the small structure were weathered and faded a charcoal gray. The metal roof had a nice brown patina, and a tiny stone chimney, made of flat river rocks, ran up one side. It boasted some new latches and clean boards, so I knew Rourke had recently put some time into it.

"Wow, it's so cute," I said as we entered the clearing. "It's amazing, actually. How'd you find it way up here in the middle of nowhere?" The backdrop to the cabin was the continuing side of the mountain we were on, framing it like a fantastic painting.

"I've spent a lot of time in these mountains," Rourke answered. "When you spend as much time as I do exploring the woods, you're bound to find something." He gestured to the right of the structure. "There used to be a rough trail leading to a deserted mine, located a few miles east of here. I figured this cabin must've belonged to one of the miners who decided to live here year round." He shrugged. "Or at least that's my best guess."

"How come no one else has discovered it?" Meaning humans.

"A few people have stumbled in here and there, but there's no easy way to get here other than what we just did." Which had been a heavy climb up the steep side of a mountain. "The land sheers off in every direction eventually. The old mine was lost to a landslide years ago, effectively eliminating any easy routes that could've run up here long before I ever found it. I've tried to buy the land, but it's owned by the state and there's too much bureaucracy involved. There's no record of the cabin at all, so when and if they ever find it, I'll move on."

The tiny structure reminded me of my home in a strange way. It didn't have much in common with the elegant Lodge of my upbringing, but the cabin, edged by rolling green on all sides, surrounded by a forest of old growth, felt good. Really good. "You said you had food?"

"Right inside." He headed toward the door, chuckling again. It wasn't nice to know everything I did was funny, but at least he had a nice baritone. Marcy was right. Listening to it wasn't the worst thing in the world.

He turned the knob and headed inside.

"No lock?" I followed him through the door.

"Not necessary. If someone wanted something badly enough, all they'd have to do is break a window. Hauling glass up the side of a mountain is a pain, so I figured if I had to replace some of the food once in a while, it's easier than bringing up more glass."

Inside, an old wooden countertop ran along the left wall with a cutout for a sink, but an aged plastic basin balanced in its place instead. Homemade cabinets hung on the walls above the countertop, framing a lone, four-paned window in the middle. The doors to the cabinets were long gone, exposing rows and rows of canned goods.

I made a beeline for the sustenance. "Corn, beans, fruit, chili," I read, twisting a few of the labels so I could see what they were. "Rourke, you could open your own restaurant up here: Cute Cabin Cuisine." I grabbed a can of chili. "Mind if I eat this cold?" I eyed the small propane camping stove in the corner, but honestly, it would take too long at this point.

"You can eat anything you'd like. Have at it." Rourke's arm threaded around my waist, surprising me enough to jump. *Dammit.* I had to quit reacting to him.

He slid an old, rickety drawer open right next to where I

stood and pulled out a can opener. He handed it to me, eyes dancing. "You may want to use this instead of your teeth. It's a little more civilized."

I ignored him, swiping the opener from his hands.

While the drawer was still open, I plucked out a fork and headed for the small table. I sat in one of the two chairs. "I'll show you what civilized looks like, cat." I used the can opener, and once the lid was off, I dipped my fork in and immediately drew out a big fat forkful. With a full mouth, I asked, "Ith that where you theep?" I used the tip of my fork to point upward in case he couldn't catch my meaning.

His gaze flicked to the small loft. A single mattress of indeterminate size lay there, covered in what appeared to be an aged patchwork quilt. "Yep, that's where the bedroom is."

"Ith cute," I said over another mouthful.

Rourke pushed off the countertop where he'd been standing and came to sit in a rocking chair by the fireplace. The only other furniture in the room. He looked massive and out of place in the obviously fragile antique. It'd probably been hand-crafted by the cabin's original owner.

He looked like Gulliver sitting in a chair leagues too small.

I stifled a giggle with another bite of chili.

Then I sat back and ate the rest of the cold meat and beans. As my brain calmed and my stomach stopped aching, I sobered considerably. It'd been easy to focus on the tough climb and trying to lose our scent trail, but what the hell was I doing here?

This wasn't a happy vacation in the mountains with my lover. My Pack was at war—a war sparked because of me—and I had to quit screwing around. I'd followed Rourke up here, like a good girl who'd been ordered by her father, but now it was time to figure out my next move. And in order to do that, I had to gather some facts.

Starting with Rourke.

I finished the chili, set the can and fork down on the table, and turned decisively toward him. He seemed to be patiently waiting for me to finish my meal. His face was quiet, almost brooding. It seemed we'd both fallen into the same what-the-fuck-do-we-do-now mode.

I cleared my throat. "Okay, Rourke. It's time to figure this thing out once and for all. I think our happy-talk quota is all used up, quite possibly forever. You got me here, saved me in a strange sense, made sure I stuck with you, and I've played along. Now I need you to give me the real reason why you're helping me. This isn't a game, this is my life, and I want to know the real deal. A trained mercenary does not help a damsel in distress, he avoids her like the plague. I am a burden to you, and mercs hate burdens. James's sudden paradigm shift to trust you was abrupt. He had to have a good reason, or a damn good hunch about something. I want some answers to why you're playing nice."

Rourke shifted in his chair, his muscular arms gripping the rails as he slid himself forward until he rested at the edge. It was a miracle that thing held him. He set his elbows on his knees and waited a few beats before answering. "Irish was right to trust me. I brought you here because I owed your father a debt."

Not what I was expecting.

He continued, "It hadn't been my original plan, but it came along, so I took it."

I narrowed my eyes. "My father didn't mention you owed him any debt, and believe me, we discussed you in depth. If he felt he could've trusted you because you were beholden to him in some way, we wouldn't be sitting here having this conversation. He would've arranged a closed meeting in a safe place. End of story. What you're saying doesn't ring true, Rourke."

His mouth went up on one side, making him look cocky. "Cats and dogs play by different rules, sweetheart. What your father did for me had nothing to do with battle or war, which I believe a wolf holds above all else. After he did what he did, I made an oath to pay him back in kind. Irish must have found out about it somehow, or heard the rumors, or just guessed, but it doesn't matter. This opportunity came along, so I took it." He shrugged. "That's all there is to it."

"That doesn't explain our meet-up in the first place. Saving my life because a war dropped unexpectedly into your lap, and you just happened to have a debt you needed to repay, doesn't equal meeting me for drinks because you were hired to extract information. Those are two very separate things." I sat straighter. "Listen, Rourke, I'm not expecting you to divulge every single detail to me, but I'm looking for answers to help preserve my life. Nothing more." He stared at me so intently, my breath caught for a moment. I cleared my throat. "Please, I need to know," I said softly.

"What specifically do you want to know?"

"Who hired you? I need to know, because the details of my shift shouldn't be out yet. It's only been a few days, and that most likely means we have a traitor in our Pack. If I want to survive, I need information." I tried another tack when he didn't answer. "If keeping me alive a little longer counts toward repaying the debt you owe to my father, consider telling me what I need to know as the final payment. After I have that, I'll go on my way and you can be done babysitting me for good."

Rourke stood and started to pace.

It was a move so like my brother's, my heart jumped into my throat suddenly and my thoughts rushed to Tyler. I brushed my mind, but there was only dead space there. The same dead space I'd gotten all day.

Rourke stopped in front of the countertop and propped himself against it. There wasn't exactly any place else to go. "It's not as easy as all that."

"I didn't think it would be easy. In fact, I was thinking it was going to be very, very difficult."

"Jessica, I'm bound by a very powerful client, and there's more to this story than I can share with you now—or quite possibly ever." He broke his gaze and I took the meaning intended.

My heart raced again with the proper use of my name, but I pushed it to the farthest reaches of my mind. My wolf howled her delight again at hearing, and I had to quiet her before I went on. *This is not the time. You have to cool it.* "You mean somebody would've taken the job who didn't owe a life debt to the Alpha of the U.S. Northern Territories? Somebody who could've extracted the 'by whatever means necessary' information by ripping out my fingernails or running a silver blade across my neck?"

"Yes."

"So you went into this knowing there was a good chance you would have to save me at some point, even though it meant double-crossing your powerful client?"

"By 'saving you,' I'm not double-crossing my client. I'm simply bringing you to another location to obtain what I need."

"And if I refuse to give it freely?"

"The only way to do that would be to escape me." His eyes sparked.

I raised an eyebrow and ran my head pointedly around the small room. "Hmm, I'm thinking that may be a likely scenario, Rourke. But the minute I make my masterful 'escape,' you'll be back to hunting me, correct?"

"Yes," he said, not bothering to look abashed as he crossed

his arms. "Most likely in a day or two, after I've had some time to recover from the serious injuries you inflicted on me in your overzealousness to escape."

I couldn't help but laugh. The thought of fighting him suddenly sent my libido skyrocketing several octaves. *Damn cat.* My wolf yipped. *Quit. I know you're behind this. We're in serious discussions here and I need to stay focused. Can you please keep your mind off sex for two freaking seconds? It's getting to be on the insane stalkery side.* She growled and snapped at me. "I'm assuming once you've recovered from all my crushing blows, your debts to my father will be paid in full?"

He glanced down at his boots, a lock of hair fell over his eye. "Yes."

"Interrogating women isn't your thing, is it?"

He looked up, surprised. "No. I don't make it a habit to shake down women."

"But you fight them on occasion, right?" There were some nasty-ass supernatural women on the planet. Not all were created equal.

"When duty calls."

"You mean when you're paid enough?" I didn't wait for an answer. "If I choose to give you enough information freely, will your client back off?"

He dropped his arms and paced to the door. "I don't know. My client tends to be attracted to the unusual. Once the entire supernatural world learns about you, there may be no end to the curiosity. Right now, I'm being paid to gather necessary information only. The next job may be a bit more...*detailed.*"

"Nobody's putting a gun to your head to take the next job, Rourke."

He turned, covering the small room in a few short strides, grabbing on to the back of my chair, putting his face right next to mine. It took everything I had not to shrink back. His eyes were sparking, green arrows of light shooting like beautiful starbursts in his irises. My wolf jumped to attention immediately, but instead of snarling, she ran her typical circles. "If I don't take it there's always someone next in line who will." The scent of him thickened around us, making my head dance.

"Why do you *care*?" I breathed.

Both of us stilled.

He backed off, dropping his hands from my chair. "I don't."

His scent said otherwise, but the markers were so unique it was hard for me to really tell. He was giving off something new, and I couldn't sort it fast enough, but whatever it was, it was heady and strange and it was all over the place, pinging around in my mind like a pinball drenched in honey. He didn't smell like a wolf or a human. *He smells incredible, richer than before.* I was beginning to get light-headed from it and my wolf was beyond frenzy. I had to find a way to shut her out of my mind completely so I could concentrate.

I shook my head, but it didn't help. "So if someone else took the job, your debt to my father would be forfeit? Is that why you took it?"

He ran an absent hand through his hair. "Dammit, having you here complicates everything." He strode toward the door and reached for the handle.

He so didn't get to storm out of here.

I was pissed. I jumped up, my anger wiping away the last tendrils of whatever scent of his that had lingered in my mind. "If you *remember* correctly, I didn't want to be anywhere near here. I wanted to stay with my Pack and fight. I was a complication you didn't need to act on. It was *your* choice to bring me here. You could've dropped me in the next town over and my father would've called it good, your life debt paid in full."

"Dropping you off and leaving you alone wasn't in the cards," he ground. "My honor is one of the only things I have left to give freely, and I don't give it lightly."

I stalked toward him. He dropped his hold on the door and faced me. "All the stories I've ever heard about you in the past have been full of hard edges, but honestly, Rourke, you've turned out nothing like them. Now I'm left wondering what's true and what's a goddamn smokescreen. I'm beginning to think everything is a lie and you're just one big, badass kitten under all that muscle." I got in his face. "Are you trying to gain my trust so you can pull one over on me, or are you really just a nice guy masquerading as a stone-cold killer?"

All in one motion I was up against the doorframe, his body flat against mine.

His mouth covered mine, his lips soft but firm, the kiss deep and full. His mouth felt hot against my lips; his strange, wonderful scent pouring over me in waves, making my whole body ache with need.

My body responded on its own, my mouth opening up to his. My tongue found his warmth; my nails sought his back. *Gods, he's hard and soft at the same time.*

"It shouldn't be. This shouldn't be right," he growled into my mouth, then covered my lips again fiercely, his grip tightening on my hips. He groaned, pulling back a few inches, his eyes fully dilated. He took my mouth again, his hands sliding up to tangle in my hair, his body full of power as he leaned into me, pressing me farther into the jamb. The currents of his power radiated into my body, throbbing everything deliciously. *"Jessica."*

My body seized and all my synapses exploded at once.

Reality came back slowly, like waking from a dream. *No. What did he just say? I have to stop this. What was that?* I tried hard to clear my head, but instead my hands slid to his still naked chest, caressing, feeling, my brain too foggy to concentrate on anything but pleasure. His delicious scent was overpowering me and I let it.

He nipped at my lips, his teeth pulling, tasting, his tongue lapping me.

I moaned.

"Jessica," he murmured as his mouth covered mine again in a deep, sensual kiss.

I froze. *No. No. No. What's happening?* It took everything I had, but I braced my hands against his chest and shoved.

He stumbled backward, dazed.

"What was that? I…I…" I ran a forearm over my bruised mouth. I tried to refocus. Everything was blurred. "That wasn't a normal kiss, Rourke. I know you're hot, and my wolf's been going apeshit over you, but holy crap. I've never…that was… I…" There were no words.

Rourke stared at me without speaking, his irises a full blaze of green. He appeared as stunned as I felt.

My wolf howled, angry with me. She shot a picture into my mind of Rourke looking down on us like he just had, but this time we were licking and biting his chin.

Ohmygod.

No. My wolf danced around excitedly, like she'd been doing all day. *Rourke is* not *our mate.* She snarled and bared her teeth. *No! It can't possibly be right. That would be insanity.* She howled. I shook my head. There had to be some mistake.

"Jessica." Rourke closed the gap between us and tried to reach for me again.

I stepped to the side, pushing him away. "You knew," I said accusingly. "You knew what was happening—what had been happening to us all day—and you didn't say a damn thing."

"No." He shook his head. "I had no idea until right now. Until I just tasted you. Something shattered between us when we came together and I know you felt it too." He gazed at me in open wonder. "Your blood is calling to me right now. Just being this far apart is making me crazy. I need to touch you."

He felt different to me too, but I wasn't ready to admit it. It was too much. "How could this happen?" I scooted away. I needed some space. "Cats and dogs don't play together, and if this really is true, the universe is playing some kind of cruel joke on us."

"It's no joke," Rourke said, taking another step toward me. "Jessica, when I first saw you striding toward me in the bar, all confident and headstrong, it was all I could do not to bend you over a barstool and take you right there. But I marked it up to a regular male response to a gorgeous woman. I didn't think about it any more than that." His eyes were still wild, firing a beautiful green. "When I realized you hadn't set me up, and you were in real trouble—my beast went crazy trying to get you out of there and out of harm's way. I had trouble controlling his impulses, and it pissed me off. That has never happened to me before. It seems I've been denying him the whole time I've been with you, pushing him back, scolding him. He never stopped urging me, fighting with me, until this very moment. When you got in my face, I finally gave in to what he's been pushing me to do all along."

"And what was that?" I asked warily.

"To taste you."

I knew in my bones what he was saying was true. I'd been denying my wolf just as hard. But that didn't make it any easier to swallow. Rourke was nothing like any of the wolves had thought, but I still wasn't ready. I'd just turned into a wolf— now I had a mate? It was too much, an insane amount of too much. "I can't think. None of this is making any sense." I put my hand to my forehead. "Why us? Why now? It takes some a thousand years to find their true mate." I turned. "I need some air." Before he could object I darted out the door, slamming it firmly behind me.

My wolf had gone quiet for once, her head angled at me like she wanted to ask a question. *I cannot talk about this with you. I know where you stand, you've been abundantly clear on all fronts. You accept him. I get it. But I can't deal with this right now. His scent is still inside me, driving me crazy. His taste is still on my lips. I crave him even now.* Holy shit, I had a mate. And he was a cat.

I ran headfirst into the woods.

20

I followed a well-worn path leading away from the cabin. It ran without stopping straight into a wall of densely packed pine trees. I had to duck my head and pull apart low branches to get through.

Inside was a tiny clearing, ringed tightly with tall trees. The grassy field in the middle was so perfect and green, it appeared to have been freshly mowed. That was inconceivable. Rourke didn't come up here and mow lawns.

I paced into the middle and looked up. The trees were entrancing, like a beautiful forested cathedral made of swaying boughs with a rooftop of the purest blue. The edges of the sky were fading to orange with the setting sun.

We have to do something, I told my wolf. *I have to get my mind off of all this.* She mimicked lying on the ground and barked. *You want to shift?* She yipped. *What if I can't shift all the way?* She snapped the air in front of her and flicked her muzzle. *It's not a stupid question. We did that whole Lycan thing, and I have no idea how it happened, or how to do it again.* She turned away from me like it wasn't any concern of hers. *What if I'm not in control as a wolf? I'm not ready for a repeat of the last time we were in our full true form.* My wolf turned around slowly, her eyes clear as she put her paw up against the opaque barrier between us in my mind. I had dropped it momentarily when we'd fought the rogue, but it was still there. She was telling me it still held, it was still strong.

I was in control whether she liked it or not.

Okay, let's try it then. I've really got nothing to lose.

I shimmied out of my clothes quickly and lay down on the grass, pushing Rourke and the kiss from my mind. It took gargantuan effort. All my body really wanted to do was run back to him.

I closed my eyes and focused on my wolf, which wasn't hard because she had situated herself front and center, waiting for me to get with the program. *Okay, this is all you. I'm trusting you to know what to do.* She growled, urging me along. *Fine, fine, I'm going.*

Once I was settled, I pushed out to her. I wasn't sure if I was doing it right, but it felt comfortable. The barrier between us bowed, but held. Power flowed through me, transferring to my wolf through the screen. She howled fiercely as she accepted it. Shivers shot though me as my muscles started to dance and move. Slowly at first, and then more rapidly, like my body was yielding on its own.

My back arched, my spine lifting off the ground, starting to shift beneath me. Soft fur sprouted along my arms and legs, my canines and claws elongating to full length. My legs bent and twisted as they changed.

There was no shock of pain this time. My father had been right.

Instead, a constant pressure mixed with liquid heat ran through my veins. Raw energy transformed my body; it shaped me and shook me with need.

My body wanted this, it welcomed it.

When it was over, I sprawled on my stomach panting heavily. My paws spread out in front of me. *I have paws.* I laughed. It was funny to think of myself with anything other than hands. I blinked a few times, adjusting to the field of vision, which was sharper and much more precise than before. I pushed out to my wolf and found her sitting right next to me, panting with me, seeing everything I saw.

How can you be here with me at the same time? As she barked, our mouth opened and the sound of a wolf's calling reverberated in the air. *You told me you wouldn't be in control!* She sniffed the air, and as she did, our snout absorbed the scents around us. The smell of Rourke hit me immediately. He was near. In my wolf form, his scent called to me immediately, signaling our connection clearly. There was no mistaking it. It screamed *mate*. No wonder my wolf had known. I wanted to go to him now, so he could comfort me, soothe me. But I didn't.

Instead I jumped to my feet and stumbled a few paces. I wasn't used to working a body with four legs. I had to get out of here. I needed to think somewhere I couldn't smell my mate. *I don't get it. Why won't this work?* My wolf took a step forward in my mind, and I felt a pull to step, my paw lifting off the ground on its own. *No!* My foreleg froze in place. I focused all my concentration and my paw went down, and as it did, I understood.

I *was* in control, but the shift of power in this form hung on the tiniest thread of thought. We were melded here, almost one and the same. Nothing like my human body. She bit the air in my mind, but my muzzle stayed shut in my physical form. *I get it. Let me get used to it first.* She huffed, but sat back on her haunches. I moved forward cautiously, feeling out my new body on my own. The last time, I'd been in shock and she had taken over, so it was my first time.

I crept out of the ring of trees.

Rourke stood fifty paces from me, watching me intently.

I ran.

I raced toward the creek, where the smell of sweet water beckoned me like a tinkling bell. I was hungry and thirsty. Once I got there and took my fill, I followed it to the end, picking over rocks and boulders, taking time to explore my new form. My wolf was patient with me, even though I knew she wanted to run and hunt.

I settled us on a big boulder at the edge of a small waterfall, the cliff sheering off below us. I didn't want to think about Rourke, but he'd been the only thing occupying my mind. My wolf flashed me a picture. It was the same one she'd shown me before of Rourke towering over me, us biting and licking his chin. *I know that already! But we need to talk to our Alpha right n—*

Jessica! My father's voice came screaming into my consciousness. *Can you hear me? Damn it, answer me! Jessica!*

I sprang up so quickly I stumbled back, almost losing my balance and tumbling off the rock. I had to use all my faculties not to plunge over the waterfall.

Dad? Dad! I'm here! I can hear you!

There was a pause. *Jessica, are you in your wolf form?*

Yes.

Your full wolf form?

Yes, I just shifted.

Are you in danger right now? Jessica, answer me quickly!

No. I looked around me, but there was nothing but woods. *At least not anything immediate. I'm somewhere in the Ozarks, at a cabin up in the mountains. We lost the Southern wolves for the time being, but I'm certain they'll find us soon. We have, at Rourke's best guess, till morning.*

I felt my father's mind shift as he said something to someone else; it was like being on hold during a phone call when you heard murmuring in the background. *We're on the road somewhere in Missouri. Tyler saw you get on the highway and we followed as soon as we could.* There was another brief interruption. I waited patiently. *Jessica, listen to me, there's something else going on here. When you left with Rourke, the Southern faction pulled out of the fight immediately. And when I say that, I mean, to a wolf they abandoned the fight. They had several U-Hauls, and they came around quickly, gathering up their wolves midfight. Never in my life have I ever left a fight, and I've certainly never seen any other wolf do it either, especially during a war. We stay and fight, it's our instinct to do so.*

If they left, does that mean no one on our side was hurt? I was anxious to know if everyone was okay. I felt a heavy burden on my shoulders, thinking there was a possibility wolves could've lost their lives because of me. Especially anyone I loved.

I heard what amounted to a scoff in my head. *We're fine, don't worry about us. Danny got a few bones broken and it pissed him off, and some of the younger wolves have some bumps and bruises, but there were no major losses.*

I was relieved. *Is Tyler with you?*

Yes, he and ten others. The rest are going to rendezvous with us once we pick you up.

I don't know how you're going to find me. We crossed a small river with a sulfur stream and we hiked up a steep slope all day. You're going to have to follow our stinky trail. I can change back and ask Rour—

Jessica, I will find you. I can promise you that. There's nothing on this planet that will keep me from finding you—but you have to listen to me closely now. Intensity stressed his words. My blood jumped, reacting to his emotion.

I'm listening.

The implication of the Southern wolves changing their tactics and pulling out is extremely serious. It means they're working with another Sect, maybe even more than one. There's something going on here that we don't fully understand yet. And it's highly organized, Jessica. I've been a fool not to think something like this wasn't a possibility. His regret flowed though me. *I'll be sorry until the day I die, but I promise I will make amends to you. I swear it on my very life.*

My heart thudded in my chest. I wanted to be with my Pack, to alleviate my father's worry. *I can leave now, try to meet you through the forest. I can try to find my way out in my wolf form. Or Rourke may be able to guide me there if he's willing.*

My father stilled. *Has Rourke told you anything? Has he told you who sent him? Or why?*

No, he only hinted they were "very" interested in me.

Jessica, he cannot be trusted. He's a great warrior, one of the best I've ever seen, and I will owe him a life debt for getting you out of the fight, but he is not *one of us. He is not* Pack. *If he's led you into a trap by bringing you there . . . he's also a dead man.*

The thought of Rourke dead choked me. I couldn't breathe.

Jessica? Do you hear me?

I shook myself. *Yes, I hear you.* Now was not the time or the place to explain what had happened between Rourke and me. That would have to wait. *I don't think I'm in any danger from Rourke, as of right now,* I said carefully. *He's been on the level as much as he can be. When I change back, I'll try to get more information. He may be willing to share more with me now.*

Jessica, I think we're close to the point where you entered the mountains. Tyler is reading the map as we speak and the base of the Ozarks is roughly a twenty-minute drive from where we are. If you climbed all day, we can make it in a fraction of that time. We have your scent. We'll find you soon.

I can change back into my wolf form after I talk to Rourke. I can be waiting and ready in an hour. That should give you enough time to find my trail.

Heavy emotion pulsed in my blood. There was something my father wasn't telling me, and it weighed heavily on him. Then he spoke. *Jessica, the Southern faction is ahead of us. It took us some time to round up our wolves and get organized. There's a strong possibility... they will make it to you before we do.*

But they don't know where to go, and you do, I told him with a confidence belying my feelings.

It doesn't matter. If they're working with another group of supernaturals, it's possible they have information we don't. And they have your scent. They could be working with anyone: witches or demons or any of the goddamn Sects, very likely the same one who hired the cat. A string of angry curses tumbled around in my brain. *You have to arm yourself. Right now. Change back and get yourself somewhere safe. Don't stay in the open. Go someplace unpredictable. Start moving. We'll find you.*

I'm heading back right now. We'll leave as soon as I shift back.

When we draw closer, your link with your brother should be intact. Just get yourself to a safe place. My body tingled, the blood order searing through my veins, solidifying.

I'm leaving now. I'll see you soon. I told him.

I love you, Jessica.

I love you too.

I jumped off the rock. *Okay, this is going to be all you.* I shifted control over to my wolf on a thought and she took off, picking up our pace, speeding through the forest. It was exhilarating— a feeling so pure and free, I'd never experienced anything like it. For the very first time since my change, I finally felt like the animal I'd become. It was wonderful.

She skillfully bounded over and through obstacles like she was a part of the natural flow and of the woods. She managed to snag food for us on the way, not even needing to slow in order to hunt. Never in my life did I think I'd enjoy the taste of squirrel, but it was actually delicious. At this point, anything would've tasted good. If I'd thought my hunger had been annoying in my human form, it was nothing compared to the empty, gnawing feeling in my wolf form.

We bounded back toward the cathedral of trees.

Rourke was there now. I could smell him, his powerful scent concentrated inside the tree line. Even though it mixed with the pungent smell of sulfur, which was much more sensitive to me in this form, I could've found him blindfolded. I needed to tell him a threat was coming sooner than we'd expected. I still didn't know who had hired him and what was going on, but he'd taken the job before either of us knew there were going to be . . . *personal complications.*

I wondered for a moment how all this would play out, where the loyalties would fall.

At the edge of the trees, I shifted gears and took control from my wolf. She relinquished without a fight, satisfied with her run, both of us becoming more at ease in our roles. The barrier still stood in my mind, and she was indeed behind it, but I knew there would be a time when it came down for good.

I peered through the darkness, searching for him as I padded into the cathedral.

He leaned against a tree, staring at us carefully, not moving. The vibration of his power enveloped me, calling to me like no other. He was strong. A warrior of his kind. And he was here, waiting.

For me.

I felt his gaze on me as I lay down, finding the spot where I'd made my first shift. I closed my eyes and shifted back. It was a smooth transition, with little pain. When it was over, I pulled on my clothing and stood.

He walked to the edge of the grass. "Jessica."

I strode toward him, my eyes flashing violet as they connected with his. He returned my stare, his irises igniting.

"They're com—"

"—I need to touch you and know you're all right." He reached for me, leaning down to take me into his arms. It felt right to be in them, my hands immediately tracing around his neck, cupping his back. My body had missed his, craved his taste, even though we'd been separated only a short time.

His mouth seared mine. Images of licking and tasting him, caressing his smooth skin, wrapping my legs around him, and being filled by him shot into my mind. I dragged my nails along his collarbone, luxuriating in his incredible strength.

His taste was a trigger, it fed me. It also made me lose coherent thoughts.

I understood now about our saliva, but it wasn't just intoxicating to humans—it was our identifier. What his body produced was meant for me, and me alone. Mine was meant for him.

It took just one kiss.

I had to sever the connection. "Rourke...just wait." I tried to push him backward, but didn't succeed. "I want to do this...I do." He stilled at my words. "But we can't right now." I glanced up at him, trying to blink away the haze that filled my brain, tried to force my eyes back to normal. "We can't do this now...at least not right here...I mean..." I stammered.

His lips were on mine again, hot and soft. They tasted like sweet cinnamon mixed with molasses. "You're mine," he murmured into my mouth. My fingers threaded into his thick hair, my arms brushing against his stubble. My fingers pulsed as they twined through his locks. I grabbed a fistful tightly. *Mine.*

He locked me firmly to him, every contour of my body touching his. His hands splayed tightly across my back and my ass, his arms around me like a clamp.

No, no, no. We have to get out of here. Help me stop this. I pulled back again, this time I pinned my forehead to his chest. "Listen!" I drummed my fists on him. "Stop kissing me, I need to tell you something!" I was definitely intoxicated with whatever he was giving me. I shook myself.

Rourke strongly opposed in the form of a snarled growl as his arms locked around me again. "Jessica." His tone was low, feral, and hot.

"Rourke!" I stepped away from him with effort. He let me go this time. "I need you to listen right now. I just talked to my father and we're in more danger than we thought. Not tomorrow or the next day, but right now. We need to arm up and get the hell away from here. He said—"

Rourke's demeanor shifted instantaneously.

His reflexes went from relaxed to tense; he took one step forward and cupped his hand around the back of my neck, angling my head softly until I met his gaze squarely. His irises glittered fiercely. "Jessica, what else did he say?"

Mine. I blinked. "He said they were close to the river, but the Southern faction is ahead of them."

He cursed and broke away from me, turning in a slow circle.

"That's not all." His eyes pinned me. As a predator he took my breath away. Hairs stood on end as his face transformed into something hard. "My father's convinced they're working with another supernatural Sect. He said the wolves voluntarily surrendered the fight after we left. He said he's never seen a wolf leave a fight in his entire life. Whoever is pulling the strings is very well organized."

Rourke grabbed my hand and ran with me out of the trees. "We need to get our stuff from the cabin and leave right now. There's a cave about four miles from here where I have additional weapons stashed. We'll arm ourselves, and then we'll make our way out of the forest to meet your father."

"Rourke." I stopped, dragging him back, trying to accurately read his urgency. "What do you know about this? Do you know who the Southern wolves are working with? Who else is after me?" Panic brewed just below the surface. My wolf let out a low growl. Having our mate betray us was not a good way to start off this relationship.

He let go of me and turned, raking both hands through his hair. Not a good sign. "I'm not sure, but I have an idea. But I swear to you, this wasn't the plan." I stayed silent, my mind racing. His hands sought my body again, his fingers tightening around my forearms. "Jessica, you have to believe me. I didn't lure you up here to trap you. I had no idea you were my mate when all this began." His eyes were fierce. "Say you believe me. Please."

"I...I..." I wanted to say it.

"Jessica!" he shouted. "I didn't bring you here to trap you! I brought you here because it was the best place I could think of to keep you safe until I...I mean we...could figure everything out."

"Okay," I said, moving around him to start toward the cabin. "I get what you're saying. But if you don't mind I'd like to reserve my judgmen—"

"Jessica, please." He ran a hand over his mouth, his eyes pleading. "You have to listen—"

Suddenly there was a shout in the distance, followed by something that sounded close to a *whoosh*, followed by more *whoosh*ing sounds.

Rourke eclipsed me and grabbed my hand, racing us toward the cabin. The only place where we had any weapons. "Rourke!" I shouted as I ran. "What's coming? What the fuck is going on?"

He slid to a halt so suddenly I crashed into his back. I righted myself, but his hands were gripped on to mine so painfully, I'd lost blood flow. He'd stopped right at the edge of the clearing. I peered around his shoulder, his stress and fear radiating into me in angry currents. My wolf reacted to him, barking and growling.

If Rourke was stressed, I knew I wasn't going to like what I saw.

I gasped.

Creeping into the clearing from all around us were unfamiliar wolves, still in their human form, snarling, moving slowly, eyes pulsing yellow, each one on the cusp of change. All of them with clear intent to harm.

But that wasn't what got my attention.

Five shrouded figures in dark capes stood in the middle of the yard like they were frozen in time. Even though it was full night, and they were all wearing black, they gleamed oddly in the moonlight, somehow reflecting the very darkness around them.

One of the hooded figures glided toward us.

It didn't seem to touch the ground.

"Rourke," it hissed as stark white hands slowly drew its hood back to reveal a shockingly beautiful face, seemingly carved out of ivory and bone, the edges too defined to appear normal in any realm. Its two eyes glowed like wet mercury as they pierced the darkness for the first time. "The Queen is very unhappy with you," it tsked as it opened its mouth to reveal two of the longest canines I'd ever seen—which was saying something. Its smile filled me with horror and loathing, its mouth twisted at an odd, unnatural angle. "You were supposed to deliver the female werewolf to us *yesterday*. You've been a very bad boy."

Vampires.

21

"That wasn't the deal, Valdov," Rourke snarled. "You know it as well as your *Queen*. My job was to extract information only. It never involved kidnapping or delivery."

Pain shot though my fingers as Rourke's grip on my hand tightened to the point of breakage. His muscles began to pulse underneath his forearms in a dangerous way.

I frantically searched my inner database for what I knew about vampires, which wasn't a whole helluva lot. I knew about as much as the rest of the supe community—that the vamps operated out of one large Coven headquartered in both New Orleans and France. It'd been ruled for the better part of four hundred years by the powerful Queen Eudoxia, rumored to be sired by Ivan the Terrible.

Vampires, as a rule were reclusive, powerful, and ridiculously dangerous. They had a long, sordid history of cruelty, but since they conveniently viewed themselves as entirely above the caste system of all supernaturals, they tended to keep to themselves.

Which was lucky for us on all counts.

Needless to say, vampires had never needed any help from Hannon & Michaels to solve their problems—and although my father had fought them on and off over the past few centuries, usually because one of theirs picked a fight with one of ours, I'd never seen one up close.

Technically, as a lowly wolf shifter in their eyes, I should be well beneath their notice. They had no use for other Sects.

I had no idea what they wanted with me, and the fact that they'd obviously hired Rourke, and already knew of my change, was nothing short of terrifying.

"*Ah, ah*, Rourke, our *agreement*"—Valdov steepled his fingertips together in front of his icy visage—"was for you to gather information for us by whatever means *necessary*. Of course, necessary *clearly* implied bringing the girl to us if you were… shall we say…*unsuccessful* in your quest." Valdov peered over his pointy nails at us, his steady mercurial stare completely unnerving. "And it seems…your *quest* has indeed been waylaid…by what is this…" He lifted his perfectly chiseled face, stonelike and eerie in its careful definition, into the air and inhaled an exaggerated breath. "*Ahh*," he exhaled as he leveled his gaze fully back on us. "…*Lust*, is it?"

Rourke vibrated with power. It licked at me, wrapping me in its tendrils.

"I'm doing my *job* just fine, Valdov," Rourke said. "I'm doing *exactly* what you paid me to do, and nothing more. You'll have all the information you need as soon as I have it. And make no mistake, I will get it. So you can go ahead and scurry back to your Queen like the lapdog you are, and you can tell her to go fuck herself if she tries to change the rules on me halfway through a valid contract."

Valdov hissed at Rourke, a deep visceral sound that made

my skin itch. Then, right before our eyes, Valdov's features began to shift and change. I watched in horror as his lips slowly peeled away from his mouth and his canines grew longer and sharper, dropping well past his bottom lip. His face elongated, impossibly stretching, his cheeks receding inward as his chin dipped downward.

It looked like his skin was going to slide completely off his face.

Holy horror show.

Then, as the final gruesome capper, his eyes bled to full black, leaving no trace of white showing at all. Then a wave of his anger hit me. I shrank against it as it pummeled me with a taste of magic I'd never experienced before. This vampire was ancient, and his powers were completely off the charts.

My wolf sprang at him inside my head, snarling and gnashing her teeth. My muscles started to jump and twist as the adrenaline she fed me charged its way through my bloodstream. I had to rein her in quickly or we'd be dead before this fight started. *Hey, I know you're itching to fight Creepy here, and I want to too, but we can't take him and all his cronies at once, so you're going to have to cool it down.* She snarled at me, her teeth flashing, showing me an image of us sinking our teeth into his bone-white neck. *Even if we managed to take out the vampires with Rourke's help, we still have the Southern wolves to deal with, remember? If we attack now we lose. Get it? We need a better plan, one that doesn't include going balls out on a horde of powerful supernaturals. Just give me a minute.* She barked loudly but backed off, her frustration echoing around me in angry waves.

Rourke squeezed my hand in warning, acknowledging my sudden influx of power. I took it to heart. We were going to have to wait this out as long as we could. If anything, I hoped we'd be able to outrun them somewhere in the mountains.

Angry Southern wolves mixed with scary vampires did not tip the odds in our favor.

Valdov gained control of himself with effort, obviously having a change of heart about tearing Rourke's neck out. As he organized his features back into place, he flashed us a wretched smile. Locking his gaze on Rourke, he managed, "It looks as though we will no longer be needing your…*assistance* after all." He drew out his esses like a serpent. "You may consider your contract with us null and void from this moment on. You will be paid in full, of course, but we will take the girl now and you can go back to your den, or wherever it is you slink off to." He gestured breezily with his dead hand, like he was flicking away an irritant. "Now run along before I change my mind and decide to kill you just because I can."

"That's not going to work for me, Valdov," Rourke said. "I'll tear your head off your shoulders if you take so much as one step closer. You don't have the authority to dismiss me that easily, and you know it." Rourke's voice went eerily calm then, dangerous and cutting in its intent. "If you lay one dead finger on her you will be *begging* me to end your life. Do you understand? You will *beg* me."

The energy in the clearing jumped at Rourke's words. The wolves had slunk in closer, forming a ring around us. They chattered and growled, riled at the prospect of a good fight.

Valdov didn't seem cowed in the least.

Instead, he shifted his beady little stare to me, cocking his head like a bird. "*My, my, my*, what do we have here?" A grim smile played on his face as he clapped his hands together. "And here I thought it was only your constant need to rut! My Queen will be ever so interested in this new development. Come out and play, little werewolf," he addressed me directly. "Or are you too frightened by what you see standing before you?" When I didn't respond, he shook his head in mock sympathy. "It's too bad your daddy is so very far away, isn't it, little werewolf? It's such a shame he couldn't be here in time to catch all the fun."

He was challenging me.

I couldn't shrink away from it, even if my very human side wanted to flee. If I let myself appear weak, it would hurt me in the long run, plus it wasn't something I could do—my wolf *wouldn't* do. She now resembled a raging lunatic on a short leash, snarling, gnashing her teeth, rearing her legs up. I squared my shoulders and pried my hand from Rourke's grasp with great difficulty, since he wasn't interested in letting me go anywhere near Valdov.

I disengaged and stepped forward. Rourke growled, a low, steady sound full of menace and hatred. I stared Valdov straight in the eye, and in the strongest voice I could muster, I said, "The last time I needed my *daddy's* help was when I was seven, *Valdov*. And just so we're clear, I prefer to dirty my own hands. So whatever you think you've got, feel free to bring it now. I'm not scared of you." I ended with a smile, flashing full white teeth, my wolf's warning to stay the hell back or there would be trouble.

Right as I uttered the last words of my pretty speech, my body surged with power.

My wolf's idea of backup. She fed me just enough juice to send a rough pulse through me, but not enough to start anything moving.

Perfect.

She barked.

Valdov inhaled again, closing his eyes in some kind of awful ecstasy, ignoring my bravado completely. "*Ahhhh*, such raw power, little werewolf," he breathed. Then his eyes snapped open, cunning and superiority written all over his face. "Unfortunately, it won't be enough to withstand all of us, poor female, no matter how *dirty*...you manage to get yourself. However entertaining that might be to witness, we will regretfully have to decline this time."

I was about to tell him exactly how much dirt I was willing to shovel down his throat when he snapped his fingers, and almost immediately a figure stepped from the deep shadows across the clearing.

As it traipsed forward, I realized it was a woman.

She had long, flowing red hair, and as she sauntered confidently to us, her tresses danced wildly behind her like she was caught in a wind machine I couldn't see.

She was outfitted head-to-toe in black leather. A short cropped jacket covered a skintight bustier, hugging her tiny waist so completely it was a wonder she could breathe. Both the jacket and corset were studded with sharp, angry metal spikes. The whole ensemble was accompanied by a pair of extremely tight, hip-hugging leather pants that stopped just below her belly button. Over the pants were thigh-high black boots. She also had what appeared to be a bullwhip attached to her hip.

Geez, now I knew who was in charge of bringing sexy back.

The mystery woman laughed as she drew near. "Did you miss me, my sweet? It's been entirely too long since our last rendezvous, don't you agree, *Rourke*?"

I tore my gaze from her as Rourke lunged at Valdov.

He stopped himself a foot shy of the vampire, who hadn't even so much as blinked at Rourke's sudden reaction. "How dare you bring her into my woods, *vampire*," Rourke raged. "We all know you are a weakling, forever hiding beneath the folds of your Queen's skirts, but hiring werewolves and witches to do your bidding? That is a new low, Valdov, even for a vampire rat like you."

The witch in question, because she obviously wasn't a shifter, seemed bored. She picked at her nails as she planted her feet directly in front of both the angry vampire and a molten Rourke. When she was firmly rooted into place, she placed her hands on her hips and drummed her fingers against her teensy studded waist.

She was absolutely stunning.

What a total bitch. I can't wait to wipe that insipid smile right off her lips. My wolf snarled in agreement.

She was flawless, like a porcelain doll, complete with a set of perfectly pouty heart-shaped lips and high, rounded cheekbones.

Leaning forward, she purred into Rourke's ear, "I'm a Sorceress, not a witch, darling. But you already knew that, didn't you? Did you miss me?" When he kept his eyes fastened on Valdov, she seemed mildly put out. "I don't work for vamps," she spat. "But, my dear, I wouldn't have missed this party for the world—and you know how I *love* a good party. And if the Queen wants to part with a few trinkets in the end, who am I to challenge her generosity?"

Rourke didn't so much as breathe in her direction.

It was a damn good thing, because if he had my wolf would've thrown down all over her perfect tiny ass.

The witch brought her hand to Rourke's face, her dark red nails flashing as she slowly caressed the back of her knuckles down his cheek. "What's the matter, kitten? Wolf got your tongue?" She laughed, a perfectly pitched voice tinkling like bells on a hot summer night.

My wolf surged in me so fiercely, my claws formed to vicious points and my incisors dropped instantly. I managed to hold her back before it went any further, but only because Rourke still hadn't responded. *Just wait! We can't do this yet!* If I freed my wolf, the whole yard would go ballistic and we would likely die. We were going to have to shift at some point, but it had to be exactly right. *We still have to assess the situation. We don't know what that witch is capable of, but I'm sure it's something terrible, because Rourke is wary of her. Maybe if we stall long enough backup will arrive.* I knew that was wishful thinking. "Daddy" and his band of werewolves would clearly be our ace in the hole tonight.

My wolf snapped the air repeatedly, throwing me a graphic picture of her teeth sinking into the Sorceress's hands, the same ones that had just traced down our mate's face, and ripping them apart. *Right on, but let's hold on to that thought for just a few more minutes.* She snarled her answer, clearly not on my side of the waiting game. She did have a point. Every molecule in my being detested that red-haired bitch on sight, even before she'd approached, and seemed to know, my mate. Now I wanted to kill her and watch her die a slow, painful death.

Mine.

Rourke's body trembled with rage. His scent was so strong and menacing a few of the wolves in the clearing took a step back. "*Selene*," he snarled. "I will give you five minutes to get out of my sight. You made a grave mistake coming here tonight and aligning yourself with the *vampires*. If you don't leave right now, I will kill you this time. I swear it."

This time? Selene? The Lunar Goddess? The Grand Patron of magic and witchcraft? Surely he wasn't talking about *that* Selene.

"Oh, Rourke, don't be such a party pooper." She snickered. "I'm not only going to stick around, but I'm going to enjoy this little show more than anything I've done over the last… um…millennium…and that includes *you*, lover." She tapped the edge of her fingernail into his chest.

Rourke was a statue. He didn't move a muscle, or even

pretend to look her way. *He's not paying attention to her. Calm down. We'll bite her fingers off soon.*

Selene's voice changed to a shrill. "Did you really think I would *ignore* what you did to me? Let you just go about your *business* without some sort of revenge?" She leaned in close, her anger searing. "Listen to me when I say this, Rourke. This time it will be *you* who will pay. And I'm planning to start with this little wench over here." She nodded frivolously at me like I was nobody. "Then I'll move on to bigger and better things." Her irises sparked red to match her hair, naturally. "I *swear* it."

My hackles rose and I growled without any aid from my wolf. Was she kidding? The tension in the air had become unbearable. *Steady*, I told my wolf. *Only a few more seconds.* My blood danced in anticipation. *Then we'll rip her goddamn heart out.*

"Ahem," Valdov broke in. "I do hate to break up this charming little reunion, but we must be off. The sun will be rising and my Queen is anxiously awaiting our return." He turned toward Selene. "Get on with the binding then, witch, and we'll leave you the cat for your troubles."

"I'm not a witch, you filthy bloodsucker, I'm a *Goddess*." She glared, her irises a pure, fiery red now. "Goddess of the Moon, to be exact. Or if you prefer, a powerful Sorceress of Enchantment. Take your pick. But I am most certainly not a *witch*."

It was Valdov's turn to look bored. He flicked his wrist at her. "Just get on with it."

She sneered at him, raising her hands. A low chanting erupted from her lips and her fingertips began to glow.

Christ, the plan was to have the Sorceress bind me? So the vamps could whisk me away to hell knows where?

I don't think so, dollface.

But before I could react, Rourke roared, whipping his powerful leg around, striking Selene squarely in the chest with the force of a Mack truck. At the same time, he swiped his curved hand, full of claws, at Valdov's throat, just missing the vampire by a millimeter as he slid out of the way.

Selene flew into the darkness with a satisfying crash.

It would be wishful thinking that she'd somehow find her true death on the side of a boulder, but it was fun to hope. She'd likely return unscathed within moments, no doubt terrifying us with her scorn. Rourke had effectively stopped her spell in its tracks, however, which had been his intention. But there were plenty more spells where that came from.

We were going to have to work fast to eliminate the vampires and exit this mad scene before the wolves shifted and the Porcelain Doll from Hell shook off her injuries.

"Now you're going to pay with your sorry little life, Valdov." Rourke sprang at the vampire, catching hold of his cape before he could escape.

The wolves around us howled in unison and dropped to the forest floor to make their change.

Now.

My wolf responded in a rush of delicious power, adrenaline shooting like a fire hydrant through my veins. My wolf was ready and my partial change into my Lycan form was almost instantaneous. My muscles transformed into a thick, hard mass coated with smoky fur. My throat issued a deep snarl and I stood taller within seconds. My muzzle expanded to accommodate my canines.

I focused on Rourke. The fight between him and Valdov was happening so fast I could barely track it, even in my new, enhanced form.

The other vamps stood off to the side, still cloaked, watching Valdov with seemingly little interest. They didn't appear anxious to join the party.

I stalked forward, keeping an eye out for Selene. I was in the mood to do some damage, and my plan was to start with the vamps, even if they hadn't joined in yet. The wolves would be up in a few moments, and Rourke and I would need to be free of the vamps before we could fight the wolves and have a chance to get away.

I was almost to the group, who didn't even seem to notice my advance, when a figure barreled out of the trees. It buzzed straight toward me with menace and it wasn't Selene.

It was a werewolf in human form, and the anger coming ahead of him was intense.

It only took me an instant more to recognize him.

My eyes narrowed.

Traitor.

My wolf howled.

I could taste his hate as he approached. It was dry and rancid, like something dead. My wolf danced in a rage. There was nothing a werewolf abhorred more than a loss of honor.

I called to him as he came forward, my vocal cords rough but audible. "Well, well, I guess I'm not surprised to see you here. You've always detested me, so I guess it makes sense. Do you like what you see, Stuart?" I snarled, delighted as he gave me pause, his eyes widening a flicker before he recovered. "You filthy piece of shit," I growled. "You're lucky my father's not here to rip your sorry head from your shoulders. He'd make damn sure you understood the depth of your betrayal." I grinned, flashing him my new, lengthy canines. "But lucky you, you get me instead."

Stuart Lauder, son of Hank, looked at me, his furor bubbling over. "You're an abomination," he foamed. "A blight on the great race of werewolves. You've always been a freak, and it was just a matter of time before you brought the whole race down. I'm not about to let that happen. I chose to take a stand. Not even my father was brave enough to stand up, but I am." He spat on the ground. "The old generation was content to wait, sitting on their asses with their thumbs in their mouths, until you finally ended us. But the next generation of wolves aren't going to sit back and take it. We're ready to rise up and fight as one united Pack, *one* force. We're not going to wait around until it's too fucking late and you destroy us all." He halted a few paces from me, his yellow eyes firing, brown fur sprouting along his forearms.

"Stuart, this is your war, not mine. You're bringing the race down by pitting wolves against each other because of your own stupid fear. It has nothing to do with me. I'm not a threat to any wolf. And do you honestly think our Pack—excuse me, *my* Pack—isn't going to win? The Southern wolves are no match in strength to us. They never have been. You picked the losing side, asshole." I liked the sound of my voice; it sounded tough, like I ate rocks for breakfast. "The Northern Territories are stronger, and we will remain strong. There's no contest. You are going to die for absolutely nothing, not that I give a shit, mind you, I'm just pointing out the facts."

He sneered. "These aren't the Southern wolves, you dog bitch in heat, these are the *New Order wolves*."

Not the Southern wolves? *Who the hell are the New Order wolves?*

I tried to process what he said.

Stuart laughed at my confusion. "That's right, we are the new order of things. The wolves you see before you have gathered from all over the world to unite as *One Pack*. And we *will* dominate, make no mistake about it. We are stronger, and when the dust settles all the other wolves who weren't brave enough to join us before will be forced to join us, or die," he proclaimed. "The old generation is officially over and the new generation has begun. We hold the power."

"The power to pimp yourselves out to the vamps and witches, you mean? You're delusional," I replied. "Do the *Newbies* enjoy playing backup to the creatures of the night? Or do they prefer the role of pandering seeing-eye dog to the witches?"

He gave me a wicked smile, his incisors growing longer by the second. "The *New Order* will do whatever it takes to get the job done."

He jumped.

I swatted him away like a fly.

He rolled several feet and was back up.

"You mistake my femininity for weakness, Stuart." I laughed. "Now get over here, you slimy piece of shit, and fight me like a wolf... Excuse me, an oh so powerful *New Order* wolf."

Even though he pulsed with the change, he would be incapacitated for a few precious moments if he chose to shift. More than enough time for me to kill him, and we both knew it.

He circled me slowly. "You're not stronger than me. I can fight you in my human form just fine."

"Suit yourself, asshole." I lashed at him, my claws tearing right through his shirt, drawing thick dark furrows of blood. "Looks like you're going to get cut. Or do the New Kids on the Block need to put on their chest protectors before they fight?"

Loathing filled his eyes. "I don't need *any* protection from you. I could kill you with one hand tied behind my back."

"Let's find out." I beckoned him with a curl of my claw.

He sprang. We went a few rounds, him managing to land an occasional blow and me making sure it hurt on the return. The wolves had begun to finish their shifts and stalked around us, forming a tight circle. I was surprised they hadn't jumped into the fray, but I was thankful.

Stuart was quick and played dirty and he was stronger than any human, but it was almost too easy for me. My wolf hung back in my mind, leaving me to fight since he hadn't shifted. But she did let me know with a rousing bark when I landed a particularly good shot.

He stumbled backward again as I landed another powerful blow to his chest. "Had enough yet, Stuart? Or would you like to take a little break?" I taunted.

He bled profusely from his face and chest. The wolves around us snarled in earnest, snapping their jaws and rending the air in their impatience. The scent of their combined aggression threatened to short-circuit me a few times, but my wolf parceled the scents away as quickly as she could, saving me from complete overload. Getting used to this scent thing was crazy intense.

The entire time I'd been tussling with Stuart, Rourke fought a snickering Valdov. The vampire moved too quickly, and was proving hard to catch. Rourke bellowed as he threw the vampire to the ground, only to have him pop up again in a new spot laughing it off.

I needed to tie this up with Stuart quickly, because it was going to take both of us to finish off Valdov—if that was even possible. Then we had the other vamps to contend with, but so far none of the other cloaked wonders had joined the melee. They stood off to the side watching. I had no idea why, but I hoped it wasn't because they were so powerful this fight looked like a romper room brawl. They must be following orders of some kind.

I wasn't going to stop fighting. Wolves didn't go down without a fight. Our instinct to win was ingrained too deeply. When Stuart stopped, I responded, "What's the matter, Stuart? Not willing to die for your new cause?"

Blood dripped from a gash on his forehead into his eye. He swiped it away with the back of his hand. "You're the one who's gonna die, bitch. Even if you manage to take me down, these wolves here are going to rip you to shreds." To emphasize his point, several of the wolves snapped their teeth in agreement.

It'd actually been a miracle they hadn't joined in thus far. The smell of blood and fear was a fuse to the powder-keg trigger of their base instincts. They must have had some military connection to their leadership, enough power to make sure they stayed in line. Either that or Stuart had given them some previous command. But either way, the wolves around us were staying put and I wasn't going to argue.

"Aren't your new employers going to be pissed when your New Order wolves tear me to pieces? I thought when you took on a job as the 'hired help' you were supposed to honor your contract? Oh, wait... I'm sorry, I said the word 'honor' by accident." I tried to even my tone for the last part, to make sure it hit home. "That word obviously has no meaning to you."

"I have *honor*!" he screamed, his lips curling in a feral way. "Which is why I'm going to enjoy killing you so much. We don't work for the vamps, you filthy slut, we struck a mutually beneficial *alliance*. We just happened to get to you first." He shrugged. "The Queen will just have to deal with it."

He kicked out with his leg, landing a blow high to my thigh. I rolled twice, the two wolves nearest me nipping and growling, and was up on my toes. I circled Stuart, trying to figure out the best move to end this quickly, when a soft flutter hit my brain.

It immediately intensified and I waited, circling more. But nothing but dead space came through. I pushed out. *Dad?*

Nothing.

I pushed out again. *Tyler?*

Jessica! Thank gods! Tyler screamed. *I've been trying to get through for the last twenty minutes. We're almost to you; we were a lot closer than I'd thought. Your scent is all over the place down here, even with the fucking sulfur shit plugging our noses. We've all changed already. I can smell the goddamn Southern wolves too.* I felt his energy and his speed as he ran. My brother could run twice as fast as any other wolf. He would be here in a moment.

Tyler, the wolves aren't Southe—I lost the connection as Stuart leapt, my brain switching back to full fight mode, slamming the door on all other thoughts. I gave a hoarse shout and threw my weight at Stuart's oncoming body. We clashed in the middle. He gave a strangled yell as my claws tore into his neck, slashing at his jugular. I was more than ready to be done with him. "I'm finished playing with you, Stuart. It's time for you to die."

He staggered back, his hands grasping at his throat, trying in vain to stanch the wound. His mouth moved but produced no sound.

"It's too bad you won't be here to see your New Kids get annihilated." I walked up to him as he fell to his knees. "Yep, that's right. The Northern wolves—*my* Pack—are on their way up the hill right now. These wolves here don't stand a chance. I don't care where you dug them up from, they're all going to die."

Stuart clutched his neck with both hands, blood flowing freely down his shirt. I crouched next to him. "Was it worth it, Stuart?" I rasped. "Was betraying your Pack and everything you stood for worth an ending like this?"

Something lit in his eyes and he dropped both hands to his sides, blood racing from his throat. The side of his mouth went up in a half-crazed smile as he struggled to find words. "You . . . *ack* . . . are going to die . . . bitch." His teeth were stained a dark red. He tried to laugh but fell short, instead he coughed up more blood. "You...have no idea...*ack*...what's...waiting for you. You are...the true daughter of...Cain..."

A slashed jugular wasn't enough to kill him, but this would be. With a scream, my wolf slid into the driver's seat and my hand shot out like a lance. She tore the rest of this throat out in one swift motion, spine and all. He collapsed in a heap at my feet.

We were both so focused on the now dead Stuart that neither of us processed the other snarls.

A roar of fury erupted. "Jessica! *Fight!*" Rourke raced toward me at full speed. Valdov stood just behind him wearing a wicked grin, seemingly no worse off than he'd been before.

The wolves, who'd crept in closer while I'd watched Stuart die, shifted their attention for a brief second on the new threat barreling straight at them. A few of them turned, choosing their aggressor over their prey.

But most stayed completely focused on me.

This was going to be a Pack attack.

The lesser wolves would wait for the most dominant to spring first, and then they would all gleefully join in the fun of tearing me to pieces.

Rourke reached the first wolf in the circle, picked him up like he weighed nothing, and tossed him away like a bag of garbage. He was moving toward another when a loud crashing noise sounded from the woods behind us.

The wolves halted their forward progression, lifting their heads in unison, scenting the new threat.

Tyler launched himself into the clearing like a missile fired from a cannon.

He was beautifully powerful in his wolf form, and more than a foot taller than any of the wolves around us. His face was set in a gruesome snarl, his eyes flashing with an eerie menace promising swift retribution. There was a reason he was an unparalleled fighter. Few wolves were his equal. By the change in scent around me, every one of them knew it too.

Tyler tossed his head and gave a terrifying howl.

Within moments, our other Pack wolves returned his song. By the sound of it, they were only a short distance away.

The cavalry had officially arrived.

The wolves around me snapped and snarled, furious at the sudden intrusion. One of them lunged forward, his teeth latching on to my arm. His fangs sank deeply into my flesh. I'd been half hoping they'd all run with their tails between their legs when my brother had arrived in all his glory, but by the looks of the teeth embedded in my arm, they clearly weren't going to be easily swayed from their target.

I twisted my body, dragging the wolf along with me, my Lycan form incredibly strong, grabbing on to its scruff with my other hand so my arm didn't get shredded, and flung it straight into another oncoming wolf who was vying for a piece of me.

My arm was torn and bleeding, but more sweet energy raced through me, dispelling the pain quickly. My body rushed to fix the damage, and I was grateful.

Rourke was three feet from me, fighting the other wolves in the circle. "Is that all you got?" he roared again as he grabbed another wolf by his throat, cracking its neck with more physical power than I'd ever seen a supernatural being possess without changing. "You will not fuck with me or mine! Do you hear me?" He shook the wolf and tossed it away.

I lowered my body into a fighting stance, putting my back to Rourke's. A savage growl rent the air from somewhere above me and I tilted my head to catch Tyler as he crashed down onto the pile of wolves in front of me, scattering them as effectively as if he'd dropped a load of dynamite. He grabbed the nearest one in his jaws and gave a powerful snap.

Two wolves inched in around him, and advanced toward me intent on harm. They saw their opportunity and they weren't going to miss it. *We got this*, I told my wolf. She happily agreed. *No need for the boys to have all the fun.*

They both vaulted at the same time, springing in tandem.

I flicked the switch in my mind, handing the reins to my wolf. She howled once and sent us to the ground, skillfully turning and lashing in a motion I couldn't track in my human mind. *Thank goodness, you're in charge.* The two were back on us in a flurry of motion. I shot my fists out, grabbing them both by the throats before they could sink their teeth into my neck. My arms were strong—stronger than they should be—and I marveled for a moment. This really shouldn't be this easy. I was holding back two rabid wolves, one in each hand.

Am I stronger than yesterday? No time to ponder.

Before I could reposition myself, one of them flew backward out of my grasp. It yelped once before its voice abruptly cut off. A moment later the other went in the opposite direction. I stared up to find a furious Rourke, eyes so green they appeared like pools of glowing phosphorus.

He stared down at me, scanning my body for damage.

A thin coat of fur had erupted along his arms, and his nails were curled into sharp hooks, but other than that he hadn't changed. His control was astounding. His muscles literally bounced under his skin as he reached down to pull me up. I grabbed on to his extended hand and noticed the beautiful tattoos covering his forearms had melded perfectly into the patterns of his fur.

His eyes met mine and my heart leapt into my throat. *War-*

rior of Old. Without a doubt, it was true. What was he? "What are you?" I breathed.

He looked at me curiously and I realized he was seeing me for the first time in my Lycan form. Surprise crept along his features, but we didn't have time to discuss it. "I'm yours," he said simply.

I didn't push it, because there was a new commotion in the woods and my fur jumped to attention, this time in happy relief. The four vampires, who had watched the fight but had never participated, took off in a single *whoosh*, leaving Valdov standing alone.

My father's eyes blazed a blinding amethyst, looking starkly dangerous against the jet black of his fur as he thundered across the clearing in all his glory. He was so dark he absorbed everything around him.

Nine of his wolves, including James, spread in a V just behind him, all of them terrifyingly beautiful in their true forms. Some of the New Order wolves, or whatever they called themselves, crept slowly back into the shadows, obviously unprepared or unwilling to take on this new threat. Tyler growled and snapped at the retreating wolves, but held still, awaiting the next command of his Alpha.

My father was deathly focused on Valdov.

Not a muscle rippled under his fur. His lips curled in clear distaste, revealing his massive canines. A threatening rumble issued from deep within, an abyss of anger boiling under the surface.

"Callum," Valdov said briskly. "How very lucky you could join us. It's entirely too bad you're too late, after all the hard work it took you to get here."

Rourke's hand slipped into mine, squeezing as he pulled me

close again. There was an urgency in his grasp, and I glanced to my right following his gaze.

Selene leaned casually against a tree with her arms crossed in front of her, clearly amused by the new turn of events. I'm sure she'd been hoping the New Order wolves would do her dirty work for her, sparing her from chipping her pretty nails killing me herself.

We both watched as she pushed off the tree and strode confidently into the mix. Her mane flowed behind her, her eyes blinking with the first hint of red. It appeared her flight into the forest hadn't left a scratch on her. *Damn.* Seeing that creamy porcelain skin marred would've been incredibly satisfying.

But she wasn't the one standing next to Rourke, his possessive growl telling the world not to fuck with what was his.

I smiled.

I already had what she wanted most.

She sashayed over to Valdov, who looked like he'd eaten the canary as well as the whole cage. She'd clearly been his ace in the hole the entire time, and he wasn't shy about letting us all know.

"You see, Callum, it seems my Queen has invoked the favor of a *Sorceress* this time," Valdov told my snarling father in a singsong lilt. "If you so much as move one furry paw in my direction, I will have the lovely Selene strike your darling offspring dead where she stands. Are we very clear? Or shall I repeat?"

My father turned his massive head slowly toward Selene. His power rushing outward in one solid beat, making every molecule in my being leap. All of his wolves responded to it in kind. We all bared our fangs and made terrifying noises. Our Alpha had control, and we would follow. I snarled fiercely.

How Stuart and his band of ingrates thought they could

possibly take the most powerful Alpha who'd ever lived was beyond me.

My father was magnificent.

Selene kept her cool, ignoring his steady, piercing gaze as she stopped next to the vampire. Only an infinitesimally small quiver of her hands gave her away. Her fingers were already glowing with a spell, so the red tremor had been easy to detect. She steeled herself for a moment before glancing up to meet my father's stare, her face wearing the same haughty expression she'd donned before.

Honestly, Rourke had fallen for that?

"Come on, big bad wolf. Give me something to play with here," she toyed. "There's nothing on earth I'd rather do tonight than annihilate your entire bloodline. Why don't you come over here and get me?"

My father watched her, his gaze unfaltering.

"Where's the huff and puff, fella? Not so tough when a Sorceress is involved?" Selene taunted. "I thought you'd be a pansy. I guess I was right."

Tyler surged forward in a volley of snarls and barks.

Selene turned a lazy glance toward him and tinkled. "Oh, does your little wolf boy want to be first instead? How very noble of him."

My father snapped his muzzle once. Tyler stopped like someone had pulled a plug on his vocal cords.

"That's a good doggie," she crooned. "You should listen to your daddy more often." Selene turned to face my father again. "Honestly, wolf, you need to keep your pups on a tighter leash. My fingers are especially twitchy tonight and I wouldn't want any . . . *mistakes* to happen."

As far as I knew, Selene couldn't fight off multiple wolf attacks, even as a self-proclaimed Goddess. Sure, she could kill me, and maybe a few more, but she couldn't kill them all before they managed to tear her apart. Werewolves were resistant to magic as a rule, but not immune. Someone as powerful as Selene could inflict major damage before the strongest ones ripped her to pieces.

I wasn't sure if my father would be affected by her magic, but I wasn't willing to chance it. She wanted me, she could have me.

I made a move to step forward.

Rourke yanked me back to his side immediately. "Don't move, Jessica," he ordered in a harsh whisper. "Selene is unbelievably dangerous. She'll kill you if she gets the chance. Even if it means her own life is forfeit—she'll do it just to spite me. I'm not going to allow that to happen."

I locked eyes with him. This was not a good time for an in-depth discussion on the ins and outs of "allowing" me to do anything. "Rourke," I whispered, "I'm not going to stand back and let her kill my family without a fight. You can't stop me from doing that even if you tried, so don't take it too hard. If the vamps want me, they can have me, but I'm not going to let my family—or my *Pack*—go down because of me."

Right then my brain shattered into a million pieces.

The pressure of the fracture was so strong I reached out blindly and grabbed on to Rourke's arm to steady myself. He kept me upright automatically and without question.

Jessica! My father raged. *Jessica! Drop your barriers* right now!

My barriers? What barriers?

Dad...I'm here! I'm here! I clutched my head with my hand. A sledgehammer would've been gentler. The ache was incredible. Rourke held me firmly around the waist as he growled his alarm. *I think you just shattered any barriers I had left. I'm sorry. I didn't know they were up. I have no idea what I'm doing or how I'm keeping them up in the first place.*

Jessica, listen to me right now. You have to get out of here. Don't worry about Selene. Take Rourke with you and run. I can't let them take you. I won't allow it. If you leave now, we can corner the vampire and deal with the Sorceress. Do you understand me?

Dad, I can't—

Run, GODDAMN it!

My blood seized at the command and I latched on to the front of Rourke's shirt. He understood at once, pushing me ahead of him as fast as he could, his back blocking the sounds of my Pack as they jumped as one on the vampire and the Sorceress.

We'd only made it into the woods a few feet when I pulled up quickly, Rourke rocking into me from behind, his arms circling my body protectively.

There, lurking all around us, were wolves. More wolves than I could count. Each one baring their teeth, their yellow eyes dancing with excitement. There were twice as many wolves in the shadows than had been in the clearing. We could not take them on and survive.

Rourke pulled me closer and twisted us around, putting his back to the growling wolves.

Before we could come up with a concrete plan, there was a long, angry howl behind us.

Tyler.

I broke out of Rourke's grasp and ran. He pounded right behind me.

I tumbled into the clearing to a completely unbelievable sight. Valdov stood over my father, his bony finger extended, tapping my father's still muzzle like a naughty child. The rest of the Pack snarled and paced around them, too uncertain of the vamp's intent to react. None were willing to jeopardize their Alpha in any way. James howled the loudest, his anger searing the air. He was fierce in his wolf form, with a coat of blue-gray and nearly as tall as my father. It killed him not to act.

My father was locked in some kind of binding spell.

Selene looked smug, and a wave of indignant rage swirled inside me. My wolf let out a sorrowful howl, followed by a nasty snarl. I gnashed my teeth.

"Ah, Callum. Did you honestly think we would come unprepared after the last time we met?" Valdov tsked. "It looks like you're woefully outnumbered this time, and desperately unprepared for this battle. Oh well, better luck next time. We will be taking your daughter now, but don't fret overly much. I will make sure she's kept . . . *alive.*" He grinned, flashing his fangs. "At least for the time being anyway."

My father's fury raged through my veins. I felt it as clearly as if it were my own. My wolf responded with a yelp of anger.

I was still in my partial form, but a new blast of adrenaline rocked through me. I grinned. *Let's take them down.* My wolf ripped her jaws in the air.

Almost as if Valdov had read my mind, he turned to Selene, who'd been lurking a few feet away. "Enough playing, witch! Now do the deed we came for and we will be gone!"

I turned my gaze on Selene for the first time. A line of blood trickled down the side of her mouth, marring her perfection nicely.

Then I noticed something at her feet.

Tyler lay unmoving.

I strode forward, snapping, my wrath blinding me to anything else. I wanted her away from my family. "How dare you!" I shouted. "Why don't you come and get me! I'm the one you want. Or are you too scared I'll kick your sorry ass from here to the unknown? Come on, you bitch. *Fight me!*"

Selene tipped her head back and laughed. "Oh, please. This is just too easy." She glanced caustically at the fallen wolf by her foot and kicked him. Hard. "Oh, did crippling your little brother tie your undies in a bunch? Or is it Daddy over there frozen with no place to go? *Hmm?* Well, I'm sure I can finish this one off"—she gestured downward—"right after I finish *you.*"

She lifted her fingers and started chanting.

"Is that all you've got, Selene?" I sneered as I stalked forward, not caring anymore. "Too afraid to meet me without your fingers twitching? I'm not exactly surprised, since you look like the weakest piece of ass I've seen in a long time. Looks like you'd be hard pressed to keep a man interested long enough for a second run. I'm sure Rourke got tired of you the moment after he fu—"

"*Enough,*" she screamed. "You're going to pay for that!" She flicked her wrist.

I dodged her spell, feinting to the side at the last moment, but I turned, watching in horror as the shimmering lines hit Rourke, who had been standing just behind me.

"*No!*" I screamed, grabbing a hold of him before he crumpled to the ground. I dropped beside him, my fingers seeking his pulse. It was still there, thank goodness. He wasn't dead. I had no idea if the spell would kill him, but he was breathing.

I lifted my head slowly.

My lids burned as my eyes flashed a strobe of color. A vicious howl rose in my throat. "No, you have it wrong, Selene. It's *you* who will pay."

Nothing else existed. My wrath was a thick, throbbing haze. I strode straight ahead, my wolf racing back and forth in my mind waiting to tear her to pieces. Not even Selene's tinkling laugh daunted me.

I was almost to her when a flicker of fear finally registered in her eyes. She gathered herself quickly. "Little mongrel, it's time for you to go nighty-night," she said as she snapped her wrist at me, red lines racing between the few feet separating us. The spell struck me fully, but not before my hand shot out, connecting with her creamy porcelain face. There was a loud crack and she flew backward. My body went rigid.

I fell to the ground.

Red lines began to transverse my mind, streaming through me, her spell binding me.

But there was satisfaction painted on my lips as I watched red drip down her broken face as she staggered to stand. *Take that, you harlot.*

My wolf snapped and tore at the threads growing thicker in my mind as fast as she could, but it was no use. There were too many. The spell was going to overtake me within moments.

The wolves within the trees launched into the clearing and my Pack erupted in battle around me.

Valdov walked over and leaned above me like a circus ringleader, reaching down to caress my face. I cringed inwardly, my body unable to move. "Hurry, witch, she is too strong. This will not hold her for long."

A haughty voice responded, "That will hold her just fine. She is *not* stronger than I am, vampire. You'll have plenty of time to get her back to your precious *Queen*. Now get her out of my sight before I decide to kill her for real."

My body rose in the air.

Wind rushed against my face as Valdov took us into the clouds.

A terrible keening howl bellowed from below.

My father had finally broken his restraints.

22

I heard the noise before I opened my eyes. It sounded like rusty metal fingernails grating down a chalkboard. But worse. My arms bristled before my brain was fully awake. The first thing I became aware of was my wolf, who was crouched low in my mind, a ferocious growl issuing from her mouth.

Do you know where we are? I asked her before I dared open my eyes.

I could feel the threat. The power pushed down on me, oppressing me with its strength, penetrating my skin like a million sharp needles. The surface I was lying on was hard and rough, cold stone under my fingertips. I tried once more. *What's going on? Do you know where we are?*

Then I heard it again.

Scraaaape. Scraaaaape. Scraaaaaaape.

My wolf didn't have a chance to respond before a feminine voice pierced the quiet. It was smooth and held a faint echo. My blood ticked in warning. "Wake, little wolf girl. We are done playing. I grow tired of waiting." The voice was moving closer as it spoke.

I opened my eyes. It was no use pretending, because whatever was in the room with me knew I was already awake and pissing it off wasn't the smart choice. Selene's spell was gone. I had no idea if my wolf had conquered it or not, but I wasn't complaining.

My eyes focused on the ceiling above me. It was shaped in a high dome and decorated completely with stained glass. A soft glow of light ran behind it, radiating outward to give it a multi-dimensional quality. Unfortunately, the images rendered on it were not beautiful flowers or happy unicorns; instead the entire ceiling was covered in a landscape of gruesome, gory scenes—vampires depicted at their very worst, like I'd seen Valdov in that brief but chilling moment. The horde detailed above my head gleefully tore out the necks of their human prey, their faces contorted, blood flowing around them in pools of ecstasy, splashing into the bodies of their unwitting victims.

Wasn't that heartwarming.

I was clearly in a vampire stronghold of some kind, and seeing the artful ceiling depictions didn't do anything to make me feel any better about my situation.

There was movement at my feet and I slowly lifted my head.

"You are not nearly as impressive as I had presumed you to be, little wolf girl." The voice was attached to a vision of flawlessly etched skin. A face so perfectly defined it cast its own shadows. She boasted high, prominent cheekbones and a pair of wide hazel eyes, rimmed in heavy kohl. Her pallor was a true white, making her red lips look garish. A complicated pale mass of curls sat atop her head, giving the illusion of a greater age than her twenty-something looks. She was dressed in a beautiful gray silk gown, so thin it shimmered like liquid silver in the low light. As she approached me, her cape, of the same shimmering fabric, flowed out behind her.

The Vampire Queen.

A lone fingernail traced along the stone altar I was lying on as she paced forward.

Scraaaaaape.

"Um, sorry to disappoint you?" I pushed to my elbows, grateful I hadn't been physically restrained, but knowing it hadn't really been necessary in the company of the Vampire Queen and her plentiful power, which bounced around the room in strong currents. Why did she care if I was impressive or not? I wasn't looking to impress anyone, and to vamps all shifters looked unimpressive. All I cared about was getting the hell out of here in one piece with my skin still attached and all my vital fluids still in my body.

The altar I was lying on was in the middle of an ornate vestibule. The room resembled what I'd envisioned a throne room in a castle to be like, complete with a raised dais and a queenly looking chair perched in the center.

The only other people in the room were the two shrouded shapes flanking either side of the massive, and precisely decorated, door.

A private meeting with the Vampire Queen, it seemed.

She stopped a few feet in front of me and waited, her features unmoving, her head tilted at a slight angle.

I had no idea what I was supposed to do, so I raised myself to a full sitting position, with my hands bracing my weight behind me. When I was done, I met her eyes for a brief second and was rewarded with a bolt of power so strong my nails curled into the stone beneath me, gouging little moon-shaped grooves into the rock.

My wolf was issuing fairly erratic sounds in my mind, ones I hadn't heard her make before. *Easy there. We don't want to freak the Freak too soon.* Instead of answering, she responded with a small flow of adrenaline. It ran through my veins, calming me, but it wasn't enough to trigger anything. *Perfect. Just relax. We'll get out of this. We aren't tied up, and nobody else is here.* Specifically the horrid Valdov. *If she wanted us for breakfast, we'd be shackled in her dungeon or sucked dry by now.* This place so had a dungeon.

"Valdov was a fool to bring you here," the Vampire Queen snapped. She was still examining me, her eyes measuring. I felt like I was under a vampire microscope.

Huh? "From what he implied to us," I retorted, "he was only following your direct orders."

"Fool," she grated. Then she turned abruptly, ascending the steps of her dais toward her gilded chair. She whipped around with a flourish and sat, her gorgeous face set in a frown, her cape flowing gracefully around her.

Hmm. Instead of watching her brood, I brought my legs around and perched myself on the edge of the altar. I wiggled my bare toes and looked down at my filthy, torn clothing, still reeking heavily of sulfur and sweat.

The perfect picture of badass.

I had no idea what she wanted from me, but other than sensing her incredible power, I wasn't feeling the threat of imminent danger. Having her irked at Valdov worked in my favor. I just didn't know why. Someone like Valdov did what he was told. Always. I decided to venture a question. "If Valdov was disobeying you, then why am I here?" I asked.

The Queen narrowed her eyes at me like a hawk. A fleck of mercury sparked in their depths so brightly it seared like a white flame. She stood abruptly and strode forward, stopping at the edge of the steps to look down on me. I instinctively leaned back.

"Do not push me, little wolf girl. I am not something to be trifled with so easily. If you provoke me, I promise I will punish you. You are here because I wished it and nothing more." She waved her hand in a sweeping dismissal. The vamps liked their hand gestures.

You just said Valdov was a fool for bringing me here. I said instead, "I'm not trying to trifle with you, um ... *Queen*." What in the hell was I supposed to call her? "I'm just trying to figure out why a newborn wolf would warrant such an interest from you. By all rights, I should be beneath your notice. If what I know of our races are true, I shouldn't even be a blip on your radar. Our separate Sects haven't made it a habit to be involved in each other's business at any point in time."

Her voice rang out in a cold laugh. "You, little wolf girl, are very *much* my business." She floated down the steps. "My trusted servants have been keeping tabs on you since your very *untimely* birth." The vamps had been tailing me for that long? She laughed. "What? You think your father could hide you from us? The birth of a *female*? Never!"

Her eyes flickered dangerously between the purest silver to black, and back again. She came to a halt a few paces in front of me, clasping her hands in front of her torso like a demure schoolgirl. She might look the part if I wasn't hyper aware she could snap my neck between her two index fingers in the space of a sneeze.

"What exactly do you mean by 'untimely'?" I asked. "I wasn't aware there *was* a good time for a female werewolf to be born."

She inclined her head, peering at me closely. I shifted

uncomfortably, hating the feel of her weighted stare—it made my skin crawl. Then she tilted her head to the side, like a bird listening for a worm, just like Valdov had. Vamps were totally creepy. Every movement they made was unnatural. There was no way the Queen went out in public. Very little about her resembled anything human.

She abruptly straightened her neck and a wicked smile crept over her unsightly red lips. "You do not know what you are, do you, little wolf girl?"

"I have no idea what you're talking about," I answered. "What do you mean, 'what I am'? I'm a lone female in an all-male race—a freak, an anomaly, something to fight about." I was leaving out the violet eyes, the Lycan abilities, and communication via brain waves with my sibling, but she shouldn't know any of that. She couldn't possibly know about that.

Her canines were retracted, because when she opened her mouth in a macabre kind of glee all I saw were rows of straight, neat teeth. "I had not thought it was possible for you to be— how shall I say?—*unaware* of your...situation." She put her hands together in a pseudo clap and paced away from me, toward a mural of torture painted along one huge wall. Lovely. "This is very interesting indeed. It puts us in a decidedly different position."

I didn't like the eerie glint coming from her voice and neither did my wolf. *What's going on? Do you know what she means by my "situation"?* My wolf paced agitatedly. She raised her hackles and continued to emit a low growl, essentially telling me this wasn't exactly the right time for a heart-to-heart. I took the hint.

That the Vampire Queen knew more about me than I did was less than optimal. It was actually sucky, and put me at a huge disadvantage. "It seems I'm at a bit of a loss here. If you could—" I started.

"They come." Her head snapped to the doorway and the two shrouded figures simultaneously drifted toward her.

"Who's coming?" How long had I been out anyway? I looked around, but there were no clues to what time it was.

"I have little interest in starting a war with your...*kind*." She curled her lips. "But I am very certain we will meet again, little wolf girl, and that time may be very soon indeed."

My kind? There was some faint commotion coming from outside the room now. My heart sped up. It took me a second, but the final puzzle pieces of my kidnapping snapped clearly into place. Valdov hadn't mistaken his Queen's request. His plan had simply been foiled by a rather large and furious Alpha werewolf. If my father hadn't arrived on the scene, I'd probably be cuffed in a dungeon right now being snacked on like a canapé.

I was tired and pissed off. So far my Pack had gone to war, I'd been hunted down and taken by the vampires, a splinter werewolf group was highly organized with a detailed plot to kill me, Selene the Evil had struck down my new mate, whom my body ached for right this minute, and to top it off, it all pointed to me being exactly what everyone had always feared I'd be: The End of Things as We Knew It.

I wanted no part of it anymore.

Shouts echoed along the corridor, coming closer every second. I glanced at the Queen, who seemed to be entranced by the commotion, apparently gearing up for the werewolves to bang her door down. She'd forgotten me, or I was beneath her notice, either one worked.

My voice came out in a snarl, surprising us both. "Hey, Queen." Her head shot to me in a snap. "I take it when my father arrived in the woods it put quite a crimp in your plans to blame my unfortunate 'disappearance' on the *New Order* wolves—or whatever the traitors are calling themselves?"

Her eyes narrowed to slits.

"Isn't that how all this was supposed to shake out? I bet it took some patience on your part to incite fear over the years to a few well-placed wolves to form your precious 'alliance.' But it's not an alliance at all, is it? You've been running the show the whole time, orchestrating your puppets along the way."

"The witch has taken your *lover*," she hissed, completely surprising me once again. Then I watched in horror as her features changed ever so slightly as they began to slide down her face, and then, without warning, her power hit me fully in the chest like a bolt. I doubled over instantly, gasping for breath, clutching my front.

Holy shit she's powerful.

"*You pathetic little girl*," she spat. "You tarry where you do not belong. You do not *question* me. I only allow you to sit here—*a weakling of a shifter*—with the air still in your lungs because I deem it to be so. You should be prostrate on your knees in homage to my kindness. I will not tolerate your insolence, and I certainly do not answer to you for my actions."

I had no time to do anything other than hold my chest and try to breathe again when the doors burst open and my father bounded into the room, followed by, to my relief, James *and* Tyler, and about fifteen other wolves who were unfamiliar to me. All of them in their human form.

"Eudoxia," my father snarled as he strode forward. His wolves fanned behind him, all of them growling.

Crowding into the room just behind the wolves were a large number of vamps, many of whom wore corset-style gowns and tailored jackets with big, shiny buttons. But others were decked out in skinny jeans and hipster shirts. As a group, the vamps ran a serious gamut of style. If Marcy were here, she'd have a field day with the bevy of fashion choices in the room. My best guess was each style choice denoted a rough age of the vamp, because putting an eighteenth-century vamp into a pair of jeggings would take a leap of faith most vampires were likely uninterested in taking. If these vamps were as arrogant as their beloved Queen, each thought their style choice was the right one.

But this wasn't a happy day at court. The vamps bared their fangs, their faces twisted at the intrusion into their lair.

There was also no Rourke. My heart clenched. Our bond had already manifested into something beyond me, beyond my wolf. The physical distance from him was taking a toll already. I craved him in a way I hadn't known could exist in this world.

Eudoxia raised one finger and the mass stilled instantly.

I slid off the altar so I could stand in front of my Pack, my back resting against the rough stone as I fought to shake off the last of the Queen's blast. My wolf had been feeding me power and was still snapping continually at the cloud of residual white mist lingering in my system, which I guessed was the manifestation of the Queen's magic. When my wolf bit down on the cloud, it evaporated into nothing. As the power disappeared, I began to get my strength back. The same thing had happened with Selene's freaky red lines. I had no idea how my wolf was doing it, but I was glad she knew how, because being beholden to magic made me vulnerable.

The Queen, flanked by her guards, marched confidently toward my father, stopping right in front him. "*Callummmm*," she purred. "What a wonderful surprise to see you here. Welcome to my home." She gestured grandly at her room of decorated macabre, the walls and ceiling were accompanied by ornate vases on priceless lacquered sideboards, all of the furnishings ominous in their stark harshness. "Are you not impressed by what you see before you? It's only taken me a few short centuries to get it to my exact liking. Though I'm lately rethinking the color of the velvet drapes. Blood red would go so much better with the furnishings than gold. Don't you agree?"

My father growled in response. "My daughter is coming with me immediately or I will kill you where you stand, Eudoxia. Make no mistake."

"But of course she is," Eudoxia purred again. For the first time, a bit of her Russian accent strayed into her voice. "That was quite understood, was it not? Otherwise, Callum Sèitheach McClain, leader of Wolves, you would have not made it so far into my sanctuary. You must not mistake my leniency at your intrusion for passivity." Her voice became steely, her eyes flashed dangerously as power cloyed the room, filling it with a sticky repulsive sweetness. "You see, very few individuals pass through these doors uninvited and remain . . . *alive.*"

Before my father could answer, she turned on a dime, marching toward me with an air of nonchalance. She reached for my cheek, almost touching me, but pulled short when fifteen wolves ramped up their snarl. It took everything I had not to flinch back.

"Your little wolf daughter"—she angled her head at my father—"and I were just having a chat about a few precious things before she bids us a fond farewell. And you know what? I've just discovered that it's of the *gravest* interest for her to find out where that bad, bad kitty has gone. Is he here with you by chance?" She mocked standing on her tiptoes and looking over the shoulders of the wolves to the back of the room. "*Hmm.* I don't seem to see him," she said, turning with pouted lips to me. "Poor, poor little wolf girl. What are you to do?"

"The cat is of no use to us," my father said slowly, reading her mood carefully.

Pressure pushed into my mind, but nothing came through. My father was trying to communicate, but the room must be spelled in some way. The Queen wouldn't want any communication she couldn't hear among her disciples, and odds were several of the vamps had mind-reading talents. They weren't uncommon among supes. I tried to concentrate on opening up, but it didn't work; all I came up with was dead space.

My father continued out loud, "The cat was taken by the witch soon after my daughter was *kidnapped* by your drone. Once they left, the remaining wolves scattered like thieves."

"Kidnapped is such a strong word, don't you agree?" the Queen replied airily. She positioned herself at the end of the altar, running her hands along it in what could only be considered a loving caress. "I prefer to think of it as merely *borrowing* her for short while. No harm has come to her, as you can plainly see. I blame my curiosity for coveting new things, of course, and a *female* wolf is such a unique thing, don't you agree... Callum?" She met my father's full gaze for the first time. The direct collision of contact between the two put a cringe-worthy burst of energy in the room. Nobody could stare at my father for long, and clearly the Queen had a crazy powerful stare of her own.

The Queen broke contact first. I smiled inwardly.

Not so tough now.

My father continued to stare without answering. She acted unfazed by her misstep, and said instead, "She's a diamond among plain stones, one should think." She waved her hand behind her, dismissing her next thought as she twirled around, floating her way up the dais. "Valdov overreacted, you see. He took my need to gather curiosities quite literally, but I promise you he will be soundly punished for it. In fact, his torture commences as we speak."

"You don't fool me, Eudoxia," my father said, taking a few steps forward to even the gap. I wouldn't have been surprised if he'd actually leapt up on the dais to level the playing field. See-ing Eudoxia shrink back would've been delicious. As an Alpha wolf, instinct dictates you put all your enemies beneath you. Eudoxia being above him had to be infuriating. And she knew it. Instead of leaping, he growled. "I don't know what game you're playing yet, but I promise you it's not a game you will win. The mere act of your henchman taking my daughter, whether it was sanctioned by you or not, gives me the right to declare war on *all* vampires. If I were you, I would consider yourself lucky I'm feeling very magnanimous today. I will not declare war. *This time*." He turned toward me, holding out his hand to me. "Jessica, it's time to go."

I moved forward, not anxious to add anything to this heady mix of power. My chest still stung and I knew drawing myself into it now would be a mistake, especially since it seemed we were leaving with the upper hand.

"It's such a shame your daughter will never lay eyes on her *mate* again." The Queen's voice rang out in a bored tone just as I stepped in front of my father. "Don't you agree? And what was his name again?" She paused, tapping a long silver-coated nail against her lips. "Oh, that's right...silly me...*Rourke*, isn't it?"

My stomach dropped as the wolves behind me lost it.

The Queen smiled, her morbid red lips animated. "Yes, you heard me correctly, little wolf girl," she said. "Your *true mate* won't make it out of Selene's lair alive. He doesn't stand a chance against her. This time she will be well prepared." *This time?* The Queen giggled then. "Most likely Selene is enjoying a nice game of cat and mouse with him right now. Either that or she has him tied to her infamous whipping post already. Whatever it is, she will not let him go again. Ever."

My lungs stopped working as the vision of Selene with her hands on Rourke's body made my nails elongate and a snarl issue from my chest without my consent. At least from what the Queen was telling me, the spell I'd inadvertently let him take hadn't killed him. If it had, Selene would have nothing to torture. *Thank gods he's alive.* My father grabbed on to my arms, effectively pulling my attention from the Queen back to him. "What is this?" he asked quietly, his tone fierce. "Is what she says correct?" Anger flashed in his eyes.

There was no way the Queen could know for sure that Rourke was my mate. She'd been grasping at straws, obviously going on a hunch of Valdov's—but whatever she thought she knew, she'd gotten damn lucky. She'd laid down her ace and now it was my turn to play.

Did I really know for sure? We'd only known each other for such a short period of time. Before I could get my thoughts straight, my wolf slammed her paw down in my mind, snapping fiercely at me. *I know exactly how you feel, how you've felt from the beginning, but are we willing to throw down now and risk everything for him? The Queen clearly wants something from us in return, and it won't come cheaply. If we do this, we go against our Alpha.* She gnashed her teeth at me, no indecision whatsoever.

"Jessica, answer me," my father demanded. The room had gone completely silent.

"Yes, what she says is true." I closed my irises and clenched my fists. "And it seems...my wolf and I are prepared to fight to get him back."

My father focused on me hard, his irises jumping to a deadly amethyst. As we stood together, his hands still gripping my arms, the wolves deathly still, the vamps behind us started to twitter and snicker.

It was a distinct possibility it was happening because we were touching, but my father's blood connection to me suddenly amplified, racing though my bloodstream, triggering jumps and starts like little waves cresting and tiding.

There was no mistaking the Queen's intent to use this information to its fullest. Both my father and I knew it without having to communicate. There would be a steep price to pay before we were allowed to exit these walls if she had anything to say about it.

"When?" my father finally asked, his jaw set tightly.

"It seems my wolf recognized him immediately, but I ignored the cues she was giving me. I didn't realize it until"—*he kissed me senseless*—"I made my full change. The vamps arrived immediately after. There was no time to process anything." Then I said simply, "I will do anything to find him."

The Queen cleared her throat as she descended the steps slowly, reveling in the show. "Dear, dear," she murmured. "This is such a quandary. How will you ever find him on your own?" she mocked. "Do you know where Selene keeps her lair? Or I should say lairs, really. She has a number of preferred haunts, because she is a very powerful Goddess, you know." She placed a bony white hand over her unbeating heart. "But how silly of me. Of course you know she's powerful. She has already defeated you once." But I'd made her bleed. I smiled, remembering. "I'm left wondering how you will ever conquer her and win back your mate all on your own. That seems an immeasurable mountain to climb for what meager strengths you've shown thus far."

"I—"

"She won't be alone." My brother stepped forward, his voice hard and angry. "Her Pack will assist her, as our law dictates." I watched Tyler struggle with the next bit, obviously trying to reconcile a number of things for himself. "We are duty-bound to accept all mates... even if they... even if they're... of a different... *Sect*." He rolled his shoulders back instead of shuddering, and I loved him more in that instant than I ever had. "She will not be alone in her search. Her Pack will assist her."

The Queen glared at the interruption, looking vaguely put upon. "It does not matter in the least if every one of your wolves joins in the hunt, boy." She waved her arm as a dismissal. "You will never find them in time—and even if you manage to bumble your way in, Selene's protection is as vast as a deadly ocean. She will kill you on sight if her multitude of traps don't kill you first." She laughed, bright and hard, tracing her mercury stare to me. "Your only choice, little wolf girl, will be to swear an oath to me for one small favor of my choosing, and I will grant you two of my best and brightest trackers to aid you in your quest. Without them, you will fail. There is no other way."

23

"*Impossible*," my father's voice boomed over the din around us. That one word held incredible power. Everyone quieted whether they wanted to or not. He dropped my arms and marched directly to the Queen. "Werewolves do *not* swear anything to *vampires*. Or anyone else for that matter. We have always fought our own battles and we always will."

"Is that so?" The Queen stayed just out of arm's reach, her accent even thicker now. "Why just last week a pack of mangy wolves, some of your very own precious young, eagerly *swore* their oaths to me. In return, I vowed to track down your daughter and bring her here." She smiled shrewdly. "In fact, they were so taken with themselves, and swore so quickly, they didn't even bother to ask me if I intended to end her life or if I was merely interested in *chatting* with her."

My father's expression stayed stoic, leading me to believe he was already well aware of the fracture across Packs and the new splinter group of wolves. I wondered for the first time where

Hank and some of the younger wolves were, because they weren't here with us now. I know I'd seen Hank in his wolf form behind my father in the clearing. Once he learned I'd ended Stuart's life—his level of hatred toward me would sky-rocket into the upper stratosphere. I wasn't looking forward to seeing how that manifested itself.

"I can assure you, Eudoxia"—my father's voice strummed low and fierce—"the wolves who allegedly *swore* to you were simply rogues and nothing more. They were wolves without honor and no longer members of any Pack. They will be hunted down by our own. No wolf with any notion of self-worth would ever seek the help of vampires. Wolves with honor have always fought their own battles, and we will continue to fight them in the future. No one will be *swearing* anything to you."

"Really, Callum, how very old-fashioned and positively down-right *male* of you. I think you will soon find that persons of the…*feminine* persuasion may feel differently about such things." The Queen turned her bird stare on me. "*Hmm*, little wolf? Are you agreeing with Daddy here? Or do you actually wish to *find* your mate…*alive*?" Her power thrummed through the room.

No more playtime.

I bit the inside of my cheek.

The bitter taste of iron swirled on my tongue. I could feel my father's anger weighing on me. I knew that with our current resources we had no clue how to find a powerful Sorceress quickly, even coupled with Devon's vast computer skills. Wolves con-cerned themselves about wolves. Evil Goddesses, imps, demons, or vamps were completely ignored until a problem arose. Hell, I didn't even know Selene was real until I saw her in the flesh. I'd only heard rumors, but had dismissed them like everyone else.

If I declined the Queen's help, I would be going home cold. It could take me weeks of interviews to come up with any viable way to track Rourke. If Selene had multiple lairs, it would take longer. We had her scent, but could only track her accurately on the ground. If she could fly, which I was assuming without a doubt she could—flight being a credential of card-carrying high-level supes—Evil Goddesses included—by then it would be too late.

I knew it in my bones.

If I played this game correctly, I could bind the Vampire Queen to keep her end of the bargain, which would include *not* killing me. I knew whatever she wanted from me mattered a great deal to her, or we wouldn't be dancing together right now.

I shuddered, knowing the price might be too steep for me to pay, but if I didn't try, I would lose my mate.

"What would it cost me?" I asked the Queen.

"*Jessica*," my father roared. He turned to me, his fury pinging around the room. "I forbid this!" His command swirled in my blood, teasing me at its edges, but it was a command from the Alpha—not a blood-request from my father—and even though it tried to capture me, to make me obey, it didn't hold me. It seemed my father and I had entered into a complicated relationship when we had unwittingly swapped blood. His Alpha commands still did not affect me, but as a father he could manipulate our new blooded bond if he chose. But, clearly right now, as a father he loved me, even if his Alphaness was furious with me. I had to hope that as a father he would ultimately understand what it meant to have a mate and what I had to do to get him back.

"I'm sorry," I said, my voice pleading. "Please forgive me, but I have no other choice. I have to do this or I will lose him. I owe it to him to try."

"Jessica, there is nothing in this world worth binding yourself to them for. We will find your mate on our own, with our own kind." My father's blood danced in my body, rich and angry, but no other command came.

"I will accept that," I said quietly, dropping my eyes, giving him my full submission. "If you can tell me where Selene is right now. Do you, or any of your wolves, know anything about her? If you know where she is, I will follow you from here without pause. I promise to leave this place and never look back. If not, you must understand I must do this."

My father grappled with the knowledge that his Alpha command hadn't taken. The wolves behind us started to become agitated. This would not go unnoticed. I had just defied my Alpha in a very public arena, in front of our enemy.

I had a stark moment of regret.

I was on a very dangerous ground. Everything I'd done so far had screamed something was wrong with me, that I wasn't a normal wolf. The Pack was already fractured, and I was putting them in danger by showing that weakness to our enemy.

My wolf shot to the surface, growling as menacingly as I'd ever seen her. *I know. You don't have to remind me. This is a clusterfuck, and we choose Rourke. It doesn't mean I'm not sorry it turned out this way. We're going up against our Alpha, my father, in front of the whole damn world. It's going to come back and bite us, I know it will. No wolf is going to trust me when they know the Alpha can't control me. It's a big deal.*

She huffed.

I had no other choice. My wolf and my body both demanded I find him. There was no other option. "I can't explain it"— unfamiliar emotion erupted as I spoke—"but I know Rourke only has a short amount of time. If we take too long, I will lose him. Give me another choice, and I will gladly take it." Then I said very, very quietly, "There may be some things in this world worth binding yourself for."

My father ran a hand over his face. He had incredible control, but I could see a faint line of fur erupting on his forearms. He was trying hard to contain himself. I didn't even sneak a glance at the Queen, who was likely elated with her soon-to-be victory.

The wolves behind us growled and shifted uncomfortably. There was also a low murmur running through the crowd of vamps. They weren't familiar with our ways, but they knew enough to know that this interaction between us was wrong. It was likely physically impossible for most of the vamps to go against a direct order from their Queen.

My father still said nothing. My eyes pleaded with him to understand.

After a moment, I felt a shift. His eyes flashed a deep violet, and calmness wove its way through me. He'd made his decision. Whatever it was, I'd have to live with it. His voice was strong and final. "Jessica, you leave me no other choice. If you take this path, you will receive no help from us. You make this choice separate from Pack, acting on your own as an individual." He was giving me an option. He was trying to fix this.

"I understand."

"I can grant you this only because there has been no official ceremony tying you to Pack...*yet*." Not the truth, since I was blood-born and needed no ceremony, but the vamps likely didn't know. "You are still separate from us." He gritted his teeth and forced out, "*This time.* If you are successful in finding your...mate...and return to us alive...you will *immediately* be given the proper ceremonies, and will henceforth be expected to follow Pack Law to the *letter*." His irises flashed, telling me all I needed to know. I would follow orders. "If you fail to do so, you'll be labeled a rogue and cast out. There will be no more chances. My decision on this is final."

That was it.

"I accept those conditions."

My brother strode forward and knelt in front of our father, his head bowed, his voice clear. "I request permission to aid my sister in her quest as a Selective. I will act solely as her human bodyguard. I voluntarily forswear all of my rights as Pack during this journey."

A Selective was a paid position wolves took outside of Pack for extra cash. The jobs usually consisted of some kind of bodyguarding or some other muscle. It was understood a Selective couldn't shift, ever. They could not call any attention to themselves, use any powers, and anything that happened to them on the job wasn't Pack business.

In a nutshell, if you were stupid enough to get yourself into trouble it was all on you.

It was extremely clever of Tyler, and extremely dangerous. He'd be forced to stay human for the duration of the journey. I would never allow it. I started, "Tyler, that's—"

"Granted," my father said before I could finish, clasping Tyler's shoulder as he stood up. "You have my permission to act as a Selective, along with Daniel Walker, if he so desires. All restitutions will be made in full by Jessica on the eve of your return. Our standard hourly rates apply, of course," my father said with his very first hint of a grin.

My father had just hired two bodyguards who would likely cost more than I made in two years.

"I hate to interrupt this adorable family moment," the Queen snapped. "But the sun will be breaking the horizon shortly and we must act quickly if we are to move forward."

I turned toward her and said, "I accept your aid."

The Queen stepped from behind the altar and snapped her fingers. "Eamon, Naomi, come forward."

A pair of vampires, both dressed in period costumes, came

forward. It was clear they were siblings. They stood almost the same height, same brown hair, same lilt to their enamel features, dark eyes, and arching brows. Both looked like they'd been frozen in death in their early twenties, which seemed to be a common trait among the Undead.

The Queen directed her response at me next. "These two share a kin-bond and each has a particular specialty, one in tracking and the other in sensing. They are not only capable of getting you to your destination safely, but they will be able to detect Selene's many defenses." Her voice turned hard. "I do not lie in telling you this is the only way you will have a chance to succeed. After you breach Selene's lair, it will be up to you, and you alone, to save your mate. Selene is a very dangerous being. None but your cat has ever bested her before. She will not relinquish him easily. You will have to kill her."

"And what do you ask of me in return?" The billion-dollar question. If the price was too high, I would be forced to leave here with little chance of success.

My father stiffened beside me. Every fiber of his being rebelled at what I was about to do, but he stayed quiet, honoring his decision.

The Queen stepped up beside me, her lips parted without shame, flaunting her delight. The upper hand was hers, and if I refused—well, she would happily take glee in my sorrow. "It's nothing really." She gave another dismissive wave of her hand. "You will swear to return to me here in New Orleans, on the eve of our annual celebration of Ţepeş, to provide your service of guard as we enjoy our…*festivities*."

My mouth fell open a teensy bit without my consent. "You want me to serve as a guard dog at your annual gala?" I asked incredulously. She didn't want my firstborn? Or my blood drained hourly? Or primal torture at the hands of Valdov?

"Oh, it isn't merely a party, little wolf girl. It's an...*event*. It lasts for a full fortnight, and the revelry can get quite...out of hand. We have hired mercenaries in the past, like your cat, to keep things in check and away from human knowledge. But this year we will require a more *civilized* crowd, for this year marks the five hundred and fiftieth year of our celebrations, and we plan to...*outdo* ourselves."

Creepy chills slid up my spine. I didn't want to know what they were going to outdo. My brain raced as I tried to process. There was a catch. There was always a catch. My coming back here, under this horror-filled roof once again, would be a major stroke in her favor. Anything could happen to me in fourteen days. Plus, if she was willing to take the measures she had to get me here this time, I was clearly missing something about the good Queen's interest in me.

I planned to remedy that as soon as possible.

My father glowered at the Queen, distaste pulling his lips. The Queen crossed her arms and tapped her foot.

Apparently I was taking too long. "If I agree to swear to your demands, it will come with several of my own stipulations," I rambled, thinking fast, "or I walk out now and take my chances."

She shrugged like my meager requests meant nothing. "Name them and we shall see."

"After my duties are fulfilled at the...party"—it sounded so ridiculous—"I will leave here *alive* and...untouched." My skin crawled. "I stay no longer than fourteen days."

The Queen appeared bored. "Yes, yes, you will be alive. You have my solemn word."

"During my time here, I won't be your prisoner. I will enter and leave the premises freely, showing up for my duties when necessary."

"Yes," she ground out, her bored look changing to a glint of anger.

Here was the kicker, something I was going to insist on. "And if my mate lives, he will be allowed to accompany me." I was a realistic gal. There was no way Rourke was going to agree to let me romp around with vamps without him. Plus, once I got him back, I planned on enjoying him.

Before the Queen could answer, Tyler strode to my side. "And she will also be allowed ten bodyguards. To ensure you intend to honor your agreement about her safety fully."

The Queen's eyes dilated to full black, her incisors dropping in an instant. There was a horrible hissing as she shrieked, "How dare you question my honor!" The power in the room rose to a suffocating degree and my hand shot to my throat.

My father calmly stepped in front of her and bellowed, "Enough!"

The Queen came up short, still hissing, her fingernails curved to hideously sharp points. Her skin slipping again. Man, I was never going to get used to that.

"Eudoxia"—my father was an inch away from attacking—"you come too close in your threats."

The Queen trembled with fury. She struggled to tamp it all down. She'd pushed her power too far, now she risked losing her prize. "I will not . . . I will not tolerate being called without honor in my own home."

The vampires in the room started to hiss, crowding themselves in behind the wolves. Everyone was on edge.

"Eudoxia, you fool no one," my father snarled. "It's very clear to all of us standing here you want my daughter, for some reason I don't quite understand. But rest assured, henceforth I will make it my greatest quest to find out." His eyes flashed a brilliant violet. "Understand this now, my daughter is not yours to take. I will never let her go without a fight. We have been forced into an agreement at this time, but the terms she has already brought forth *will* stand, and in addition, *you* will *hire* ten of my wolves as your . . . *guards*," he spat, "and personally guarantee their safety. Make no mistake, Eudoxia, by the time my daughter arrives back here to fulfill her oath to you, she will be full *Pack*. And she will be protected as such."

The Queen's eyes had returned to their normal silver glow, but her incisors stayed put. "Five," she snarled through her fangs.

My father started to respond, but I interjected quickly, "Five! I agree to five wolves, a werefox, and a witch. Well, a minor witch. If this is going to play out like a job, I want my team." I added for good measure, "That's my final offer. Take it or leave it."

The Queen snapped her furious glare to me, her long canines so white they stood out like ivory knives against her red lips.

"It is done." Before any of us could react, she swept up the dais. "My vampires will begin the hunt at nightfall. They will first go to the mountains to ascertain Selene's trail. Expect them at your door in two eves from this day. Be prepared to leave then." I didn't want to ask how she knew where my door was. "Now swear an oath to me, little wolf girl." Her lips spread into a hideous smile, her teeth ridiculously long and sharp, her eyes flashing danger.

Am I really going to do this? "I swear to . . ." I recited everything we agreed on carefully, and for good measure I threw in, "And if your two vamps kill my mate, or any other vampire tries to for that matter, my oath to you will be considered forfeit. And I will come back and kill you instead." Then before she could interject, I added, "This is my Oath of Honor. I give it freely to Eudoxia, the Queen of the Vampires."

From the screams following us out, it seemed my end of the bargain wasn't looking so bad after all.

24

Hank was missing. It was the only piece of news I'd received since we'd emerged from the vamp hold. No one knew what had happened to him. My father had decided to give him space to grieve his son before he ordered him found.

Hopefully that would happen before Hank came for me in the middle of the night, hell-bent on revenge for his son's demise. It wasn't a stretch to assume Hank knew what his son had been doing, and keeping that kind of information from his Alpha carried a hefty punishment, if not death. But I had enough to worry about without adding Hank into the mix.

After a plane ride home, the wolves dispersed. Tyler and I headed back to my apartment in a cab, my father and James back to the Safe House. We would meet in the morning to come up with a plan.

I'd snagged a T-shirt and some sweatpants at a boutique in the New Orleans airport, so I was presentable enough. I couldn't help my smell, however, even though I'd given myself a half-assed rinse in the restroom. Luckily, the cab's greasy takeout stench masked any of my unpleasantness for the time being.

I laid my head back against the headrest and shut my eyes. I was tired and hungry. "So Danny's been staying at my place, right?" I asked.

Tyler stretched out his legs, jostling me a little. "Yep. He was injured during the attack, broke a few ribs, gushing head wound, so Dad put him at your place to look after things. He was pissed he couldn't come along."

I raked my hands through my hair and tried to energize myself. So many things needed my attention I didn't have the pleasure of curling up and going to sleep. The manhunt for Rourke would take resources and he was my first priority. "God, it feels like I've been gone for at least two months, and it's only been a day and a half," I said. "I should've called Nick when we reached the airport. I was just too tired."

"Nick was put in charge of the Safe House while we were gone. He's been updated regularly. He wanted to meet us at the airport, but I told him we were fine." Tyler cleared his voice, which got my attention.

"What?" I asked.

"Well, there's been..." He paused for a long second. "...Well, I guess you could say there've been some issues concerning that cop Ray Hart. Nick's sort of been forced to...cover for your absence again."

My head snapped off the headrest so quickly I had to brace my hands on the seat in front of me to stop my momentum. "What did you just say?" When he didn't answer immediately, I shot a fist into his shoulder. "Come on! What are you talking about? What issues with Ray?"

"It seems he's gone missing," my brother said carefully, glancing out the window, not meeting my eyes.

"What do you mean, *missing*?"

"It means," Tyler grumbled, turning toward me, "he clocked in at work yesterday and was scheduled to come by your apartment first thing in the morning, and wasn't seen again. When he didn't show up at the end of his shift, they tracked his car... to your lot. Nobody knows what happened to him."

"Nobody *human*, you mean?" I said, my voice low and angry. "Why wasn't I informed of this before right now? You know how this is going to look—they'll be all over my ass now. I can't just waltz back into my apartment, into my life, completely clueless. There could be a whole SWAT team waiting to arrest me."

"I didn't tell you on the plane because there wasn't a damn thing you could've done about it. Plus, you were too busy trying to convince me not to help you as a Selective, remember?"

I gave him a searing look. "Well, what did Danny say? If he's been at the apartment this whole time, he must've seen Ray." I lowered my voice. "You didn't tell Danny to..."

"No." Tyler shook his head. "There haven't been any official orders about what to do about the cop yet. But there will be at some point. That man is a nuisance."

"What did Danny say?" I urged.

"That's the problem," Tyler said. "I haven't *exactly* been able to get a hold of him in the last twenty-four hours."

"*What?*"

"He's not answering his phone."

I rocked my head backward and closed my eyes. "Tyler, you have got to be kidding me. And you haven't told any of this to Dad either?"

"No, I haven't. Dad has more than enough to deal with right now. Plus, this is a *minor* issue."

"*Minor?*" I lowered my voice because the cabbie had started to glance back at us in the rearview mirror. "A detective is *missing*. The very same detective who wants a chunk of my soul. If a fully competent *wolf* doesn't answer his phone, that equals B-I-G trouble—trouble I don't need right now." I whined at the end, but I couldn't help it.

Before Tyler could answer, the cabbie stopped in front of my building. I peered out the window, eyeing the redbrick façade for anything amiss while Tyler paid him.

Once we were out, we waited for him to drive off before either of us said anything, both of us sampling the air. There were no traces of supe, Marcy's spell still in action.

Tyler turned to me. "Listen, Jess, you're going to have to trust me on this one. If Danny was in serious trouble, I'd know it. Something must've happened when Ray showed up, but it couldn't have been that big or we would've found out one way or another. The two of us are just going to go up there and find out what it is and solve it ourselves." He cocked his head at me pointedly, and then brushed my mind: *And we're going to have to do it quietly.*

I finally understood.

The real reason Tyler had waited so long to clue me in. *Okay, I get it now. If Danny has somehow hurt Ray without orders, you want us to figure it out and cover it up on our own? Right?* Immediate visions of another body-shaped duffel being launched out of my apartment popped into my brain. I brought my fingers up to the bridge of my nose. *And then we're supposed to tell our father . . . what, exactly?*

We'll tell Dad whatever he needs to know when it's all done. Once it's all shored up there can be no complaint, and there's no reason he needs to know right this minute anyway. Most likely nothing's going on; it's all just pure speculation at this point and we don't need to bother him with our speculation. He read my face. *Danny's on probation almost all the time because he goes off on his own too much. If he's killed a detective without orders there will be serious repercussions for him. It doesn't matter if he's one of the Pack's best fighters. I'm just saying it might not be a bad idea for us to see for ourselves what happened here first. Get a handle on the situation. After all, we're just on our way home from a long flight, what do we really know for sure?*

"You're playing with fire, little brother," I said out loud. "Not your typical style, but I kind of like it." I grabbed his shirtsleeve. "Come on, let's go get this over with."

The smell of fear and something unknown permeated my hallway as we rounded the top of the landing. My wolf was alert, searching for any potential danger. There would be no repeat of the rogue attack.

My brother and I edged cautiously down the corridor, my nose working to categorize the strange scents. *Do you know what that smell is? It's almost like rotting peaches.*

Tyler answered. *Nope. I don't recognize it other than it's definitely a supe of some kind.*

That did not bode well for us—or for Danny—or Ray, for that matter, if he was indeed tangled in this. And how could he not be?

Strangely, Juanita's voice broke the silence, her hearty laugh ringing out in the hallway, followed by a low male murmur. My stress level relaxed somewhat. I glanced at my brother. *That just came from my apartment, right?* Juanita's jubilant tone mixed with Danny's smooth alto became more clear as we continued down the hallway, but since our apartments were directly across from each other, there was a slight possibility my ears were picking up on some kind of echo.

Yep, seems Danny has company. Whatever's happened can't be that bad, then, and that means I was right.

He better not have tried anything on my neighbor. Other than those two voices, the hallway was quiet. Our flight out of New Orleans had left at six a.m. It was now ten-thirty in the morning on a workday. Most of my neighbors were at work.

Please. Tyler snorted. *Danny can have anyone he wants, he's not making a move on your elderly neighbor.*

She's not elderly! And she happens to be voluptuous and sexy for her age. He'd be lucky to have her. But he better not have. I'm just saying.

Tyler snorted again.

As we approached my door, I motioned for Tyler to stand behind me. The rotten peach smell was all over, clogging both of our senses. I put my ear to the door to make sure there were only two voices inside and grabbed on to the handle. I gave it a slow turn. There was movement, no catches. I eased it open. "Hello," I called. "I'm home."

"Hello there." Danny gave a little salute from his place on the floor, on what appeared to be a plaid picnic blanket full of empty plates and a couple of red-stained wineglasses. "Glad to see you back in town so soon."

"Um, it's good to be back." I tentatively made my way into the strange scene of my apartment, followed closely by Tyler.

Danny ran his gaze over me from head to toe and smiled, not bothering to get up from his spot on the floor. "Too bad about the outfit, then. But I'm certain flip-flops are going to make quite a comeback this season."

Juanita sprang to her feet. "Oh, Chica, es so good to see you!" She ran over and embraced me, and I let her because everything was a bit surreal.

"It's good to see you too, Juanita, but what are you doing here?" I had to ask.

"After all the loud noises," she said, "I rush over here to check on what es going on, jus like you told me to do, and I find him here alone"—she pointed at Danny—"and he es so nice and tell me he es protecting jour home for you. I believe him after all the bad break-ins and troubles, so I bring him food because he has none. We are keeping watch together, you see, so now jour apartment weel be safe." I followed her logic fine, even though it wasn't even close to what I had told her to do. She could've gotten herself killed coming over here alone; she'd been very lucky. I was glad she was safe, but the cloying stench of rotten peaches was so intense now that we were inside I had a hard time concentrating on anything she said.

"That's great, Juanita, and thank you for bringing food and helping keep watch." I met Danny's eye over her shoulder. I arched a single brow. Ignoring the horrid smell was not an option and I wanted to know what was going on.

Tyler cleared his voice behind me. "So everything's okay in here? Right? No problems that you know of?"

Before Danny could answer, Juanita walked over and started stacking empty dinner plates together. "Oh, sí, everytheen es fine. Nobody or nothing bothered us here."

Danny grinned as he finally stood, his brown hair falling in his eye. "You two must be tired after such a last-minute trip," he said, placing a plate onto Juanita's stack. "I was explaining to your neighbor about your sick grandmother, but she's as good as new, right? Recovered from that frightful injury?"

"Um, yes," I said, picking up the thread. "She's a sturdy old goat, so she's already back on her feet. Turns out she didn't need our help after all, so we came home."

"That's such a relief, Chica." Juanita solemnly nodded. "Grandparents are so fragile."

Danny put a few more dishes onto Juanita's stack, then bent

down and folded the plaid blanket, turning to us. "You two look like you could use a bit of a freshen-up. You know, to get rid of jet lag? Perhaps a shower? Or maybe your teeth need a good solid brushing? And while you're tending to that, I'll just help the lovely Juanita back to her apartment."

I glanced at my brother. His face was stony. Neither of us was going to like what we found, I guaranteed it. "Um, okay, I'll go first," I said. "I'm dying to...brush my teeth." I started toward my tiny bathroom. "And, Juanita, thanks for taking care of Danny. But you have to promise me one thing: the next time you hear any noises, please call first. Or better yet, lock your door and don't come out. I would never forgive myself if you got hurt on my account."

"Okay, Chica. I call first next time." She winked and headed for the front door.

The bathroom door was shut and I eased it open, listening before I slipped inside. The smell was so thick I coughed, covering my mouth with the palm of my hand as my eyes landed on the only place they could possibly go in the small space—the bathtub. There, lying naked and dead, was my super, Jeff Arnold. He looked awful, his pasty skin and thinning hair only accentuating his crumpled pale visage. "Oh my gods." I pushed my hand tighter to my face. I knelt down by him, and the stinky peach mixed with death made me produce bile. I had no idea what kind of supe he was, but it was obvious he'd been one.

The front door of my apartment clicked shut, then Tyler was crowded behind me, followed by Danny in the now open doorway.

"What the fuck is all this?" Tyler turned toward Danny. "When you didn't answer your phone I thought that asshole detective Ray Hart put a bullet in your brain."

"No bullet, mate," Danny said. "The reason I couldn't call

you is this guy here"—Danny gestured toward Jeff—"broke my bloody phone during our brief interlude. I couldn't very well leave and go out and make a phone call, now could I? Then I had to deal with your neighbor well enough after she heard all the commotion. Though she makes an excellent pie. It was truly delicious."

"Danny, what happened here?" I pushed by them and made my way out of the bathroom. I had to get away from the stench. They followed me into the living room. I placed my hands on my hips and turned in a full circle, trying to get my brain back on board with what I just witnessed. "I'm having trouble understanding why my super is lying dead in my bathtub."

"Well, it's a very simple story actually," Danny started. "I was minding my own business, convalescing as ordered by your father. My wounds were quite severe, as I'm sure you were informed—not to worry, though, all shipshape now—when I heard someone sneaking into your apartment as bold as day. He wasn't technically breaking in, you see, since he had his own *key*, but nevertheless he woke me out of a perfectly lovely sleep. I'd been dreaming about the Dallas Cowboys Cheerleaders, who are, for the record, a naughty lot of—"

"Danny," I said sharply. "Please stay on topic."

"Of course. So naturally I did my duty and came out to investigate the disturbance. Our man was toting a rather large bag of very suspicious goods, and when he saw me he had the nerve to pull out a *gun*." Danny infused some outrage. "Which I kindly knocked from his hands as quick as you like, and I was about to break his sorry little neck when out of nowhere he dropped to the floor and began shifting into a bloody weasel."

"A *what*?" Tyler and I both balked.

"A bloody weasel shifter the size of a large dog." Danny spread his hands to indicate a hefty size. "Then he jumped on my back like a possessed little fuck and went after my flesh like a piranha...scenting blood."

Jeff was a shifter? Never in a million years would I have guessed that. The peach smell, obviously his signature scent, wouldn't have meant much to me as a human, and he'd definitely stayed clear of me since. He must have had a lackey deliver my new set of door keys, because I would've picked up the peach scent if he had brought them himself. But the million-dollar question was, what did he want? And who was he working for? There was no way a guy like Jeff Arnold was a one-man operation. He didn't have enough motivation in one of his pinky fingers, let alone enough brainpower to hatch a plan to catch a wolf. He was likely recruited for the job or someone had forced him into it. Either way, it shouldn't be too hard to track down the trail.

"I've never heard of a wereweasel before," my brother said. "And I'm positive I've never smelled one." He wrinkled his nose. "I would've remembered that stink anywhere."

"Well, I can assure you they bloody well exist," Danny bristled. "But what the little shite wasn't expecting was a werewolf counterattack, and I'd like to kindly point out that a weasel and a wolf make a highly unbalanced fight. After I shifted, it took me under three seconds to take him out."

"You shifted? Right here?" I asked. "In my apartment?"

"Of course I shifted," Danny said indignantly. "I had to shake off the bloody wereweasel who was ripping chunks out of my back with his devilish little claws and sharp, pointy teeth. I couldn't get the bastard off without shifting. But, of course, that's when the detective came sniffing around, so I—"

"*What!*" I shouted, grabbing on to his arms. "Danny, you said this happened last night. Ray came here in the *morning*. Please tell me he did not see you shift!"

"No, I never said it was at night, you just assumed it was. And yes, he did see me, but I had almost fully finished by the time he came round, so he didn't get to see the lot of it. But he did see me toss a weasel—the size of bloody Benji—against the wall. After that I had no choice—"

"Danny," I half yelled, half begged. "Please tell me you did not kill Ray Hart."

"Of course I didn't kill him!" He had the nerve to look shocked like poor Jeff wasn't lying in my bathroom lifeless. "I don't kill people who don't threaten me directly. No need to worry your pretty little head about it. I haven't killed him, I've just tied him up in your closet for the time being. Not that we won't be killing him later, because he's uncovered our secret, but I couldn't just let him walk out of here, now could I?"

I stood there frozen. Ray was tied up *in my closet*?

Danny continued without pausing, "Damn well nearly pissed his pants when I launched myself at him. It was lucky for me he fainted dead away. Always makes the job of securing them a whole lot easier when they go limp. But I didn't actually realize it was the detective until Nick came by just in time to fob off the police when they came to the door searching for him. Nick convinced them they'd already checked this apartment thoroughly. Bloody convenient, persuasion is. Wish I had that knack. It's quite handy in a mess like this."

I didn't bother to answer, since I was already running down the hallway toward my bedroom.

My bed had been well slept in and the floor was littered with takeout bags and empty plates. It seemed poor Danny hadn't been without resources after all.

I approached the closet doors slowly and stood there for a full minute gathering myself. I wasn't sure what I was going to see when I whipped them open, and visions of the recent dead man in my bathtub gave me pause.

My fingers grazed the knobs and in one motion I yanked the accordion doors back. To my immediate relief there was a very angry, but very *alive*, detective sitting on a pile of my shoes.

He was gagged with what looked to be a pair of my pantyhose. Both Ray's hands were tied behind his back with something I couldn't see, but it seemed to be holding him well enough. He glowered at me with so much hatred and loathing—if he'd been a wolf, I might have shied away for a second.

But he wasn't.

I squatted down to his level. "Hi, Ray. So glad to see you're alive and well. Are you enjoying your little stay in my closet?"

He didn't try to move, which meant he must've been sufficiently freaked out by what he had witnessed with Danny and the canine-sized wereweasel. Instead, he unleashed a string of curses I couldn't fully understand due to his gag but immediately recognized in their entirety anyway. His faced turned beet red with each effort and saliva pooled along the corners of his mouth.

"Ray," I chastised. "I'm going to need you to calm down. I know you're incredibly agitated right now, but look on the bright side—you're still breathing. That's a very big accomplishment at the moment. Most people in your current position wouldn't have breath left in their bodies after what you witnessed."

More swearing and some agitated movements.

"Listen, as much as I'd love to have a big heart-to-heart, you're going to have to hold on to those thoughts for now," I told him. "I just came back here to make sure you weren't dead. Now that I've seen you with my own eyes, I've got to get back to my living room and sort out another round of chaos that's become my normal life. If you can believe it, I have bigger things to attend to than you right now, so you're just going to have to hold tight."

I stood up right as Ray's leg struck out, connecting solidly with my knee.

The blow staggered me back a foot, but I recovered in a snap. Furious didn't even come close. I sprang at more-than-human speed right into Ray's personal space. His eyes widened in surprise and fear leaked out of him like air from a punctured tire.

I growled to enhance the effect. "Listen to me very carefully, Raymond Hart. You have forced your way into something that was *never* any of your business to learn. Do you understand me? You're a self-centered, egotistical, thick-necked, mean-assed cop. One who could never leave well enough alone." He winced at the force of my words. "I never, and I repeat *never*, deserved your dogged pursuit of me. Nothing has warranted your extreme hatred of me, and now you're in way over your head, and guess what? It's become my fucking job to dig you out. Do you understand the irony of this whole situation? It's certainly not lost on me."

He blinked.

"Now, in a normal scenario you don't live to see tomorrow," I said, my voice icy calm. "That's just how it works. So if you don't want to end up dead, you're going to have to start treating me like I'm your best friend until I have a chance to figure this out, and it's going to take me more than seven seconds to do it. Understood?"

More fear swirled in the air, accompanied by slight annoyance. Ray gave me a few more rapid blinks. He was a piece of work, that was for damn sure.

"Contrary to what you might think, I don't want to kill

you." He deserved to know that much from me. "You can choose to believe me or not, I don't really care. But right now, you have no choice but to wait patiently. If you make any move to escape, or do anything stupid, we will know it immediately. Don't test us. The big guys in the other room won't hesitate to take you out, and I won't be able to stop them." I couldn't resist adding, "Blink twice if you understand me."

If he could've killed me with his brainpower alone, I'd already be dead. But very slowly he blinked twice.

"Good. See you in a few minutes, Ray." I shut the closet doors. Garbled curses followed me back into the living room.

My brother was on the phone calling for a cleaning crew to deal with Jeff.

I got down to business. "Okay, Danny, were you able to get anything off of Jeff before Juanita came in? We're going to have to figure out who he's working for and why he was here in the first place."

"His pockets were clean and other than some low-level surveillance equipment and a few cheap bugs, there was nothing of value in the bag he carried. I'd planned to sneak down to his apartment as soon as the detective was settled, but your lovely neighbor waylaid my carefully made plans."

"His apartment's a good place to start. I'm assuming it shouldn't be too hard to piece it together. Jeff was not the brightest bulb—" A force slammed into me, knocking the breath out of my body as I hit the living room wall. My wolf howled, springing at the red lines that had suddenly emerged in my mind, snapping her jaws fiercely.

It was one of Selene's spells.

Why now? No time to ponder, we had to get rid of it. *We conquered the last one, we need to get this one too.* My wolf growled and lashed at the red amassing quickly in my mind.

I gasped for air, sliding down the rough brick into a sitting position, trying my best to breathe. The spell was cutting off all my bodily functions.

"Jess, Jesus Christ, look at your hands." Tyler knelt beside me and grabbed a hold of my wrists.

Danny squatted next to him. "That looks like trouble if I've ever seen any."

I forced my neck down so I could see my hands lying in Tyler's grasp. Red veins were spreading upward at an alarming rate, starting from the very tips of my fingers like an oil spill, slowly seeping up my forearms. Pain raced up to my shoulder, ahead of the spell, and back down my spine, zinging it with fire. This wasn't the same spell she'd hit me with in the clearing. This spell was different.

The bitch gave us two.

She must have snuck one in under Valdov's nose. This one must have had a waiting period before activation. If the vampire knew she'd put a spell in my body to kill me, there would've been backlash. Sneaky witch.

All my limbs stiffened; I couldn't move anything.

Inside my head, my wolf kept hacking at the spell. I pushed power into her, trying to feed her control. My arms throbbed and burned with a searing heat. My body's instinct was to change, but it was too risky. The spell would probably kill me before I could shift. I had to defeat it now.

"Jess, can you hear me?" Tyler voice echoed in my ear. "What's going on? You have to answer me."

My eyes were open, but I couldn't blink.

Tyler turned to Danny. "Get my father on the phone. We need help."

No. "No," I managed on a harsh breath. Both boys turned to stare at me. "Don't." I had to deal with this on my own. If my father found out, there was no way he'd let me leave town. I had to find my mate. At all costs. No matter what was going on with Jeff, or any of the other craziness, finding Rourke was my priority. My only priority. "No." It came out slowly. "*Please.*"

My brother and Danny waited, both of them crouched next to me, concern on their faces.

I battled the insidious spell, pushing more control at my wolf, trying to draw power from my body and direct it at her, pumping her full. She ripped and struck at the red mass in a fervor, too fast for me to follow. I gasped for more air, my lungs barely inflating. *We have to do this*, I told her. *We have to be stronger than her or we lose him forever. It's giving a little, I can feel it. We're almost there. I promise you she's not going to win this. We are* stronger. My wolf snarled, gnashing her teeth, forcing the lines back into submission, tearing the spell apart before it could fully metastasize in my body, which was exactly what it was trying to do.

I channeled one last burst of power, using everything I could gather, and aimed it at my wolf. A moment of clarity hit my mind, a bright concentration of power, and the spell snapped once and for all. The lines broke apart, dangling limply in my mind like a tattered spiderweb swaying in the wind.

Then very slowly all the color dissipated, seeping back the way it'd come, like eels sliding back into their holes.

My wolf continued to growl, lashing at the retreating lines until no red remained. But the ugliness hadn't gone away forever. The spell was still there.

It'd just gone dormant.

When the last remnant of red vanished I fell forward, coughing for air, taking in short deep breaths. After a solid minute of panting, I finally looked up, sweaty and spent. "She's trying to kill me."

"Who's trying to kill you?" Tyler asked. I'd forgotten Tyler had been out cold when Selene had blasted me in the clearing.

"Selene." I rested my head back against the wall. "It seems she left me a fun parting gift from our party together in the woods."

But she wasn't going to win.

"It looked a bit touch-and-go there for a second," Danny said, his face worried. "You're not talking about Selene the *actual* Lunar Goddess, are you?"

"The very one." The whore was trying to kill me.

"What kind of a spell is it?" Tyler asked. "It looked like it was going to consume your entire body."

"I think it was a…death spell of some kind," I said quietly, knowing Tyler wasn't going to take that news well.

"What the *hell* does that mean?"

"It means I have to kill the bitch before she kills me."

The End of Book One

The story continues in book two of the Jessica McClain series:

Hot Blooded

extras

www.orbitbooks.net

about the author

A Minnesota girl born and bred, **Amanda Carlson** graduated from the University of Minnesota with a double major in speech and hearing science and child development. After enjoying her time as a sign language interpreter, she decided to stay at home and write in earnest after her second child was born. She loves playing Scrabble, tropical beaches, and shopping trips to Ikea. She lives in Minneapolis with her husband and three kids. To find out more about the author, visit www.amandacarlson.com or on Twitter @AmandaCCarlson.

Find out more about Amanda Carlson and other Orbit authors by registering for the free monthly newsletter at www.orbitbooks.net

interview

Have you always been a writer?

Yes, ever since I can remember. I started writing in junior high, using my yearbook to add faces to my stories. Over the years, I've written humorous essays about my kids, articles for various publications, but did I consider myself a "writer" before the publication of this book? Not really. For me, it's one of those validation milestones that has made all my other endeavors feel worthy. Now I feel like I can call myself a writer, and it feels damn good.

What do you do when you're not writing?

I have three kids, so it's safe to say when I'm not writing I'm trying my best to keep up with my motherly duties. I usually wrap my writing day when they get home from school, but my kids are understanding and give me extra time when I need it. Minneapolis is full of beautiful lakes and I love to walk with pals. By the end of the week I need to escape, so movies are a delicious treat. The more action-packed the better. I also love playing Scrabble—to a slightly unhealthy degree. There's nothing better than flipping from my WIP to make a move on the Scrabble board. It clears my mind, and when I jump back, I'm ready to write again.

World building is such a big part of urban fantasy. How did you build your world in *Full Blooded*?

To me, world building is the best part of writing urban fantasy. Being able to invent the rules and bring readers into your universe is so much fun. I had a blast creating *Full Blooded*. The biggest question I started with was: Do humans know my characters exist? Once I decided their world was a secret, it shaped the book. For the individual characters, the imps, the witches, the vamps and wolves, I asked myself, how much magic do they have? How do they wield it? When all the details were fleshed out, the key was to open up the world in front of the reader and make sure they weren't bogged down with too many details at once. Selene, the Lunar Goddess, is an actual Greek deity. I enjoyed working her into the story. There's never a dull moment writing urban fantasy. I absolutely love this genre.

Why the "only female werewolf"? Where did the inspiration for Jessica come from?

All my books start out with a solid visual first scene, which plays out in my mind like a sequence from a movie. Jessica started in my mind with her shift, and once she was done, I knew she was completely "different" from all the other wolves. She stood out, but she also craved a strong family unit. As the books progress, you'll see Jessica's friends and family play a big role in her life. She made herself unique in that first scene—and people often fear what they don't understand. Not so different from the wolves in my story. After that, everything fell into place and the story line unfolded.

How did the Cain Myth come to be?

Werewolves in my world are superstitious to an incredible degree. Jessica wasn't supposed to exist, so to solidify the Pack's fear, I felt they had to have something tangible. Preferably something they could hold on to and see. The Cain Myth was a great place to start…but be careful…all may not be what it seems.

How much of you are in your characters?

All of my characters come into my mind fully formed and stubborn. I can't say any of them *are* me, but they are definitely a combination of the way I view the world. As a writer, I think most of the time we're writing characters we'd love to sit down and have a drink with, rather than writing subconsciously about ourselves. At least that's true for me. Jess may have a little bit of me infused in there somewhere, but really, she's someone I just want to hang out with.

There are all different types of weres, witches, vampires, and more in your story. If you could be one supernatural creature, what would it be?

I'd love to be a shifter of some kind. Possibly one with wings so I could take myself to the beach at a moment's notice. I have a deep weakness for sunshine and sand. Having magic abilities would also be interesting. Being able to conjure a spell anytime, anyplace would be incredible. The world would be a much different place with a little magic in it—and, I think, a lot more fun.

Rourke is a powerful character and so gorgeous. But so is James. Why did you pick Rourke for Jessica's mate?

I love James. There are no two ways about it. But Jessica demanded something different. The standard-issue Pack member, even a strong, capable one, wasn't going to suffice. She's a one-of-a-kind wolf who needed an original mate. Rourke is amazing and sexy, and he's completely devoted to her. Jessica hasn't gotten to explore him ... yet. But when she does, there will be no question in the reader's mind of why he's The One.

Will we ever find out what Rourke really is?

Absolutely! But don't get your hopes up too soon.

What's next for Jessica and Rourke?
Jessica and Rourke are in for some extreme adventures together. But first Jessica has to fight an evil Goddess to get him back, and if that's not bad enough, trouble manifests itself in a whole new form—one that Jess and Rourke had no idea was coming...

if you enjoyed
FULL BLOODED

look out for

UNCLEAN SPIRITS

by

M. L. N. Hanover

1

I flew into Denver on the second of August, three days before my twenty-third birthday. I had an overnight bag packed with three changes of clothes, the leather backpack I used for a purse, the jacket my last boyfriend hadn't had the guts to come pick up from my apartment (it still smelled like him), my three-year-old laptop wrapped in a blanket, and a phone number for Uncle Eric's lawyer. The area around the baggage carousel was thick with families and friends hugging one another and saying how long it had been and how much everyone had grown or shrunk or whatever. The wide metal blades weren't about to offer up anything of mine, so I was just looking through the crowd for my alleged ride and trying not to make eye contact.

It took me a while to find him at the back of the crowd, his head shifting from side to side, looking for me. He had a legal pad in his hand with my name in handwritten letters—'JAYNE HELLER.' He was younger than I'd expected, maybe midthirties, and cuter. I shouldered my way through the happy mass of people, mentally applauding Uncle Eric's taste.

'You'd be Aubrey?' I said.

'Jayné,' he said, pronouncing it *Jane*. It's actually

zha-*nay*, but that was a fight I'd given up. 'Good. Great. I'm glad to meet you. Can I help you with your bags?'

'Pretty much covered on that one,' I said. 'Thanks, though.'

He looked surprised, then shrugged it off.

'Right. I'm parked over on the first level. Let me at least get that one for you.'

I surrendered my three changes of clothes and followed.

'You're going to be staying at Eric's place?' Aubrey asked over his shoulder. 'I have the keys. The lawyer said it would be okay to give them to you.'

'Keys to the kingdom,' I said, then, 'Yes. I thought I'd save the money on a hotel. Doesn't make sense not to, right?'

'Right,' Aubrey said with a smile that wanted badly to be comfortable but wasn't.

I couldn't blame the guy for being nervous. Christ only knew what Eric had told him about the family. Even the broad stroke of 'My brother and sister-in-law don't talk to me' would have been enough to make the guy tentative. Much less the full-on gay-hating, patriarch-in-the-house, know-your-place episode of *Jerry Springer* that had been my childhood. Calling Uncle Eric the black sheep of the family was like saying the surface of the sun was warmish. Or that I'd been a little tiny disappointment to them.

Aubrey drove a minivan, which was kind of cute. After he slung my lonely little bag into the back, we climbed in and drove out. The happy crowd of families and friends fell away behind us. I leaned against the window and looked up into the clear night sky. The moon was about halfway down from full. There weren't many stars.

'So,' Aubrey said. 'I'm sorry. About Eric. Were you two close?'

'Yeah,' I said. 'Or . . . maybe. I don't know. Not close like he called me up to tell me about his day. He'd check in on me, make sure things weren't too weird at home. He'd just show up sometimes, take me out to lunch or for ice cream or something cheesy like that. We always had to keep under my dad's radar, so I figure he'd have come by more often if he could.'

Aubrey gunned the minivan, pulling us onto the highway.

'He protected me,' I said, soft enough that I didn't think Aubrey would hear me, but he did.

'From what?'

'Myself,' I said.

Here's the story. In the middle of high school, I spent about six months hanging out with the bad kids. On my sixteenth birthday, I got very, *very* drunk and woke up two days later in a hotel room with half a tattoo on my back and wearing someone else's clothes. Eric had been there for me. He told my dad that I'd gotten the flu and helped me figure out how to keep anyone from ever seeing the ink.

I realized I'd gone silent. Aubrey was looking over at me.

'Eric was always swooping in just when everything was about to get out of control,' I said. 'Putting in the cooling rods.'

'Yeah,' Aubrey said. 'That sounds like him.'

Aubrey smiled at the highway. It seemed he wasn't thinking about it, so the smile looked real. I could see why Eric would have gone for him. Short, curly hair the color of honey. Broad shoulders. What my mother would have called a kind mouth. I hoped that he'd made Eric happy.

'I just want you to know,' I said, 'it's okay with me that he was gay.'

Aubrey started.

'He was gay?'

'Um,' I said. 'He wasn't?'

'He never told me.'

'Oh,' I said, mentally recalculating. 'Maybe he wasn't. I assumed . . . I mean, I just thought since my dad wouldn't talk about him . . . my dad's kind of old-school. Where *school* means *testament*. He never really got into that love-thy-neighbor-as-thyself part.'

'I know the type,' he said. The smile was actually pointed at me now, and it seemed genuine.

'There was this big falling-out about three years ago,' I said. 'Uncle Eric had called the house, which he almost never did. Dad went out around dinnertime and came back looking deeply pissed off. After that . . . things were weird. I just assumed . . .'

I didn't tell Aubrey that Dad had gathered us all in the living room—me, Mom, my older brother Jay, and Curtis the young one—and said that we weren't to have anything to do with Uncle Eric anymore. Not any of us. Not ever. He was a pervert and an abomination before God.

Mom had gone sheet-white. The boys just nodded and

looked grave. I'd wanted to stand up for him, to say that Uncle Eric was family, and that Dad was being totally unfair and hypocritical. I didn't, though. It wasn't a fight I could win.

But Aubrey knew him well enough to have a set of spare keys, and he didn't think Eric was gay. Maybe Dad had meant something else. I tried to think what exactly had made me think it was that, but I couldn't come up with anything solid.

Aubrey pulled his minivan off the highway, then through a maze of twisty little streets. One-story bungalows with neatly kept yards snuggled up against each other. About half the picture windows had open curtains; it was like driving past museum dioramas of the American Family. Here was one with an old couple sitting under a cut glass chandelier. One with the backs of two sofa-bound heads and a wall-size Bruce Willis looking troubled and heroic. One with two early-teenage boys, twins to look at them, chasing each other. And then we made a quick dogleg and pulled into a carport beside a brick house. Same lawn, same architecture. No lights, no one in the windows.

'Thanks,' I said, reaching around in the seat to grab my bag.

'Do you want . . . I mean, I can show you around a little. If you want.'

'I think I'm just going to grab a shower and order in a pizza or something,' I said. 'Decompress. You know.'

'Okay,' he said, fishing in his pocket. He came out with a leather fob with two keys and passed it over to me. I took it. The leather was soft and warm. 'If you need anything, you have my number?'

'Yeah,' I said. 'Thanks for the lift.'

'If there's anything I can do . . .'

I popped open the door. The dome light came on.

'I'll let you know,' I said. 'Promise.'

'Your uncle,' Aubrey said. Then, 'Your uncle was a very special man.'

'I know,' I said.

He seemed like he wanted to say something else, but instead he just made me promise again that I'd call him if I needed help.

There wasn't much mail in the box—ads and a water bill. I tucked it under my arm while I struggled with the lock. When I finally got the door open, I stumbled in, my bag bumping behind me.

A dim atrium. A darker living room before me. The kitchen door to my left, ajar. A hall to my right, heading back to bedrooms and bathrooms and closets.

'Hey,' I said to nothing and no one. 'I'm home.'

I never would have said it to anyone, but my uncle had been killed at the perfect time. I hated myself for even thinking that, but it was true. If I hadn't gotten the call from his lawyer, if I hadn't been able to come here, I would have been reduced to couch surfing with people I knew peripherally from college. I wasn't welcome at home right now. I hadn't registered for the next semester at ASU, which technically made me a college dropout.

I didn't have a job or a boyfriend. I had a storage unit in Phoenix and a bag, and I didn't have the money to keep the storage unit for more than another month. With any luck at all, I'd be able to stay here in the house until Uncle Eric's estate was all squared away. There might even be enough money in his will that I could manage first and last on a place of my own. He was swooping in one last time to pull me out of the fire. The idea made me sad, and grateful, and a little bit ashamed.

They'd found him in an alley somewhere on the north side of the city. There was, the lawyer had told me, an open investigation. Apparently he'd been seen at a bar somewhere talking to someone. Or it might have just been a mugging that got out of hand. One way or another, his friend Aubrey had identified the body. Eric had left instructions in his will for funeral arrangements, already taken care of. It was all very neat. Very tidy.

The house was just as tidy. He hadn't owned very much, and it gave the place a simplicity. The bed was neatly made. Shirts, jackets, slacks all hung in the bedroom closet, some still in the plastic from the dry cleaner's. There were towels in the bathroom, a safety razor beside the sink with a little bit of soap scum and stubble still on the blade.

I found a closet with general household items, including a spare toothbrush. The food in the fridge was mostly spoiled, but I scrounged up a can of beef soup that I nuked in a plain black bowl, sopping up the last with bread that wasn't too stale. The television was in the living room, and I spooled through channels and channels of bright, shining crap. I didn't feel right putting my feet on the couch.

When I turned on the laptop, I found there was a wireless network. I guessed the encryption key on my third try. It was the landline phone number. I checked mail and had nothing waiting for me. I pulled up my messenger program. A few names appeared, including my most recent ex-boyfriend. The worst thing I could have done just then was talk with him. The last thing I needed was another reminder of how alone I was. I started typing.

Jayneheller: Hey. You there?

A few seconds later, the icon showed he was on the other end, typing.

Caryonandon: I'm not really here. About to go out.
Jayneheller: OK. Is there a time we can talk?
Caryonandon: Maybe. Not now.

His name vanished from the list. I played a freeware word search game while I conducted imaginary conversations with him in which I always came out on top, then went to bed feeling sick to my stomach.

I called the lawyer in the morning, and by noon, she was at the door. Midfifties, gray suit, floral perfume with something earthy under it, and a smile bright as a brand-new hatchet. I pulled my hair back when she came in and wished I'd put on something more formal than blue jeans and a Pink Martini T-shirt.

'Jayné,' she said, as if we were old acquaintances. She

pronounced it *Jane* too. I didn't correct her. 'This must be so hard for you. I'm so sorry for your loss.'

'Thanks,' I said. 'You want to come into the kitchen? I think there's some tea I could make.'

'That would be lovely,' she said.

I fired up the kettle and dug through the shelves. There wasn't any tea, but I found some fresh peppermint and one of those little metal balls, so I brewed that. The lawyer sat at the kitchen table, her briefcase open, small piles of paper falling into ranks like soldiers on parade. I brought over two plain black mugs, careful not to spill on anything.

'Thank you, dear,' she said, taking the hot mug from my hands. 'And your trip was all right? You have everything you need?'

'Everything's fine,' I said, sitting.

'Good, then we can get to business. I have a copy of the will itself here. You'll want to keep that for your files. There is, I'm afraid, going to be a lot of paperwork to get through. Some of the foreign properties are complex, but don't worry, we'll make it.'

'Okay,' I said, wondering what she was talking about.

'This is an inventory of the most difficult transfers. The good news is that Eric arranged most of the liquid assets as pay-on-death, so the tax situation is fairly straightforward, and we get to avoid probate. The rest of the estate is more complicated. I've also brought keys to the other Denver properties. I have a copy of the death certificate, so you only need to fill out a signature card at the bank before you can do anything with the funds. Do you have enough to see you through for a day or two?'

She handed me a typewritten sheet of paper. I ran my finger down the list. Addresses in London, Paris, Bombay, Athens . . .

'I'm sorry,' I said. 'I don't want to be a pain in the ass, but I don't understand. What is all this?'

'The inventory of the difficult transfers,' she said, slowing down the words a little bit, like maybe I hadn't understood them before. 'Some of the foreign properties are going to require more paperwork.'

'These are all Uncle Eric's?' I said. 'He has a house in London?'

'He has property all over the world, dear. Didn't you know?'

'No,' I said. 'I didn't. What am I . . . I mean, what am I supposed to do with this stuff?'

The lawyer put down her pen. A crease had appeared between her brows. I sipped the peppermint tea and it scalded my tongue.

'You and your uncle didn't discuss any of this?' she said.

I shook my head. I could feel my eyes growing abnormally wide. 'I thought he was gay,' I said. It occurred to me just how stunningly underqualified I was to execute anybody's will, much less something complex with a lot of paperwork.

The lawyer sat back in her seat, considering me like I had just appeared and she was maybe not so impressed with what she saw.

'Your uncle was a very rich man,' she said. 'He left all his assets specifically and exclusively to you. And you had no idea that was his intention?'

'We didn't talk much,' I said. 'He left it to me? Are you sure? I mean, thanks, but are you sure?'

'The majority of his titles are already jointly in your names. And you're certain he never mentioned this?'

'Never.'

The lawyer sighed.

'Ms. Heller,' she said. 'You are a very rich young woman.'

I blinked.

'Um,' I said. 'Okay. What scale are we talking about here?'

She told me: total worth, liquid assets, property.

'Well,' I said, putting the mug down. 'Holy shit.'

I think lottery winners must feel the same way. I followed everything the lawyer said, but about half of it washed right back out of my mind. The world and everything in it had taken on a kind of unreality. I wanted to laugh or cry or curl up in a ball and hug myself. I didn't—did *not*—want to wake up and find out it had all been a dream.

We talked for about two hours. We made a list of things I needed to do, and she loaned me six hundred dollars—'to keep me in shoes'—until I could get to the bank and jump through the hoops that would give me access to enough money to do pretty much anything I wanted. She left a listing of Eric's assets about a half inch thick, and keys to the other Denver properties: two storage facilities and an apartment in what she told me was a hip and happening neighborhood.

I closed the door behind her when she left and sank down to the floor. The atrium tiles were cold against my palms. Eric Alexander Heller, my guardian uncle, left me more than I'd dreamed of. Money, security, any number of places that I could live in if I wanted to.

Everything, in fact, but an explanation.

I took myself back to the kitchen table and read the will. Legal jargon wasn't my strong suit, but from what I could tell, it was just what the lawyer had said. Everything he had owned was mine. No one else's. No discussion. Now that I was alone and starting to get my bearings, about a thousand questions presented themselves. Why leave everything to me? Why hadn't he told me about any of it? How had he made all this money?

And, top of the list, what was someone worth as much as a small nation doing in a bar in the shitty part of Denver, and did all the money that had just dropped into my lap have anything to do with why he'd been killed?

I took out the keys she'd left me. A single house key shared a ring with a green plastic tag with an address on Inca Street. Two storage keys for two different companies.

If I'd had anyone to talk to, I'd have called them. My parents, a friend, a boyfriend, anyone. A year ago, I would have had a list half as long as my arm. The world changes a lot in a year. Sometimes it changes a lot in a day.

I walked back to the bedroom and looked at my clothes, the ghost of my discomfort with the lawyer still haunting me. If I was going to go face Christ only knew what, I wasn't going in a T-shirt. I took one of the white shirts out of the closet, held it close to my face, and breathed in. It didn't smell like anything at all. I stripped off my shirt, found a simple white tee in Eric's dresser, and put myself together in a good white men's button-down. It classed up the jeans, and if it was a little too big, I could roll up the sleeves and still look more confident than I did in my own clothes. More confident than I felt.

I felt a little weird, wearing a dead man's shirt. But it was mine now. He'd given it to me. I had the ultimate hand-me-down life. The thought brought a lump to my throat.

'Come on, little tomato,' I told the key ring. 'You and me against the world.'

I called a taxi service, went out to the curb to wait, and inside forty-five minutes I was on Inca Street, standing in front of the mysterious apartment.

2

In the middle of the afternoon there wasn't much foot traffic. The address was a warehouse complex converted into living space for the Brie and wine set. Five stories of redbrick with balconies at each level. Tasteful plants filled the three feet between the knee-high wrought iron fence and the walls. According to the paperwork, the apartment Eric owned—the one I owned—was valued at half a million.

I tried to look like I belonged there as I walked in and found my way to the elevators. It was like sneaking into a bar; I didn't belong there, but I did. I kept expecting someone to stop me, to ask for my ID, to check my name against a list and throw me out.

Why, I asked myself, does someone have a house and an apartment both in the same city? It wasn't like he could sleep in two beds at once. Maybe this was his getaway. Maybe it was where his lover stayed, assuming he had one.

The elevator chimed, a low, reassuring bell, like someone clearing their throat. I stepped out, checked the number on the key ring, and followed the corridor down to my left. I started to knock, then stopped.

I stood there, silent, my breath fast. The door shone like lacquer. I could see my reflection in it, blurred and imprecise. I put the key in the lock and turned. I felt the bolt open, but I didn't hear it.

The inside of the apartment was gorgeous and surreal. Wooden floors that seemed to glow, bronze fixtures, windows that made the city outside seem like it had been arranged to be seen from this vantage point. The ceilings were raw beams and exposed ductwork so stylish they looked obvious. Books were stacked on the floor, on the deep, plush couch. History books, it looked like. Some of them were in languages I recognized, some weren't. A whiteboard hung on one wall, covered with timetables and scribbled notes. A huge glass ashtray held the remains of at least a pack of dark brown cigarettes, the scent of old smoke tainting the air. And the art . . .

At each of the huge windows, a glass ball seemed to float in the air. It was only when I got close enough to breathe on them that I saw the tiny cradles, three hair-thin wire strands for each, hanging from the high ceiling. When I turned around, I saw there was one above the doorway too. Candles in thick brass candlesticks covered the dining table in three ascending rows, and a picture framed in burnished metal hung at the mouth of a hallway. It was a picture of a young woman in nineteenth-century clothes, and I wasn't sure from looking whether it was a photograph or a drawing. It seemed as real as a photo, but the eyes and the way she held her hands looked subtly off.

Silently, I went down the hallway. A fair-size kitchen with white tiles and a brushed steel sink and refrigerator and stove. A breakfast bar with ironwork stools to match the fence outside. A bathroom with the lights out. A bedroom, and on the bed, laid out as if in state, a corpse.

I could feel the blood leaving my face. I didn't scream, but I put my hand on the door frame to keep steady. My stomach tightened and flipped. I stepped forward. Whoever he'd been, he'd been dead for a long time. The skin was desiccated, tight, and waxy; the nose was sunken; the hands folded on his chest were fleshless as chicken wings. Blackened teeth lurked behind ruined lips. Wisps of colorless hair still clung to the scalp. He was wearing a white shirt with suspenders and pants that came up to his rib cage, like someone from a forties movie.

I crouched at the side of the bed, disgusted, fascinated, and frightened. My mind was jumping and screeching like a monkey behind my eyes, but there was something wrong. I had touched my nose before I figured it out, like my body already knew and had to give me the hint. He didn't smell like a corpse. He didn't smell like anything. He smelled *cold*.

I had started to wonder if maybe it wasn't a body at all but some kind of desperately Goth wax sculpture when the eyes opened with a wet click.

This time, I screamed.

'You aren't Eric,' it said in a voice like a rusted cattle gate opening.

'I'm his niece,' I said. I didn't remember running across the room, but my back was pressed against the wall now. I tried to squeak less when I spoke again. 'I'm Jayné.'

He repeated my name like he was tasting it. Zha-*nay*.

'French?' he asked.

'My mother's side,' I said. 'People usually say it like Jane or Janey.'

'Monolingual fuckwits,' he said, and sat up. I thought I could hear his joints creaking like leather, but I might have only imagined it. 'You're here, that means something happened to Eric?'

'He's dead.'

The man sighed.

'I was afraid of that,' he said. 'Explains a lot. The little rat fuckers must have sussed him out.'

The skeletal, awkward hand rubbed his chin like it was checking for stubble. When he looked at me, his eyes were the yellow of old ivory. In motion, he didn't look like a corpse, only a badly damaged man.

'Hey,' he said, 'where are my manners, eh? You want a drink?'

'Um,' I said. And then, 'Yes.'

He led the way back to the kitchen. I perched on one of the stools while he poured two generous fingers of brandy into a water glass. I'd seen pictures of people who survived horrific burns, and while he didn't bear those scars, the effect was much the same. I could see it when his joints— shoulder, hip, elbow—didn't quite bend the way they were meant to. He walked carefully. I wanted to ask what had happened to him, but I couldn't think of a way to phrase it that didn't seem excruciatingly rude. I tried not to stare, the way you try not to look at people with harelips or missing hands, but my eyes just kept going back.

Guilt started pulling at me. Even if it was officially my place, coming in the way I had was rude. Clearly Uncle Eric had been letting the guy crash here. He poured a glass for himself, then took a wood cutting board from the cabinet beside the refrigerator and a knife from its holder.

'So,' he said. 'He didn't tell you a goddamn thing about all this, did he?'

'Not really,' I said, and sipped the brandy. I never drank much, but I could tell that the liquor was better than I'd ever had.

'Yeah. Like him,' the man said, and put a cast-iron skillet on the burner. 'Well. Shit, I don't know where to start. My name's Midian. Midian Clark. Your uncle and I were working together.'

If I pretended I was listening to Tom Waits, his voice wasn't so bad.

'What on?'

A scoop of butter thick enough to make a dietitian weep dropped onto the skillet and started to quietly melt.

'That's a long story,' Midian said.

'Was it why he got killed?'

'Yeah, it was.'

'So you know who killed him.'

Midian shifted his head to the side, his ragged lips pressed thin. He sighed.

'Yes. If he got killed, I know who killed him.'

'Okay,' I said. 'Spill it.'

He frowned quietly as he took a yellow onion, half a red bell pepper, and an egg carton out of the refrigerator. I drank more brandy, the warm feeling in my throat spreading to my cheeks. I cleared my throat.

'I'm not blowing you off. I just think better when I'm cooking,' he said. 'Okay. So. There's a guy calls himself Randolph Coin. He came to Denver about a year ago. He heads up a bunch of fellas call themselves the Invisible College, okay? They think that all the ghoulies and ghosties and long-legged beasties you've ever heard of really exist. Vampires, werewolves, zombies. People doing magic. You name it. You like onions?'

'Not really.'

'Not even grilled? Tell you what, just try this. If you don't like it, I'll make another one. So the Invisible College, they also think they know *why* all these things exist. It's about possession. Something coming out of this abstract spiritual world that's right next to ours and worming its way inside people and animals. Hell, sometimes even things. Knives.' He held up the cutting blade. 'Whatever.'

'Demons taking people over,' I said. He looked up, smiling at the skepticism in my voice, as he sliced the onion in neat halves, peeled away the skin, and started dicing the pale flesh.

'Well, yeah, a lot of it is about demons. Or spirits or loa or whatever you want to call them. Seelie Court, Unseelie Court, Radha, Petro, Ghede. Ifrit. Hungry ghosts. All kinds of them. The generic term's riders. They get inside a person, and they change them. Make them do things, make them *want* to do things. Give them freaky powers. Normal people who've got a feel for it and the right training—call 'em wizards or witches or cunning men or whatever—they can do some pretty weird shit, but *nothing* compared to what riders are capable of.'

'So not just demons, but magic too,' I said. He dropped the onion into the spreading pool of butter, where it sizzled angrily. The pepper was next for the block.

'Thing is, kid, the folks that believe that shit? They're absolutely right. That's exactly how the world is. Let me give you a fer instance. I know you're wondering what the fuck happened to me, right? Well, how old do you think I am?'

'I . . . I don't . . .'

'I was born the year they stormed the Bastille. The year of our Lord seventeen hundred and eighty motherfucking nine.' His voice had taken on an angry buzz. The blade in his hand flickered over the cutting board. 'I crossed the Invisible College, and they cursed me. I've been wandering around ever since. Coin is direct apostolic line from the pig fucker who did this to me. He's the only one who can take it back.'

He put the peppers in with the browning onions. Wisps of smoke and steam rose from the black metal.

'I came to Eric because he's the kind of guy who knows things. Helps people. I needed help.'

'You're telling me that a bunch of evil wizards killed my uncle?' I could hear the raw disbelief in my own voice.

His yellowed eyes locked on me. He took an egg from the carton and cracked it deliberately on the countertop.

'I'm telling you the world's more complicated than you thought,' he said. 'And I'm not wrong about that.'

While he whipped eggs in a tiny steel mixing bowl, I sat hunched over the breakfast bar, brandy in my hands. I felt like I'd been on an amusement park ride one too many times. Confused and dizzy and a little sick. We both knew he was giving me time to think. Time, specifically, to decide he was a nut or a liar. My first guess was both. But he was the only thread I had that might lead to Uncle Eric and whoever had killed him.

'Okay,' I said as he poured the yellow-white froth over the peppers and onions, 'let's say I buy it. What were you two going to do? Track this Coin guy down and give him a good talking to?'

'The Invisible College is here for a reason. Every few years, they have to come together to induct new people into the club. They have to call up a rider, open the poor sucker who's signing up for the horror show, and infect them with it. Things start moving just outside the world like sharks coming up for chum. When you get too many riders bumping around, the barrier between the physical world and the abstract gets . . . well, not thin exactly, but *weird*. That started in April. While that's happening, the Invisible College has its hands full. Eric and I were planning to disrupt things before they could eat the new crop of people. And while we were at it, kill Coin.'

'You were going to murder someone?'

He put his hand on the handle of the skillet, flinched back from the heat, and reached for a dishcloth to protect himself.

'Coin's dead, kid,' he said. 'Coin's been dead since the

day they made him Invisible. We were looking to kill the thing that's living in his body.'

He lifted the skillet, and a flick of his wrist spun the omelet in the air, folded it, and caught it. The ragged lips twisted into a satisfied smile. He waited a few seconds, then flipped it to the other side.

'That's how it works with them,' he said. 'You take the unclean spirit inside, and it devours you. It's not always like that. Other kinds of rider, you maybe don't need a ceremony. You get bitten, you pick up the wrong guy at the bar. You get assaulted. Maybe it kicks you out of your body, puts you someplace else. Or it just hangs out in the back of your mind, making suggestions or taking over in little ways so you won't even notice.'

'That's . . .' I didn't know whether I was going to say horrible or gross or implausible. Midian shrugged.

'Yeah, well,' he said. 'Thing is, the Invisible College bastards? They're strong, and they're smart, and they're organized. Every one of them that penetrates into the world makes Coin stronger, and the stronger he gets, the more he can protect his own. Think Amway, but for demonic possession.'

'And killing the thing inside Coin would fix you?'

'Killing that fucker would undo everything it's done in the physical world. Me and a whole lot of other things besides. He's the center of the whole damn infection. Here, lemme get you a fork. Blow on it a little, it's still hot.'

The taste was more than a few eggs, onions, and peppers seemed to justify. It was lush and hot and rich. He smiled at my reaction and slid the rest onto a plate for me.

'That's really good,' I said through my mouthful.

'There's a secret to it. Always drink some brandy first. There. Enjoy. So, yeah, we were looking to break the Invisible College's back. Get rid of Coin, disrupt the induction. It'd be just like penicillin taking out a case of the clap. We both knew it was dangerous. I don't know how they got to Eric, but I'm dead sure they did. Your average mugger would have been out of his depth with him. Guys like Eric don't die at random. He got hit.'

I took another bite of the omelet, chewing slowly to give myself time to think. On the one hand, everything Midian said was clearly insane. A two-hundred-year-old man cursed by demons. A cabal of evil wizards planning to engineer the demonic possession of a new batch of cultists. And my uncle in the middle of it all, dead because someone caught wind of his plan.

On the other hand, if anyone had asked me a week before what my uncle did, I would have guessed wrong. And even if every word coming out of Midian's mouth was crap, it seemed to be crap he believed. And so maybe this Coin guy believed it too. I'd had enough experience with the kind of atrocities that blind faith can lead to that I couldn't discount anything just because it was crazy. If Coin and the Invisible College believed that they were demon-possessed wizards and that Eric was out to stop them, that could have been reason enough to kill him. Things don't have to exist to have consequences.

I was lost in bitter memories for a moment. The flare of a match brought me back. The deathly face was considering me as he lit a cigarette.

'I'd think it was bullshit too if I was you,' he said. 'You doubt. I respect that. Doubt's important stuff.'

He took a long drag, the coal of his cigarette going bright and then dark. Long, blue smoke slid out of his mouth and nostrils as he spoke. It didn't smell like tobacco. It was sweeter and more acrid.

'Thing is, kid, you gotta doubt the stuff that *isn't* true. You go around doubting whether pickup trucks exist, you'll wind up on the curb with a lot of broken bits.'

I put my fork against the side of the plate and looked up at him.

'I'm taking this to the police, you know,' I said.

'Won't do you any good. They're just going to think you're nuts. They have an explanation that suits them just fine.'

'All the same—'

A hard tap came from the front room. Both of us turned to look. The little glass ball that hung over the door had fallen. It rolled uneasily along the unseen slope of the floor-boards. While we watched, the ones over the windows fell too, one-two-three. Midian grunted.

'When you came in,' he said, 'you didn't drop something behind you? Ashes or salt, something like that?'

'No,' I said. 'Nothing.'

Midian nodded and took another drag of his cigarette.

'That's too bad,' he said.

With a bang like a car wreck, the front door burst in.